Gonzalo S. Rey

The Calling

The Calling
Gonzalo S. Rey
www.thecallingnovel.com

English edition of the novel "La Llamada" by Gonzalo S. Rey

1st Edition: October 2.017

Published by: Gonzalo Simón
ISBN: 978-84-944772-1-8
Legal deposit: TO-730-2017

Book registered in the Registry of Intellectual Property - Toledo, Spain

Composition of the cover: Gonzalo Simón
Illustrations of the cover: Sky - Evgeny Karandaev / Shutterstock
                            Toledo - Hebstreit / Shutterstock
                            Sun logo - Created by Freepik

Editing: Mara Melton, Marliss Melton and John Brozak
Layout: Ana M. Juan and Gonzalo Simon

www.thecallingnovel.com
E-mail: info@thecallingnovel.com

To my Mother

Special thanks to Warren Kenton

Contents

Part One

1. Light 15
2. Life 23
3. Family 31
4. Transition 39
5. Readiness 45
6. Soul mate 53
7. Dreams 61
8. Business 69
9. Conflict 77
10. Departure 85

Part Two

11. Courage 99
12. Chase 107
13. Modesty 115
14. Arrogance 123
15. Path 131
16. Retreat 139
17. Mirages 147
18. Ballads 155
19. Adventures 163
20. Arrival 171

Part Three

21. Discovery 181
22. Learning 189
23. Intrusion 197
24. Hope 205
25. Pretending 213
26. Opportunity 223
27. Temptations 233
28. Door 241
29. School 249
30. Encounter 257

Part Four

31. Indiscretion 267
32. Love 277
33. Emptiness 287
34. Guidance 295
35. Peace 305
36. Pressure 315
37. Loneliness 325
38. Preparation 335
39. Trial 343
40. Ascend 353

Foreword

Throughout our lives, we all experience, consciously or unconsciously, a spiritual journey. Our, joys, sufferings, hopes, and despair are all part of this journey. The purpose of this way is to help us to become fully realized human beings, so we can return to the source from which everything emanates. This novel narrates the path of an individual as he traverses the different stages of this journey. The story is set in 13th century in Spain, but it can equally apply to us today; the form maybe different, but the essence of the journey is to the same for all humanity.

My spiritual search started when I was twenty years old. A teacher recommended that I sat every day to listen to my breath for ten minutes. After a year of practicing this exercise, I heard the silence! It was an unforgettable experience and that moment changed the way I perceived reality. Since then, that experience goes with me everywhere, even though sometimes I am not fully aware of it.

Writing this novel has been a great adventure and has brought me many gifts. I have had the opportunity to delve into an extraordinary period in Spanish history, the 13th century, which is not familiar to most people. It was incredible to make a 400 km. pilgrimage between Teruel and Toledo, which allowed me to discover many inspirational places. It enabled me to research the history of Spain in a way that I would not have otherwise been afforded. The novel also has helped me to discover the history of Toledo.

I want to thank those who have helped me to write, edit, illustrate, print, and distribute the book. Especially I want to thank to Mara Melton, Marliss Melton, and John Brozak for their extraordinary help editing the book. They all were very helpful, kind, and generous. Thank you very much for your kindness.

I also want to thank my mother, to whom I dedicate this book, for her constant loving presence and dedication throughout her life. This book is the result of her constant care, love, and kindness. Thank you so much, Mother.

I also want to express my gratefulness to Warren Kenton, thanks to whom, after an extraordinary trip to Spain, the idea of writing this novel emerged. He is a constant source of inspiration and helped me very much during the process of structuring and writing the book.

I also thank my sister Mercedes for her help in editing the Spanish edition of the novel. I would like to thank all the people that have already read the book in Spanish and with their valuable critics encouraged me to continue writing and working.

Finally, I want to thank the Holy One for the awesome privilege of writing this spiritual book. Without His Will, nothing can be done. Love governs existence. Thank You.

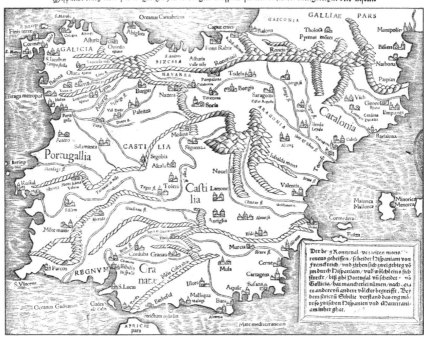

Figure 1

• Part One •

I. LIGHT

*A*n extraordinary white light prevails in the World of the Spirit, and a sublime celestial music plays softly in the background. Lower, where the souls live, the spiritual watchers observe the presence of the hand of Providence in Teruel, during the spring of 1214. A man of destiny was about to be born, and his life required a detailed preparation from the heavens.

Diego Garcia Pardo, one of the most important sheep farmers in the city, managed to sell a large quantity of wool to the buyers from the Kingdom of Navarre. The negotiations were tough. "I will be one of the richest men in Teruel, and everybody will respect me," he said to himself while heading for the main tavern. He wished to celebrate his good luck with his distinguished friends, the noblemen of the city, a group to which he yearned to belong.

Diego was thirty-seven years old. His robust body, his brown-gray hair, and his round face were the signs of a hard-working life dedicated to the wool business. His serious work allowed him to buy an expensive house within the city walls. His dream was to become one of the eight aldermen on the city council, and he spent a great deal of money courting the noblemen, trying to buy his way into the privileged group. He did not know his new friends looked down on him, seeing him as inferior. As long as he paid for their indulgences, they allowed him to believe he could become a member of their exclusive group. "A sheep farmer can never be a nobleman," they whispered in secret.

It was already night and a heavy downpour was falling in the cold sunset. While Diego was walking toward the main plaza, thinking about the money he just made, an old man came out to meet him. He was startled when he saw a gentleman appear from nowhere. The man had a long white beard and wore an impeccable white tunic with an outstanding blue cape. The old man asked Diego for directions to Montalban. The wool trader thought the old man was out of his mind; only a crazy person would wander the dangerous paths of Aragon at night. Diego did not want to waste any of his time with the stranger, so he gave him brief directions and waved him on his way. But the old man did not move. Standing still in the rain, he scrutinized the wool farmer. Suddenly, Diego felt unwell and his ears felt clogged. He felt compassion for the gentleman. "Today I was fortunate in my business, so I am going to escort him on his way," he thought, and postponed his celebration for another occasion. "The path to Montalban is near my home. I can show you the way if you wish," he suggested.

The two men headed towards Diego´s home, which was situated near Saint Michael´s Gate. As the rain stopped, a mist arose from their bodies and blended with the gathering fog. They walked through the dark night, in silence, along the streets of Teruel. The old gentleman moved with unusual grace and agility, faster than Diego, who could not keep pace with the gentleman.

"Where are you coming from, sir?" he asked, breaking the uncomfortable silence. "I have never seen you in Teruel."

"I am coming from far away. I am here to complete a specific task, and then I will leave".

"By the way," the sheep farmer continued, "the cloth of your cape is extraordinary. I have never noticed such quality in this region."

The old gentleman said nothing. As Diego spoke, a high-pitched ringing filled his ears and he blinked to clear his vision as the street before him blurred. He asked himself if he had been drinking for he felt disoriented. His vision cleared, and without realizing how he had arrived there, he found himself in front of his house. Confounded, he looked around to get his bearings, and gave directions to the gentleman.

"You can leave the city walls via that street," he said, pointing ahead. "Then take the path north. In approximately three days, you will reach Montalban." Diego paused and then concluded: "Those roads are dangerous, especially at night. Be very careful"

The gentleman bid Diego goodbye and set off. Diego entered his house, and paused to look back. To his astonishment, the old man had disappeared into the mist.

While marveling at the man's peculiar character, Diego heard his wife calling him. He hurried to join her, pleased to see her looking especially attractive. She wore a long elegant violet dress that suited her slim body and her long blond hair. A peaceful feeling washed over Diego, relaxing him. His two sons were already asleep, which was rare for that time of the evening. Admiring his wife's big bright eyes, Diego remembered the first day he met her. He thanked Fortune for having met and married this extraordinary woman. Heavenly powers led them to the bedroom where they undressed. In a trance the miracle of conception took place without their being aware.

That night, a rare silence befell the city, lasting all through the night. Diego and Elvira sensed that something beyond their understanding had happened. The presence of a special atmosphere in the room confirmed it. An extraordinary light, only perceivable by sensitive souls, shone through the rafters. Two columns of light breached the physical structure of the room, and a dim face of a blond child took shape upon the ceiling.

Elvira had a profound dream, in which the precise features of the son she had just conceived appeared to her. The woman knew she was pregnant with a light-eyed child of Germanic appearance. He was just like her grandfather. She prayed, thanking God for her new child.

The next morning, after Diego left home to meet his shepherds, Elvira remained in bed, luxuriating in the certainty she was pregnant. Dreaming again, beings of light visited her, and assured her they would protect her and her son during her pregnancy. Then she dreamed of her son, who revealed his name: "Lorenzo", which she knew it meant "he who has been laureated by God." Convinced she was about to conceive an extraordinary son, Elvira awoke to enjoy one of the happiest days of her life.

A few months later, Elvira announced the good news of her pregnancy. Diego wondered if the conception of the child happened the day of his meeting with the mysterious gentleman. Diego's intuition confirmed, that, in fact, the two incidents were connected; but his pragmatic mind prevented him from seeing their significance. What could be the connection between the stranger and his son? "None," he concluded.

A few days later, Diego went to the Jewish quarter to pay off one of his loans. He used the occasion to visit Daniel, the main astrologer, considered the wisest man in town. Daniel had an excellent reputation among his neighbors, not only for his wisdom, but also for his kindness and politeness. His large beard, and sharp bright eyes denoted his knowledge of life. His studies about the influence of the stars helped him to understand human affairs. That morning, Daniel was deeply focused on his work in his study, in the upper part of his house. He was drawing up astronomical tables, so he could contrast them with the tables of the members of the Astrological School of Aragon.

Diego, upon entering the room, was awe struck by the unique atmosphere that permeated the study. It was presided over by a sublime Menorah, the seven-branched Jewish candelabrum. The sheep farmer, astonished, also appreciated the best library in Teruel, composed by astrological essays of Ptolemy, Abraham Ibn Ezra, and Abraham Bar Hiyyad; Arabic translations of Greek books of Philosophy; metaphysical volumes; copies of the writings of the Rabbinical School of Cordoba; and, of course, the Torah.

"Hello, Diego, nice to see you. How's business?" the astrologer asked, lifting his gaze from the table while holding an astrolabe.

"Very well, sir. Our wool has an excellent reputation in the northern kingdoms. I have just received payment of a lot. So I came right away to pay back my loan."

"You have made a name for yourself as an excellent borrower. This will allow you future credits. Last year, during the harsh drought, you fulfilled your obligations under adverse conditions. Not everyone honored their debts."

"Prompt payment is my motto."

"That is how it should be. And, how is your family?" the astrologer, who had a great fondness for Elvira, asked.

"My wife is pregnant again," Diego said. "That is the reason I have come to see you."

"Congratulations. When is the baby due?"

"Before the year's end. Could you ask your daughter to assist my wife with the birth?"

"Of course, but, are you aware the Church does not allow Christians to have Jewish midwives assisting at births?" Daniel reminded Diego.

"I understand, but your daughter is the best midwife in Teruel and I do not want to take any risks. The life of my wife is of far more importance than a rule of the Church."

"All right then. I will tell my daughter, but be discrete. I will project the natal chart of the baby when he is born," the astrologer promised. Then he once again concentrated on his meticulous work with the astronomic tables.

Nine months later, Diego visited Daniel once more. It was the night before Elvira went into labor. It was freezing cold, usual for Teruel's harsh winters. Daniel, his daughter, and her assistant headed to Diego´s. The astrologer lit their way with a torch, and as he walked, he noted the position of the planets in the sky: he was already composing the child's horoscope in his head.

Diego's two small sons, Martin and Fernando, were home; filling the house with excitement as they sensed something important was about to happen. A crackling fire burned bright in the hearth. The midwives, upon entering the house, perceived the subtle light, characteristic of a childbirth. Examining the intensity of the light, they predicted the birth would occur at dawn. They waited near Elvira the whole night.

Just before sunrise, Elvira started to gasp. The midwives prepared themselves for the birth. Everything seemed normal, but without warning, a sharp pain exploded in Elvira's chest, paralyzing her. The midwives panicked as the mother fainted and her heart stopped! As they worked with desperation to revive her, Elvira slipped into a deep coma. In this dream state, she saw herself outside her body; she could watch the scene from above, as a spectator. She observed the midwives frantically massaging her heart, her husband yelling, and her two sons weeping over the imminent loss of their mother. All at once, a tunnel with a gleaming bright light of a lighthouse at the end of it, drew her closer. She realized she was about to die. Just before releasing herself to that immortal force, she heard a solemn voice:

"You must regain consciousness and give birth to the child. Lorenzo has an important mission in the world. You cannot falter."

Elvira sensed, next to her, the magnificent figure of a luminous being who spoke to her. Hovering between life and death, she understood the meaning of her life. In that indescribable space between two realms, she decided to resist the force that pulled her to the other world. Through sheer force of will, she returned to her body, determined to give birth. That encounter with another dimension of reality lasted just a few moments, but it forever marked the life of the good woman, who would never forget the mysterious voice of the unknown being.

Lorenzo, while in his mother´s womb, sensed how his mother's heart had stopped. He experienced, for the first time, a suffocating terror. The oxygen was not reaching him, and he had to fight for his life, kicking with all his strength. Fearing for his survival, he strained to come into the world but with his mother's body frozen, he could go nowhere. The same being of great luminosity called to him from outside his mother´s womb, showing him the way. Still, he could do nothing if his mother did not respond.

At the same time, two bizarre creatures of spiritual evil, attracted by the light of the scene, tried to enter the baby´s body. Benefiting from the confusion of the situation, they sought to possess Lorenzo´s body. There were two sprite beings who refused to face their past actions. Their aim was to live through the bodies of others. The luminous guide blocked their ways with his strength, and after a fight, they left the room.

The midwives, with great effort, revived Elvira. She pushed hard using the last of her energy. Lorenzo breached, and the exhausted midwives pulled his body forth from his exhausted mother. Lorenzo, once free of the womb, observed the strange scene and began to cry. The midwives cut the umbilical cord and put it under his mother's pillow. Elvira, exhausted, looked at Lorenzo tenderly, and realized her son's face matched the blond boy whose face she had seen on the ceiling the day of his conception. Then his mother spoke his name. The rest of the family, now happy after the dangerous birth, started calling the baby Lorenzo.

Just after his birth, the child remembered a sublime dialogue with the bright being who had assisted with his birth. The conversation had taken place long before his conception.

"Now, you should again experience being an incarnated human being," the guide told him.

"I have suffered in purgatory for my past actions and I have experienced profound loneliness in that place. I feel this is the moment to open myself up to physical reality," Lorenzo's soul answered.

"The earthly experience is not easy. You know that. To be born on Earth is a heroic act."

"I yearn to continue learning and evolving. I want to develop to my full potential."

"All right then. We will help you on your path. Remain still during the difficult moments. You will receive signs so that you will not lose yourself, although we cannot interfere with your free will."

The guide showed the boy's soul the most important people he would meet during his life, imprinting their faces onto his mind for his lifetime. After Lorenzo had accepted his fate, divine energy filled his spirit and enlightened his entire being. His soul thanked God for the new journey he was going to undergo.

"Lord, allow me to serve you and lead me not into temptation. Thank You, My Lord, for allowing me to live this new life," the soul expressed.

And his accompanying being of light proclaimed:

"Lord Almighty, help this man of destiny to be able to develop to the fullest and to keep alive the flame of the Tradition. Holy, Holy, Holy."

In that moment, the light of the sky brightened. The laws and principles of the universal manifestation were about to be fulfilled; a soul had just incarnated into a physical body to contribute to the evolution of humanity.

2. LIFE

The baby's face was that of a mature person, as if he were an adult, despite his few hours of life. When Daniel, the astrologer, saw the child's serious face and profound eyes, he predicted Lorenzo would be a wise person. Without a doubt, the baby was an old soul.

Daniel projected the child's horoscope. He was curious about Lorenzo's fate, born at eight thirty on the fifth of December 1214. First, he positioned the sun in the sign of Sagittarius, and close to our star, he placed the moon in the sign of Capricorn. He then put Mars and Venus side by side pointing towards the south. To finish the horoscope, he used his astronomic charts to place the unseen planets.

Daniel, looking at the horoscope, analyzed Lorenzo's life. The chart presented favorable aspects for the distant planets, but less promising outcomes for the nearer ones. Lorenzo would need to abandon some of his comforts to progress along his path, which was spiritual. Reflecting more deeply, Daniel saw that Lorenzo would develop an intense inner life, would travel, and would fight to become a free man. The child would ask deep questions to learn what lies beyond the physical world. His ascendant in the sign of Capricorn would give him a practical sense of life, and would help him to keep his feet on the ground; this would prevent his becoming mad.

Diego showed interest in his son´s fate, but the astrologer avoided discussing the horoscope with his father. It was necessary to wait until Lorenzo grew up before showing the chart to the parents;

he did not want them to interfere in the child's natural growth.

Lorenzo found it difficult to adapt to the physical world. He could not get used to the cold room temperature or light given off by the candles. Even after a few months of life, he felt like a stranger in his body; it frustrated him not being able to move freely. Although he tried to communicate with his family, they could not understand him. When his older brothers and his father were close to him, he felt as if they were attacking him. He was, essentially, a stranger in a strange land. For that reason, he decided to just eat and sleep.

During his first year, Lorenzo's soul tried to form a permanent union with his body, but its density was too heavy for his soul. The boy needed to sleep for long periods to recuperate from the effort of being awake. Meanwhile, he was forgetting where he came from. Lorenzo took refuge in his intense dreams during which he communicated with a disembodied, luminous figure that helped him adapt to the physical world; it was the same figure that had spoken to him before his birth.

"When you are awake, try to remain calm," the being said.

Lorenzo protested. "I am in stress when they approach me. I do not know what to expect," he said, revealing his feelings of powerlessness. "They project aggressiveness towards me. Just a simple heart felt gesture from them would be enough to communicate with me."

"It is normal for you to feel invaded. Some humans, after a few years of life, forget where they have come from and they behave primitively. Adapting is part of your learning process."

"So, where do I come from?" Lorenzo asked.

The being took him to the heights and showed him his pre-birth state. He saw how different guides had planned his life before his birth, choosing a precise place, date, and family for him.

"Your life was designed with great care. You will be able to develop to the fullest and become an example for others."

Lorenzo understood what the guide was saying; however, upon waking, he forgot the message. The effort required to negotiate the physical world was immense.

In his first years, Lorenzo interpreted the world as undefined masses of colors. Therefore, when his father was near him, Lorenzo perceived a grey cloud in his father´s solar plexus, which generated a great rigidity on the left side of his body. Although Lorenzo tried to talk to him, his efforts were in vain.

When with his brothers, Lorenzo could see a red aura emanating from their bodies, which indicated their violent energy. His mother, on the other hand, gave off a white light, something Elvira had cultivated with her constant prayers; the only time Lorenzo ever felt at peace was when he was close to his mother.

At the age of three, Lorenzo's frustration reached its limits; no one understood him, and he could no longer tolerate life in the physical world. His body demanded more attention, the noise of his environment was excessive, and he found his helplessness distressing. "This does not make sense," he said to himself and decided to put an end to his life.

In his desire to end his suffering, he allowed a virus to infect his body and he spent several days comatose. The high fevers caused him to experience intense dreams, where he once again encountered the light being.

"Lorenzo, what is the problem? Why have you decided to die?" his spiritual guide asked him.

"I cannot remain in my body any longer. There is so much violence around me, and my physical body's demands are extreme. This requires a monumental effort. I cannot connect with humans like you!" Lorenzo complained.

"This is part of the human experience. Remember you are not alone. When we incarnate, we go through a stage where we are defenseless, and we experience a crisis of the body. Each crisis is an immense challenge. Do not give up."

"Why do I sense this violence around me?"

"In contrast to the refinement of the place where you were before your birth, your earthly manifestation seems brutal. Some of your relatives have lost their connection to the source and have not regained it. Less harmonic forces have overtaken them," his guide explained.

"I need to decide whether I want to live."

"Before you were born, you decided to live this life. Now you have the possibility to break the contract you made with yourself, but keep in mind this may not be the best decision," the guide warned him. "Remember that in every difficult moment, you will receive spiritual help. Everything will be part of your learning process."

Lorenzo reflected deeply in his fevered state. Meanwhile, his body reached its limit. His parents, desperate, called the most prestigious Jewish doctor of Teruel. The expert, after examining the child, did not give much hope to Diego and Elvira.

In his despair, Diego called Arturo, one of his eldest shepherds. Arturo knew a great deal about medicinal plants. He was the representative of the Shepherd's Assembly and the best healer in the region. During the seasonal pasture changes, Arturo healed his fellow shepherds with natural remedies. After the shepherd observed Lorenzo's condition, he realized the child was determined to die.

"Nothing can be done if someone does not want to live. Lorenzo wants to leave us," the wise healer said.

Elvira, who knew that Lorenzo had come to carry out an important mission, did not accept his judgment. It did not make sense that her son would die. His mother prayed for Lorenzo, without realizing the process Lorenzo was going through. During the days that followed, the child hardly moved. In Lorenzo's dreams, the guide appeared again to explain the seriousness of the situation.

"Lorenzo, your physical body is debilitated, and it will not hold up much longer. You are reaching a point of no return," he told the child.

"I feel a great deal of pain while I am incarnated, and I cannot familiarize myself with this world. I want to return to my true home," Lorenzo explained.

"The pressure of the physical world makes us learn and evolve," the light being explained. "The body only holds you, but remember that you are much more than your physical body."

"The body is heavy and dense. I miss the mobility I had before I was born. I depend on people who do not understand me! Besides, their aggression gives me so much pain!" Lorenzo protested.

"This is part of life. The conditions will never be perfect. You must adapt and learn from situations."

"How can I keep in touch with you? You give me peace. Our conversations provide me hope and keep me alive," Lorenzo muttered in his dream.

"I will send you signs, and I will come to you in your dreams. As you grow, you may think our connection is lost, but that will not be so. I will always be close to you."

"And what will be my mission in life?" Lorenzo asked.

"During the first part of your life you must rise above the control the community seeks to exert over you. If you succeed, then you will need to learn how to earn your living. After that, you will be able to acquire knowledge about the higher worlds, and then you will communicate the lessons you have learned.

"Is that the way my life will be?"

"That is the general plan, however you have free will to decide whether you want to fulfill it. You will face tests and will have to make difficult choices. To do the right thing is usually the most difficult choice. Each situation will test your inner strength, your maturity, and your ethics. Furthermore, you will encounter your soulmate..."

"My soulmate?" Lorenzo asked with curiosity.

The guide asked permission from the heavens to show him the face of his soulmate. He knew it would have a positive effect on his protégé. A vision appeared to Lorenzo, with a face as pure and angelic as any he had ever seen. The need to be near her erupted like a wave, giving him, the will required to regain his health and confront his hardships.

"And will I find her during my life?"

"Perhaps, but you must work hard," his guide answered. "Both of you must learn specific lessons, which are unique to you as individuals. Although the goal is the same, each path is different. Now you must decide," and the guide disappeared.

Over the course of that day, Lorenzo reflected upon his life plan. His body had shrunk to a quarter of its original mass. Everyone thought the baby would die within the next few hours. Diego and his brothers understood the gravity of the situation and remained silent. Elvira lost all hope and focused only on praying for her child`s soul. His mother's heart was breaking. She touched her little one, trying to warm his cold limbs, but it was impossible. Aside from his beating heart and the air flowing in and out of his lungs, Lorenzo was a corpse.

"Oh, My Lord, if you want to take this child, take me first," the good mother begged.

The child meditated on his possibilities. He could die and lose the opportunity to evolve, or he could fight and try to live as a human with dignity. He knew his life was not going to be easy but he chose the second option. In that dream state, he affirmed his decision to his guide, who applauded his courage.

In seconds, the child`s immune system defenses were working once more. The body returned to a normal temperature, the fever dissipated, and the baby`s antibodies defeated the virus. Lorenzo opened his eyes and smiled at his mother. Elvira studied him closely. Something had changed in the look of her child. He seemed another person and no longer presented the appearance of a grown man. His face was now the face of an innocent child.

Joy flooded Diego and Elvira`s home, and the parents gave a joyous celebration of thanksgiving for their son`s recovery. His mother gave credit to God for the baby`s healing, on whom she cast an occasional admonishing look for putting her through such an agonizing trial.

His mother`s immense love for her son lightened the house`s atmosphere and Lorenzo reciprocated his mother's loving looks. Through his will, he had initiated his life in the family laid out for him.

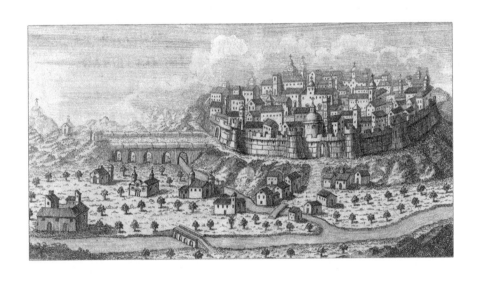

Figuere 2

3. FAMILY

*L*orenzo continued to communicate with the ethereal, luminous figure in his dreams. When he spoke with his guide he felt at peace; however, when he was with his family, he could not tolerate their violent energetic fields.

"I will not speak to anyone until I am understood," young Lorenzo promised himself. He anxiously awaited the time when he would be treated as the adult.

"Come on, you calf, speak!" his brother Martin, eight years older than he, provoked him pushing and shoving him.

His father blamed his wife:

"You are spoiling the child. You treat him like a girl. That is why he doesn't speak," Diego accused his wife.

"Leave him alone. The boy understands everything, but he does not want to talk. He must have his reasons," Elvira answered.

"I think he is disturbed. If he continues like this, I will consider him mad and I will tie him at home as the law compels," Diego threatened. "Or I will send him out with the shepherds, so they can educate him like an animal!"

"Be patient. The boy will speak," Elvira answered, trying to placate her husband.

Lorenzo was happy only in his little world, imagining he

lived among of the stars. In those moments, he felt part of the universe, amongst the constellations, in a place where he did not use the words. "The stars and the wind talk to me," he stated.

Curiosity stirred within him when he heard his elders speak. He had a powerful urge to learn from them. From the little nook of the dining room, he overheard his relatives discussing his father's life.

"Diego, it is time that you take over the family business. You are the eldest son," Garces, Lorenzo's grandfather, urged him.

"Father, I will not disappoint you," Diego promised, while his chest expanded with pride from his father's confidence.

"The business is healthy. I am leaving you a generous legacy; however, I am worried about the hostility towards the Jews and Arabs in Teruel. The Hebrews finance our activity, and we sell a considerable part of our wool in Arab territory. If the Jews leave, our business will be in danger."

"The persecution of the Cathars in France is generating resentment against the non-Christians in Aragon. This is harmful for us," Diego agreed. "If the Jews stop financing us..."

"The Pope's Crusades pursue peaceful people. The French Cathars have arrived in Aragon, escaping from the French Church, and the French Inquisition. The tribunal judges burned the heretics alive. However, another thing worries me," Garces paused.

"Tell me, father."

"You are drinking, heavily."

"I know," Diego, said, bowing his head in shame.

Lorenzo's grandfather, still in remarkable physical shape, became a role model for his grandson. Garces, through effort and dedication, had become the most important wool farmer in Teruel.

He had learned the profession from his ancestors, who worked at it, generation after generation. The cloth he produced was of such quality that northern wool traders traveled to Teruel to buy it. Garces made a fortune selling his wool to Christian merchants from Aragon, Navarre, Castile, and Leon. During the winter, he walked with the shepherds to their grazing lands, so that he traveled from the cold of Teruel to the warmth of Valencia and Alicante, territories under Arab authority during his youth.

"Walking is the best medicine," his grandfather told Lorenzo on one occasion, advice the child remembered for the rest of his life.

When Alphonso II "the Chaste" conquered Teruel, he made it a Christian city. Garces acquired citizenship, which had been his childhood dream. He married Ines, the daughter of a leather artisan, and had three sons: Diego, Gonzalo, and Ramiro.

After the conversation with his father, Diego took over the family business. It seemed an excellent opportunity for Lorenzo's father. Nevertheless, he was not aware that it would turn into an inescapable trap of ambition; Diego's plans to expand the business were endless; he wanted to be the largest wool seller in Aragon. He conceived a plan in which Lorenzo, upon growing older, would help him, but Lorenzo's refusal to speak was not part of his plan. Diego ordered the two brothers to annoy the little one until he spoke. Each time Lorenzo saw his brothers' approach, he hid to avoid being tortured.

"So, he is our business's successor!" Garces proclaimed in another visit, watching Lorenzo with great interest.

"The calf will have to talk first," said Diego. "My other two sons will be good men! One will be a soldier and the other a priest. Lorenzo will take charge of our business if he becomes a human as God intended. Let us hope he does not insist on being a mute animal," Diego said, strong slapping Lorenzo's neck.

"He seems bright enough. I think he understands what we

are saying, but I do not know why he does not speak," Garces said while staring at the silent three-year-old.

"I will make him talk!" Diego said threatening, hitting the child again.

Lorenzo's other grandfather, named Alvaro de Marcilla, was from Huesca. His ancestors were Vandals who had conquered the Iberian Peninsula in the fifth century. Don Alvaro's aggressive temperament, paired with his Germanic appearance, made him a formidable warrior. He served the king of Aragon, fought in the battle for Nice and in the conquest of Cuenca. Don Alvaro, knighted by the king for his valiant service, was granted land in the conquered village of Teruel. Don Alvaro became one of the Councilors, and organized the city into a military stronghold. He also led clandestine attacks into the Arab held territories in search of slaves. Alvaro had five children: Froilan, Jimena, Sancho, Elvira, and Pedro.

Elvira, Lorenzo's mother, had inherited her father's physical beauty. She was a woman of great purity, who always attracted attention, not only for her physical beauty, but also for her inner beauty and kindness.

Elvira and Diego met in the year 1202 and they married in June of the following year. The marriage benefited both families. For the groom's family, it connected him to the aristocracy of Teruel; for the bride's family, it offered financial security, as Diego owned a successful wool business. The bride's wedding dress was beautiful but modest, accentuating her youthfulness. The first happy years of marriage, the couple had two sons, Martin and Fernando.

When Lorenzo was three years old, Elvira gave birth to a daughter, Leonor. The life of the boy took a turn: now he could communicate with his sister heart to heart. Lorenzo, Leonor, and Elvira developed an unbreakable bond; the three of them counterbalanced the violence of Diego, Martin, and Fernando. Every night, Lorenzo, Leonor, and Elvira prayed together, creating a protective spiritual cloak, helping them to withstand the punishing abuse of the father and the two oldest sons.

When Lorenzo turned four, Daniel, the astrologer, took him for a walk. It was a Thursday, the day of the street market in the main plaza. That was a remarkable experience for the boy; Lorenzo enjoyed watching the shopkeepers, shoemakers, craftsmen, and leather workers. The two also met a group of soldiers who had come from fighting in a jousting tournament. The soldier's horses and swords astonished the little boy. Daniel walked Lorenzo through the hospitals, and to the Kosher Jewish butchers. The astrologer introduced Lorenzo to the hidden corners of the Jewish quarter. To end the memorable day, they went to the city wall, from which they could see the nearby fields and contiguous small towns.

That night his guardian angel appeared to him in his dreams:

"You just had your first contact with the Jewish quarter," the radiant human guide told him. Then, the guide showed Lorenzo the spiritual chain of the Oral Tradition. The spiritual chain that had existed since time immemorial, and included extraordinary men, such as Enoch, Abraham, Jacob, and Moses were part of it. Lorenzo nodded. His soul understood the meaning of that chain.

"You are a mature soul on the path of return to the point of light from which everything emanates," his guide explained, but Lorenzo once more forgot the dream upon waking.

Soon enough Lorenzo reached the age of five, and Diego was worried, for his son was still mute. His father chose to use increasingly punitive methods in the hope of forcing his son to speak. Diego, ignorant of his son's inner motives, believed if his son did not talk, it was because he was an animal, so he treated him like one. Diego ordered Martin, the greatest nightmare of Lorenzo's childhood, to inflict pinches, kicks, and punches on Lorenzo.

"Please, do not let my brother near me," Lorenzo prayed each time he saw Martin approaching him.

Soon, Providence listened to his prayers. Lorenzo's grandfather, Don Alvaro de Marcilla, announced some good news:

"Martin is going to join the king's army! He will be a member of the Royal Guard in Huesca!" grandfather exclaimed, after having spoken with the monarch.

The aristocrats had betrayed the adolescent King James. They had convinced him to attack the independent manor of Albarracin, although it was part of an ally's domain, Pedro Fernandez de Azagra. During the battle, the aristocrats abandoned him and his loyal men died. The traitors set fire to the king's camp and the king left devastated.

James I took refuge in Teruel where he arrived deeply depressed, after realizing the extent of the betrayal he had suffered. The monarch wished to forever remain in the Hospital of the Holy Redeemer, since he did not want to resume his kingly duties. His few remaining loyal nobles worried that the young king had decided to abdicate. Despite their valiant efforts, the royal doctors failed to heal the king.

Don Alvaro thought that Arturo, the healer-shepherd, was the only solution. The shepherd realized the king`s condition was critical. He recommended the use of mandrake as the only solution. Since the time of Hippocrates, mandrake was commonly used to combat depression and suicidal impulses. The noblemen of Teruel understood there was no other alternative. However, mandrake was dangerous; if applied improperly it could kill the king.

The shepherd prepared a mixture of boiled leaves and gave it to the king in small doses. After a few days, the monarch, started to see life from a more positive perspective. As his depression lifted, he understood adversity could help him to be a wiser and better king. He acknowledged his mistake of trying to take Albarracin from Pedro Fernandez de Azagra, who had always been loyal. Following the depraved noble`s disastrous advice was a foolish move.

Once the king had recovered, he offered the shepherd Arturo a job at court among his Jewish doctors. Arturo declined the offer. The king appreciated the shepherd`s wisdom and promised him he would never lack for anything. Arturo thanked him silently, but he already had everything he needed. The shepherd said goodbye, admired by everyone for his humility.

The king then spoke to Lorenzo's grandfather,

"Don Alvaro, I want to thank you for your loyalty to me. You have helped me in my campaigns; you have remained faithful to me and have confronted the traitors. Also, you have brought me this shepherd who has cured my illness."

"Your Majesty, I have only fulfilled my duty," Don Alvaro insisted.

"I wish there were more nobles and soldiers like you, whom I could trust without hesitation I need loyal people by my side."

"Your Majesty, I am too old to go with you, but my grandson will serve you with honor.

"So be it," the king proclaimed.

Martin joined the Royal Militia. Finally, freed from his tormenting brother, Lorenzo felt his prayers answered. Despite all the suffering his brother had inflicted upon him, a sense of loss swept through him at Martin's departure. As with all losses, there came the opportunity for personal growth.

Lorenzo, thanks to Providence, could escape brother`s violence. He would still face the pig-headedness of his father, unless, of course, he abandoned his own stubborn decision not to speak. He needed to relate as a human being or pay the consequences for not wanting to communicate with others.

4. TRANSITION

Since Teruel having become a Christian city in 1171, the town's people had enjoyed thirty years of prosperity. Still, the forces of corruption began invisibly advancing. The misuse of their excessive wealth had attracted decadence and the original citizens watched their dreams evaporate.

"The atmosphere has changed. People are not helping each other. There is no longer a sense of community," an elderly gentleman lamented in the main plaza.

"Nobody challenges the corruption. There are huge differences between the classes. Nobody cares. The noblemen scheme and place their friends in positions of power'," his wise gentleman answered.

"To top it off, we lack a true king. James I was crowned at the age of six, and the noblemen continue to plot against him."

"It is better to have this child-king than his father, who died drunk on the battlefield. His reign was disastrous. The price of goods kept climbing, and he was forever minting new coins."

"Look at the city: It is crowded with swindlers, wandering minstrels, prostitutes, and hustlers," the first gentleman continued.

"You're right. Teruel now means feasts, and drunken orgies. The streets are full of vagabonds and card sharks. Everyone ignores The Legal Code of Laws given by the king in 1177."

"And look at the priests. Some of them use the church offerings for fancy clothes, playing dice, and getting drunk. They have no shame."

"We can only pray to God, hoping that He will intercede for us. We need to return Teruel to the good city we built with our sacrifices."

The celestial watchers, in charge of the prosperity of the city, sent several warnings to correct their destructive ways. The warnings were ignored. Now they needed to send an even more powerful sign to rein in the destructive forces created by their excesses. If the people of Teruel heeded the warning, they would regain the path of justice and fairness; if not, depravation would annihilate the city.

This warning was, in fact, imminent. Fifty Arabian Almohad riders, all dressed in black, met in a small tearoom in the nearby town of Sarrion. Half of them had fought in the Battle of Navas de Tolosa, where they suffered a humiliating defeat. They still could acknowledge that loss which changed the course of history. The Christian soldiers were about to lose that battle, but adorned with papal insignias, they adopted the desperate strategy of "do or die", which allowed them to defeat the fearsome Arab army. The Arabs had not devoted themselves in body and soul to the combat because they were confident in their army's superiority. The Arab knights criticized their petty kings for not risking their lives as the Christians had. The repercussions from the defeat were disastrous for the Arabs of the Iberian Peninsula. Since the Battle of Navas de Tolosa, their kingdoms collapsed.

The bravest of Arab soldiers could not accept this humiliating situation, which had already lasted for more than a decade. They preferred to die as warriors than to pay higher and higher tributes to the Christians. These courageous soldiers had wanted to obtain revenge for many years; however, their weak petty kings did not allow them to initiate any battles.

The horsemen gathered in Sarrion decided to lead a secret

attack on the frontier town of Teruel. They thought the moment was perfect, noting the weakness and corruption in Aragon.

"Tonight we attack! We will set fire to their houses!" their leader shouted.

The riders cheered his decision. A guitar and a drum accompanied the celebration. A unique beat prevailed in the melody. The voices of the horse riders repeated the name of God:

"Allah! Allah! Allah!"

"Our king condemns our actions, but a coward cannot be our king!"

"Allah! Allah! Allah!"

Their shouts became louder, as did the timbre of the drum. Everyone yelled in unison, expressing the repressed rage of the recent humiliations.

"Allah is the only king," the leader cried.

"Allah! Allah! Allah!" the knights responded, raising their arms to the heavens.

"Death to the infidel! Death to the infidel!"

The riders reveled in the repetition of those words. Year's earlier, Christian soldiers used to surrender with just the mention of that phrase. Recalling that phrase filled them with adrenaline.

"Allah! Allah! Allah!" the enraged knights repeated.

Intoxicated by emotion, they left the tearoom ready to give their lives. Before them lay the main street of Sarrion, and to the northeast lay Teruel. Before starting the ride, they spent a few solemn moments in prayer. The oldest of the group knew they were going to die that night, but he encouraged them to chant louder:

"Allah! Allah! Allah!"

The riders took their swords and mounted their horses. An immense dust cloud formed in Sarrion as the fifty riders galloped away. The musicians, after returning from their trance, played a farewell song to honor the men whom they would never see again.

The knights rode until they reach the outskirts of the Teruel. They realized there was no sentinel guarding the Gate of Valencia. Teruel was celebrating its town festival, and the event was at its peak. The village gates had not been closed and the sentinel had left his post. All the citizens, regardless of social class, were mingling intoxicated, and absorbed by the music. Nobleman, landlords, traders, wandering minstrels, gamblers, and vagabonds were all drunk together. The Christian soldiers were also celebrating, bathing in wine.

The Arab knights paused outside the city wall, awaiting sunset. They dismounted and formed a circle. After a moment of silence, they prayed, offering their souls to God. Just after sunset, they lit their torches and advanced on horseback. The sound of the drum still was resonating within them. A violent force possessed the leader, who voiced his rage.

When they reached Valencia's Gate, they slew the drunken sentinel, who had just returned to his post. Without hesitation, they set fire to the houses, the shops, and to the drunken people lying on the ground. The Christian soldiers, back from their tournaments, tried to fight back, but their efforts were futile in halting the relentless destructiveness. The specter of blood and fire raised the Arab's morale, determined to kill and to die. Beyond vengeance, their own lives meant nothing to them.

Diego was with his wife and second son in a tavern when the sounds of attack reached him. He hurried to the door, watching in dread as the assailants arrived in the plaza. Panic seized the locals, who ran for their homes in terror. The bells of the cathedral rang out in warning, and the few sober soldiers hurried to arm themselves.

The attackers spread out, rampaging through the city, with their eyes reflecting the fire in their torches.

Lorenzo had stayed at home with his little sister Leonor. A commotion attracted his attention, prompting him to look out of the house's rear window, where he saw a black garbed Arab horseman, who fixing his gaze on Lorenzo set fire to the house with the two children inside.

Flames leapt up immediately, blocking their escape through the doors. Lorenzo's heart pounded, yet he could still hear the powerful inner voice who advised him to stay calm if he wanted to save his and his sister's life. A sudden lucid state enveloped him, which connected him to the inner voice that offered instructions. He understood if he did not follow the directions to the letter, they both would be burned alive.

"Go find your sister," the voice commanded.

Lorenzo, confident, hurtled the flames and entered his sister's room, where she lay sleeping on a cot. He felt, despite being just five years old he was in control of the situation. Thanks to the confidence inspired by the voice, the fire and horror seemed a simple imaginary scene that could not hurt him.

"Leave the room with your sister and then run to the stable door," he heard.

Lorenzo, carrying his sister in his arms, lumbered towards the exit.

"Get out of the house and run away," he heard.

As Lorenzo heeded the voice's instructions, he spotted his father and mother running desperately toward home. Though he had been mute up to that very moment, Lorenzo called to them. Shocked and profoundly relieved to find their children safe, Diego and Elvira were stunned by Lorenzo's fluency and the clear and precise way he described the horseman's attack.

As Diego went to fetch water from the well, Elvira hugged and kissed the son who had saved both himself and his sister. Lorenzo soaked his mother's dress with his tears.

When the excitement passed, the child contemplated the burning house. He could not help but think that a part of his own being, the stubborn child who had refused to speak, had also been destroyed in the fire. Twice Lorenzo had been near death, and each time he had risen above the situation. Lorenzo was no longer a child.

From the moment he started talking, Lorenzo became part of the community. Helping his sister allowed Lorenzo to realize he could be useful to other people. His father was proud of him. When he tried to explain to his father who had guided him out of the fire, he did not understand him. "Maybe that voice only talks to me," he determined. Yet, years later, he would discover that many people also hear similar voices which help in saving their lives in dangerous situations.

Diego saw Lorenzo as the real heir to the family business. Now that Lorenzo was able to speak, he could determine Lorenzo's destiny according to his own ambitions and delusions of grandeur. The child had escaped the fire, but he was oblivious to his father's powerful influence which he would still have to endure.

Meanwhile in Teruel, the fire woke the townspeople's conscience, and the sense of community returned. Most of the houses emerged unscathed. The citizens, after the shock wore off, returned to their lives. The Arab horsemen were tracked down, captured, and their throats cut.

5. READINESS

*T*he king's sickness and the Arab attack had left a strong impression on the people of Teruel. Thanks to those events, they found strength within themselves to overcome their corrupt lifestyles and to discard unnecessary things.

Lorenzo's paternal grandfather, recognizing the valuable lesson the fire taught the community, said to a friend, "What looked like a disaster is in fact beneficial. The fire helped to transform consciences. The previous years' excesses are corrected."

"Superfluous things are gone, and the citizens are working together again as a real community," the old friend replied.

"Even regarding the drought, instead of provoking new conflicts, it is having a positive effect. People are more united than ever!"

"And the corrupted leaders, tax collectors, and priests who only worried about their personal wealth have been exiled."

Diego's wool business also went through a rough period as the cost of moving animals to seasonal pastures increased. The petty Arab kings, aware of Aragon's weakness, required more heads of cattle to graze in their territories. In addition, Diego had to hire armed guards to prevent attacks on his flocks. Thanks to Daniel's intervention, the Jewish moneylenders extended the length of his loans. This allowed Lorenzo's father to pay his shepherds and feed his family during the difficult years.

Lorenzo grew up unaware of his family's and the kingdom's difficulties. Nonetheless, he was intelligent beyond his years. Thanks to his ability to observe his parent's weak points, he knew how to exploit them to get what he wanted, which made him the king of the house. In school, he became a natural leader and was smarter than the noblemen's sons. As a result, his confidence swelled.

Several people taught Lorenzo about what matters in life. One of them was his paternal grandfather. Garces not only taught him how to play chess, but also took him on long distance walks. The walks helped Lorenzo establish a strong connection with nature. Sometimes they played in the seven gates of Teruel, where Garces narrated different tales of the city.

Another essential person in the education of Lorenzo was the shepherd, Arturo. After school, Lorenzo joined the shepherds who worked for his father. Lorenzo sang traditional songs with them and danced around the fire. Arturo taught him how to prepare different medicinal remedies, such as henbane or belladonna.

"And what are those concoctions for?" Lorenzo asked him.

"Some of them alleviate pain, others cure illness, and others arouse joy…"

"Are they magic potions?"

"No, they are plants with healing properties. But some people use them to create potions for their personal benefit," Arturo said.

"And why do they do that?"

"To gain personal profit, as a Catalan monk I met," Arturo finished explaining with contempt in his voice. "He used to take large portions of his own potions, and became a victim of his own creations. He ended up going mad," the wise healer answered, ending the conversation. He did not want to arouse the child's curiosity.

Daniel, the astrologer, who had recognized that Lorenzo was different from the other children, sought to influence his childhood. He taught the value of speaking several languages, emphasizing Arabic, which was the language used by the greatest philosophers and scholars on the Iberian Peninsula. Daniel often took Lorenzo to the top of the city wall to contemplate the sky, the planets, and the stars. During the mild summer nights, they drew figures in the sky, joining stars with imaginary lines, which gave Lorenzo a sense of unity with the universe.

"Who created the world?" Lorenzo asked him on one occasion, taking Daniel by surprise.

"God, the Holy One, of course."

"Is He the same God as the Christian God? My grandfather says the Christian God is the only true God.

"God is God," Daniel answered. He did not wish to explain further. "In the future you will be able to explore the great mysteries in greater depth. You are still young," the astrologer said, leaving Lorenzo eager to know more.

The period of material shortages passed, and Lorenzo's second brother departed to Zaragoza to join a religious order. He fulfilled, in an unconscious way, but with mathematical precision, the desire his father had had for his life. Now, the biggest concern for Diego was to teach his third son the family business. By 1226, Diego had twenty flocks of a thousand sheep each, an extraordinary number. Although he had many assistants, he could not run the business on his own. Once Lorenzo turned twelve, Diego knew it was time to have a serious talk with him.

"Your brothers have all left home. One is a soldier and the other is dedicating his life to the Lord. I want you to take care of our sheep business," he said.

Lorenzo sat astonished. He had not expected his father to

give him such a large responsibility at his tender age, but Diego's ambition and impatience made him foolhardy.

"What about my schooling?" Lorenzo asked.

"You do not need to go there anymore. This is the real world! You will be with me in the mornings and learn everything about the sheep business," Diego insisted. His son's lack of enthusiasm puzzled him.

Lorenzo's heart sank. His father's dictates overwhelmed him, making him feel as if he had lost his very freedom. Diego showed him various aspects of the business and introduced him to the Jewish moneylenders and to the merchants who came to Teruel to buy their high quality wool. Each time Diego spoke to someone, he mentioned Lorenzo would be running the business in the future.

But Lorenzo had no interest in learning his father's profession. He knew this was not his calling. He persisted in spending his free time pondering life's deep questions, knowing he would not find meaningful answers while working for him.

One-day Daniel watched Diego explaining essential details about the wool business to his son and how Lorenzo failed to pay attention. The astrologer noticed Lorenzo's lack of enthusiasm and returned home to ponder the boy's future. He examined Lorenzo's horoscope and saw it was a favorable time for him to learn a profession and get a practical sense of life. Daniel sought out Lorenzo and had a serious talk with him.

"You must learn a profession, although you might not like it. I have seen your apathy when your father is teaching you," Daniel reproached him. "It is necessary that you learn how to make a living. Apply yourself. This learning is good for you."

"I am not born for the profession of sheep herding. I love being with the shepherds, except when they take care of the sheep. I like when they sing, dance, or make musical instruments. I also enjoy training the dogs to defend us against the wolves. But the sheep…"

"Then learn the profession with your father during the mornings, and do the things you like in the evenings. Come with me and we will look at the stars together," the astrologer invited.

Lorenzo understood he had no other choice but to accept his father's wish. "At the end of the day, it is not so bad," he thought. Working in the fields allowed him to spend more time with the shepherds, and during the summer nights, he could eat cheese and honey with them.

One hot summer evening, an event occurred that taught Lorenzo the fragility of life. A strong storm broke over them. "Run, Lorenzo, run home! This storm is dangerous," Arturo yelled.

While Lorenzo was running, a bolt of lightning struck a tree near him. He panicked, and his heart was filled with fear. The rain fell with indescribable force.

When he arrived home, soaking wet, his mother embraced him. Elvira lit candles all over the house and prayed with Lorenzo and Leonor as they waited for Diego, who had not yet returned. The torrential downpour pounded the roof of their home and the ground outside. It was as if the sky was pummeling the earth.

The boy wondered if God was punishing him, for something he might have done wrong. "What if a lightning bolt had struck his father?" he thought. He prayed with all his soul for Diego's life.

A few hours later, Diego arrived, soaked from the rain. He explained when the rain did not stop, he had decided to seek shelter in Santa Maria's church. Elvira rejoiced to see her husband safe, and thanked God with all her heart.

"The city is flooded. Many are praying in the church," Diego informed the family.

Approaching the fire Elvira had prepared, he brought up the

names of his eldest two sons, at that time away from home. Lorenzo thanked God for his family, as he had come to the realization it could have swept them away in just a few seconds.

He basked in the special moment and felt closer than ever to his family. Until then, he had taken for granted an essential element in his life, his family.

Throughout the night, Lorenzo suffered several fear fueled nightmares; even so, when he awoke the next day, he felt liberated. The sun rose brightly over the drenched soil. Lorenzo exited his home to admire an astonishing rainbow. It gave him the idea to visit Daniel, whom he found reflecting on the covenant God had made with Noah, sealing it with the sign of the rainbow.

"Why such a strong storm yesterday?" Lorenzo asked Daniel.

"Nature must balance itself," Daniel replied. "When there is too much tension, it builds to a force which must be released."

"But many people could have died yesterday!"

"Fate protects the people who must live," Daniel told him, believing in the will of God over everyone's life.

"Am I also protected?"

"Of course! However, do not take it for granted. If you forget who you are and become overindulgent, your protection will disappear. Fate cannot protect people who forget themselves," Daniel said earnestly.

Lorenzo was intrigued by these statements, which he finally understood years later. However, at that moment, a great will to live vibrated within him. He was certain nothing was impossible for him. Life was full of exciting and rewarding experiences. He knew that God loved and protected him.

He frequented a centenary tree, his favorite place to sit and rest while contemplating silently. The tree was in a peaceful place deep in the woods, a place where he felt calmed by his surroundings. Lorenzo thought this place had been created just for him. When he lay down in the rays of the sun, he was infused with the love of God, and he thanked God for this contentment. However, Lorenzo did not realize the profound loss he would soon suffer, for his innocence was about to end.

6. SOUL MATE

*I*n 1227, the king of Aragon, James I, who had just turned eighteen, launched a campaign against the kingdom of Valencia, which was then controlled by a Muslim ruler. Young King James wanted to show to the European Christians that though he was young, he was a strong ruler. The moment was favorable, due to the weakness of the petty Arab kings. Teruel was full of enthusiasm. Conquering Valencia would mean a significant increase in trade with the Mediterranean cities. Teruel welcomed hundreds of soldiers into its midst, and enormous tents were set up in the outskirts of the city to accommodate the warriors.

Martin, Lorenzo's brother, came home for the first time in six years. The family was thrilled to greet the eldest son, now transformed into a handsome gentleman. Lorenzo was startled to realize he hardly recognized his brother. The man who made his life a nightmare now was an admirable figure. Martin was still energetic, but elegantly dressed and spoke like a nobleman. Instead of behaving with violence and disdain toward Lorenzo, he addressed him with polite consideration.

The return of his brother was not the only event that shocked Lorenzo in the summer of 1227. Martin had invited a veteran military officer to accompany him. The veteran, widowed years before, also brought his daughter with him.

The afternoon he met Ariadna was unforgettable. When he arrived home following a long day with the shepherds, he noticed more people than usual were in his home. He acknowledged the older gentleman talking happily with his father, but his eyes did not remain long on the pair. Instead, they fixed with fascination on the young lovely presence, in the back of the room. His beating heart seemed to stop as she turned her head and her gaze met his.

"Hello, my name is Ariadna," the young woman introduced herself, smiling angelically.

Lorenzo could scarcely remember her name. He was so smitten. When he opened his mouth to introduce himself, he found that he had lost his voice. His heart pounding in his chest felt as if it were in danger of exploding.

"This is our son Lorenzo. He is going to oversee the family business," Diego said proudly, thinking about his son's promising future. "He will be the most important wool producer in all of Aragon."

Lorenzo paid no attention to his father's words. Ariadna's presence captured all attention, for he had never before met someone like her. "Who is this angelic creature?" he wondered.

That night, in bed, Lorenzo was unable to focus his thoughts on anything else but Ariadna. Sleep eluded him. He spent the entire night recalling her long dress, her blond hair, her sweet look, and her gracious manners. His introduction to Ariadna had thrust Lorenzo into a new dimension. That night, he learned what love was.

In the days that followed, Ariadna enthusiastically helped Lorenzo´s mother. Lorenzo watched her with rapt curiosity. The more he saw of her, the more enamored he became. He noticed each step, each expression, never overlooking a single detail. Lost in thought, he could not focus. His obsession with Ariadna followed him to work, where he bungled even the simplest tasks. When Diego asked what was wrong, he answered vaguely, without revealing his true feelings.

Ariadna was never alone at home, and when the families met, Lorenzo was afraid to look in her eyes. Meanwhile, his nights were a mixture of torment and devotion. He could not stop thinking about the girl with such an irresistible name, Ariadna. The more Lorenzo tried to understand her body language, the more confused he became. The way she moved, the things she said with her eyes seemed part of an unintelligible language.

In the heavens, Lorenzo´s guides knew the meeting of soulmates required a great deal of nurturing and should be dealt with care. The force of attraction was powerful, however, such a strong desire required mastery, so that physical impulse did not ruin the idyllic situation. They set up Lorenzo and Ariadna's first real encounter with great care.

One day, Elvira sent Ariadna on an errand. That same morning Lorenzo felt a powerful urge to visit the center of town. As Ariadna was about to descend the stairs near the main plaza, Lorenzo started up the stairs. They gazed into each other's eyes and their souls recognized each other. They knew they were sharing the same journey on the path to wholeness. Time seemed to stop and Lorenzo and Ariadna entered another dimension. There was no need for words; they spoke through their hearts, their eyes, and their souls. That moment became an eternity, and the memory of it stayed with them for the rest of their lives.

The sound of the church bells brought them back to this world. Lorenzo then spoke her:

"Come with me, I want to show you something extraordinary, my secret place."

Walking hand in hand, he led her to the centenary tree deep within the woods. He had promised himself never to take anyone else there, but the celestial Ariadna was different. He already loved her. Urging her to lie down in the grass near the tree, the sun shone on their faces. With their eyes closed, their fingers entwined, and the tree as their only witness, they entered the subtle worlds. It was an intimate space, only accessible to people who take risks, where people are free and secure, beyond the reach of the world's troubles.

Lorenzo and Ariadna, with their eyes closed, danced in their imaginations. They recognized that they had known each other before. After mesmerizing moments, the noise of a flock of sheep startled them. It was time to return to the physical world and Ariadna remembered Elvira's errand.

"I have to hurry home. Your mother is waiting for me."

When they arrived safely home, Ariadna brushed a kiss across Lorenzo's cheek and rushed into the house. Lorenzo's joy surpassed anything he had ever known. His afternoon with Ariadna had left an unforgettable impression on his soul.

Lorenzo passed the next days preoccupied with thoughts of her. When their paths crossed at home, they concealed their feelings for each other. They used every free moment to sneak away, together, to go Lorenzo's favorite place. There, they lay under the sun, holding hands, and dancing in the subtle worlds. Those were the happiest weeks of Lorenzo's life.

"Thank you, God, for allowing me to be so happy," he said when he prayed each night.

The heavenly plans for Lorenzo and Ariadna were different then they imagined. One afternoon Lorenzo found her crying. He could not tell if she was crying out of happiness or sorrow.

"What is wrong?" he asked.

"I do not know. I have a bad feeling," Ariadna answered. She could not explain it, but she felt the bond between them was weakening.

Lorenzo did not pay attention to Ariadna´s omen; nonetheless, he worried. Some days later, Ariadna's prediction came true. Lorenzo stumbled upon Diego and Ariadna´s father together in the main room of the house. He thought it was odd to see the gentleman home at that time of day, for he ought to have been drilling with the rest of the army. Standing out of sight, Lorenzo eavesdropped on their conversation. The more he listened to the officer's discouraging words, the more his heart was breaking.

"How is the situation?" Diego had asked. "Is Aragon attacking Valencia?"

"There has been another coup against the king," the soldier answered. "The battle of Peniscola was a disaster. Consequently, the noblemen have withdrawn their support from the king. He has had to call off the attack on Valencia."

"Once again, James I has been duped by traitors. The noblemen had urged him to attack Peniscola, even knowing that victory was not possible. Its geographic location is tricky. They should have gone with the decision to attack Valencia first, but they did not."

"The king is devastated. His wife has left him and has asked the pope to annul their marriage. What's more, the king has lost the aristocrat's trust. Now they are withdrawing their financial support of the war," Ariadna´s father sighed.

"This is like the Albarracin situation," Diego commented. "The evil noblemen, who wanted the monarch to fail, have fooled him again. Many people in Teruel went into debt, hoping for a quick victory over Valencia, and now they are in bankrupt."

"The Valencia campaign will be postponed for several years, if it happens at all. It will be difficult to rally enough troops to carry out such difficult attack."

"The people of Teruel are disappointed," Diego agreed. "It will be impossible to excite the people to support another war. As it is, the noblemen will oppress the farmers and ranchers, extorting money from them to gain back what they have lost."

As we speak, the soldiers are breaking camp. In a few days, I will return to Huesca with my daughter. If the attack on Valencia takes place in a few years, I will be too old to participate. I wanted to retire with a glorious victory, and now that is not going to be possible," the soldier said with sadness.

"I wish you a safe trip back to your home, sir."

"I am grateful for your hospitality. You have a home in Huesca."

Lorenzo had turned cold while listening to the conversation. Life was betraying him for no apparent reason. His pain was extraordinary. "Just because of a political problem, my love is leaving me. What do I care about the Valencia campaign or the battle of Peniscola?" he wondered, tortured by the cruel turn of events. He knew, once in Huesca, Ariadna's father would promise his daughter in marriage to another gentleman, and he would not see her again.

Devastated, Lorenzo cried in his room. He did not have dinner with his family, and hardly slept.

At five o'clock in the morning, he went out to the garden to meditate amongst the stars. He observed the constellations, Polaris, Ursa Major, and the belt of Orion. This activity calmed him. He also noticed the moon had been near Jupiter throughout the night when his emotions where overwhelmed. He tried to get an explanation from the cosmos, but there were no answers.

Ariadna saw Lorenzo in the garden and slipped out of the house without her father's knowledge and took Lorenzo's hand. They spent their last bittersweet hours together.

"My father has told me we are leaving soon," the young girl, sobbed.

Gazing at the sky, they held hands tightly and identified themselves with two stars. They promised that when they looked at their stars, they would remember each other and wish the other each the very best, regardless of where they were.

"It is possible we will not see each other again. Your father will promise you in marriage to a soldier in your region," Lorenzo said, trying not to believe his own fatal prediction.

Ariadna felt Lorenzo was part of her, although an inner voice told her they had to separate. She held his hand tighter, and they stood together, in silence, until sunrise. Ariadna then entered in the house and Lorenzo felt her loss. The pain within him was beyond anything he had ever suffered.

Lorenzo hardly spoke during the subsequent days. Sorrow kept him so profoundly silent that he doubted he would ever speak again. The day Ariadna and her father left, he did not say goodbye to her. He watched them leave from a distance. Then he turned toward the fields and continued into a pine forest, where he wandered aimlessly, weeping as he went.

During the following weeks, he remembered Ariadna every moment, and tried picturing what she was doing. He fantasized that she would return, but she never did. To overcome his devastation, Lorenzo required divine help, and it was granted through the shepherd Arturo. Lorenzo's overwhelming feeling of loss gave him the opportunity to enter the world of dreams and to understand why life punished him as it had.

7. DREAMS

*A*fter Ariadna's departure, Lorenzo was left feeling devastated. He could not focus or concentrate on his work. During his free time, he walked great distances through the natural places near Teruel. One evening, while wandering, he met the shepherd Arturo, who appeared as if from nowhere. Lorenzo did not realize that the meeting was fateful, so he could hear the words he needed to hear.

"Lorenzo, what is wrong?" Arturo asked him, sensing his weakened emotional state.

Lorenzo could not say anything. Arturo, with his innate ability to understand the soul's problems knew Lorenzo was feeling lovesick. He consoled him by saying:

"When sorrow and anxiety take over me, I sit and listen to my breath. Do this every day, in the same place, at the same time. As you practice, a new vision of life will unfold before you."

"I sit and focus on my breathing, is that all?" Lorenzo asked without understanding the exercise.

"That is all. Listen to your breath. Nothing else."

When he got home, Lorenzo tried the exercise, but he could not do it. His grief repeatedly overcame him. He could not stop thinking about Ariadna. Although he tried to concentrate on his breathing, it was impossible to get her off his mind. Every night he watched her star near his, shining. Looking at the stars together gave him a glimmer of hope that he might see her again.

Another day, Arturo showed Lorenzo how to live with his sorrow.

"It is inevitable that sadness comes into our lives at certain moments. It is not the feeling, but what you do with it. Rhythmic breathing will help you transform the sorrow into something positive."

"But when will this heartbreaking pain leave me?"

The shepherd insisted on the importance of the breathing exercise.

"When you listen to your breath, your soul rests. The anxiety of the loss becomes gratitude for the experience."

The young man did not want to listen. He was determined to be a victim, instead of trying to understand the meaning of the situation.

"Why does God let me suffer? They have snatched my beloved," Lorenzo said angrily.

"The feeling of lost love produces intense suffering, yet it is possible both of you have a destiny to fulfill. If this separation has occurred, it means both of you need to take different paths. Each of you must learn your own lessons," the shepherd said.

"And what is my destiny?" Lorenzo asked angrier, realizing he was not getting the answers he was looking for.

"It is good for you to be angry. It means you are transforming the pain. The next step will be to transform the anger into understanding," the shepherd pointed out.

Arturo did not want to answer Lorenzo's question. He knew each person must discover their own destiny by their own means, which happens through the process of personal development. However, Arturo did clarify an important question related to his encounter with Ariadna.

"Meeting the girl was inevitable. For reasons beyond my understanding, you are both united. Those kind of encounters are unavoidable and leave permanent impressions for the rest of your life. Experiences like these help you remember where you come from."

"But I wish so much to be with her again, with my beloved Ariadna," Lorenzo cried out.

"Your encounter had a specific purpose. If you had stayed together, your learning would have stagnated. If she had stayed in Teruel and you had married, you would have had at least half a dozen children. You would have spent all of your time and energy on raising your children. Maybe God wants you to do something other than raise children."

Lorenzo had not thought about their situation in that way. He once again appreciated Arturo's insightful intelligence. Being with Ariadna maybe was not the best thing for him right now. It was hard to admit, but the shepherd was perhaps right. He decided to follow his advice and do the breathing exercise. While he concentrated on his breathing, an infinite number of thoughts about Ariadna bombarded his head. Finally, after repeating the exercises day after day, the pain began to subside.

The positive side of being lovesick was that Lorenzo could connect with his soul. On the days he practiced, he had more vivid dreams. One of his dreams astonished him. He was a big white bird, locked in a cage, in the middle of a field. The iron bars of the cage did not allow him to escape. He gave up, but other birds flying by said to him:

"Lorenzo, dare, fly!"

"But I cannot leave the cage."

His unhappiness grew. His sadness was so intense that he was dying in the cage. Because of his anguish, he stood up and took an audacious decision.

"I am going to get free of this cage, even if I die trying. I would rather die than languish inside," he said to himself.

He gathered his strength, closed his eyes, and started flying inside the cage. Just before touching the iron bars he stopped. He was afraid of hurting himself and gave up. His despair trapped him and touched bottom, but he was not going to die a slave. He flew again and prepared himself to die from hitting the bars, but death never came. To his amazement, he found himself outside the cage. He could not explain what had happened. He looked back, confused, and realized that the cage had not existed. His imagination had created it.

Lorenzo woke up scared, wondering about the meaning of the strange dream. He felt as if had been real, so different was it from all his previous dreams. He ran to see the astrologer Daniel, hoping he could help understand the dream. The wise man listened attentively, but did not say anything. Lorenzo grew frustrated and demanded an interpretation. After much pondering, Daniel said,

"This is a prophetic dream. In time you will find the explanation."

"I do not understand what this dream has to do with me," Lorenzo protested. "I am not a bird and I cannot fly."

"At the right moment, do not be afraid of flying. This is all I can say to you," Daniel said, ending the conversation.

Daniel would rather be silent. He had seen people who took the first step towards freedom, but then they gave up. They were not brave enough to continue on the path, and had to create fantasies to cover up their cowardice. For that reason, the wise man decided to remain silent; when Lorenzo was ready, he would risk flying.

Still, the astrologer realized Lorenzo was awaking up to other dimensions and decided to share some of his knowledge. He invited him to the baths on Friday, the day reserved for Jews. Daniel told the owner of the baths Lorenzo was almost family and he entered with him. In the first room, Lorenzo experienced the hot water; in the second room, he was massaged with flowing water; and he ended in the third room with cold water. Then he met with Daniel in the resting room with the rest of his Jewish friends, some of whom were members of the Aragon Astrology School, a school of royal counselors. They spoke for hours about astrology and Lorenzo was delighted to be in their presence.

Daniel, observing Lorenzo's enthusiasm, invited him every Friday. The only condition was he had to not speak, only listen. Lorenzo obeyed. He enjoyed the conversations about planets, signs of the zodiac, and the political situation. Each Friday he was stunned with the depth of their knowledge. On many occasions, the intellectual conversations were much deeper than he could understand. He took great delight in listening to them. He learned about the battle of the Navas de Tolosa and the consequences for the Jews: they had to flee Andalusia and settle in Toledo. "Toledo." That was the first time that he heard the name of the Castilian capital. He felt an immediate connection to the city.

On another occasion, in the baths, the men talked about women. Lorenzo dared to tell his love story with Ariadna, whom he remembered every day. The Jewish bathers smiled at his innocence. That night, after his breathing exercise, Ariadna came to him in his dream, walking with him hand in hand. Lorenzo saw the two of them together from a distance, illuminated by the sun. Lorenzo knew Ariadna was his soulmate, but that they should live separately for reasons he did not understand. A sense of peace and understanding came from the heavens filling his spirit. Arturo also confirmed this to him,

"Lorenzo, if you had not experienced the pain of the separation of Ariadna, you would not have started the breathing exercise, and would not be able to enter the world of dreams."

This was Lorenzo's the first initiation, which helped him develop his intuition, and make good decisions regarding his life.

"Intuition is essential in instructing us how and when to act," Arturo told him another time. "For us shepherds, it is essential. We use intuition to know when to let the sheep roam free and when to corral them. The breathing exercise will help you connect with the voice of your intuition."

Lorenzo nodded. After much practice, he could attune to his "small voice", which subtly told him when was the time for action and when it was better to wait. It was the same voice that had saved him from the fire years before.

He also learned the consequences of not heeding it. On one occasion, when his father was traveling some well-dressed buyers asked him if they could buy some wool on credit. As they introduced themselves as good friends of Diego, Lorenzo accepted their word, even though his inner voice warned him not to. As predicted, they never paid. Diego became angry and punished his son, making him carry heavy loads, in payment for his mistake.

Days later, Lorenzo tried to explain Diego about his inner voice; however, the astonished look on his father's face was such that Lorenzo never spoke of it again.

During his time off, Lorenzo visited Daniel, who taught him basic concepts of astrology. On another Friday, Daniel recited poems to his friends. They were verses from Oriental lands, written by Jalal ad-Din Muhammad Rumi, also known as Mevlana. The poem's theme deeply touched Lorenzo's soul:

One went to the Beloved's door and knocked.

A voice asked, "Who is there?" He answered, "It is I."

The voice said, "There is no room here for me and thee."

The door was shut.

After a year of solitude and deprivation

this man returned to the Beloved's door.

He knocked once more.

A voice from within asked, "Who is there?"

The man said, "It is Thou."

The door was opened for him.

Lorenzo pondered the mysterious words. He tried to ask Daniel about the poem's meaning, but Daniel kept quiet. He would only say that the poet was a mystic and a man of knowledge. It was the first time the young man had heard such words, and he pondered them deeply.

The reality was Lorenzo's father had many other mundane things to teach Lorenzo, which would become obstacles on the path of knowledge that waited for him.

8. BUSINESS

The Kingdom of Aragon became peaceful in 1228, following a difficult period for King James I. The defeat at Peniscola, the failure of the Valencia´s campaign, and the divorce from his first wife had put the king in a weak position. Some powerful noblemen met secretly plotting his overthrow. The chief nobleman, Don Pedro Ahones, and sixty of his followers agreed to depose the king, who was in Daroca at that time. Don Pedro's intention was to duel the king. He had the advantage, thanks to his being a skilled swordsman. He never considered that his younger and inexperienced adversary could defeat him. Don Pedro already saw himself as king.

When James I discovered Don Pedro's plans, he decided to face his enemy in a life or death battle. The monarch knew he would receive protection from the heavens. And sure enough, despite his physical inferiority and lack of experience, James I killed the traitor Don Pedro in an epic duel.

Victory in the face of such a stocky and expert rival meant a turning point in his reign. From that moment on, the people considered him an extraordinary figure, protected by the Holy One. All noblemen had to promise loyalty in a solemn ceremony in Daroca.

Once the people believed James was the rightful king and that he was protected by Providence, the internal squabbling ceased, creating an era of peace and prosperity. As a result, Lorenzo´s family business experienced unparalleled prosperity. Unfortunately, the economic success did not bring psychological stability to Lorenzo´s father; on the contrary, it had the opposite effect. Diego's ambition grew. He became more miserable and irritable and exploited his shepherds to make ever more gold. There was never enough to satisfy him.

One of Diego´s methods was bribing tax collectors. He was so proud of his "art", that taught it to Lorenzo. The king had just imposed a new tax of five percent of their goods to pay for the disaster of the battle of Peniscola. To put the new levy into effect, a tax collector came to the city. Diego used the tax inspection to teach his son a masterful lesson about taxes.

"When you meet a tax collector, the first thing is to determine if he can be bribed. Most of them are honest. If you see this, pay as soon as possible. This will save you a lot of time and energy."

"And what if the tax collector is dishonest?" Lorenzo queried.

"You need to make him feel important. Thus, you must look like impoverished. You need to flatter him and let him speak. He must believe that you are his friend. Tax collectors do not have many friends, as you can imagine. If you lie, you must do it firmly, looking him in the eye."

Lorenzo watched his father's charade. It was a completely new experience for him. Having spoken with several colleagues, Diego had discovered the tax collector was not honest. That delighted him. He told Lorenzo to come with him to meet the civil servant and to pay close attention. Before leaving, Diego dressed in an old, moth-eaten jacket, ratty sandals, and a dirty cape. The wool trader invited the tax collector to eat and drink with abundance, so he could feast on unknown foods. During the hearty lunch, he hung on every word the tax collector said, making him feel important.

"I have heard that the life of a tax collector is a lonely one," Diego said to him,. "You travel such dangerous roads."

The short, heavy-set tax collector shrugged. "I am just a legal officer. I only collect what the law determines," he replied.

Lorenzo´s father continued with his flattery while waiting for the alcohol to take effect.

"If you only knew the number of problems that come with this job," the tax collector complained.

Upon hearing those words, Diego smiled, as he realized it was possible to bribe him.

"I can imagine," he replied, feigning interest in the man's problems.

"We travel all day, we must evaluate the businesses, and everyone complains. Then, they turn against us. Meanwhile the Crown and the main tax collector always want more, not caring that I must transport the collected gold and the cattle on my own and at my own risk. And do you think that anyone appreciates it?" the tax collector shook his head.

Lorenzo watched his father fake sympathy with the man. He nodded as the tax collector spoke, conveying empathy. By the end of dinner, the civil servant had drunk enough. Then he mentioned Diego's tax bill.

"According to my information, you own twenty thousand sheep. This means that you must deliver one thousand to the Crown."

Diego's expression turned indignant. He threw his hands in the air as if he had absolutely no idea what the collector was referring to. Diego shamelessly lied. Lorenzo watched his father's charade astonished.

"I do not even have half of that amount! It must be a huge mistake!" Diego protested.

The tax collector did not know how to respond to Diego's indignation. Diego's tone made him doubt of himself and question his information.

"Tomorrow we can inspect my flocks and I will prove it to you! Meanwhile, take a room in the main lodge of the city at my expense. This will compensate for your extra time. We can meet at sunrise," Diego proposed.

The civil servant accepted joyfully. Sleeping in a feather bed was more than he accustomed to. That night, Diego sent him wine and female companionship. The tax collector had one of the best nights of his life. The next morning, Diego went to the lodge, and found him suffering from a terrible hangover. He asked Lorenzo to wait outside the lodge,

"When you bribe someone, you must do it without witnesses," he said to his son.

"Are you all right?" Diego fussed over the man.

"I did not sleep well," the tax collector admitted.

"It is rather late to inspect the flocks," Diego pointed out.

"How many sheep do you say you own?"

"No more than seven thousand," Diego insisted. At the same time, he showed him a sack of gold coins.

"To count all your sheep would require three days."

"Trust me, I will give you three hundred sheep in payment and you can stay in the lodge for three days at my expense. Do me this favor, I beg you. Here, you have a small present for your expenses in the city," Diego said, handing over the sack of gold.

"I am sick of doing favors from everyone!" the tax collector grumbled, eyeing with disdain the sack of gold.

"I thank you, sir, for your kindness and understanding," the wool trader continued.

"I will make an exception just for you. I will not inspect the flocks, but bring me three hundred and fifty sheep!"

Diego hid a smile for he had just saved himself six hundred and fifty sheep of the original one thousand requested by the Crown.

"I will deliver the sheep to you before you depart Teruel," Diego promised.

Feeling immensely proud of himself, Diego counseled his son all the way home.

"Lorenzo, have you learned how to deal with the tax collectors?" Diego asked.

"Is it always so easy to bribe them?" Lorenzo asked instead of answering.

"It depends on the economic situation. If the Majorca campaign is successful, the defeated Arabian kings will defray most of the war's expenses. Then, the tax collectors will have no extra pressure and the next inspections will be easy. However, if James I fails to capture Majorca, then we will be more heavily taxed. That is how it works. So, let us pray for the success of the Majorca campaign," Diego told his son laughing and winking his eye.

Lorenzo father's cunning astonished him, and he wondered where he had learned it. He realized that his father's life, although it seemed exemplary, was in fact corrupt. His father had fallen victim to his basest ambitions.

Diego could not bear to see the shepherds happy. He felt terrible when he saw their happiness. To punish them he lowered their salaries blaming it on the disastrous war, the increase in taxes, and the apathy of buyers. The truth was Diego oppressed the shepherds to exert obstinate control over them. The shepherds, although they felt sorry for their boss, formed a union to halt the abuses of wool ranchers like Diego. They asked him for better conditions and after days of negotiations, they reached an agreement for half of what Diego was ready to pay.

"I have tricked those ignorant shepherds and they believe they have negotiated well," he said to his son. "Do not keep company with the shepherds anymore. It is better that you learn the code of laws and become a good businessman. The shepherds are only our employees."

That night Lorenzo was anxious and could not sleep. He saw himself trapped as a wool trader, receiving orders from his father with his unlimited ambitions. All of the sudden, he remembered the cage dream. He understood its meaning. He was living the dream! That realization sent shivers through his body. The premonition had come to fruition.

The prospect of following in his father's footsteps contradicted what Lorenzo knew of his destiny. He thought if he followed Diego´s example he would have a comfortable life; he would own a nice house, would be the owner of a successful business, and would become an influential man in Teruel. On the other hand, he knew he would not be happy, he would be lowering himself to practicing all his father tricks, ultimately oppressing the shepherds, his friends. He would become a cynic.

One afternoon, catching Lorenzo by surprise, Diego asked him to accompany him to the village of Gea. He wanted to hire Arab dying experts. Gea had belonged to the aristocratic Arab family Beni-Razin and since the year 711, the village survived paying by fees to whomever protected it, as the Cid Campeador had done two hundred years before. The people of Gea lived under the threat that some nobleman would conquer them and, then, they would find themselves slaves or worse, murdered. For that reason, they regularly paid a large ransom to the lord of Albarracin, who protected them against possible Christian attacks.

Traveling those roads was risky. Elvira, worried about the trip, prayed for her husband and son. Meanwhile, Lorenzo's excitement over leaving his native city for the first time soared. He rode a mule and his father a horse. The mountains, miles away, beckoned him. He pondered, what might possibly be beyond them.

When they reached Gea, Lorenzo noticed how the town really was. Life was harsh. The local inhabitants had become a cheap workforce for the Christian landowners. Diego took advantage of their poor circumstances and haggled mercilessly over their future salaries. Lorenzo had never before observed the hiring process. After the successful negotiations, they lodged in the village's best lodge. The inn was magnificent, decorated with calligraphic and geometric motifs. There was a big warm tea salon, and on Thursdays, most of the town's inhabitants gathered there.

That night, a new Persian, was going to perform a stellar act in the lodge. The expectation in the town was high and everyone came to the tea salon to see him. The owner of the inn mentioned the dancer came from a Persian mystical school. He was a disciple of Rumi, also known as Mevlana, the most renowned spiritual master of that part of the world. Lorenzo then remembered the poem that Daniel had recited.

After a period of meditative preparation, the Persian whirled to the music. He wore a white tunic and a tall conical hat. A flute, a guitar, and a small drum guided his movements. While dancing, the man pointed with his right hand heavenward. His left arm had the palm down. In that position, he turned around himself, following the music.

"What is he doing?" Lorenzo whispered to the owner of the inn, while marveling at the movements of the dancer.

"He is receiving God's love with the right hand, and distributing it to the world with the left."

"And why is he doing that?"

"To be united with God and share His Love with the world."

The atmosphere of the lodge changed as the Persian turned. Regardless of how many times he turned, the man did not become dizzy. When he finished, the Persian entered into an ecstatic state. Then he exclaimed, crying out in joy,

"Allah, Allah, Allah!"

Possessed by the love of God, he glowed. His eyes were the eyes of a child, and at the same time were alight with the serenity of a person of great spiritual development. His glance touched Lorenzo deeply.

When the dervish had completed the Sema, all the townspeople came to embrace him. The owner of the lodge asked Lorenzo and his father not to tell anyone what they had seen, as the orthodox Almoravids attacked those who embraced mystical practices.

This shocked Lorenzo.

"Reaching God through dance!"

He thought some Christian priests might see it as heretical, but it seemed that the Holy One loved the Persian.

"Could the Church be wrong?" he wondered confused, questioning the words of Teruel's priests.

Back in his room at the inn, Lorenzo reflected on what he had just seen. "Maybe God has a unique face that presents Itself with different forms," he said to himself, thinking about what Arturo and Daniel had taught him, trying to embrace the greatness of what he had felt that evening.

Just before sleeping, Lorenzo experienced a crescendo of emotions, and he asked God:

"Do you love me?"

A subtle affirmation came from deep within. He fell asleep in a state of deep peace, knowing that he could trust life.

In his peaceful state, Lorenzo was not aware that his conflict with his father would soon bubble to the surface. Denying the path Diego had laid out for him would become the hardest test faced so far by the young Lorenzo.

9. CONFLICT

On his way back to Teruel, the young man meditated on how to reach God dancing, but his father's voice shook him from his revelry.

"Look at these three gold coins," Diego said. "Yesterday, while the town's people were watching the Persian, I closed several deals. I sold them a lot of wool at a good price."

Lorenzo realized how one could experience a situation based upon different perceptions.

"In business it is important to seize opportunities. Always consider the people's mood," Diego continued, unaware of his son's thoughts. "Yesterday was one such opportunity. The people were ecstatic watching that lunatic dancing, and I acted. Today, when they realize how foolish they were, it will be too late. And, who has the three gold coins? Your father, Diego Garcia Pardo!"

Left speechless by his father's greed, Lorenzo could only nod. He remembered the face of the Persian dancer broadcasting God's love. His eyes were shining while his father's eyes were darkening. Lorenzo realized Diego could not see with God's eyes, as he had blocked the manifestation of the Spirit.

"This is the important thing in life. Look at these coins. Are they not beautiful?" Diego asked his son, so proud of them, showing them off.

To celebrate the deal, Diego ordered two expensive waistcoats and two extraordinary capes when he arrived home. He also ordered a new sword of the best Toledan steel. He wanted so much to impress the town's leaders.

Lorenzo, on the other hand, disappeared in to his room. There, he tried to dance like the Persian dervish, but he only got dizzy. He wondered what the Persian's secret was. After trying a few more times, he fell to the floor. The noise attracted the attention of his father.

"What are you doing on the floor?"

"I was dancing," Lorenzo said, getting up slowly.

Diego's thick eyebrows drew together, "Don't tell me you were imitating that lunatic."

"Yes, father," admitted Lorenzo "I want to whirl like him."

"Don't be stupid. Look at the amount of sheep and wool that we own. Look at our remarkable business! Focus on what is real! Soon, all of this will be yours. You will be able to parade in front of the whole city! Those dances are for lunatics, for people that do not live in the real world," Diego reprimanded his son.

Keeping silent, Lorenzo swallowed his protests. He didn't know if his father were right or wrong. Certainly, Diego's life seemed successful enough.

"You should have seen the envious looks on the faces of the council members when learned out that I had ordered two new expensive waistcoats! What fools they are! Now they realize who is in charge!" Diego continued, still pleased with his recent purchases. "Soon I will become one of the council mayors, which will add to my stature. I will welcome the king when he visits, and I will discuss the different taxes and levies. The Royal Adviser of Teruel will appoint me as his helper. Life is beautiful, is it not?" he said reveling in his good fortune.

Lorenzo remained quiet. Diego seemed pleased with his achievements. In that regard, Lorenzo was happy for him, but did not know what to say.

"You must know everything I do, I do for you. If it were my choice, I would live tranquilly with your mother, away from this dirty commercial life. One day everything will be yours, Lorenzo!"

His father's comment confused him. "So, all of my father's problems and business issues are because of me", he thought to himself, suddenly stricken with guilt. Diego continued with his speech without paying attention to Lorenzo.

"Look at our family. One brother is a soldier and the other a monk. Your sister soon will go to the convent, and you will be left to oversee the family business. We will become an example for all our neighbors. The family name, Garcia Pardo will ring throughout the country. My name, Diego Garcia Pardo, will be acknowledged as the greatest wool producer in Aragon and as the head mayor of the council. Everyone will know who I am! I will show your grandfather who I have become."

Listening carefully to his father, he sensed Diego's rage. He realized Diego had put distance between people. When people came close to him, they were afraid. Watching him talk, Lorenzo remembered his childhood, and the violence Diego had used to make speak.

Following his rant, Diego retired to the tavern to drink wine. He would not drink anything but the best wine. He invited his friends from the council and returned home inebriated. Lorenzo was eating in the kitchen when his father returned.

"Lorenzo, look at me," Diego said as he moved about the kitchen, inebriated. "The king will honor me and everyone will envy us. You are my son and you will inherit all this" Diego gestured out the window at the mountains, as if those, too, belonged to him.

It was the moment of Lorenzo's big test. A symbolic door through which only he could pass was about to open; it was the door leading to freedom. If Lorenzo chose to cross that threshold, he would live an adventurous life with all of its risks and rewards; but it would be a free life. If he chose not to walk through it, he would resign himself to living the life chosen by his father. Lorenzo had no way of knowing that, the door only opens once in a lifetime.

Perhaps sensing Lorenzo's lack of commitment, Diego decided to marry the young man to the daughter of a noblemen.

"It is time that you settled down, Lorenzo. You are an adult now," Diego said a short time later. "We are going to betroth you" he announced.

Diego's words stunned Lorenzo. "Who is she?"

"She is the daughter of one of the mayors, Montcada. He is the most important lawyer of the council," Diego said filled with pride. "In exchange for betrothing you to his daughter, I will become a council member. The money I already give to the council is not enough. Your marriage will secure my appointment."

Lorenzo was confused. His father was so adamant about how his life should unfold, that he did not know what to say. Without any delay and as if it was just another trade, Diego sealed the deal on Lorenzo's marriage to the daughter of the most influential lawyer in the court of Aragon. Montcada was the most difficult opponent Diego had ever negotiated with. Not only did he know the local laws, as his ancestors had written the codes of laws of Daroca and Teruel, but he also had a great network. Montcada had financed the successful battle of Majorca. Diego, who eagerly wanted the wedding, accepted unfavorable conditions and agreed to pay a large payment in the event he should cancel the wedding. It was set for 1st of May 1232.

The wool trader explained his decision to his son, and he, went to meet his future wife. Sabina, his betrothed, although only fourteen, knew exactly what she wanted. The young man still recalled his time with Ariadna. Lorenzo realized there was no real connection between him and Sabina, not even a physical attraction. Sabina immediately sought to establish her role as his future wife, trying to change Lorenzo's character; her husband would have to learn how to conduct himself amongst highclass society.

"Do not dress that way," she told him showing the kind of cloths he should wear as a highclass gentleman. "Greet that man. He is my father's friend," she murmured, lowering her eyes demurely when they encountered the nobleman. "Do not speak to the shepherds," she scolded Lorenzo when she caught him joking with the men whose company he had kept for many years. "It will cause some noblemen to think less of you."

Lorenzo wondered if Sabina were not thirty years old instead of fourteen. Living with her for the rest of his life would be unbearable. His father, on the other hand, applauded her comments and encouraged him to follow her advice.

"She is a lawyer's daughter, and has been educated by them and knows how to behave," Diego asserted.

"But I would not change her family for ours."

"Her father will teach you the law. You will create the laws for the wool commerce! Remember, he who makes the law, knows the tricks!"

"But I don't want to be a lawyer! She wants to change me!" Lorenzo protested angrily.

"Nonsense! You will be both a lawyer and the premier wool trader in Teruel! You will get used to Sabina! It does not matter whether you like her or not. The marriage raises our social status. And all women are the same," Diego added, for he no longer recognized Elvira's worth, even though his wife had kept her faith and dignity, despite of the destructive path her husband had chosen.

Diego seemed certain of his opinions, but Lorenzo did not agree that all women were the same. He knew from his experience with Ariadna, that she had been unique, and he would never experience anything like it with Sabina.

The night the young man turned seventeen, he celebrated his birthday with his betrothed. When he returned home, he went to sleep straight away. A being of light appeared in his dream, frightening Lorenzo with its vivid presence.

"Do not be afraid," his guide told him.

The guide whispered a single word in his ear, but Lorenzo did not understand it. Then he transported him to a magnificent city. There he saw wide streets and lofty, beautiful buildings, and even a fortress! The reality of the dream convinced him it was real. He saw spiritual guides watching over the city. The atmosphere was sublime and uplifting, lifting Lorenzo to a state of rapture.

The being of light told him with firmness, "This city is your true home. Leave Teruel and go to Toledo!"

Immediately, Lorenzo woke up with the luminous being's last words still resounding in his head. Stunned, he analyzed his dream. It had a special quality impossible to ignore. His guide's face returned. He knew the tall being had been guiding him his whole life, even before he was born. The dream gave him insight into the deepest longings of his soul. He knew his life's purpose went far beyond taking over the family business.

"My home," he said to himself when he thought about Toledo.

Lorenzo knew his place was in the Castilian capital. The feeling was more certain than anything he had felt before. It compelled him to visit Daniel, the astrologer. Daniel, though he knew what

Lorenzo would face, had kept silent all these years. He knew Lorenzo would have his own revelation and it would put him at a cross roads, where he would need to decide whether to live a life chosen by others, or to follow, in an act of faith, the signs of his dreams.

"Now it is the time to become a real man." Daniel laid a hand on Lorenzo's shoulder, conveying pride over Lorenzo's sudden maturity. After meditating for a few more moments, Daniel added, "Your life is yours. No one can decide for you. You have the gift of free will. Do not waste this opportunity."

The symbolic door towards freedom had just opened for Lorenzo. Daniel stepped aside and did not interfere. He only prayed for him.

"Providence can open doors, but each person must walk through by himself," and Daniel warned Lorenzo the door would not remain open forever.

"Destiny cannot wait for someone who does not dare to leap."

Lorenzo left the meeting in a meditative state.

"Toledo is not that far from Teruel," he considered. Now he was ready to follow his own path. All he needed to do was to overcome the pressures imposed upon him. If he failed to claim his freedom, other's expectations would defeat him, and he would remain enslaved forever.

10. DEPARTURE

*L*orenzo could not ignore his dream. "Toledo" kept echoing in his head. At the same time, he imagined how it would be to live in the capital. The young man asked Daniel about Toledo. The astrologer spoke about the many translations of classic books. He also mentioned the extraordinary beings who resided in Toledo; seekers of knowledge who wanted to find answers to deep questions.

"The most highly developed people of the world live there," Daniel assured.

"Do they translate books?" Lorenzo asked, eager to know if there was a place where he could do more than managing a family business.

"Those books explore who we are, our free will, and the universal laws. In Toledo you can find translations of books by Ibn Gabirol, Al-Farabi, Plato and Plotinus," Daniel answered.

He then showed him his own manuscripts. Lorenzo was amazed to behold the best library of Teruel.

"I wonder if we actually do have free will. I have contemplating this question for years."

"Yes, we do. We are free people, but only up to a point. However, we are also determined because we live in a relative world. Nevertheless, this discussion is premature. In Toledo, you will meet with metaphysicians and philosophers."

"And, do they translate these books? Lorenzo asked.

"Yes. They translate and compile the great treaties written long ago by the great philosophers, intellects, sages and saints. They adapt universal principles to our contemporary languages so everybody can access it."

Daniel took down book about Toledo and showed him some of the illustrations. The drawings exactly matched his dream images.

Lorenzo said good-bye to Daniel. He was not sure how he could have seen that reality in his dreams. The idea of going to Toledo strengthened him. It represented something meaningful. A new possibility he had never thought of opened before him. "Maybe I can find the wise ones and learn from them," he thought.

Lorenzo compared the life his father had designed for him with the lives of the Toledan translators of magnificent works. "Why hasn't anyone mentioned Toledo to me? Is no one in my family interested in these subjects?" he asked himself.

The young man spent the next few days pondering the decision he was about to make, even his father noticed something was not right with him.

"Lorenzo, why are you so quiet?" he asked him.

The young man felt extremely nervous because he recognized the consequences of his decision. Fear almost won, but he dared, without looking into his father´s eyes, to tell him the news,

"Father, I am going to Toledo."

"This is wonderful news, my son! The kingdoms of Leon and Castile are one with King Ferdinand III. Toledo is going to be the most important city of both kingdoms, and the richest people will live there. If the son of Ferdinand, Alphonso, gets married to daughter of James I, then Castile, Leon, and Aragon will be one kingdom. And

Toledo will be the capital!"

"Father," Lorenzo tried to speak.

Diego was proud of his son, and did not let him finish the sentence. He thought Lorenzo had just made an extraordinary business decision that he even could not conceive. Diego said to him,

"In Toledo you will be able to see the kind of clothing they make and their pricing. You can take some garments from here and sell them there. The trip will be a long one; it could prove dangerous, but it is worth the risk for the future of our business."

"I think that you have not understood me well. I am going to live in Toledo," he said fearfully.

"Live?" inquired Diego, astonished!

"Yes. I want to meet the Toledan translators," Lorenzo said, trying to remain firm.

"Is this a joke? Where did you get this idea? Daniel must have influenced you! He has no right to interfere!

"It was not Daniel. I had a dream and I wish to move there."

"So, you are telling me that you had a dream and that you are going to leave the family business and your wedding?"

"Yes…" he answered frightened by his father's reaction.

"Look, son… When I was your age, I also thought of leaving, but I decided to stay. Look how well things have turned out. Soon I will become a city councilor. I did well not to follow my youthful fantasies."

"And how are you going to make your living?" Elvira intervened, worried about her son.

"I will do something. I am strong and young."

Diego became anxious. He was not ready to accept that his plans would not unfold as he expected. He tried to understand his son's words as youthful rebellion. Then, he threatened him,

"I do not want to see you until you abandon this ridiculous idea! If necessary, I will put you in chains!"

Lorenzo was distressed by his father's reaction, although not surprised. He tried to understand Diego's reasoning, and even tried to convince himself that Diego was right, but a stronger pull from within was calling to Toledo. It was something beyond his life. Then he went to his room and contemplated his death. In that moment, he did not mind dying as the price for following his dream. If he did not leave, he would castigate himself for the rest of his life. Despite his father´s resistance, Lorenzo was determined to go. An impulse made him speak to his girlfriend. Lorenzo took Sabina to a quiet place to speak privately with her.

"Sabina, I am sorry to tell you that I am leaving for Toledo," he said, frightened by how she might react.

"And when are you coming back?"

"I do not know if I am coming back."

"Don´t you know when you are coming back? What about our wedding? The preparations are already underway! My whole family is anticipating our marriage.

"I am sorry, but I want a different life. I want to explore other cities. I don't want to be a wool trader," Lorenzo answered, now firmer.

"We could be the most powerful couple of Teruel! Everyone will envy us. You can´t do this to me! You were not going to be a mere wool trader. My family was prepared to make you a lawmaker! And why are you going to Toledo?" Sabina demanded, emphasizing each of her words.

"I am not exactly sure why I am going, but I am leaving. I want to know Toledo. I feel that there is something there calling me, although I do not yet know what it is," he answered firmed again.

Lorenzo was surprised that his fiancée's annoyance did not affect him.

"Do you dare to reject me before our wedding to go to a city in which you do not know what you are going to do? You are insane! Besides, this is not acceptable for a Montcada. My father will never forgive this insult. Your father will have to pay for this!"

Lorenzo realized, even though she seemed annoyed, she was not. After Ariadna's departure he had experienced a tear in his soul and Sabina was not in pain at this news. He realized his fiancée was happy the wedding had been canceled. Her annoyance was due to the mask she would have to present before the community. Lorenzo thought, because the marriage was not consummated, it should not be a case of repudation; it would be a just simple cancellation. With economic compensation to her father, Sabina's name would remain untarnished.

After the conversation, he experienced a paralyzing fear. His confidence evaporated when he understood the consequences of his decision. He was fully responsible for the first time in his life. He did not want to hurt anyone, but he had to stop living the life that others had chosen for him. A deep anxiety overtook Lorenzo, when he realized he had thwarted his father's plans. Diego would disown him and he would never see him again. His fiancée's family would require a public apology, and a large payment.

"If I go to Toledo I will never see my mother again," Lorenzo realized, overcome with sadness. "I will be an outlaw, the community will expel me, and I will become a vagabond."

When Lorenzo returned home, he went to his room and cried. There was enormous pressure on the seventeen-year-old young man. A multitude of thoughts filled his mind and he could not breathe. He had an easy life in Teruel, and he was about to abandon it. Maybe he could take back what he said, apologize to everyone, and stay in his native city. Everything for that dream... Damn the dream! He prayed and asked for guidance, but none came. Nothing...only silence. The way to freedom lay before him. Still, he felt a profound loneliness; it was the solitude that any human being faces when has to make such an epic decision.

The next morning he woke up depressed. He could not motivate himself. He was devastated. His father did not greet him and Lorenzo went for a long, solitary walk.

"Going to Toledo was not a simple adolescent craving," he thought. It was his soul's longing!

He then went to lay down near his favorite tree. He contemplated the sun and calmed himself. He spent the whole day watching the sun and its precise movements. He realized many people had experienced the same dilemma. And he remembered Ariadna. He had lost his beloved, and did not want to lose his life as well. Whenever he felt his extraordinary love for her, he knew that there were other dimensions to life. Life was a mystery, and he wanted to understand it; he wished to meet those who shared the same longing for freedom. He would be a slave if he stayed in his Teruel.

In the days that followed, his father increased the pressure on him. Diego's plans would collapse because of a young man's decision, and he was not going to allow it. He would use violence if necessary, to prevent Lorenzo's leaving.

"Lorenzo, come back to work, and stop being stupid! I have met the father of your fiancée and he is furious. Your decision means that I will have to compensate him with a fortune. This will ruin us," he said to Lorenzo, exaggerating.

Lorenzo did not know what to answer and merely nodded and worried. Reading his father's expression, he observed a cold cunning look in his father's eyes. A destructive force had possessed the man. Once that force would come out into the light, it would destroy him and everything around him.

"But father, I do not love Sabina," he answered not mentioning Toledo.

"It is not good for us to have such an important person as an enemy. He is going to approve the new laws regarding the wool trade. I need someone who will benefit me. If he becomes our enemy, it will mean bankruptcy," Diego explained, holding out a glimmer of hope.

Lorenzo did not understand why his father kept speaking in plural tense. He did not have anything to do with the business. Lorenzo thought for a moment and did not answer. He then remembered Daniel had advised him the new projects should start a little after the new moon, and which would occur the next day.

He disguised his real thoughts, and came back to work, waiting for a favorable moment to tell his father his true intentions. Lorenzo's silence filled Diego with hope , who believed his son had at last come to his senses.

"Lorenzo, prepare the lots to hand over to the agents from Navarre," his father ordered to him.

After observing Lorenzo doing the work, Diego ran to meet Montcada. They talked about the new military campaign being prepared to once more attack Valencia. The royal militia, the king, and the nobility of Aragon would come back again. The majors of the council would have the privilege to meet the monarch, and Diego fantasized about being one of them.

"By the way, my son is back to work. It seems he has come to his senses," Diego mentioned offhandedly, downplaying Lorenzo's actions.

"We all have rebellious moments. This is even good, but it would have been bad for both families if the wedding had been canceled," Montcada warned.

Diego was delighted. He had only one thing on his mind: to have the opportunity to welcome the king in person. Then he spoke to Lorenzo.

"I have met your father-in-law. I have told him he should not worry; the wedding is back on," he winked in collusion. "I knew sooner or later, you would listen to reason."

Lorenzo kept quiet. He was not brave enough to talk face to face with his father. He prepared the wool lots and left him believing whatever he wished. It was the last job for his family and he carried it out with great care.

The morning of the new moon he went to say good-bye to Daniel.

"Tomorrow, I am leaving to Toledo", said the tearful young man.

"First go to Albarracin, and from there, keep going until you reach Cuenca. Then continue to Ucles. I will have you hold you in my prayers," he said.

"Thank you very much," he hugged him crying, knowing he would never see again the man who had been a second father to him.

"I wish you all the luck in the world. Remember you are not alone. If you do not turn away from righteousness, you will be protected. Do not engage in nonsenses and God will be with you. He will guide your every step."

"Thank you very much," Lorenzo answered in a faltering voice.

"This is a list of friends in the different Jewish quarters of the cities that you will pass through. Ask for the rabbi when you get there. Tell them that I have sent you. They will welcome you. Good people are always welcomed by good men."

Before leaving, Daniel gave Lorenzo his natal chart.

"Here is your horoscope. Always keep it with you. Memorize it. As you learn more about astrology, you will be able to find what you need to know. In Toledo you will meet great astrologers, and you might become an expert."

Daniel blessed Lorenzo, and set him free. The young man's feelings were on edge.

Next, he went to say good-bye to his favorite tree. He sensed the tree also was saying goodbye to him as well. He hugged it and felt his friend's emotions. Then, he went to see Arturo, who explained in detail the path to Albarracin. The shepherd informed him he should pay a high tax to enter the independent manor,

"Only the rich men and the noblemen can live in Albarracin," he advised the shepherd.

Arturo knew Lorenzo was a mature man. The shepherd thought it was natural for a person at the age of seventeen to make this decision. Arturo bid him farewell.

Once Lorenzo got home, he ran to his room. He would leave the city at sunrise once the gates opened. He would leave as a criminal, hidden, by the Gate of Guadalaviar. This excited him, although he was also fearful. He prepared his bundle with the essential clothes: his best shoes, a waistcoat, a single pair of trousers, a cape, and a little bit of food. Since he had no spade, he took a small dagger for protection.

The idea of not saying goodbye to his mother distressed him greatly, however, Elvira was thinking about Lorenzo. She felt her son's fear and went to his room. She hugged him with all the love in the world. He took her hand, and felt it soft, as always, while she gave him unconditional love. She knew Lorenzo's intention, and experienced a mother's love for her son, that with all the pain in her soul, set her son free. She knew Lorenzo would not be happy living the life determined by her husband, because her son was born for something greater. Elvira prayed for God's help. She would never see him again and felt enormous grief at letting him go.

Diego came home happy. He kissed his wife after telling her their son would stay with them forever. Elvira remained quiet, knowing what was about to happen.

Lorenzo soon retired. He could not sleep, struggling between his inner sadness and the excitement of his immediate future. He turned all night long on his straw mattress. Something was pushing him onward.

It was thirty minutes before sunrise. He took his bundle and left his room. His mother, alert to the house's noises, arose and met him. Without saying anything, she hugged him.

"Son, I love you with all my heart. I hope you will be happy in Toledo," his mother said crying, trying not to awaken Diego.

Lorenzo hugged his mother in farewell.

"Take these three golden coins. I took them from your father. Use them to overcome difficulties," his mother gave him the money, heartbroken at the departure of her son, whom she would never see again.

Lorenzo was also crying. He hugged his mother one last time. He loved her with all of his soul, although he had never told her. He said goodbye, feeling an immense sadness.

Lorenzo departed his family home. As he headed southeast, he said goodbye to all the buildings and people he knew. He said goodbye to the hospitals, the churches, and the cathedrals; to the mosques and the synagogues. He said goodbye to the city wall and its seven gates, to the main plaza and the stairs where he met Ariadna. He said goodbye to his favorite place and his tree. He said goodbye to the shepherds, to Daniel and Arturo. He said goodbye to his sister and his mother. He bid farewell to his childhood...

He left the city through the Salvador Tower of the Guadalaviar Gate and headed towards Albarracin. He stopped and looked back at Teruel for the last time. He felt sad and alone, but he knew what meant to follow his dream.

Daniel, the astrologer, climbed up on to the city wall. He saw a young man accompanied by an invisible figure who was guiding him. With his guide were three figures, also invisible, protecting him. He nodded and blessed him one final time. He knew Lorenzo was following his calling, and through his hard work, he would help with the unfoldment of the Divine Plan. Daniel congratulated him silently for his courage; he was proud of the young man who had been like a son to him.

Lorenzo continued walking and left his home town like a fugitive, knowing he could never return. For an instant, he worried about the result of his actions, but he heard a clear voice coming from his soul.

"Lorenzo, fear not. You are not alone."

He was grateful for the voice that would become his spiritual adviser during the dangerous path he was setting out on. Lorenzo now, would have to face the path's difficulties, with its inner pitfalls and external threats. But with enough inner strength, he would overcome them with dignity and arrive in Toledo to fulfill his destiny.

Figure 3

• *Part Two* •

11. COURAGE

Lorenzo began his walk to freedom with swiftness and enthusiasm. The sun shone brightly on a wonderful spring day. He felt strong. He was proud of himself. However, after his long hike, he was exhausted. His inner voice encouraged him to continue.

"Keep going, Lorenzo, this is not the time to stop. You are only half way to completing your first stage. You can rest in Gea."

His initial euphoria faded when he realized he had to face his new reality; life was no longer a game. He was thirsty and his feet were blistered.

"Must I follow this path?" he doubted. "If I end the adventure, nobody will miss me. In a few hours I can be back home in Teruel."

Lorenzo left his bundle on the ground and admired the view. The route was not well traveled and seemed endless. He looked back and could no longer see Teruel. He was alone, surrounded by the impressive mountains of Albarracin. Beyond those mountains lay Toledo, his ultimate destination.

He continued on his way, but felt tense and worried. The experience was different from traveling with his father. Lorenzo thought about his mother and became sorrowful, realizing he would never see her again. He knew his mother was praying for him with all her soul for his fate. He could feel Elvira's suffering. He cried. All of the sudden he let out a loud piercing wail from deep in his soul. The accumulated tension of the last weeks emerged and even the birds scattered with fear when they heard the agonizing scream of the young man. He kept yelling, until he could yell no more; he felt liberated. Once he released his tension, he saw his situation clearly: he was now responsible for his own destiny. There was no one to accompany him, and he needed to find a way to support himself. Now he would live as a true individual.

He pondered going back to Teruel, but he realized it would be a fatal mistake. If he returned, he would become his father's puppet, and nobody would take him seriously. He knew stopping half way on this path would leave him suspended in a limbo. He would hate himself if he did not have the courage to follow his inner longing; if he returned to Teruel, he would be condemned to live as a cynic.

The young man continued on his way, feeling excited, fearful, vigorous, and tense. In the distance, he heard horses galloping. They were five soldiers returning to Albarracin feeling victorious after the battle of Majorca. They halted in front of him. Dressed in the colors of Aragon´s militia, they wore shields with red and yellow stripes, spades, and lances. They also carried an abundance of gold, silver, jewels, and gifts for the young ladies of Albarracin, the independent manor.

"Young man, salute the hosts of Aragon. We have triumphed across the seas!" the leader, with long hair and an aggressive demeanor shouted.

Lorenzo looked at the riders not knowing their intentions. He knew walking alone on the routes of Aragon was dangerous and his first reaction was defensive. The soldiers soon realized the young man was not a threat.

"Enlist yourself in the army of Aragon! We have won the glorious battle of Majorca! God protects our king, James I! Only someone immune to death by the Grace of God can win such extraordinary battle!" the soldiers shouted with great pride.

For those knights, James I was a great figure: colossal, distant, and exemplary. They risked their lives to follow him and enlisted in the biggest naval adventure in the history of Aragon. James I was no longer a child-king manipulated by noblemen. He was in fact a well respected ruler.

"Gentlemen, would you be as kind as to give me a little bit of water?"

"Drink wine! It is much better! We have just conquered Majorca, Menorca and Ibiza have surrendered! Let us celebrate the victory with the drink of the gods! Let us toast for the health of the king!" the soldiers laughed and danced around with their horses.

As a courtesy, Lorenzo drank wine and toasted to the king; however, he knew his destiny was not to be a military knight. It was humiliating for him to ask for the essential things his family had provided. How much he missed his mother!

The knights continued on their way. Intoxicated by their victory, the soldiers anticipated a rousing heroic reception in Albarracin; parties, presents, and pretty young women awaited them upon their return.

The encounter with the knights changed Lorenzo´s perception. The warriors came from Majorca after an extraordinary naval adventure, and he just needed to reach Toledo. It was a minor deed.

"It is just a route with a destination," he said to himself.

"Do not worry. God is with you. Step by step you will walk the path," he heard from his familiar spirit whisper, which gave him hope and the energy to continue.

On the ground, just a few steps from him, he spotted a small shining object. He moved closer and found that it was a miniature seven branched candlestick. It was a Menorah. According to Daniel, it was the spiritual symbol of the Jewish tradition. Daniel had told him God had revealed to Moses the Menorah's design, telling him its place within the Tabernacle.

"The soldiers must have dropped it, believing it was worthless," Lorenzo thought.

It was a good omen to find such a precious object. He kept it, sensing he was on the right path, guided by Providence.

After walking further, he approached Gea. His first objective was in sight, which brought great relief. He looked up and noticed a flock of birds accompanying him. He thought they were as free as he felt now. The feeling of freedom was unsurpassed.

All of the sudden, a sense of danger overcame him. He knew his father would follow him! Many people in Gea knew Diego, and they would inform his father of his whereabouts. Lorenzo felt paralyzed by fear. His father might even kill him! From a high hill, he contemplated the view. His heart was beating fast, and tension gripped his body. Despite his exhaustion, blisters, and his painful feet, he had to find a place to hide.

Lorenzo entered the village with caution and listened to his inner voice, "look for water in the town, and then, leave fast. Your father is looking for you!"

His inner voice was right. Diego, possessed by anger, rode at a gallop. Elvira, worried for her son's life, tried to stop her husband, once Diego realized Lorenzo had left the city. Diego took out his wrath on his wife and hurled insults at Lorenzo. He would not allow Lorenzo´s stupidity to interfere with the prosperity of the family business!

Lorenzo felt uneasy being in Gea. He was visible to everyone and needed to find a safe place to hide. Suddenly, he ran into the owner of the lodge, who recognized him. He asked him uncomfortable questions,

"Have you come with your father to hire good workers?" the man asked, happy to see the young man again.

Lorenzo kept quiet, not knowing what to say.

"Tell your father that not only are there good workers in Gea, but we also have wonderful vegetable gardens. He might be interested in buying some," the owner of the lodge suggested.

"My father is in Teruel. I came on my own. Where are the vegetable gardens? I would like to see them," Lorenzo thought the gardens might be a good place to hide.

"They are near the aqueduct," the lodge owner answered, proud of the largest roman construction in the region.

"The aqueduct?"

"It runs from Albarracin to Cella. It is very long and has many stretches excavated into the rock. It is magnificent. It is in the upper part of the town."

"Thank you, sir. Would you be so kind as to offer me some water? I am thirsty."

"Come to the lodge with me."

The lodge owner, not only gave him water, but also bread and cheese. In the blink of an eye, he ate most of the food, but kept some for later.

Lorenzo went to the upper part of the town and found the aqueduct. He grew excited contemplating its Roman construction, built a thousand years before, water no longer flowed through it. Tunneled into a mountain, the aqueduct made a perfect refuge for Lorenzo. He examined the aqueduct closely and went over its different sections, until he found a perfect spot to spend the night.

He paused when he saw several inscriptions on the rock, an indication other people had hidden there before. He looked at the inscription of two names together. One of them was a Christian name, Araceli, and the other was an Arab name, Latif. Those were the names of a young couple, in love, who escaped from their families, and the persecutors. The relationship between an Arab man and a Christian woman was punishable with death.

"Would God find justification in that? Two young people, of different religions, being burned at the stake because they were in love," he asked himself.

In that moment, he remembered Ariadna. The first letters of the Arab and the Christian woman were the same as the first letter of his name and his beloved. Ariadna would be proud of him. He remembered when they were holding hands, and he let his imagination fly.

A trumpet's call awakened him from his daydream. He went down to see what was happening. As all Thursdays, the people of the town met in the tea house to dance as the Persian did on that unforgettable day. From a safe distance, he heard the rhythmic music.

"Protect me, God! Protect me!" a man, directing the session, shouted.

"Allah, Allah, Allah," the whole town repeated with enthusiasm and devotion.

"Protect me, God! Protect me!" the man repeated with a melodic tone.

After a long period chanting Allah, the people returned to their homes and Lorenzo went to his refuge. The Arabic chants produced a calming effect on Lorenzo. He thanked God for being alive. His fears had disappeared, although he was alone in a cave, had no belongings, his body was in pain and did not know how he would feed himself.

"God will provide," he heard within.

The young man remembered the breathing exercise that Arturo, the shepherd, had taught him. He took a breath, inhaling and exhaling, filling his lungs to their maximum capacity. As he was breathing, he saw everything clearly, and felt secure. Everything was fine and and going according to plan. He was certain he would fulfill his destiny, whatever it was.

Lorenzo contemplated creation. Who had created the sun and the sky? Who was he? Was he real? He entered a deep state within himself. He felt great compassion. He prayed to God to bless the town, the region, and the rulers.

He then had a vision from the past, which seemed real. In his vision, he saw a Roman centurion ordering several slaves to break stone. He also sensed the presence of other refugees in the aqueduct, fugitives who prayed and asked God for help escaping from the village, and couples who went there to make love,

Lorenzo left the cave and observed the immensity of the night sky. He loved the world, and a great peace enveloped him. He realized his infinite capacity for love. He understood the beauty of the universe. He thanked God for opening the path to freedom for him, realizing he was part of the cosmic dance. He slept well that night, unaware of the many adventures, blessings and obstacles that lay ahead on his way.

12. CHASE

The dawn light woke Lorenzo. His entire body ached. Lorenzo knew he had to leave the cave, as staying there was dangerous. He tightened his clothes, attached his dagger to his belt, picked up his little Menorah, and started walking towards Albarracin. The blisters on his feet did not allow him to go fast. The previous night's calm had passed Thousands of thoughts raced through his mind, but one worried him the most: the fear of confrontation with his father.

Diego was following the same route. Lorenzo could sense him. He could hardly breathe. His heart was beating irregularly, and he feared he might be having a heart attack. He knew that if his father found him, the consequences would be brutal. He rushed ahead and asked directions to Albarracin, and some shepherds directed him. As fast, as his hurting body would allow him, he followed the instructions.

The initial part was easy, but all of a sudden, he confronted a crossroads. It was a life changing moment. Lorenzo questioned which path he should take; unaware either would lead him to Albarracin. The road on the right looked direct and well-traveled; the one on the left looked more difficult and narrow. Lorenzo did not know his father was on horse on the right hand path; Diego sought to punish him severely.

Lorenzo noted that the path on the right ran downhill, while the one on the left went uphill. He tried to consult his inner voice, but there was no answer; only a frightening silence. Time stood still. Even it seemed that the wind and the trees awaited his decision. Lorenzo was not aware that his life depended on a seemingly trivial choice. If he chose the wrong path, his father would find him, his journey would be at an end, and he would return to Teruel and marry the lawyer's daughter; if his soul were ready to assume responsibility for his freedom, he would follow the correct path.

After much reflection, with great relief to his spirit, he opted for the longer route and started to move again. Soon, he found himself in the middle of a pine forest, which brought him a sense of tranquility, replacing the anxiety and trepidation that had been strangling him. Something within told him he had made the right decision and his father would not find him.

The path became steeper. According to the shepherds, the distance between Gea and Albarracin was about half day's journey; however, it was already evening, and he still was in the midst of the forest, unable to glimpse of the village of destiny. No one else was on the path, and he worried. He questioned his decision at the crossroads, not knowing his choice had saved him from a fatal meeting.

Lorenzo found a fountain of spring water from which he drank and ate the last of the food he had saved. Backtracking to find the crossroads would take him a long time, and he lacked the strength to turn back. The young man lost all hope and broke down shouting expletives; he was exhausted and in the middle of an unknown wood. He hoped someone would hear him, but no one did.

He calmed down and assessed his situation. He discovered several caves which seemed to make a good refuge; they were full of drawings, drawn thousands of years ago. The extraordinary drawings cheered him up, and confirmed the cave was the right place to spend the night.

"If other men have been here, it must be a safe place."

As soon as he decided to stay in that cave, he collapsed. It seemed an eternity since he had left home, but it was only two days! He missed his family and friends, and even, at that moment, he would not mind seeing his father, despite of the beating he would suffer.

Lorenzo made a fire to keep any dangerous animals away. During the night he hardly slept He wanted to hug his mother and tell her he loved her. That same moment in Teruel, his mother was thinking of him, praying to God for his well-being. The two had a spiritual connection, formed at his conception.

"My Lord, protect me," Lorenzo prayed. "I have doubts and I am not sure if I am doing the right thing. I need encouragement."

Lorenzo sensed an invisible figure who nodded and told him how proud he was of him. Lorenzo thought he was going crazy, although he felt a great inner peace. This allowed him to sleep for several hours. He was surprised there were no threats of wild animals that might attack him, in truth, wild animals respect those who walk the path of freedom.

When he woke up, he started walking. Instead of returning to the crossroads, he tried to reach Albarracin on the same road. Without assessing his strength, he applied much of his strength to his journey. The path was difficult to follow in the middle of the pine forest, and he became lost. In his frustration he swore, unaware that his stubbornness was working in his favor; his father backtracked on the other road many times, desperately seeking Lorenzo.

After half a day of walking through the mountains, Lorenzo lost his confidence and sat down. He cried, near a tree, which reminded him of his tree friend of Teruel. He regretted his decision; if he had stayed in Teruel, he would be with his family, eating well and feeling no fear. He prayed again.

"Lord, protect me. I am desperate and lost. Please do not leave me here. Lead me out of this forest," he begged.

In the middle of his shouting, not knowing how, he felt the Divine Presence in the woods. He knew God was with him and He had not abandoned him.

"Lord, protect me! Protect me..." he begged again, and again, crying.

Lorenzo looked up, and saw the sun, the valley, and the mountains, all illuminated. His soul felt the beauty of the landscape. Regarding the landscape he calmed down and pondered the wonders of creation, and how lucky he was. "Only in the present moment, can one find God," he thought, absorbed by the natural beauty all around him.

Meanwhile, Diego was in Albarracin awaiting his son's arrival. He knew the path to Toledo passed through the independent city and decided to wait for him. However, Lorenzo's soul was guiding the young man. There was a reason behind Lorenzo's getting lost in the forest. If he had arrived a day earlier in Albarracin, he would have encountered his father. Without his   realizing it, the time that he spent lost in the woods had been a blessing.

Lorenzo finished his prayers and continued on his way. The young man decided not to stop until he arrived in the city. Exhausted, he walked and walked as a lost soul. After expending the whole day in the forest, he could see several houses in the distance. He became joyful and hopeful. Finally, he had reached his goal!

Lorenzo's intuition told him to carefully study what he was seeing. After observing the place in detail, he realized something was not right. He knew this place! He had been there before. He was in Gea, the town he left the previous day. Lorenzo collapsed and cried with anger and desperation. He was devastated. He felt he was the most miserable man in the world. The forest had defeated him.

He considered returning Teruel to accept his fate but he suppressed the thoughts of giving up. An inner voice, firm clear, told him not to despair. There was no time to feel sorry for himself. Lorenzo decided to spend one more night alone before deciding on his future. He returned to the aqueduct and once the sun had set, he went into the town and bought some food. He looked terrible and the local people were suspicious of him. After buying some food, he ran to hide in the aqueduct. As soon as he lay down, he fell into a deep sleep. His spiritual guide appeared in his dream, and with the utmost compassion told him,

"We are taking care of you."

Lorenzo's soul thanked the invisible being. In his dream, spiritual healers came and healed his wounds. The abrasions on his body disappeared while he slept. It was indeed a miracle.

When he woke up, he said to himself, "What is the worst thing that can happen to me?"

Looking at the beautiful day, he pondered that thought. "I will set out once more. I can always return to Teruel and ask for forgiveness," he rationalized.

He started walking again, but this time, in the crossroads, he took the path of the right without hesitating. The heat was intense. He walked all morning and did not stop until he reached a hilltop, where he heard the sound of a horn. He hid in the underbrush and watched as group of elegant gentlemen strode along the path. King James was with them; indeed, it was the royal entourage! The monarch was hunting wild boars with some aristocrats from Aragon.

Hidden, he observed the elegance of the king and his entourage. There was something about the monarch that was different than other people whom he had met before. The king shone. He remembered the legends about James I, and upon seeing him, he knew a superior force protected him.

Lorenzo saw himself as dirty, starving, and lost. He compared himself with the great lords hunting with the king. "How can there be such a great difference between two human beings?"

He followed the royal entourage from a safe distance. Late in the evening, once the king and his guests had finished hunting, they left at a rapid pace. Lorenzo followed them. The young man sighted a magnificent city, shining in the mountains. Lorenzo rejoiced for finally arriving. The city's beauty amazed him; it was in fact Albarracin.

He waited until the king had entered the village, and went to the main gate where guards were suspicious of Lorenzo and charged him an exorbitant toll to enter the town.

He had completed the first stage of the way and Lorenzo's soul was filled with joy and happiness.

Meanwhile, his father returned to Teruel believing someone had given Lorenzo a ride to Toledo. He gave his son up for lost and cried at his stupidity; the anger that he felt against his son transformed into rage. Diego blamed himself because his son had left as a fugitive. Deep within, he was proud of Lorenzo's courage, for doing something he never risked. Still, Diego could not forgive him for abandoning his family. Now, he had to face the large payment for canceling the wedding and he would be banished from the council of Teruel. Lorenzo's courageous act had destroyed Diego's world.

From that time, Diego neglected himself and his business. He did not become one of the mayors of the council, and he never met the king. He wandered the taverns, and the noblemen turned their backs on him. His moments of glory were limited to the occasions when he treated the drunks; only then could Diego talk about his great deeds, feeding the fantasy he was someone important. Elvira tried to help him, but Diego did not return. The wool rancher did not want to face the life he had created and lived in limbo until his death. His wife, unable to stand the corrosive and raging forces of her husband, died of an unknown illness. After her death, Diego lived a life without direction. The people who approached him tried to take advantage of his fortune, which he wasted on easy women and drunks, who laughed upon hearing his silly deeds in exchange for wine. Moments before Diego passed he realized he had lived without dignity during the latter part of his life. However, he could not even apologize. He died alone attacked by thieves, who took what little he had left. Tormented for having thrown away his gifts and the prosperity he had received from heaven, Diego died alone.

13. MODESTY

$\mathcal{L}$orenzo spent his first few nights in Albarracin at a lodge. He rested and ate until he was satiated. However, without his family's support, he was exposed to life's circumstances. He had to trust his only true possessions: the guiding voice of his intuition and the spiritual connection through his Menorah. Now he should learn to make his living in an unknown city. He could not let doubt, weakness, or difficulties defeat him.

During the first days in Albarracin, he felt at peace. The refined beauty of the buildings and the main plaza fascinated him. Prominent Aragon noblemen lived in town. Lorenzo confirmed this fact as he listened to a conversation between two well dressed gentlemen:

"It seems the lord of Albarracin, Don Pedro Fernandez de Azagra, is once again a friend of King James I," an old gentleman wearing a golden tunic of excellent quality said. "Yesterday, they were hunting together in our woods."

"We are lucky to be such an independent town, since we have also signed a pact with the Arab King Lobo of Murcia," the other gentleman, answered.

"From here we can watch the battles between the kingdoms of Castile, Aragon, Valencia, and Granada, without getting involved. It is a great advantage to be in this privileged territory."

The two gentlemen sensed Lorenzo's presence and they

moved on to continue their conversation. They wanted to continue talking away from the stranger. He reacted positively, and instead of getting angry, decided to educate himself about the acceptable manners among noblemen. Lorenzo decided to stay in Albarracin for the time being, before continuing his journey to Toledo: he needed to save money, and learn the ways of a true gentlemen.

After a few days of rest and good food, Lorenzo's wounded feet healed. Life in Albarracin was expensive, so he needed to find work. The village produced and sold wool, an activity shared by Christians, Arabs, and Jews; the Christians produced the raw wool, the Arabs cleaned, dried, and dyed the wool, and the Jews financed the commercial transactions. Lorenzo thought his previous experience would help him to find a job.

He went to the synagogue to see the rabbi of Albarracin, Salomon. The rabbi, with an aquiline nose and a white trimmed beard, received him with a reserved attitude.

"Daniel, the astrologer, has given me your name as a reference," Lorenzo indicated with courtesy.

"How is Daniel?" the rabbi asked him, examining the young man in depth.

"Very well. The day I was born, he drew my horoscope which I bring with me," Lorenzo said, showing his natal chart to Salomon.

"What can you do, young man?" the rabbi inquired, taking a deep look at the horoscope.

"I have helped my father in his wool business, however I left my family because I want to go to Toledo," Lorenzo mentioned, feeling uneasy with the questions of the rabbi. "Daniel encouraged me to take the journey."

"And are you traveling alone?" Salomon asked, surprised by Lorenzo's audacity.

"Yes. I want to go to where they translate the books that answer the major questions. I want to know the real meaning of things."

"I see," affirmed the rabbi, as his interest in the young man grew.

"Is there any library in Albarracin?"

"Everything in its time," Salomon said, realizing that the young man was a mystic traveler. "I am going to speak with a wool merchant, called Pasqual Ramirez. He might need help. Go to see him tomorrow," he recommended, after pondering for a few moments.

"And do you know anyone who would like to rent me a small room?"

"There is an old lady named Higinia, who rents out rooms in town," the rabbi answered before saying goodbye.

Lorenzo thanked the rabbi for the information, although his attitude surprised him. Lorenzo was not in a position to make judgments. However, he remembered the sentence of Daniel: "The good people are always welcomed by good people," and he stopped worrying.

When he arrived at the house of Higinia Brigida, he met a, white haired, seemingly unpleasant woman. She asked him six-month rent in advance. She knew the young man was desperate to find a place and took advantage of him. Although he was not comfortable paying a lot of money to such a disagreeable woman, Lorenzo had no other option.

His depressed mood changed the moment he entered the room in the upper part of the house. He loved the view from which he could contemplate the starry sky at night. He settled in, and placed his little Menorah on a table beside the only candle in the room.

As the rabbi had advised, Lorenzo met with Pasqual Ramirez, who was a forty-year-old man, heavy set, almost bald, and with a lively disposition. He was half drunk when Lorenzo met him.

"So, you are recommended by the rabbi?"

"Well...I have met Salomon. He told me I could be helpful to you."

"I need someone in Albarracin to manage my business while I am away selling the wool. But I am not sure if I trust you," he said, laughing, and finishing his glass of wine. Then he looked in Lorenzo's eyes scrutinizing him.

"Test me for a period," Lorenzo answered with courage.

"I am in debt to the Jews. Since they recommend you, I will hire you. If you fail, I have the perfect excuse to renegotiate my loans with them," the trader continued laughing, opening another bottle of wine.

Lorenzo was disconcerted, dealing with such a strange character.

"Drink, boy, drink! Life is good for me! Or are you one of those people who do not drink?

Lorenzo wanted to make a good impression and so had a glass of wine. Pasqual kept laughing.

"I like you, young man! I never get it wrong with people. I know you will never betray me. I will hire you!" he exclaimed patting Lorenzo's back.

Lorenzo left the room bewildered. He realized the man was crazy, but that he would get along with him. He started working for the businessman. Ramirez was delighted with the young man's ability to deal with the shepherds. On top of that, he soon learned how to stack the wool for transportation. Pasqual, realizing the natural intelligence and ability of the young man, allowed him to make his own trading decisions.

Settled in Albarracin, with a job, Lorenzo's life took an unexpected turn. One morning, after finishing a bottle of wine, Pasqual became elated. He looked at Lorenzo in a strange way, and then he yelled as if crazy and agitated.

"I am going to be the richest man in town, I will be rich, rich, rich!"

"But sir, how are you going to do that?" Lorenzo asked, knowing Pasqual was drunk.

"Young man, there is going to be a shortage of wool production in the northern part of the kingdom. No one is producing wool anymore there. The ranchers are settling in the south."

"So, your wool will be selling well in the north of Aragon."

"Exactly."

"But, Pasqual, I do not understand. You can make a little bit of money, but how are you going to become the richest man in town?"

"Young man! Not only I am going to sell my existing wool, but also I am going to sell wool that I do not own!" he yelled rejoiced, thinking of his extraordinary commercial venture.

"I do not quite get it..."

"I am going to buy all the wool production in the region in advance and, you know what? The Jews are going to finance the deal!" the businessman said while he laughed and laughed.

Lorenzo had never seen a person be so excited. He compared it to a hunter who had his prey in front of him, waiting for the hunt. Pasqual Ramirez imagined himself as the richest man of Albarracin, and, in fact, he was going to be. To his astonishment, the Jewish lenders gave him the money. He also negotiated an excellent price for the purchase of the wool production in the region for the following year, 1233.

Once Pasqual had made the purchase, he followed the news about the battle of Valencia with great interest. Pasqual was overjoyed when he heard the soldiers from Teruel had conquered Ares and Javalambre. Then he praised the courage of James I, who conquered Sarrion and Burriana, dividing the Kingdom of Valencia in two territories, leaving the upper part of the kingdom without food. Pasqual was astonished when he heard how the royal doctors removed an arrow from the king´s head. The Arabs took this event as a sign that God was protecting the Christian King, and their morale sunk. The new wife of James I, Violante of Hungary, accompanied her husband into battle, which was a great sign, since the queens only accompanied the kings to the most important battles.

To Pasqual's delight, Valencia's fall was imminent, which brought even greater wealth to Aragon. The demand for wool from Albarracin multiplied. In just a few short weeks, Pasqual Ramirez sold all the wool production he had purchased at an extraordinary profit. After paying back all the loans, the businessman had become the richest man in Albarracin. Lorenzo had learned more about the wool trade in a few months with Pasqual than with his father during his life.

This was not the only lesson that Pasqual taught Lorenzo. He also taught him what not to do with a fortune. Pasqual Ramirez stopped working and left Lorenzo in charge of his business. He bought unnecessary luxuries, spent a fortune on women, and lost thousands in card games. Nevertheless, he was laughing all the time. Since he had made so much money, he did not worry that gamblers were cheating him, or that loose women took advantage of him.

Lorenzo felt Pasqual was entering into dangerous territory but he kept silent; he remained focused on performing the duties of his job. Pasqual thanked Lorenzo for his dedication, and impulsively, he increased Lorenzo's salary tenfold, which allowed him to save money in a steady pace.

Pasqual's lack of self-control himself turned his attention to the beautiful wife of one of his shepherds. Her name was Agueda and she had a flamboyant presence. She was tall and voluptuous. While the shepherd was away working, Pasqual pursued her. His generous spending became an enormous temptation for Agueda, who lived in a modest home, such as the one that a simple shepherd could afford.

Blinded by passion, Pasqual spent a large amount of gold trying to win her. He did not care what other people thought about him; his only obsession was to be with the most beautiful woman in town. During the day, they paraded publicly, and Agueda, dazzled by the Pasqual's presents, did not even care about covering up their meetings. When the villagers confronted her about the affair, she denied it, saying she was not doing anything wrong. The whole town watched them, and gossiped about the disaster that was about to happen.

Pasqual became very drunk one evening after losing a large amount of money in a game of cards. After doing his business, as a personal revenge, at the gambler's door, he went to his lover's house. He began to serenade her with a popular love song, and shouted her name. When he reached her bedroom window, Pasqual yelled,

"Agueda, come out of your bed! I am Pasqual, the richest man in town and I have come to get you!"

Agueda peeked out the window. She smiled with delight. All the commotion Pasqual made in the street woke up the neighbors, who witnessed the tarnishing of the shepherd's honor. In the morning, when Pasqual left the shepherd's house, an ominous shadow followed him; it was the shadow that follows those who will die soon. From then on, Agueda began to mourn unconsciously; she began dressing in black, in anticipation of her fatal end. Meanwhile the whole town waited in silence, for the shepherd to return.

A month after the fatal encounter, the shepherd returned from his pastures. The shepherd's joy of seeing his wife again was quashed by an inner pain. The moment he saw her, he noticed a radical change. She had become cold, arrogant, and demanding. Agueda forgot everything the shepherd had provided for her. He had taken her from a little town near Cuenca, and offered her a good house and a peaceful, easy life in Albarracin.

The people of the town held their tongues. They just sat and watched, for the inevitable disgrace. One night, the footsteps of a group of shepherds, walking in the darkness, broke the silence. A woman's cry pierced the night. Then the shepherds set fire to Pasqual Ramirez's home. He died. In the morning, Agueda was also found, dead. No one mourned her. Only the groaning of deep sadness of the shepherd confronting his wife's betrayal broke the eerie silence that darkened the town. The Lord of Azagra, who had the authority to impart justice, did not investigate the case; the killing of two adulterers was not a crime. No one paid homage to Pasqual after his death. Only Lorenzo grieved his passing.

Lorenzo now found himself running a prosperous business, but now he would face the temptations that come along with success and wealth. Commercial success and all its temptations was not the plan set up for him; however, the desire of riches could derail Lorenzo´s spiritual progress.

14. ARROGANCE

*T*wo years went by, and Lorenzo settled in well in Albarracin His wool business was prosperous, and he repaid Pasqual's gambling debts. By doing so, the Jewish money lenders came to trust him

It was a prosperous time for the village, due to the excellent management by the lord of the manor, Pedro Fernandez de Azagra. Not only he had created the community of Albarracin, but he also donated part of his lands to the peasants, sharing his wealth among his people. The result: he repopulated the territory and established a regional code of laws for communal living. The people were delighted with the humane treatment by their lord.

The Jewish community of Albarracin also prospered at this time. They profited greatly through financing the wool trade. Salomon, the rabbi, studied the astrological configuration for the Albarracin Jewish community. He confirmed the next three Jewish generations were going to live in peace. Salomon was also an adviser to Don Pedro. He advised him to support James I, which was a wise decision. Salomon also maintained correspondence with several Jewish communities of Aragon, and in particular, with the Rabbi of Gerona, Nahmanides who was King James principal adviser.

Salomon tried to maintain good relationships with the Christian bishop of Albarracin. To be the Bishop William's enemy, who had a considerable number of military knights at his service, would not have been wise. Even so, they had spirited discussions when they met in the center of the village.

"Good morning, Bishop. Have you captured and burned all the Cathars in Provence?" the rabbi asked, worried by the Church's persecutions of minority groups.

"Have you been excommunicated by the other Jewish communities of Aragon, dear rabbi?" the bishop said, knowing about the great differences between the rabbis of the Iberian Peninsula.

"How is your military campaign against the bishop of Segorbe? Have you killed many Christians to climb the ladder of the hierarchy?"

"By the way, is there a new Messiah among the Jewish people? Let me know, so I can pay him a visit," mocked the bishop.

"If I were you, I would not talk about those things in public. The pope has declared anyone who speaks about faith issues in public a heretic. In France, they burn people alive for doing such a thing."

"Have a wonderful day, Rabbi. I see you are better than ever."

"Have a good day, Bishop. I also see you are well".

Lorenzo was invited to the meetings organized in Salomon´s home. During those meetings, the rabbi answered questions about the political and economic situation in the kingdom, the petty quarrels within the Jewish communities, or the dispute between reason and faith. Salomon became a mentor to Lorenzo.

"The middle way leads to inner peace. Avoid excesses. Remember, everything in moderation," the rabbi warned the young man. "The art is to find the right balance."

Although Lorenzo learned a great deal from Salomon, whose character was more guarded than Daniel´s, the young man still missed the enjoyable conversations from the baths of Teruel. Salomon watched his obsession with the wool trade, and warned him. He realized Lorenzo's spiritual development could stagnate in Albarracin, and in fact, after two years in the village, he had forgotten his dream of Toledo. The only things on Lorenzo's mind were the wool transactions.

"Do not obsess over your job or the money you are making," he warned him.

Lorenzo did not recognize he was fulfilling the life his father had planned for him only in a different town. He had become a prosperous wool trader, he dealt with the shepherds, and the money lenders respected him. The only thing left to fulfill his father´s plan was to marry a nobleman's daughter.

Lorenzo thought that business was a game in which he would always win. His lack of life experience had not yet taught him any important lessons Lorenzo fell into the temptation of making a great fortune in a short amount of time. Therefore, he tried to do the same thing as Pasqual, but on a larger scale; he would buy the wool production of the region of the next two seasons, and would negotiate the price with the shepherds. He explained the deal to the Jewish lenders, and since they made money with Pasqual, they financed Lorenzo´s transaction but at a higher interest. This did not worry Lorenzo as he felt he was invincible. Lorenzo fantasized about all the money he was going to make, not realizing he was moving away from his calling.

On the day that he was to meet the shepherds to close the deal, it was cold and raining. Soon after leaving home, he slipped and twisted his ankle. The omens did not favor the deal, but Lorenzo ignored the signs life was sending him.

The pain caused him to walk more slowly, and he arrived late for the meeting. While he was negotiating with the shepherds, he felt dizzy; something inside was warning him, he should not sign the deal, but he continued anyway The shepherds asked for a twenty percent increase over the current price for the first year of wool production, and a forty percent increase for the second year production. Lorenzo ignored his inner voice and accepted the deal. His pride assured him the price of the wool would rise much more during the following years. After signing the deal with blood, he felt uneasy. He was unconsciously hurting his soul. He had gone into debt doing business contrary to his true life's purpose. In that moment, the words of Daniel and Salomon echoed in his head, but in his mind, he was already dreaming of becoming the richest man in town.

At first, business went well for Lorenzo. The price of wool rose in Aragon during the next year, and Lorenzo made a substantial profit. He paid half of the loans back and bought a house in the most prestigious part of Albarracin. The day he left his little room, Higinia dressed in her best clothes to say good-bye; the landlady looked seductively at Lorenzo, but Lorenzo felt only disgust.

Lorenzo, at the tender age of twenty-two, had already made his fortune. He owned a house and a horse, he dressed with fine clothes, and had a superb sword. The young man's success attracted the attention of the village lord, who invited him to have dinner at his residence. The lord's wife and the daughter joined them for the evening. Don Pedro wanted his daughter, Teresa, to marry the son of a European Christian King; however, Teresa was impulsive and flirted with Lorenzo to annoy her father. The young man was flattered and let the flirtation continue.

"If I become engaged to the Lord's daughter, I will be a great nobleman," Lorenzo thought, proud of being a powerful and respected man.

It sounded like his father's voice was talking through him and controlled his thoughts. Lorenzo became obsessed with riches and the possibility of making Teresa fall in love with him. In that moment, the beautiful memory of Ariadna disappeared and Toledo was now just a faint memory.

"Sometimes success brings misfortune," the rabbi Salomon warned him once, knowledgeable regarding the love of money on a person's psyche and ego. "It is not succeeding that is important; it is what you do after becoming successful," he warned.

Every year, by the end of April, there was a celebration of "May Day" to commemorate the arrival of spring in Albarracin. The young ladies of the town were "auctioned" to the young men. In exchange, the young men would "sing the mayos", as it was called, to publicly court the women. The money collected was used to benefit the community, and the winner of the auction had the right to walk with the lady for a full year. The whole village awaited the arrival of festival.

The girls did not dare going out without prearranging the bidding. Being left alone without any bid was a humiliation to bear the rest of the year.

"Lorenzo, are you going to bid for me?" asked Teresa, the Lord of Azagra's daughter.

"I will think about it," Lorenzo answered with a roguish smile.

"My father wants me to marry the son of a Christian king, but he has not yet found a good candidate."

Lorenzo laughed and winked at Teresa. He had no feelings for her, but he was attracted by her status and name.

The day of the bidding, the whole town was in the main plaza. The ladies went out to the balcony, one after the other, to be "auctioned", and the young men eagerly awaited them. The climax came when the daughter of the lord appeared on the balcony. The master of ceremonies called out her name, and waited for several minutes for the first bid. The young men of the town were afraid to court the daughter of Don Pedro. After waiting for what seemed like an eternity, a voice came from the middle of nowhere.

"I offer ten thousand maravedises," Lorenzo shouted from a porch on the main plaza.

This was the highest amount of money ever offered for a lady. After hearing the bid, a solemn hush fell over the crowd; everyone was astonished over the amount offered. Then, the crowd began to cheer, and the offer was accepted. Lorenzo became the most famous man in town. He was proud and full of conceit.

During the following months, he went out with the lord's daughter and behaved with great arrogance. The neighbors treated him with respect, as if he were a true nobleman, although they gossiped behind his back; their envy of Lorenzo was hidden behind their glib words. Rabbi Salomon looked after Lorenzo, but Lorenzo distanced himself from the rabbi. He gave him another warning about the consequences of arrogance and creating unnecessary envy, but Lorenzo failed to heed him. He was behaving like a spoiled child, acting as if he were the center of the universe.

In his heart, Lorenzo knew he was mistaken, but the praise of the entire town was a powerful force that encouraged his air of superiority. One day, he met the rabbi on the street. Lorenzo did not dare acknowledge him and an unacceptable thought came to his mind, "Who does this man think he is?" he told himself with delusions of grandeur. "He should be greeting me."

The situation had peaked. Lorenzo needed to correct his course. From the heavens, they decided to teach him a hard lesson. After receiving the wool production agreed for the second year, Lorenzo tried to sell it. Northern traders came to Albarracin, and offered him less than he had paid for the wool. The hoped for payments from the battle of Valencia had not arrived yet and the demand of wool had fallen in Aragon. If Lorenzo accepted the deal, he would take a large financial hit but still he could continue with his business. But his pride would not allow him to lose! He had his mind set on coming out a winner. The wool traders did not accept his conditions and the negotiations faltered.

"They will not trick me!" he stated defiantly. "If they do not want my wool, I will sell it myself in Cuenca."

The young man loaded up a cart with several bales of wool, and headed for Cuenca. As soon as he departed, soldiers stopped him, demanding the payment of a toll. Lorenzo protested, explaining the kings of Castile and Aragon had established a unique toll for the wool loads. The soldiers did not care and demanded payment if he wanted to keep going. Lorenzo insulted them and the knights beat him. After Lorenzo asked for clemency, the soldiers left him, but not before dumping the cart; ruining the wool and leaving Lorenzo battered and bruised.

Furious, Lorenzo returned to Albarracin. He was soon desperate. The loan was due, and Lorenzo had failed to sell the wool. Anxious, he asked for help from the noblemen, but they all refused. When Teresa learned of his economic difficulties, she also stopped seeing him. In a few weeks, his life had turned upside down. Whereas before he was the most envied man in Albarracin now he was an outcast. Nobody wanted to be seen with him, knowing that had forfeited on his loan.

The Jewish money lenders demanded the payment of the loan, but Lorenzo could not honor it. He asked Salomon to forgive him, hoping he would intercede for him; however, the rabbi knew Lorenzo's mission was not to be a wool trader, and refused to help. Salomon knew Lorenzo needed to learn a painful lesson.

Lorenzo was desperate. New businessmen came to talk to him. When they realized his fear, they made an offer for the wool at an absurdly low price. The young man knew the transaction was hideous, but he had no other option. With the money from the transaction, he paid part of the debt. Lorenzo went to speak with Salomon again to get help to negotiate a postponement, but the rabbi was firm.

"I will speak with the lenders. They will take your house as collateral for the rest of the loan, but even that will not be enough."

"But my house is worth much more," Lorenzo protested knowing he was on the verge of bankruptcy.

"They do not want your house. So, this is the deal I can negotiate: you give the house as payment of your debt, and you agree to leave Albarracin," the rabbi said.

"And where should I go?"

"Don´t you remember why you came here?" the rabbi smiled.

In that moment, Lorenzo's eyes were opened. He had been a fool and had completely forgotten his purpose.

Lorenzo met with the lenders, who received him coldly, although they were thrilled with the agreement; they would get much more for the house. Lorenzo asked for a few gold coins so he could continue his journey, and the lenders granted his request.

Once the deal was finalized, he went to say goodbye to the rabbi, who advised Lorenzo:

"The road to Cuenca is difficult. It passes over the mountains. From Cuenca to Toledo the terrain is flat and dry."

Lorenzo left Albarracin as poor as he had arrived, but he had gained valuable life experience. He had experienced the results of a fast and undeserved success. A force, maybe ambition, maybe greed, had possessed him, but luckily, it had not destroyed him. He was young and alive. Three years after arriving in Albarracin, he was headed for Toledo, feeling forlorn but also liberated. He had left Teruel as a fugitive, running from his family, and now he was leaving Albarracin having learned from his mistakes. Lorenzo, now, would have to live with integrity on this part of his journey. This was the lesson he needed to find his true self.

15. PATH

*L*orenzo felt alone and abandoned on his next journey. For days he traveled, grief stricken. He felt embarrassed, ashamed, and sad for the mistakes he had made in Albarracin.

"Why did I behave so foolishly? I am not that kind of person!" he said to himself. "Trying to seduce the lord's daughter, just to feel important," he criticized himself while walking. "And throwing away all that money in such a wasteful way." He felt like an idiot.

As Salomon had warned him, the route towards Cuenca from Albarracin was a steep climb. Suddenly, the narrow path ended, and he was on the edge of a cliff. Alone, facing the slope, he broke down. "I am alone! Alone!" he shouted helplessly in the middle of the desolate land.

He felt insignificant and used the last tool of a desperate man: prayer. In Albarracin, he had lost the habit of praying and giving thanks as his mother had taught him. He raised his hands pleaded to heaven. God was listening.

When he finished praying, he assessed the situation. Albarracin was banned for him; his only solution was to climb down the cliff. He saw the steep slope and trembled. He could be injured or die of starvation. He didn't realize that beyond the steep hill there was a drinking trough, and from that point, he could take the straight path towards Cuenca.

"Lord, I have forgotten you. I do not understand how it happened. I am lost. Lord, help me!" Lorenzo begged, crying, frozen with fear, in front of the cliff.

Lorenzo's cry came from the deepest part of his soul. He was sincere, and he was heard. A little farther along, a shepherd decided to change his direction, knowing it was time to water his sheep. The young man heard the sound of bells coming from the lower part of the cliff. His inner voice encouraged him to take the risk. He gained speed on the descend, as the slope became steeper. Lorenzo could not stop and threw himself to the ground to avoid falling even more quickly; he rolled over and over, tumbling down the cliff. When he stopped, he stood up and to his astonishment, he was in front of the watering trough.

The shepherd was shocked to meet a man who appeared as if from nowhere. Lorenzo was overjoyed to meet someone after walking alone for so long. The shepherd saw the young man's condition, and knew he was in serious trouble. He guided him to the nearest town, Torres. Walking with in silent communion with the shepherd relieved Lorenzo of his anxiety. When they reached the town, he thanked the shepherd, and continued on his way.

Lorenzo needed to leave his past behind. He quickened his pace, as he tried to leave his misfortunes behind. Being in nature helped to remove his negative thoughts. In the middle of the woods, he sensed somebody walking with him; it was his guardian angel, who had come to protect him.

After a long stretch, he arrived in Tramacastilla, and spent the night there. Everybody was celebrating. When he went to the tavern, he found out the reason.

"King Ferdinand has conquered Cordova!" the peasants shouted, proud of the victory.

"Valencia is now part of Aragon! Castile and Aragon are making history! We are the example for Europe!" another man shouted celebrating the Aragons victory.

"Even the pope has sent crusaders to Castile and Aragon," the tavern keeper said, looking at two French men who had come to Castile seeking their fortune.

"The Valencian victory was not easy. The noblemen abandoned the king so he took it upon himself; he was tired of dealing with their manipulations. The night before the crucial battle, the king went to a chapel, entered into a trance, and imagined himself as a king-priest. Dedicated to his role, he promised God he would not leave without conquering Valencia," the town's priest stated, "This also shows that both James I and Ferdinand III are protected by the Holy One."

After those victories, there were just three territories remaining under Arab control on the Iberian Peninsula, each in a precarious position; Granada, whose king had just been poisoned by an Arab enemy; Murcia, which after the victory of Valencia, would soon be conquered; and Seville, Ferdinand III's next objective.

In the lodge of Tramacastilla, Lorenzo met a wise man who carried an astrolabe. The young man, surprised to see such a man, could not resist talking to him.

"I have noticed you carry an astrolabe, sir," Lorenzo said.

"Yes, young man. I am an astrologer," the well-dressed man answered.

"I have met several astrologers, and all of them Jews."

"Yes, I am also Jewish. Since Abraham, in Ur of Chaldea, many Jews have practiced this science. But there are also good Arab astrologers."

"Daniel of Teruel is an astrologer of the School of Aragon. Do you know him?"

"Yes, of course. He is a great astrologer."

"And where are you going, sir?" Lorenzo asked, hoping he could travel with the wise man.

"I am coming from Toledo, and am going to Gerona. During my trip I will visit the Jewish quarters of Albarracin, Teruel, Guadalajara, Medinaceli, Soria, Zaragoza, and Barcelona; I hope to meet astrologers of the great School of Aragon, to discuss our tables. We are living in interesting times. And where are you going?"

"I am going to Toledo."

"Oh! In Toledo there is a great astrological community. They come from all over."

"And do they advise the king?"

"Yes, they do. Ferdinand III of Castile is well advised by his astrologers. Although the church forbids the astrology, the king ignores the ban. We also used to advise the Arab kings, but they stopped listening to us a hundred years ago and expelled us from Granada, Seville, and Cordoba. They blamed the deterioration of their kingdoms on us," the astrologer told Lorenzo, sensing he was saying too much.

"And, how is Toledo?"

"It is an extraordinary place, with many translators of philosophical, scientific, and historical books from the libraries of Cordova and Alexandria. In Toledo you will meet astrologers, spiritual philosophers, Jewish, Arab, and Christian translators, as well skilled financiers who are in charge of the kingdom's accounts."

While listening to the him speak about Toledo, Lorenzo realized that he belonged in the Castilian capital. He then told him his adventures.

"I have made mistakes since I left my beloved Teruel,"

Lorenzo acknowledged.

"You must learn from your mistakes, young man; but do not lose the focus of your intention. Never forget who you are," said the astrologer, who could see the goodness in Lorenzo's soul and his guide behind him.

Lorenzo was disappointed the astrologer would be traveling in the opposite direction. His company would have been remarkable. The conversation with the astrologer left a strong impression on his soul; the meeting was a blessing and he regarded the encounter as a sign he was once again on the right path.

The next day, Lorenzo continued walking and he arrived in Guadalaviar. In the main plaza of the beautiful town, he saw a group of shepherds who had joined together to defend themselves against the Castilian noblemen. They were talking about the four hundred thousand arrobas of wool they had produced during the season, an all-time record for the region. Lorenzo asked permission to join their conversation.

"Excuse my brazenness, I am just a man speaking with good intentions. I know that the price of wool is falling in the north of Aragon. If you have produced so much wool, maybe you would like to sell it before the news reaches here."

The shepherds were suspicious of the young man, but their instincts told them Lorenzo was telling the truth. To thank him for the information, they invited Lorenzo to stay with them for a few days.

The young man continued his trek towards Tragacete, the next town on his way to Cuenca. The path went through areas of astonishing beauty. During his walk, he had an amazing sense of freedom that made his journey pass quickly.

Soon he arrived at the path's summit. The main road

traversed the side of the mountain. Lorenzo saw a shortcut, but it required descending another steep cliff. Before starting his descent, he heard his inner voice warning him, "No, no, no." It advised him it was not worth taking the shortcut; however, he took it anyway. He gained speed, lost control, stumbled over a stone, fell and began to tumble. He twisted his ankle. "Why did I not listen to my own voice?" Lorenzo cursed himself.

His inner voice spoke again, "There are no shortcuts in life. This is the result of going on a path that looked easier and quicker. You will be protected as long as you do not make foolish choices..."

The young man stood up and continued with great difficulty. His pain was unbearable and after half day, he arrived in Beamud, exhausted. He collapsed as soon as he entered in the village. He was dirty, downhearted, and defeated. A polite family, seeing his perilous state, offered him accommodation and food. They insisted he stay until his ankle was healed, and asked nothing in exchange. Lorenzo enjoyed two weeks of tranquility. He pondered his life, thanking God for the good people in the world.

Once he had recovered, the family provided him with food and he set off for Cuenca. The path from Beamud to Cuenca went through lush green country side. Lorenzo delighted in the nature's magnificence. Suddenly a herd of bulls appeared in front of him, blocking his way. He knew the bulls were noble, but he should not startle them. He waited patiently until they moved on, but one wild bull refused to move. The bull looked at Lorenzo with the intention to charge at him. Lorenzo knew one false move would make the bull rush towards him. He tried to remain calm, and he looked at the bull for several minutes. Then he whispered:

"God loves you,"

Lorenzo remained motionless for a long time in front of the animal. Suddenly the bull looked at him with a profound look of understanding in its eyes. The bull put his head down, and left with the rest of the herd, unblocking Lorenzo´s path. Lorenzo had communicated with the bull in a loving manner.

He felt pleased and knew he had passed an important test. He felt he was invincible, which made him lower his guard: the animal threat would appear again.

Soon, Lorenzo arrived in the next town. A chill ran through him when he entered in the village. He did not feel well, but he ignored the sign. He heard a loud noise from the main tavern in the town, and curiosity lead him to investigate. He opened the door and entered the packed tavern. The patrons, surprised, looked at Lorenzo with disdain; they did not like strangers. They stopped talking and everyone looked at Lorenzo. The silence was frightening. Some drunken men confronted him.

"Have you lost anything here, young man? Have you come to take our women?"

Lorenzo tried to leave the tavern, but a drunk blocked his way out.

"You're not going anywhere," a man with a sword threatened Lorenzo. "You must buy us drinks."

Lorenzo was more terrified than when he encountered the bull hours before. Two other men drew their swords and took all his money.

"The young man will buy us all drinks!" one of them shouted, waving all Lorenzo´s money in the air.

The drunks applauded with delight. Lorenzo tried to leave the tavern again, but another man hit him in the stomach and face. Lorenzo head was bleeding.

"We do not like foreigners here. Is that clear?" they warned him.

Lorenzo, shocked and bleeding, left the town as fast as he could. Those men were uncivilized beasts. He spent the night outside, unprotected. The beating he had received, hurt him both physically and emotionally, but looking at the stars helped him to contemplate what had happened to him. In less than two months, he went from being a rich man in the best manor in Iberia, to being robbed, beaten, and homeless. He had experienced both sides of fortune, and to his surprise, he did not even feel any resentment towards the drunks. In Albarracin, he thought he was the king of the world, and now he had regained his humility. The guilt he felt at being so pompous made him feel he deserved the beating.

The next morning, he started on the path towards Cuenca. His spirit dragged at the same pace as his feet. Once in the city, he went to the main plaza, which was abuzz with commercial activity.

He went to the cathedral, which had been converted to a church from a mosque. Upon entering the church, Lorenzo wept. He felt he had betrayed himself, and his soul in Albarracin, but most of all, he thought he had betrayed God.

The spiritual benefit gained from the courage to leave Teruel was wasted when he lost his dignity in Albarracin. He could not explain what had happened to him, neither the forces that influenced him.

He needed to find his way once more. He asked God with all his strength for His guidance. A solemn silence descended upon the cathedral. In a state of sincere remorse, Lorenzo placed himself before the Divine Presence asking for forgiveness. The Grace of God was present and he was heard him.

16. RETREAT

$\mathcal{L}$orenzo asked God for help in regaining his dignity. His shame was overwhelming; he had been beaten and had not defended himself. In Albarracin, he had become arrogant, egoistical, and vain. The innocent young man who left Teruel to pursue his dream was not the same man who had bid thousands of maravedises at auction for a young girl. He no longer knew himself. How had he changed so much? He cried. Not because of the beating, or for being alone, he cried because he had lost his innocence. The Divine Presence came to him, in the form of a priest, who, seeing the devastated young man came to talk to him:

"What is wrong, brother? Are you all right?"

Lorenzo could not look up, although a gentle face awaited him.

"There is always an opportunity, a new door," the priest, dressed in a simple brown robe, said to him. "Have faith. Since you alive all is not lost."

Lorenzo raised his head, as the priest gave him a hand. His face was friendly, and indeed looked familiar to Lorenzo. He felt he knew the priest.

"I feel ashamed, I was beaten, and I did not even try to defend myself." Lorenzo said, feeling better, now that he could talk about his disgrace.

"And what are you doing in Cuenca?"

"I come from Teruel and I am on my way to Toledo, but I do not have the strength to continue. I need to heal myself," he said.

"This is the best place to recover. You are in the beautiful cathedral of Cuenca."

"I need a place to stay and a job. I have also been robbed," he sobbed, and then, stood up.

"Some of the monks of our community were ordained priests and they left to preach the word of God among the Arabs living in Christian territory. We need new brothers in the congregation."

"I have great faith in God, but I do not often go to church," Lorenzo said, excusing himself.

"I will ask the community if they will accept you to live with us. Come with me. My name is Julian."

"I am Lorenzo," he said, shaking hands with the priest.

He followed Julian to a nearby building, where the monks lived, which had a garden full of trees and vegetables. Lorenzo could not tell if someone lived there, so profound was the silence. He could only hear the fall of their steps.

"If the prior accepts you, we will assign you a room. You will wake up before sunrise for morning prayers, respect the silence, and help with the community chores. The evenings will be yours."

Lorenzo pondered his options. He assessed the possibility of continuing on his way to Toledo, but he was not in any condition to resume the journey. He neither wanted to work as a wool trader, nor take on new responsibilities that would require his time and energy. He needed to heal his emotions. The spiritual discipline, and the silence of the monastery seemed an ideal place to do so.

Some of the monks, seeing his bruises all over his body, and how dirty he was, expressed their doubts. Julian proposed he would be on probation for one month, after which, they would decide if he would become a member of the community. Then, he introduced Lorenzo to the brothers. The young man had developed the ability to assess the quality of a person beyond their exterior due to his experience as a wool trader. Father Julian showed the kindness of his soul, but the prior, with twisted features, was a mystery. Lorenzo knew he could trust most of them, although he sensed some of the monks did not have a true religious vocation; some had become monks to enjoy a life without responsibilities, but God was not their concern.

Life in the community was straightforward. The brothers awoke every morning before sunrise, prayed, and meditated for a long time. After a light breakfast, they performed their communal chores. They prayed once more after lunch, and then had free time. In the evening, they met for the last prayer of the day to give thanks.

Lorenzo joined with diligence. Before sleeping, he would take out his Menorah, and focused his energy on such powerful spiritual symbol. When his probation ended, Julian, who could not hide his liking for Lorenzo, told him,

"You have done well. I do not know much about your past life, but during the last month your behavior has been exemplary. The community accepts you. Congratulations!"

"Thank you very much, father."

Lorenzo adjusted to the rhythms of the community. The routine of the monks was just what he needed. He did not mind waking up early and performing the daily duties. In the beginning, he felt uneasy during the morning meditations, since he could not concentrate well enough.

"It is normal for you feel uncomfortable," Julian explained to him. "With practice you will be able to enter a peaceful state for a longer time."

After months of practice, Lorenzo managed to control his wandering mind and often experienced a profound silence. The continuous practice of prayer allowed him to obtain a new level of clarity. So profound was his happiness that he thought about staying in Cuenca for the rest of his life; he was in paradise. Without many responsibilities, he was happy not to struggle to make a living. The life in Teruel with his father and the life in Albarracin as a wool trader were now just fleeting memories.

In the afternoon, he enjoyed many deep conversations with Julian. They talked about their inner lives, their spiritual development, and the way to God. Lorenzo spoke of the things that wise people such as Daniel or Arturo had told him.

"Personal desire is only fulfilled if it is granted by the heavens," Julian told him. "For this reason you must align your personal will with the divine will."

After a year in the monastery, Lorenzo's emotional wounds had healed. He could re-connect with the innocent young man who had left Teruel following his dream. Spiritual discipline helped him find a deep peace. Some days he experienced an extraordinary inner calm, and he no longer feared death. For several moments, he reached the mystical state that so many people long for; ecstatic unconditional love.

In his free time, Lorenzo went to the Jewish quarter to observe the merchants. There was something subtle and similar shared by the Jewish quarter's in all cities; it was the atmosphere created by the collective soul of the Jewish people. Lorenzo understood the importance of the Jews in Castile. King Ferdinand III had appointed them to important court positions. The king also had obtained a papal exemption, removing the obligation for the Jews to wear a distinctive symbol on their clothes.

Lorenzo spent many happy years in the congregation. Without realizing it, he turned twenty-nine in the monastery. He had forgotten about Toledo once more. The months passing in a peaceful routine. His idyllic state did not force him to move on and he used his time to read books of Gonzalo de Berceo, the author of the Master de Clergy, with whom he identified. He also studied Arab and Latin with Julian. Lorenzo was away from the world.

In Castile the Christians were winning the wars against the Arabs. The abbot and the monks noted with enthusiasm the advances of the Christian hosts in the Peninsula.

"James I, King of Aragon, is a hero for the Christian cause," the prior said. "Even the foreign monarchs admire him for his conquests of Majorca and Valencia."

"He is planning on expelling all the Arabs from Valencia. We will take their land and possessions and use them for our cause" another monk added.

"Now we can take everything from them. With their money we will finance new campaigns," the prior said with a little bit of malice.

"Ferdinand III, of Castile, continues his southward march. He has just taken Lucena, and Murcia has surrendered to Castile, paying a big vassalage. Castile is rich," another priest commented.

"But the noblemen are never satisfied. The most important Castilian aristocrat, Diego Lopez de Haro, has revolted against King Ferdinand." Julian replied.

"Alphonso, the son of the king, will put down the revolt," the prior answered. " Don't worry. Castile will be Christian for many years!"

Lorenzo's life was tranquil and simple, but his soul knew he had to broaden his horizons and continue his studies. His mission was in the world, not within these cloistered walls. The heavens also knew Lorenzo's destiny was not in a monastery, under a hierarchic ecclesiastic structure. Others were called to a monastic life, but not Lorenzo.

One day, Lorenzo heard some news that confirmed he was guided on this path. The lord of Albarracin, Don Pedro Fernandez de Azagra, had pawned several villages and a castle to pay his debts. The lord of Albarracin only obtained a small percentage of the Valencian territories, which was insufficient to repay his loans. The lord died leaving many unpaid debts. If Lorenzo had married his daughter, he would have had to pay those debts and would be trapped in a world that was not his. He thanked Providence for providing the circumstances, although painful, which allowed him to leave Albarracin.

Nevertheless, his happiness without responsibility had to end. The bishop of Cuenca needed brothers to join the crusades. The Inquisition, established in France decades before, had arrived in Aragon. They were now persecuting the French Cathars who hid in Aragon, Castile, and Navarre. One hundred eighty-three Cathars had just been burned in France. His companions, avoiding from the fires, settled in the Iberian Peninsula.

"I need to ordain new priests and send them to the north of the Christian kingdoms," the bishop told the prior. "At Rome´s command."

"And what would be their task?" the prior asked.

"To inform the ecclesiastic court about heretics. They also will have to convert Jews and Arabs."

When Lorenzo heard about the bishop's plan, he knew he had to leave his paradise. He had no intention of being ordained, and thereby becoming a spy for a dreadful court. Forcing people to convert through violence or the threat of burning at the stake was contrary to God's will.

The bishop kept his eyes on Lorenzo. He knew there was something special about the young man and thought he could be a great asset for the Christian cause. He informed him he would ordain him as a priest and would move to Burgos to help the new Inquisition.

Lorenzo did not want to convert people as other monks in the congregation did; he would rather be free. He felt such extraordinary love during his meditations that violence had no place in his life. He had to flee, as the church would not accept a "no" for an answer. The repercussions would be horrible: he could be considered a heretic, banned and possibly executed.

Lorenzo took his last walk through his beloved Cuenca to say goodbye to the city. He came across two lovers crying. Their parents were wealthy but the boy was a Christian and the girl was a Jew. To see his beloved, every Friday, the young man jumped the wall that separated the Jewish quarter from the rest of the city. The families had forbidden them to see each other and their brothers almost killed them in a bloody fight. Lorenzo sensed the couple were meant for each other. When he looked in their eyes, he remembered Ariadna, and the intense feeling of love returned. "Where would Ariadna be now?" he wondered. Lorenzo blessed the two teenagers and encouraged them to start a new life in another place.

Lorenzo was about to turn thirty and wished to continue his way. His body, his soul, and his spirit were in perfect conditions. He took his only true belonging, the small Menorah he had kept hidden during his years as part of the congregation. Without hesitating, he silently left the city dressed as a monk, wearing only sandals.

This time, he left calmly. He meditated and recalled the brothers with whom he had shared the paradisaic state. He felt bad for not having said goodbye to Julian; for without his help, he would not have been able to heal his body and soul. He was determined to reach Toledo. But before, he would have to face new temptations, which might entice him away from his true destiny.

17. MIRAGES

Lorenzo had forgotten what blisters felt like, however, after walking for just a few hours, he was sorely reminded. His monk robes were not suitable for the dusty roads of Castile, but he accepted the situation.

"On the road again. I pray God protects me," he said to himself.

Just then, the word "Toledo" resonated strongly in his mind. He had little food or money, yet he remained optimistic,

"God will provide. He has never abandoned me. He has always opened the right doors for me."

When Lorenzo arrived at Chillaron de Cuenca he discovered an orchard. The residents had made a shelter against the hot summer days. The garden, full of trees and vegetables, was an excellent area for resting. Lorenzo spent the night in the orchard under the canopy of stars. Free and full of life, he had a profound meditation. He awoke filled with energy.

At dawn, after thanking and blessing the new day, he continued his journey. The inner silence, practiced for such a long time in the monastery, became his source of security and self-confidence. He was happy and he trusted life.

He met several shepherds and traders, who were heading to the Burgos and Medina Del Campo fairs. They traveled the "Wool

Route", a path that traders and shepherds created for their protection.

"Hello friar, what are you doing here?" a shepherd asked him.

"I am heading to Toledo."

"Take this path." The man pointed. "The next village is still two days away. Here, please accept some bread and cheese for your trip."

"Thank you very much," Lorenzo said, thanking God for heaven-sent help. "By the way, do you know Arturo, the healing shepherd of Teruel?"

"Of course, but he is old now. He used to help the ill shepherds with his remedies. Is he your friend?"

"I used to see him in the evenings. He worked for my father."

"Do you have money?" the kind shepherd asked him.

"No, I have just left the monastery and I have nothing."

"Take ten coins. Those roads are dangerous. Let me get you shepherd's clothes; the bandits do not rob shepherds. They leave us be, as they know we have nothing; however, if you are dressed as a monk, they may attack you. The monks are known for being well off. Wait here."

The shepherd left and returned with shepherd's clothes. "Remember to help a shepherd on your way," the good man told him, waving goodbye to Lorenzo, touched by the divine meeting.

The countryside became arid, and the heat was intense, yet a strange feeling came upon Lorenzo. His body froze for no reason. In front of him, out of nowhere, a man who appeared very sophisticated passed in the opposite direction. The sky darkened and the temperature dropped. The man, with bright smile and shiny eyes, smiled and said hello. His eyes were hypnotizing.

Lorenzo was curious about who this mysterious figure could be, although he already knew the answer, but he did not want to acknowledge it. He was aware throughout history; this figure had introduced himself in a dazzling manner or with a repugnant form. To Lorenzo he chose to appear handsome. Lorenzo returned the greeting and continued walking, praying silently

He still needed half a day to reach the next town, so he picked up his pace. Soon the cold disappeared and it was hot once again. He arrived tired and thirsty and headed for the tavern. The owner of the establishment was a fifty-year old strange looking woman. She appeared strong, dressed in black, with dark hair, and a threatening look. Her husband, catered to her demands, did everything she ordered. At this point Lorenzo's fatigue was so overwhelming, that despite of his uneasiness, he requested accommodation. He ate a little bit, and went to a small straw loft, where he lay down to rest. He felt threatened and prayed for protection,

"God, protect me. Do not leave me now," he begged not able to explain his discomfort.

He fell asleep. After a short and intense dream, he awoke at midnight. He had the strange feeling of being conscious and unconscious at the same time. There were noises coming from the tavern and he went to the canteen. The patrons were drinking wine and carousing. Lorenzo looked at three excited men who were screaming and calling for bets. They were seated around a table full of gold and silver coins. Every few minutes one of them threw the dice, and if the player won, they paid them five times the bet.

Lorenzo watched for a while then he spotted an attractive young woman seated on the other side of the room. The young woman also noticed. She had dark hair and intense green eyes. He looked at her and wondered why the woman was interested in him, a simple man dressed in simple shepherd clothes.

Lorenzo's heart began beating out of control when he saw the man he had met on the road. He was smiling at Lorenzo, who was terrified. Fear enveloped him as the man came over to talk to him.

"I know what that woman likes," he told Lorenzo.

"Really?" Lorenzo responded uncomfortable with the conversation.

"She likes rich and powerful men," he laughed, looking down at Lorenzo's clothes.

"But I am neither rich, nor powerful..."

"Lorenzo, would you like to be rich?" the man asked smiling seductively. "You could spend the night with her if you wish. You could also become rich."

The young man was confused. "How did this strange man know his name? How was it that one of the most beautiful women he had ever seen was attracted to him, who was dressed poorly?" he wondered.

Lorenzo was very attracted to the woman, who was playing with her hair.

"Five," the mysterious man said before the dice were thrown.

A 5 showed. Lorenzo thought the man made a lucky guess.

"Two..." the man whispered before guessing the outcome.

"Four," and the face of the dice showed a 4 just after the mysterious man called the number.

He was predicting each of the dice outcomes! Lorenzo

thought he was conspiring with the man who threw the dice.

"I do not know the man who throws the dice," the mysterious man said, reading Lorenzo's thoughts.

"How do you do it?" Lorenzo asked, astonished.

"Come, Lorenzo. Place a bet. I will tell you the winning number. If you bet your winnings six times, you will turn your ten coins into more than one hundred thousand, which is all the money on the table."

"Are you going to help me to win all that money?" Lorenzo asked stunned.

"Yes, I will tell you the outcome of every single throw."

Meanwhile, the woman was looking at Lorenzo with great desire. The idea of having the woman was tempting.

"Who are you?" Lorenzo asked him in a moment of clarity.

"You know who I am," the mysterious man said.

Lorenzo felt icy cold, with a stabbing pain in his head.

"Do not worry, I just want to make a deal with you. I will help you win the money, you take the woman tonight, and in exchange, you will work for me."

"You want me to work for you?" Lorenzo asked, confused.

"Yes, I will help you win the money, you will sleep with the woman and, in exchange, you will have to perform specific tasks for me, from time to time."

The woman stood up from where she was and came closer to Lorenzo. She took a hold of his arm. The young man stopped for a moment to consider the situation: a stranger offering to help him win at dice easy money, and at the same time, he could seduce a gorgeous woman. Was this real?

While reflecting on the situation, both strangers pressured Lorenzo. The offer was tempting. He thought there was no harm in testing him once; however, an inner voice advised him, not to be tempted by anything these two were offering him.

"If this man knows the outcome, why does he need me? Why does he want me to seduce this beautiful woman?" Lorenzo asked himself.

The man saw Lorenzo´s doubts and signaled the woman to accompany him to the gambling table. She took him by the arm, and placed her breasts close to him. Being unable to resist, Lorenzo found himself at the betting table.

"Place your ten coins on the six!" the strange man ordered him.

"Put the money on number six," the gorgeous woman whispered seductively.

Lorenzo remained doubtful.

"Put the money on the six! You will win a lot of money and this woman will be yours!" the man shouted.

Those moments seemed like an eternity for Lorenzo. The tavern fell silent, while awaiting Lorenzo's decision. Lorenzo screamed, it coming from deep within him.

"No, no, no! Get out of here! Leave me alone!"

Lorenzo left the tavern and went to his straw loft. He lay down and after, what seemed like only a few moments, he woke up sweating. He was not sure if had dreamed, or if last evening had really happened. He then heard a rooster welcoming the new day. He went to the tavern to pay for his stay, where he met the angry tavern keeper.

"How did party end last night?" Lorenzo inquired.

"There was no party last night," the woman answered calling her husband. "This man is crazy. Let him pay for his stay and send him away. He is useless!"

Lorenzo was speechless. The tavern owner demanded a lot of money for the use of the loft, but Lorenzo did not argue. He paid the exorbitant amount, and quickly left town.

Halfway to the next village, he had another strange encounter. Several filthy men, hidden in the bushes, accosted the defenseless Lorenzo.

"Little shepherd, what do you carry for us today?" one of the men said laughing at Lorenzo, who continued his walk, ignoring them.

"Come on, shepherd, give us something, so we can eat today."

He realized they were bandits. His heart rate increased, but he continued on his way, ignoring them.

"Stop, shepherd!" said the leader of the gang, threatening him with a knife.

Lorenzo knew life had no meaning for these people, so he showed no resistance. The three thieves got angry,

"Is this everything you have, you miserable man?" one of them said. "Let us take all his clothes and leave him here. We might get something for them."

While he was undressing, the little Menorah fell down. The three bandits looked at it, and one of them took it.

"A trinket!" they said before throwing it out on the road.

"Boy, you are lucky we are in a good mood today," and they

left running with Lorenzo's clothes and his few coins, leaving him alone in his underclothes. "We are not going to take your life."

Lorenzo exhaled, relieved. However, he realized he was in the middle nowhere, with neither money nor clothes, he fell into despair. He was at the mercy of circumstances that had not turned out well. Lorenzo had saved his life and his Menorah, after encountering the thieves. Now he would be required to take on an unexpected role if he were to survive on his path.

18. BALLADS

"*Is* this what happens to me for not accepting the deal from that strange man? Look at me now." Lorenzo cried, unaware he was being watched over by his maggid. His situation was not as it seemed. There was a greater reason Lorenzo was mugged and left on the path with only his underclothes. The assault was part of his training in becoming a stronger person before starting the next phase of his spiritual path. But Lorenzo was not able to see this.

Lorenzo sat under a tree, hidden behind tall brushes. He was almost naked, with no money, with his Menorah as his only possession. He saw others traveling on the route but was not brave enough to speak to them. Suddenly he heard music and laughter from a cart full of minstrels; they were playing and singing, as they traveled. Lorenzo stopped them and asked for help,

"Gentlemen, please give me some clothes," Lorenzo begged, emerging from the bushes half naked.

The minstrels were surprised to see a man dressed only in his underclothes. They bellowed loudly and, threw water on him.

"The lord has asked for some clothes," they mocked.

"I have been robbed, have mercy, please. I beg of you."

"Take out the clown's costume and give it to him!" said one musician to another.

The costume was ghastly, and would certainly get the pub-

155

lic's attention; it was green and yellow with bright colors, with bells all over it. The musicians gave him a tambourine as well. Lorenzo conceded anything was better than being naked.

"We will give you the costume, but you must play the role of the clown," the uncivilized leader of the group spouted off to Lorenzo.

Lorenzo had no alternative. He hoped he would be safe traveling with these misfits. The minstrels were rarely attacked, on the contrary, the thieves were afraid of them: the musicians were well known for being lunatics.

"Jump! Jump! Jump, clown!" they told him from the cart, and Lorenzo tried his best to be funny.

"You must play the role of the clown, but a dignified one," another musician said.

Sometimes, spiritual teachings come in a strangest way. To be a member of a group of traveling minstrels was what Lorenzo needed to reshape his ego. The minstrels would destroy the programing that formed his ego, aggravating him until was able to become truly humble.

Wearing in the clown's costume was tedious. He tried to get into the cart, but was not allowed to. He had to walk, so the locals could see him. Lorenzo swallowed his pride, while the eight minstrels enjoyed the parade. They traveled from town to town, performing shows wherever fortune took them, and never worried about tomorrow.

"Learn these rhymes! Tonight, we perform in Huete. If you do well, you can stay with us for a week," one of the musicians said.

"At least I will have a roof over my head and will be able to eat," Lorenzo thought. "If I travel with the minstrels, nobody will call me as a stranger," he said to himself, knowing the fugitives were jailed and even executed if nobody recognized them.

Dressed as a clown, he pondered his life's path. In Albarracin, he had been rich, then he became a monk, and now…he was a clown. He was proud that at the very least he had the ability to adapt to different situations… and remain sane.

That night, in Huete, Lorenzo performed with the troupe. He was nervous and forgot his rhymes. He babbled telling his serious verses, but the audience found him funny. The performance was a success and the minstrels were invited to stay for three months. They would stay with a nobleman, and in exchange, they would perform every night. The members of the group, seeing what a success Lorenzo was with the audience, invited him to stay with them.

One night they performed at the palace of Huete's richest aristocrat. The gentleman wanted to celebrate the surrender of Murcia and the conquest of Jaen by King Ferdinand III. The minstrels played popular ballads and danced with the village maidens, seducing them. Lorenzo was assigned to take care of the instruments, while the musicians danced and caroused with the ladies.

While his companions were performing, he pondered the difference between the Ministry in the Clergy and the Craft of Minstrels. The members of the former, like Gonzalo de Berceo, composed music as a sacred act for the Lord; while the members of the latter composed music to entertain the populous and seduce women.

One of the palace maids kept her eyes on Lorenzo. It seemed strange for him that a lady wanted to talk to him, as he was dressed in such a nauseating way. The costume reeked, since it had never been washed. The girl did not seem to be bothered by the foul odor, as she took Lorenzo by the hand and lead him to her bedroom. Lorenzo could not believe what life had just gifted to him; just a few days ago he was alone and naked sitting beside the road, and now he was sleeping with a maid in the palace of the richest nobleman of Huete!

The musicians, when learning of his affair, all smiled in support. His conquest was the decisive deed to be invited to join the group; he would have food and a place to sleep in exchange for serving the musicians. Lorenzo accepted the deal.

He started liking the life of a clown. He had no responsibilities, ate well, and seduced women. It seemed the musician costumes were irresistible to women. As a clown, he could say things no one dared to say. Sometimes a nobleman, who did not want to say things to his enemy face to face, paid Lorenzo to deliver the message in public for all to hear.

Money was flowing into the kingdom. The Castilians were happy and this made life easy for the minstrels. Ferdinand III had launched an attack on Granada and the Arab king had surrendered. In exchange for peace, the Arabs would pay one hundred thousand maravedises per year to the crown of Castile.

The impressive naval victory on the Guadalquivir River eased the conquest of Seville. The victorious soldiers, loaded with plundered Arab gold, often called the musicians to play for their many parties. Lorenzo´s group made so much money that they settled in Huete for the season. They rented a villa as their base, and played in the nearby villages. The musician's fame grew and many the noblemen hired them, the women received them well dressed, and children learned their verses.

Lorenzo lost his way again. He started drinking after his performances and slept with many women. He was mindlessly enjoying life's pleasures. He ate, sang, and slept with maids. In exchange, he had to play the role of a clown and look after of the instruments. Sometimes he remembered Pasqual, his boss in Albarracin. He recalled his tragic ending for drinking too much and his affair with a married woman.

"That will not happen to me," Lorenzo said to himself, unaware the situation was already out of control.

Sometimes he had a fleeting thought about Toledo, but he was having too much fun, that he put in risk his destiny. "Toledo can wait," he said to himself one morning, while his maggid could only shake his head.

His spiritual path was once again at risk. Pride was ruling him again, but this time, it was not for money; it was for seducing women and living an irresponsible life.

In time, Lorenzo learned to play an instrument and became one of the musicians, leaving the position of the clown to the next newcomer. He became excellent lute player and he set out to become an equally adept lover. The minstrels taught him to decode the women's body language, and then seducing them while expending as little time, and energy as possible. Lorenzo became expert at telling women what they wanted to hear. In a few months, he wasted the spiritual growth resulting from his time in the monastery of Cuenca.

From time to time, a musician left the group to get married, and have children. However, they all returned; the burden of being a husband and father proving was tedious compared to the easy life of a minstrel.

Lorenzo loved women's company. He composed songs for them and played them on his lute. He had marvelous affairs with many women. Sometimes Lorenzo when felt a particular attraction for a lady, he did not stop until he seduced her. Lorenzo´s heart was frozen; he could brush off the painful weeping of a lady, who had fallen in love with him after a burning night of sexual passion, when she found him days later with another woman. A shadow stalked Lorenzo, who had stagnated.

In December, Lorenzo would celebrate his thirty-third birthday. Looking in the mirror, he saw himself in prime physical shape, but he did not like what he saw. He had changed; he had abandoned his human side to become a low life seducer. He needed to learn about women, but not become their seducer. His heavenly guardians sent him warnings from the heavens, that if he did not change his ways, they were even considering ending his life.

The treaty of Almizra between James I of Aragon and Ferdinand III of Castile was proclaimed. Thanks to the alliance, the wedding of Alphonse of Castile, son of King Ferdinand III, and Violante of Aragon, daughter of James I, was agreed to. It would take place in Valladolid. The musicians were now so famous they were called to play at the royal wedding.

The musicians happily headed towards Valladolid. Lorenzo traveled with two other musicians. They left Huete on a sunny day, but after a short distance, the sky turned dark and it began to rain heavily. The mules stopped near a tree. Lorenzo retrieved his Menorah and asked God to stop the rain. Suddenly, a strong wind blew the Menorah out of Lorenzo´s hand. He jumped from the cart and hurried to get the candelabra with seven branches. As he was picking up his treasure, a lightning bolt struck the cart killing the two musicians.

Lorenzo panicked. If the wind had not blown the Menorah away, he would be dead! The warning was clear, and as quick as the storm began, it stopped. Lorenzo dragged the two bodies off the path. They were burned. While he prayed for their souls, he heard a clear warning.

"Life is not a game. You cannot live without being responsible," he heard from his inner voice.

Lorenzo was overwhelmed by the fact he had almost lost his life. Meanwhile the presence continued to speak to him,

"Beware, Lorenzo, all things have a limit."

At that moment, Lorenzo made an important decision. He promised that he would never again live irresponsibly. Do I want to travel to Toledo to find my destiny, or do I want to continue living as a clown?" he asked himself, already knowing the answer. "I cannot keep playing with life."

He realized the life of a wandering minstrel gave him a certain degree of happiness, but it was not the true happiness of his heart. Lorenzo knew the latter would help him to live in peace, while the former brought him distress, psychological unruliness chaos, and being adrift without direction.

He looked at what he owned: a little money, a musician's costume, his lute, and his Menorah. He knew he could reach Toledo by playing in different towns.

Lorenzo was on his way again, and felt a calm joy at making the decision to follow his true path. The lightning had not touched him, thanks to Providence, and he realized this. As a show of gratitude, he decided to apply his talents in serving others, instead of using people for his immediate pleasure. For Lorenzo it was a wakeup call. Yet before devoting himself to his true mission, he would encounter new adventures, tests and challenges that would help him mature.

19. ADVENTURES

*L*orenzo continued his trek dressed as a traveling minstrel. His clothing aided his cause as the peasants asked him to perform popular songs in exchange for a few coins. On a map of Castile and Aragon, he pointed the city of Toledo, as he knew it was his destination, so he walked as quickly as he could.

Soon he reached a town ruled by a rich, insane, old landowner. The wealthy man had gone insane and the whole town was afraid of him. His children had inherited his malady and they kept the population living in fear. Those who refused to put up with the unpredictable behavior of the old man, left. The only remaining residents were the people who could not do without the little salary they received from the mad man.

The kings of Castile and Aragon had set a small toll to traverse the village of the kingdoms, but the landowner did not follow the law he charged an absurd amount to the shepherds and travelers who passed through his village.

"Why are you taking this detour when it is much shorter pass through the village center" Lorenzo asked some shepherds.

"Troubadour, the landowner is insane. If we do not pay his high transit tax, he will attack us. If you do not wish to tempt fate, go around the village," the shepherds warned him.

Lorenzo was exhausted after walking for so long under the intense sun. The next town was more than half a day's walk away, so he took the risk. Perhaps the shepherds were exaggerating about the landowner, but soon he discovered they were not. Once in the village, the lunatic's son stopped him. The young man was armed with a sword riding an elegant horse.

"Stop! You have entered the domain of Don Beltran de Villaespesa. The payment for passing through town is two thousand maravedises."

"Sir, I do not have that kind of money."

"Then, you will have to pay with your pathetic life."

"Sir, I am a simple musician, I make my living playing the lute," and Lorenzo, began to play a well-known song to the best of his ability.

The landowner's son, much to his surprise, got off his horse, and started to sing and dance to the music. Lorenzo now understood the family's mental condition.

"If you can play this melody if front of my beloved and honorable father, named Don Beltran de Villaespesa and Lagueruela de Santa Maria, we will provide you with room and board. You will also be allowed to pass through town tax-free."

Lorenzo was suspicious; nevertheless, contradicting an armed madman could be worse than accepting his offer. Lorenzo followed him to the villa. The horse looked out of the corner of its eyes feeling sorry for Lorenzo. In fact the noble animal was the sanest member of the whole family; his expression confirmed there was not much hope for its owners. Just before arriving at the lodge, the son shouted,

"A musician visits us! A famous musician is visiting us!

The old landowner had a hooked nose and a penetrating look. He was extremely thin. He jumped up and down when he saw the musician walking into his lodge.

"Play for us!" he ordered Lorenzo.

Lorenzo played his lute masterfully. When he finished there was silence, which seemed to last forever.

"Bravo! Bravo! Bravo! Where else have you played, minstrel?" the landowner asked.

"I have played in Huete, in the noblemen's palace. I was going to the wedding of Alphonso and Violante, but a lightning bolt struck our cart."

"A lighting flash, a flash of lighting! And now you are here, in my home! Listen everybody to this great musician! Eat and drink as you wish, but you will have to play for us tonight!" the mad landowner shouted.

Lorenzo spent the afternoon resting. He saw in the look of Villaespesa that he was like a mad animal who had lost part of his strength. He had been a great businessman, but now was is living in his fantasy world. Lorenzo could feel the man's hostility and knew he could explode at any moment, so Lorenzo had to choose his words carefully.

That evening, Lorenzo came down to the dining room where landowner's family awaited his arrival. They requested the same song Lorenzo had played that morning. He played perfectly, his listeners applauded, and offered him some of their best wine.

"Salute!"

Lorenzo took the cup to his mouth but he did not drink

the wine: after the death of his comrades, he had promised himself to never drink again.

"Play the same song," the owner's son of shouted.

"The same?"

"Yes, yes, the same one," his sister said, looking brazenly at Lorenzo.

Lorenzo played the melody with great skill. They applauded and offered him food.

"Musician play the same song you played this morning when we met" the owner's son requested once again.

"But it is the same one I just played…"responded Lorenzo.

"Play it again!" the crazy landowner ordered.

Lorenzo played the same song over and over. They listened attentively, as if they had never had heard it before. Between songs, they sang the verses, danced, drank and asked him to play again. It was a never ending cycle.

"Bravo, bravo! I also want to be musician. Give me your lute!" the landowner ordered.

Lorenzo thought about it twice before handing over his instrument, but there was no possibility he could refuse the demand. Losing his lute meant he would lose his source of income, but if he denied the demand, the repercussions could be horrifying. Lorenzo just wanted to leave the village.

"If you want to be a real musician, you must dress like one. I can lend you my costume," Lorenzo suggested.

"Yes, yes wonderful idea! Lend me your costume and take one of my son's. Choose the one you like. Daughter, go with the musician and give him one of our best uniforms. I will show you how well I play the lute," the landowner stated.

She accompanied Lorenzo upstairs. Lorenzo saw dozens of cages full of gold coins. Then, with brazenness, the lady sought to kiss Lorenzo, but with tact, he eased away. He then picked up a belted silver tunic with a blue hat, and gave his musician costume to the lunatic.

The landowner put on the costume, thinking he was a famous poet. He then picked up the lute, and everyone remained quiet. Beltran de Villaespesa produced the first out of tune note. Lorenzo knew, by the way how he held the instrument, the landowner had never had a lute in his hands before. A few seconds later, the landowner's mood changed.

"Good night! The party is over," and he left the room.

The young adults, terrified of their father, obeyed. Lorenzo went to his room and prepared everything to be able leave before sunrise. He hardly slept, and at the first sign of daylight, he left the lodge, being careful not to wake anyone. The landowner's daughter went to her balcony, and begged him not to leave.

"Musician, do not forget us!" When are you coming back to play again?"

"Your father is now the musician," Lorenzo answered, offering a friendly smile, before leaving the town as fast as he could.

Lorenzo continued happily along his path. Without his musician's costume, he would not be as attractive to women, and it would be more difficult to make his living but it was time to leave behind the image of someone he was not. Thinking about his life's adventures, he arrived to Ucles. There, a lavish garden formed the village entrance. The town was of unsurpassed in beauty.

The knights of the Order of Santiago had established their headquarters in Ucles. They had fought in the conquests of Caceres, Ubeda, and Jerez de la Frontera; they had also participated in the battle of Navas de Tolosa in 1212. Lorenzo went straight to the monastery where the soldier monks resided. He listened to a conversation between two of them.

"The Cathars have been exterminated in the south of France," one of the men confirmed.

"It has taken more than fifty years, but the heretics have been eliminated," the second man answered.

The two monks noticed the stranger. They welcomed him as a noble, looking at his elegant clothes.

"How can we help you, sir?"

"I am going to Toledo and I would like to stay for a few days with you at your monastery."

"We have some empty rooms for which we ask a small amount and can offer you food. The rooms belong to the monks, but many of them are in the south, fighting for Christ."

Lorenzo stayed in the amazing monastery for two weeks, watching the return of the victorious warrior monks from Seville and Huelva, and the departure of other monks to the south. He also could hear the piercing cries of the Arab prisoners held and tortured in the castle's dungeon.

Lorenzo could not understand the purpose of a Christian Militia. He believed it was contradictory that a soldier killed another person in the name of Jesus. Even giving themselves to Santiago before going into battle was awkward. The name Santiago in Spanish means Jacob and Lorenzo thought the Order of Santiago might keep fighting with the Angel of God in symbolic terms, as Jacob did.

The monk's cook stopped to talk to Lorenzo. His long white beard, his transparent blue eyes, and his clarity of thought made Lorenzo think he might be a wise man.

"Have you been to battle?" Lorenzo asked him.

"No, I am just the cook in the monastery," he said smiling.

Lorenzo observed the enormous body of the monk and he thought he was an excellent cook; probably he ate an abundance of his preparations.

"And what do you think about the crusades and the religious wars?"

"I have no opinion. For reasons we cannot understand, the Arabs and the Christians are killing each other in Iberia. The fact the Christians are gaining territory must be for a reason."

"But both religions come from the same father, Abraham," Lorenzo added.

"It is a war between brothers," the cook answered. "They believe their God is the only God, and we believe our God is the true God. I believe it is the same God. Religious wars are, in fact, political wars."

"How do you live in the presence of God here?"

"I am with God when I cook. God is present when I am preparing the food. I am lucky for the possibility to feed my brothers. Before I cook, I pray, so the food will not only nourish physically but also spiritually."

"It is embodying the spirit of God in the food."

"Exactly."

After resting for a while in Ucles, Lorenzo gathered his

belongings, and continued on his way. He looked back at the magnificent monastery-castle of Ucles. The wars of the Knights of Santiago were not his.

"The true fight is the one within against the forces which prevent God from being present in our lives," he heard from his inner voice, and he comprehended this message clearly.

"Ask me a question," his maggid said after he sat down to meditate.

"Am I on the right path?"

"Yes, but you must not allow yourself to be distracted anymore," the young man heard with clarity, while a light breeze touched his face. "You have made some bad choices that might have taken you off your path. You cannot afford another grave mistake. It could prove fatal."

Lorenzo took heed of the warning, and continued on his journey. Meditating under the tree proved enlightening. Now, his role was to maintain that state of truth, beauty, and goodness, before reaching Toledo.

20. ARRIVAL

$\mathscr{L}$orenzo had an extraordinary revelation while walking towards Toledo. He was conscious of being conscious for the first time in his life! It was an amazing state of awareness. In this state of mental clarity, he arrived in Corral de Almaguer.

After taking a short stroll around the village, he went to the synagogue. He thanked God for protecting him during his pilgrimage; however, Lorenzo sensed uneasiness in the temple. The new pope, Innocent IV, was forcing his bishops to separate the Jews from the Christians in their dioceses. In the small villages, they obeyed the order, which created a great deal of tension between the religious communities. When the rabbi noticed Lorenzo was not Jewish, he did not welcome him and Lorenzo left discretely.

Lorenzo needed to earn some money to continue his trip. He sold his fancy clothes and bought a simple blue tunic, which matched his humble circumstances. Many people, seeing his elegant garment, had treated him as someone special, which he was not. He knew, that to enter in the Kingdom of Heaven, did not require expensive clothes.

The Castilian king needed settlers to repopulate the southern territories, and many people had left the village, looking for land and fortune. Laborers were scarce, so Lorenzo quickly found work at a bakery. He had to bake bread day and night to feed the hungry travelers who could appear unannounced. His job was harsh, because he had to feed the fires with great quantities of wood, but he did not mind hard work.

Lorenzo rented a small room near the bakery, where he practiced his spiritual rituals. In his meditations, he focused his mind on
his Menorah. All during his pilgrimage, the small object had helped
him maintain a strong spiritual connection. During his stay in Corral
de Almaguer, Lorenzo lived like a cloistered monk, with discipline,
seriousness, and conscious hard work.

A food broker and his wife managed the bakery, and were
accountable to the village council. His sister admired how reliable
Lorenzo was and began making advances. Although he found her
physically attractive, he knew she was not the woman with whom he
would spend the rest of his life. To avoid trouble, Lorenzo did not
seduce her. He knew if he impregnated her, he would have to make a
compromise with someone whom he did not love. It was difficult for
him to do the right thing, but he was learning the right path is often
the most difficult one. Besides, the vision of Ariadna appeared to him
once more in a vivid form; on many occasions, he remembered the
moments he had shared with his beloved, moving in the subtle worlds,
laying down together beneath his favorite tree in Teruel.

Every Thursday, Lorenzo went to the village market where
he observed the tricks pulled by some merchants who tried to make
more money by manipulating the scales or by selling low quality products. They were unaware of the long-term effects of their actions and
that sooner or later their business practices would come back to haunt
them. Lorenzo became a committed observer in order to negotiate
the price of the flour for the bakery. Some of the sellers recognized
Lorenzo´s skills and tried to hire him, but he only wanted to earn
money to continue his journey to Toledo. He could not afford any
more distractions.

After one year's hard work, he had made enough money to
continue on his way. He looked at himself in the mirror. The innocent
blond boy who had left Teruel no longer existed: his adventures had

left their mark on him.

Lorenzo became friends with a vegetable trader who sold his goods in the region. The trader took him to Tembleque where he spent the following night. He went to the market to buy some things, but to his surprise, nobody was selling anything. The king had established a price cap for basic products, which could not be sold above a determined price. However, this produced the opposite result: the products sold on the black market for a much higher price. Lorenzo asked about that market, and some neighbors told him where to find it.

Upon arriving at the secret market, he found himself in the middle of a huge commotion produced by the excitement of the clandestine activity. In the midst of that whirlwind, Lorenzo noticed an ancient man with a long white beard, dressed in an immaculate white tunic. He also looked at Lorenzo. They acknowledged each other and the man nodded. He was familiar, as if he had known him his whole life; in fact, his father had met him many years before, near the main tavern of Teruel, on the day of Lorenzo's conception. Lorenzo moved closer to him, but when he arrived, the mysterious man had disappeared. He looked for him all around the village, but he could not find any trace of him. He gave up looking, but he could not forget his eyes.

"Will I ever have the same look as he has?" he wondered, thinking that in Toledo he might meet someone of such a high human quality.

Then, they traveled on to Mora. The trader loved Lorenzo´s company, even though they hardly spoke during the trip. Lorenzo was anxious, and preferred not to talk. He knew he was about to enter in another dimension. Meanwhile they enjoyed the spectacle of the sunflower fields and olive groves. He was overwhelmed by the size of the olive grove, which seemed to be covered by a spiritual cloak. Once in Mora, he said goodbye to the merchant.

In the days that followed, his mood changed. His happiness and enthusiasm disappeared, and he was feeling distraught for no specific reason. The thought of giving up his pilgrimage haunted him.

"What if after such a long time, Toledo is not what I was hoped? What if I do not find the answers that I am seeking? What if I have wasted my life pursuing this dream?" he wondered.

At that moment, he did not care if he lived or died. Never had he felt so forlorn, and he wondered about the meaning of life in an illusory world. He felt apathetic and discouraged. His guide, explained his state to him.

"When the goal is at hand, many give up. Despair is normal at this stage, before a profound transformation occurs," the guide advised him in a dream.

Understanding his state calmed him. Lorenzo left Mora and continued walking to Almonacid, the end of the last stage of his journey. He regained his spirit and felt that something was prodding him to move more quickly. His destiny awaited him in the most spiritual city of the world!

While he walked, he experienced visions of events that had happened near Toledo hundreds of years before. They were people who had died hundreds of years before, who thought they were still alive. Lorenzo sensed Roman soldiers, preparing for battle, who when they perceived Lorenzo, followed him with their invisible bodies. Other beings from other times, lost in limbo, joined the invisible caravan. Lorenzo also perceived with his inner eye the capital of Castile, covered with a spiritual mantle, surrounded by heavenly guides who inspired and protected the citizens of Toledo.

He arrived safely in Almonacid, where he acquired shelter and food. He remembered Daniel, the astrologer's advice; it was best to start a new undertaking on the days following the new moon, so he postponed his arrival in Toledo until the most opportune moment.

While he awaited the new lunar cycle, he felt Toledo was calling him. He knew that in Toledo he would start his new life as a new person, and he would find the answers to his longing for knowledge. He would, indeed learn who he really was, and know true calling.

In Almonacid he heard some shocking news: King Ferdinand III just died after conquering Rota. Both Christians and Jews mourned his passing, for he had been surrounded by the most skillful Hebrew advisers. During most of his reign, he brought peace, prosperity, and harmony to the kingdom. His son, Alphonso was to be crowned King of Castile and Leon, just as Lorenzo was due to arrive in Toledo. It was meaningful that his arrival to the capital of the kingdom would coincide with the crowning of Alphonso; perhaps the life of the new king and his were somehow linked.

Lorenzo had a prophetic dream in which he participated in a meeting with a group of astrologers at the new king's court. The astrologers advised the King to reject the idea of becoming emperor, as it would ruin the kingdom. He also saw that the kingdom would become impoverished by the end Alphonso's reign. Frightened, he woke up. It was absurd to think Castile, the richest kingdom in all of Europe, and where the most advanced people from all over the world arrived, would come to that fate; however, he also knew that kind of precognitive vision revealed the truth. The dream was so real, that Lorenzo accepted it as a premonition; he knew it was going to come true.

On the new moon of June 1252, Lorenzo went to the baths in Almonacid where he purified his body, his soul, and spirit.

Silence dominated the next steps on his path, where he coordinated his breath in rhythm with his steps. He reached a peak from where he contemplated the Tajo River, which watered the city. He was awed by the magnificent panorama and sensed Toledo's greatness. He was excited knowing he was approaching his true home.

Near the Castilian capital, Lorenzo rested. He was exhausted after having maintained a deeply focused state while walking. He lay back on the hilltop, and fell asleep. He dreamed of the Roman soldiers who had followed him: they ran towards Toledo, and several celestial beings were there to meet them. They flew to the village blending with the heavens, entering in another dimension.

Lorenzo woke up and continued on his way. Toledo welcomed him. As he reached the Alcantara Bridge he was overcome with emotion. The heaven beings applauded his courage and perseverance. Lorenzo cried. He knew, after so long, he was home!

Lorenzo had finished the first stage of his life and of his horizontal journey. Now he would start his vertical journey towards the spiritual realms, where new unexpected events would test his maturity. If he succeeded, he would be called to become a man of destiny in the world's most spiritual city. Toledo...Holy Toledo.

Figure 4

• *Part Three* •

21. DISCOVERY

Tears of emotion arose from the man's blue eyes. At the age of thirty-seven, he had arrived at the majestic capital of Castile. Lorenzo stopped for a moment before crossing the Alcantara Bridge. He was awestruck by the impressive panorama of the most important city in the world. An amazing monument appeared before him, sending a sign of approval: the magnificent Alcazar congratulated him for completing his long pilgrimage.

Lorenzo crossed the bridge and continued toward the main plaza. He fixed his gaze above, feeling how the sun warmed his face. On his way there he contemplated the many convents and gardens; he was overwhelmed by its beauty.

After his initial moments of fascination and excitement, he had a feeling of urgency: he should find a job and a place to sleep. He needed to act quickly in the capital. He found himself in front of the Blood Lodge, and thought about spending the night there, but he learned they executed criminals near the lodge, and looked for another place within the heart of the city. He went up the stairs and arrived at the Zocodover plaza. He watched the extraordinary movement of Toledo: there were ranchers trading their cattle, merchants selling their products in market stalls, marching soldiers, and devout religious men.

"Soldiers and priests always walk together," he thought.

He entered into the center of city. First, he explored the

metal workers street where artisans forged metal, making a deafening noise as their hammers struck the anvils. Then, he moved closer to several food stands where many people crowded together. He approached one of the stands to buy food. The owner, noticed the distracted stranger, and treated him with inconsideration.

"What do you want?" the merchant shouted, above the voice of a town crier.

"Cheese and bread," he said handing over a coin.

The hostile shopkeeper gave him the food and handed a low quality silver alloy counterfeit coin. When Lorenzo checked the metal, he demanded a genuine coin. The shopkeeper ignored him. Lorenzo became angry realizing he had been cheated. He protested to ensure the justice was done. The owner of the stand called two of the members of the Lodge of the Brotherhood, who were in charge of keeping law and order in Toledo, to remove Lorenzo from the stand. Lorenzo's inner voice warned him not to make a scene.

"You are a foreigner in a foreign city. Do not stake your claim to the bitter end," he heard from the voice of his intuition.

"Move on!" the two officers ordered him.

"The coin this gentleman has given me is made of a low alloy," Lorenzo answered calmly.

"I do not return low quality coins!" the shopkeeper lied.

"It is your word against his," the members of the Brotherhood stated.

"But what I am saying is true!" Lorenzo asserted, showing the defective coin.

"Move along and let business continue. Do not look for trouble, foreigner," they ordered him, realizing he was not a Toledan by the way he talked.

Lorenzo noticed two men with a threatening look and knifes in their hands, waiting for a sign from the shopkeeper to strike. He felt the danger and left the area: it was not worth risking his life for a coin. The episode as his first big lesson in the capital. Lorenzo was proud he had remained calm during the trick. Sometimes it is better bow out of a situation. At least the cheese and the bread were excellent. A stranger came to talk to him.

"You are not from Toledo, are you?" the man asked him.

"No," Lorenzo answered, suspicious of the man.

"You must be careful with the dealers of the city. They know all the tricks. If they notice you are not from Toledo, they will take advantage of you. The capital is difficult to survive in if you are not awake."

Lorenzo nodded, promising he would not be fooled again.

"Do you have a place to stay in Toledo?"

"I am looking for a small inexpensive room."

"Go to the Jewish quarter, near the main synagogue. There you will find the largest tavern in the neighborhood. They also rent rooms. Tell the owner that Domingo de Ervas sends you. Maybe you might find a job as a bartender there as well."

"And how do I get there?"

"Leave the city by the Gate of Alphonso VI, turn left and go around the city wall, until you reach the Jewish Gate. Then, cross another gate, near the main street of the Jewish quarter."

Lorenzo followed the good advice, and thanked the stranger for his kindness. On his way to the Jewish quarter, he met several people. The appearance, the impeccable way of dressing and walking of the Toledans amazed him. He also saw charitable friars and learned scholars carrying their books. He was even more delighted by the beautiful women showing their charm with seductive elegance. He then remembered his beloved Ariadna, "Was she still so beautiful?" he wondered.

When he entered in the Jewish quarter, he sensed a much calmer atmosphere than in the main streets. He came by a lovely street market where they sold fabulous antiques from all around the Mediterranean Sea. While he watched the exchanges in the market, he heard a conversation that confirmed they needed help in the tavern; the last barman had left for Seville to seek his fortune.

He went up a small hill from the main synagogue and reached the tavern with the following sign, "Meson y Posada del Judio." He felt nervous about what awaited him there and entered the tavern. It had a long main counter, and a large space full of rectangular tables. At the end of the room, there was a place with circular tables where groups could meet. On the right side, there were stairs connected with the upper floor.

"Are you looking for help, sir?" he asked with respect and discretion to an overweight middle-aged man.

"I need a barman. Have you got any experience?" the owner, whose name was Tirosh the Toledan, asked him.

"I have never worked in a tavern, but I am a fast learner."

"You are not Jewish, are you?" the bartender asked him.

"No, but Domingo de Ervas has sent me here. He recommended I came to this tavern. I also need a place to sleep. Do you rent rooms?"

"We can negotiate the price of your stay, which I will discount from your salary. It will be lower than ordinary as most of my clients are Jewish and they only take food or drinks prepared by fellow Jews," the owner said but also seemed pleased to hear the reference to Senor Ervas. "Since you are Christian, my wife and I will have to do part of your job."

Tirosh, who had the ability to sense whether someone was an honest person, offered him the job. Lorenzo listened to his conditions, and without thinking twice, he accepted.

"I agree, I will take the job," he said proud of himself getting a job and a place to stay so quickly in a new city.

Tirosh showed him a simple room on the second floor of the building near the client's rooms. It had a cot of straw, a small table, and a wood chair. Over the table, there was a candlestick with a candle. The shelter was not spacious, but it had a small window from which he could see the main street of the Jewish quarter.

"The job is not difficult. In little time you will learn everything you need to know. During the day, the job is easy, and you will meet distinguished people. The problems happen during the evenings, with the drunks," the owner warned him. "There have been many tax increases and drunks protest in the tavern. You will need to learn how to deal with the fights among the clients and how to treat drunk people."

"Yes, I agree," Lorenzo said.

Once settled, he set out to familiarize himself with the splendid city. The extraordinary nooks of Toledo amazed him. With every step he took, he became more and more mesmerized. He then went towards the magnificent Christian Cathedral, converted from a mosque. Inside the temple, he thanked God for being alive in the capital. Back in the Jewish quarter, he found a spot with a splendid view, and from there he gazed at the beautiful sunset; the beauty of the Tajo River and the nearby mountains astounded him.

During his first nights in Toledo, Lorenzo had many dreams. They were a source of revelation. After each dream, he awoke refreshed and rejuvenated, for in his dreams, he reconnected with his inner self. During the days, he learned from the conversations of his Jewish clients.

"Yehuda ben Moshe and Isaac ben Sid have just finished another book of astronomy tables. They were commissioned by King Alphonso," said one enthusiastic customer.

"They have worked day and night, with the help of the great rabbi Todros, in the tower of the castle of San Servando," another client added.

"This new set of astrological tables will replace the tables of Azarquiel and Ptolomeo," the first one affirmed.

Lorenzo was surprised at hearing such a philosophical conversation in a simple tavern. He remembered Daniel, the astrologer, and the tables he generated. Daniel had told him in Toledo they were obsessed with making newer and evermore precise astrological tables.

"The deceased King Ferdinand recognized the astrological work of our two companions. And the new King, Alphonso, surely will appreciate such extraordinary work, as well" a third Jew said.

"Ferdinand thought very highly of us. Even the Jews of Seville gave him the keys of the city, after the honorable king conquered the city." the first client added.

Lorenzo drew an accurate picture of what was happening in Toledo by the conversations he overheard in the tavern. He also noticed two opposing emotions by hearing people in the street. On one hand, there was a sense of pride in having the most intelligent and cultured people of the time, proud of their translators of prominent philosophical treaties, written in Arab, Aramaic, and Hebrew; on the other hand, there was a feeling of unease at the extravagant expenses the Crown was incurring, borne with stoicism by the Toledans.

"The Muslim and Jewish elites are well regarded and paid. The works of the scholars, scientists, philosophers, and artists add prestige to Castile. Toledo also attracts people from all over the world. However, the ordinary people are suffering from the never ending tax increases," a client complained during another conversation in the tavern.

"The Christians will make us responsible for the price increases, and will turn the king against us. The new laws of Castile, fostered by the bishop, are detrimental to us," a Jewish client said.

"Do not worry, we will deal with any adversity. The Church also put pressure on the previous King Ferdinand, but he confronted the pope. We are the principal lenders to the monarch, and without our money, the kingdom cannot sustain itself," a third Jew, who seemed to be a financier, clarified.

During his walks around the streets, Lorenzo confirmed what he heard in the tavern: the wastefulness of the king was obvious. The preoccupation of the people was the new king would turn the financially healthy kingdom he had inherited, into a ruin. He was already incurring extraordinary expenses, just to show off to the pope and foreign kings.

Lorenzo became worried about another matter: he was poorly educated, compared to the Toledans. Even Tirosh warned him about his primitive speech patterns, which were so different from the ceremonious dialect, the Toledan. Lorenzo promised to improve his appearance, his knowledge, and the way he talked.

"Tirosh, I want to learn, I want to know more. Where can I find books?"

"Come, follow me," the bartender told him, surprised by Lorenzo's intellectual interests.

The bartender showed him a room hidden in the back part of the tavern. Lorenzo was shocked when he saw an extraordinary library. It was incredible to see so many books in the hands of a bartender.

"If you want to take a book you can borrow one. A deceased friend gave me this collection for my scholarly clients. Although I do not read those books, I keep the library in secret. I understand some of these books have ancestral knowledge and they are not for everyone," the bartender explained.

Lorenzo thanked his employer for the offering. He approached the books and took one that caught his attention. He opened it to a page at random, and read:

"And thou shalt make a candlestick of pure gold, of beaten work shall the candlestick be made, his shaft, and his branches, his bowls, his knob, and his flowers, shall be of the same. And six branches shall come out of the sides of it; three branches of the candlestick out of the one side, and three branches of the candlestick out of the other side..."

He had the book of Exodus in his hands! It was the passage explaining the design of the Menorah! This was a true revelation. He went to his room and read the manuscript in detail. His soul had just opened another door on his path of spiritual development. The next day, Lorenzo found another book in the library, called Sefer Yetzirah, which impressed him, and then another book called "In the sources of life" by Ibn Gabirol. After reading these profound books, he prayed to God. He wished to meet these evolved human beings who travel the path of freedom.

"Here I will be able to know those things the church does not want us to know," he said, remembering the words of Daniel in Teruel. "Not even in the monastery of Cuenca was I able to have access to this extraordinary knowledge," he thought.

"Lord, I want to know, I want to understand. Help me to understand the mysteries of life," he pleaded with all his soul.

The Holy One heard his petition. From the heavens, they directed him to contact a school belonging to a living Tradition, but before that, he had to develop his spiritual discernment. He also needed to be tested.

22. LEARNING

*F*acing his new reality was complicated. It was not easy to survive in Toledo. The capital of the kingdom was action filled and the cost of living was high. The learned circles were off Lorenzo´s limits, especially for a simple barman. The possibilities of prospering were unobtainable. Many of the newly arrived failed, and left for Seville or Cordova to find better opportunities. Lorenzo was also terrified by the possibility of ending his days in a tavern. Nevertheless, he refused to think about failure and decided to look at life with optimism. "It does not make sense to have taken a lengthy pilgrimage for nothing."

Tirosh was pleased with Lorenzo's good performance. Following his wife's advice, he reduced his room price and increased his salary. It was difficult to find someone reliable during this time of massive emigration. Tirosh needed someone to remain at the tavern while he left on long trips around the region, seeking out the best kosher wine, the only wine permissible for Jews.

Lorenzo often borrowed books from Tirosh´s library. They had an extraordinarily influence on him and helped him to become insightful, and self-aware. He realized he was very reactive; he reacted to the requests of the clients, to the words of Tirosh, to the imagined opinions others had of him. He pondered on the causes of his reactions, and concluded he yearned the approval of the people he believed were superior to him; for that reason, he tried to please them.

He also tried to change others he believed were in trouble.

One day he dared to give advice to a client who was drinking too much. He had the best of intentions, but the drunk did not share his concern, hitting him and destroying tavern's furniture.

"Observe before acting," Tirosh warned him, after seeing the damage caused by the drunk.

"Sometimes I rush in, and I do not realize the effects of my actions," Lorenzo said.

"You must wait and be patient. If a client wants to get drunk, you allow him to get drunk," the tavern man reprimanded Lorenzo.

"But it is not good for his health," Lorenzo said.

"You are not his doctor! Also, if they did not drink, how do you think we would be make money?" he said annoyed.

"Yes, but…"

"I will garnish your salary the cost of the chairs the man destroyed after your wise advice," he concluded.

The wife of the bartender, who heard the reprimand, interceded:

"You should not get involved in the life of the clients. Just watch them. Soon you will develop your intuition and will know what the client wants. You will understand when someone wants advice or just wants to be heard."

"All right."

After the discussion with Tirosh, Lorenzo decided the tavern was not the right place for him.

"I have not come to Toledo to be a barkeeper. Each time I serve alcohol I'm helping people damage themselves, lose their consciousness, and ignore their responsibilities," he thought.

While pondering his future, a loud bang startled him. Shouts came from the street, with a thundering drum leading a Christian procession in the Jewish quarter, hoping to convert people.

"Christ is the King of the Jews! Convert to the Lord Jesus!" the Nazarenes yelled.

"They forgot to shut the gates of the neighborhood! Lorenzo, close the door of the tavern!" Tirosh shouted.

"It is the Holy Week! The procession is here!" Tirosh's wife yelled.

Lorenzo ran as fast as he could to shut the door of the canteen, but did not make it in time. Five Nazarenes dressed as penitents made their way into the tavern.

"Jews, convert!" a Nazarene shouted to the clients. Christ forgives you! Join the procession!

"I hope they leave soon," a client commented in Hebrew.

"Please, leave the tavern," Tirosh requested.

After uttering profanities and insults, the Nazarenes rejoined the procession, and walked in time with the drum.

"Get ready, trouble is here," Tirosh said after closing the door under lock and key.

From the neighboring windows, several children threw stones at the hooded men. One of the stones hit the face of a Nazarene who began bleeding profusely. The child's unfortunate throw resulted in dire consequences for the Jewish quarter.

"Throwing stones is the way you greet us!" the injured penitent shouted, who after removing his hood, lashed out at every Jew he met.

"Always in Holy Week, the same story. Take the day off,

Lorenzo. We will close the tavern today." Tirosh told him.

Lorenzo went to his room to watch the events unfold, while a Nazarene threw a stone against his window. At the same time, neighborhood guards brought in the dogs. The rest of the neighbors threw stones, excrement, and boiling oil over the Nazarenes, who called out other members of the brotherhood. They destroyed all the stores in the Jewish quarter. After several hours of brawling, the Jews were able to force the Christians out, and secured the gates.

"I must leave this job," Lorenzo thought.

Lorenzo was not aware, that from the heavens they thought he still needed to learn more about the human condition. The time to leave his job and conclude this phase of learning was not yet complete.

Once Holy Week ended, and the neighborhood returned to normal, Lorenzo worked in silence, following the advice of Tirosh´s wife. He noticed he could learn more about the forces and patterns that overtook his clients. He observed the powerful forces, which seemed to overcome the clients and made them drink without control. After much practice, Lorenzo learned how to calm down the drunks, before a fatal violent outbreak occurred. He also learned how to listen, without intervening, to their meaningless conversations and drunken fantasies.

Lorenzo also learned to deal with the lonely people who stumbled into the tavern, since the canteen was the only place where they could share their little world. He watched how they wasted their human potential, drifting in their lives, letting grief overtake them. Either they did not want to forgive themselves or did not want to take new risks; they shut out their opportunities in a destructive self-pitying spiral. Lorenzo often wondered if he could do something to help. He tried to give them hope but he realized only they could help themselves and stop their spiral of self-pity and loathing.

Lorenzo also witnessed the consequences of gambling. The tavern had a set aside for playing dice and cards. Some new players, who tried the game for amusement, let themselves become mesmerized by the excitement of the games. After a few hours, disreputable noblemen emptied their pockets. The plan was always the same: first they let the naive new players win small amounts of money, and then they cheated them out of fortunes. Among the losers was a priest; Lorenzo kept silent when he encountered him in the street, while the priest looked away ashamed of his disgraceful behavior.

Seeing the forces operating on his clients helped Lorenzo become a more mature person. He had already spent three years in Toledo, and his job in the tavern was the training he needed. Everything was ready for Lorenzo to take the next step in his spiritual awakening, but an unexpected visit changed his course.

"Please, pay attention, everyone!" a strange man, dressed in green, shouted in the tavern one summer morning. "My name is Tomas de Tamarite. I am pleased to inform you that tonight, coming from Cordova, the former capital of knowledge, and of the most prestigious schools of magic, Abubazar III will perform his best act. Tonight at sunset, in the Comedy Theater!

"Maybe this is the opportunity I was looking for," Lorenzo thought. "The Cordovan will teach me what I long to know," he concluded.

Convinced the magician was the person he needed to meet, Lorenzo asked permission to leave the tavern early on that hot July night. He also paid a large amount of money to attend the event. The magician, dressed in black, was smiling, showing his extraordinary white teeth. He was carrying several objects, to which he attributed supernatural properties.

"I am Abubazar III, the reincarnation of the famous magician from the 11th century. I am going to teach you the tricks that will change your lives," the black haired, dark skinned, and dull eyes

Cordovan proclaimed to the attentive audience.

Abubazar started the session with jokes. While he talked, he seduced several women, attracted by his magnetism. After his initial word play, he began to utter unintelligible words while seemingly entering into a trance.

"Now it is the moment you have been waiting for. It is the time of the fire ritual! Twelve lucky people will present their requests, and the power of fire will grant all of their wishes!" the magician exclaimed.

Abubazar chose twelve random people to participate in the ritual. Lorenzo, to his surprise, was one of the chosen ones. The magician lit a small fire in the center of the stage, while the twelve people formed a circle around the fire, holding hands. Abubazar instructed them to start walking in a circle around the fire, to the sound of a drum, played by the Cordovan. He then invoked the power of the fire, and asked the chosen ones to proclaim out loud their requests, for the spirit of the fire could hear them. One by one, they shouted their wishes.

"I want to be a rich man," a broken man said, who had spent most of his money to attend the show.

"Let the fire concede it to you!" Abubazar answered, encouraging the audience to answer at unison the request of the man.

"I want the daughter of the noble man Fernandez de Cedrillas to fall in love with me!" a young man said hoping to conquer the heart of the damsel.

"Let the fire concede it to you!" the audience yelled.

"I want the married man Juan de Briviega to repudiate his wife!" the man's lover said.

"Let the fire concede it to you!"

"I want to seduce many women in Toledo!" an old man, in a state of exaltation said, believing that he was still an adolescent.

"Let the fire concede it to you!" the audience said laughing.

When it was Lorenzo's turn, he kept quiet. All the spectators waited, but he did not speak his fantasy, which was nothing but to conquer a princess!

"The gentleman has preferred not to share his wish with the rest of us. Even so, the generosity of Abubazar is infinite. Thus, let´s say it in unison…"

"Let the fire concede it to you!" the audience exclaimed.

When the session finished, Tomas de Tamarite spoke enthusiastically to Lorenzo.

"Abubazar is an extraordinary man, is not?

Lorenzo did not know what to say, while he heard the other bewildered comments of other spectators who seemed delighted with the ritual of fire.

Abubazar, before leaving, spoke to Lorenzo.

"Your princess is on her way," he told him, smiling.

Lorenzo was shocked. "How he could know what I wanted, if I did not speak my request out loud?" he wondered

"Next week I will continue my master classes in the Hercules Cave. I will wait for you," and he said goodbye with a tempting smile.

Lorenzo thought Abubazar was the person he was looking for. He thought he had true knowledge and meeting him was the real reason for his pilgrimage to Toledo. With naiveté, he opened the door to his seductive influence. He was not aware he would have to suffer the consequences of that psychic interference. Closing that door would be an arduous task, with a costly psychological price.

23. INTRUSION

*L*orenzo let the fantasy took control his life. The first contact with the magician produced tremendous mental exhilaration. The words of Abubazar were in his mind all day long, as he daydreamed of his imaginary princess. He became obsessed with Abubazar. He even had a dream in which, after pronouncing a spell revealed by the magician, he lived in a luxurious golden palace with his beloved. He believed his fantasy was possible, even though he was a simple barkeeper.

"Tirosh, I need Saturday night off," Lorenzo requested.

"OK, then. In exchange you will work an extra full day."

Lorenzo did not mind exchanging a full day of work for a few hours with Abubazar. What was a day of work for getting anything he wished?" Lorenzo reasoned.

When he left the tavern, he found a gold coin on the floor. He looked around, but did not see anyone. He kept the coin. He thought his luck was due to meeting the magician. "If he teaches me everything he knows, I will never need to work again. The trip to Toledo would be worthwhile after all. I will be like a king. I will be a god!" he fantasized. "Let someone else be a bartender! Lorenzo Diaz will become an important Toledan!"

On Saturday, he went to the show of Abubazar held in the Hercules Cave. When he paid for the admission, an attractive Cordovan woman, adorned in a luxurious dress, told him,

"This money is not enough."

"But this is what I paid last week."

"Yes, but that was an introductory session for the general public. Today´s session is for those who Abubazar considered special. Not everyone can receive the high degree of knowledge he teaches, and you are among the chosen ones," the damsel told him with a charming smile.

"In that case…" Lorenzo answered, giving several coins to the woman.

Lorenzo was anxious to learn the methods of the magician. He loved being one of the chosen ones.

"I am sure that Abubazar has seen something special in me. The rest of the people do not know who I really am. This true magician knows the truth," these were the thoughts that were running through his head.

The Cordovan was brilliant that night and displayed all his tricks and charm. He enchanted the audience, especially the women, who were delighted with his art. One lovely spectator asked him a question, and he answered to her,

"Your question is a difficult one, it is only for an advanced person. Nevertheless, nothing is impossible for Abubazar III. We will make an incantation together in my private study after the session, to clarify the terms with you."

After saying those words, there was a strange silence in the room.

The magician then chanted nonsense as if he were channeling the spirits. He conjured spells, performed some magic tricks, while he was telling jokes that delighted the audience. Then he entered a hypnotic trance, and proclaimed the following,

"Now I will show you the spell for getting anything you want in life, whenever you need it!"

Possessed, his eyes turned all white. The magician was about to speak, as the audience waited in anticipation, thinking all their wishes would come true. In that moment, his attractive Cordovan assistant came to the center of the room. Before Abubazar continued with his discourse, she whispered something in his ear. After a moment of silence, he proclaimed the following:

"My lovely assistant, of unrivaled beauty and charm, has informed me of something important that I almost forgot. You are on the way to be the chosen ones, the one, and only, the unique ones! But I will only show the ultimate secrets of this science I practice and teach to the best among you," he exclaimed to the expectant audience. "Not everyone will have access to my knowledge! Only those who show a will of iron can possess those secrets! Let us leave for the next session the revelation of those mysteries to the ones who can truly surrender. My assistant will make a list of the people interested in coming," then he left the room, leaving his audience disappointed.

Lorenzo, ignoring the comment of a skeptical spectator, hurried to get on the list. Tomas de Tamarite confirmed Lorenzo was doing the right thing,

"Well done, Lorenzo. As you might understand, the knowledge cannot be given to anyone at random. It would be like casting pearls to the swine."

Lorenzo went back to his reality in the tavern, spending the next days daydreaming.

"Lorenzo, what is wrong with you?" Tirosh asked, "You are agitated."

"I am going to be rich and I will marry the most beautiful girl in town," he answered proudly. "This is all I can tell you."

"Are you drunk? What is all this about?"

"It is a secret. I am learning a great deal of knowledge, and I will live in a palace!" he asserted.

"Well, while your majesty finds his palace, would you be so kind to clean the tavern and take care of the clients, Don Lorenzo, your imperial majestic?" Tirosh said.

Only half of the people attended the following session of the magician. The ticket now cost double. Therefore, Lorenzo had to spend his monthly salary to enter in the show. After a never-ending performance, when it seemed that the magician was about to reveal his big secret, the Cordovan got worried:

"I cannot teach today the infallible spell that allows any wish to become true. The heavenly conditions are not propitious and the omens are not good. It is not right to defy the cosmic laws," he said.

Then he made an invocation to heavens to favor the attendants of the next session. Abubazar knelt and kept quiet for several minutes with his eyes opened without blinking. "I have received the confirmation from the heavens that on the next session the conditions will be more favorable," and he left the room marching with his head pointing upwards.

Lorenzo still hoped to fulfill his fantasy; however, after that session, everything went wrong: he was annoyed all the time, he lacked energy, and his stomach hurt. Deep inside, he knew the magician was a swindler, but he needed to believe in him. Abubazar now controlled his mind; maybe the solitude, the passing of time, the lack of good news, or the need to be fooled made him believe in that magic nonsense.

He had to ask for a salary advance to attend the following session. Tirosh thought his employee was in deep trouble. During the show, after performing some simple tricks, the magician proclaimed to the gullible attendants,

"My comment from last week was a test, and you should know now only the people who persevere will receive the definite magic spell. I cannot give it away without discernment. Therefore, I have decided to make a selection from this audience. I will make a ten-session show. The people who come to those performances and pay for them in advance will receive the full body of knowledge. In the meantime, I will practice my arts with my beautiful assistants. I also will keep an eye on the sky for further signs. For the moment, I am selling minor spells for a modest price, so you can test for yourself the power of this science that I practice and teach."

Lorenzo became obsessed with the final spell. It was a matter of self-respect and dignity. As he had paid so much money up until then, he could not let it go to waste. His ego was programmed to complete his quest. He then asked for a loan from the Jewish money-lenders to pay for the next ten sessions. During the entire month, he daydreamed on how his life would change once he knew the magician's famous spell. Meanwhile, Tirosh´s patience was reaching its limit.

The final ten sessions arrived, but once again, during the first session Lorenzo only heard jokes and absurd schemes. He learned nothing. He gathered his courage and asked the magician,

"Abubazar, when are you going to reveal the secret you have been promising for such a long time?"

"Everything will come at the right time, Lorenzo. Only those people with enough courage and perseverance will receive their reward. Who has faith in me, will obtain what he longs for."

Lorenzo´s performance at work worsened, due to his lack of concentration and Tirosh told him,

"I do not know in which business you are involved, but if you keep up like this, you will lose your job."

"I understand," Lorenzo answered.

"Take a day off, walk around Toledo, and decide what you want. You cannot continue like this. Your mind is not focused."

Lorenzo took a long walk around Toledo asking God to help him. He despaired, but the magician's power overwhelmed him. He had also paid for the ten sessions in advance, and was not going to leave before he completed the course. While he was wandering around, he met the beautiful woman who had had the private session with Abubazar.

"Why are you crying, lovely lady?" Lorenzo asked her.

"I am pregnant, with the child of Abubazar. He wants me to take some herbs which will cause me to have a miscarriage and lose the child."

"A miscarriage?" Lorenzo asked outraged.

"Yes, I am pregnant, with his child. The day of the private session, he seduced me, and I got pregnant. First, he made me feel like his princess, and then he replaced me with another when he found out I was expecting," she cried.

"And what are you going to do now?"

"If my father finds out, he will kill me. I will leave Toledo, and live in a convent in the north of Castile the rest of my life. I have dishonored my family," she said full of sorrow.

Lorenzo then realized what Abubazar did with women. The magician surrounded himself with beautiful women, and put them in competition for him. This created great tension and hatred among them. Abubazar put all his attention on one of the women until he succeeded in seducing her; once when the lady believed she was the chosen one, the magician brought a new beautiful woman to the group, casting the previous woman aside.

Lorenzo was angry with himself for being such a fool. He went to the Hercules Cave for the next session but the magician was not there. He only found the poor man who wished to be millionaire. The man, a shoemaker, was insulting the magician loudly. Crying, he told Lorenzo that after using all his spells, initially he got a small profit on a risky business. Then, he paid a great deal of money to get the final spell. His business finished in bankruptcy after applying the magic words. The man had to sell his house to pay his debts. When he asked for explanations, the magician told him,

"You need the other part of the spell. I only gave you the first one. In your haste and impatience, you forced me to hide the second part from you. It was the best for you in that moment."

"But I do not have any money! I have lost everything on the risky business that, according to you, had excellent prospects. I gave you large amounts of money for the spell. You assured me it was the final one."

"Ask for a loan and I will give you the second part of the spell! This is the final test to verify if you deserve to be rich. This spell will make you the most powerful man of Toledo, if you pass the final test," Abubazar answered him with conviction.

Seduced by the hope that the final spell would work, the man asked for a loan and put his last two belongings, his horse, and his sword, as a collateral. The shoemaker, after repeating the words of the magician with complete accuracy, got what he deserved: complete bankruptcy. The man had to hand over his goods to the lenders as repayment for the loan.

"Why I was so stupid? Even the lenders tried to convince me not to do that business," he complained hopeless in front of Lorenzo. "They knew it was a fantasy, but I insisted on my stupidity. I still recall the face of the Jewish financier, who had seen similar cases, and tried in vain to warn me. But I did not listen to him."

"The lesson has been painful, but there is always a solution. Find a job and start saving," Lorenzo told him, daring to give him an advice, although he, in fact, was talking to himself.

"I do not know why I trusted that wicked person. I am left with nothing" he regretted.

"You are not the only one. I also fell for his charm. His sessions took all my energy, and lately I had pain all over my body. I did not know why I kept paying him; maybe it was his look, or his words that fed my fantasy."

"Other people have power over us, only if we give it to them," said Tomas de Tamarite, the magician's assistant, who appeared suddenly. "He also tricked me. I left Cordova because he promised to teach me everything if I brought people to his shows. He used me as well. I left everything to learn how to manipulate the four elements and learn the secrets of the magic. Now he has departed with two of his female assistants," he reproached himself. "I will return to Cordova humiliated."

Lorenzo returned to the tavern full of remorse. As a gesture of repentance, he apologized to Tirosh, who did not make any comment. Lorenzo decided to work harder than ever to make up for his foolishness. He promised himself never to meddle with magic again. He was luckier than the others: he had only lost money. Now he needed to work in the tavern for another year to repay the money he borrowed.

Life for the magician did not end well. His tricks stopped working, and his assistants left him when they stop believing in his empty promises. Abubazar got sick and had to suffer the consequences of his actions and the manipulation of people who trusted him. He died in excruciating pain and could not escape his responsibility. Although he tried to avoid the after-life process, by creating a magic incantation hoping to possess an innocent person, he failed.

Lorenzo's spiritual awakening had stopped. He had allowed a swindler to attack his weak point. Thank God, he had survived that disastrous influence.

Once he had learned the lesson, the invisible worlds set the scene to open a true spiritual door for him.

24. HOPE

The days had turned long for Lorenzo. The initial excitement in the capital had worn off. After three years in Toledo, his life was dull. Only the time with the magician had taken him out of his routine. His life had become a routine: clients criticizing the king, discussions among scholars foreseeing the end times, drunk people trying to change the world, endless card games with innocent people losing everything, fights among peasants over women...

Lorenzo had given up hope of finding someone who could teach him the true knowledge about life. He also wanted to leave his job, but what could he do? Although he had learned much about the human condition at the tavern, he was on a dead-end street.

He pondered going to Seville to work on shipyards built by Alphonso X, who wished to build the largest navy in Europe. The king thought the nation that ruled the sea, would dominate the world; for that reason, he employed hundreds of men to build the ships on the Royal Atarazanas of Seville. But before thinking of leaving, he had to repay the loan for the magic sessions.

On the day that Lorenzo turned forty, he went for a lonely walk in the noble part of the city. He enjoyed contemplating the wealthy mansions. The views of the city were extraordinary, and with youthful innocence, he asked the neighbors about the price of the mansions. A sobering realization gripped Lorenzo when he understood that, even if he saved his whole life, he could not afford to buy a tiny portion of a house. He had to face reality: he was a lonely single tavern-man who lived in a small rented room with no hope of further prosperity. Is this the reason I have followed my dream? What have I done wrong?" he asked himself devastated.

Lorenzo was looking for a way out of his despair, but he could not see any solutions. From the heavens they decided to help him, so he could escape from this spiral of negativity. He needed to look beyond his current situation to overcome the inertia in his life. A client, who had become his friend, advised him to focus on what he had, instead of on what he lacked.

"You have your health, a keen mind, a job, and a place to sleep. You also have access to Tirosh's wonderful library. Life can bring you wonderful gifts. You are in the capital of the world. You are in Toledo!"

Lorenzo accepted the wise advice. He pondered about what he could do to live in abundance and decided to zealously study the books in Tirosh´s library. He also chose to focus on the evolved people he could learn from. He thought of a regular group that sat in a private room at the tavern. They looked different from ordinary people, they had a special human quality. When they were in the tavern, the atmosphere completely changed: the consumption of alcohol decreased, the noise faded, and the problematic clients disappeared. Each time those people came, he did his utmost to serve them and be near them.

They talked about subjects beyond his understanding ,and also about astrology. When Lorenzo saw their drawings of astrological charts, he thought of Daniel, who would have loved to take part in their conversations. How many times had he listened to similar conversations in Teruel?" he thought remembering those moments fondly.

"Have you finished the translation of the Book of Raziel?" an old white haired man, who was the great rabbi of Toledo, asked the other members of the group, while holding an astrolabe.

"Yes, the king insists on publishing it, although we do not agree with him. This is why he commissioned the Christian Juan de Aspa to do it. There are several versions in Aramaic and Hebrew, but the king wanted to publish it in Latin," another Jewish man, also older but with a sterner look, said.

"The Book of Raziel is the book of the Secrets of God. According to Tradition, this is the book the archangel Raziel gave to Adam and Eve, after their expulsion from paradise," the first man explained to a younger man, who listened with great attention.

"This is not a book for the public, but the king wants it to be translated, at all costs. The king is sending a message to the pope that he is superior to him. But I am not sure spreading this knowledge is the right thing to do," the second man said.

"The other day, I overheard the king, in casual conversation on the Chancellery, saying if God had consulted him before Creation, things would be better," said another man who had worked with Alphonso X translating books.

"I am not sure if he dared to say such a thing, but he should be more concerned about what is happening now in his kingdom rather than trying to be God."

"The Court of Castile has taken emergency measures due to the shortage of food. They also have minted low quality coins," said another one, who appeared to be an important financier.

"In the monthly meetings we have tried to warn him with diplomacy that he must set an example. If he demands sacrifices from his subjects, he needs to make them himself first," the most critical one affirmed.

Lorenzo concluded, from hearing to the conversation, that many people in the distinctive group had a close connection to the crown. The king wanted the knowledge shared by the elite groups of intellectuals to reach everybody. For that reason, he paid enormous amounts to the scholars of the three religions to translate books of knowledge. He wanted Toledo became the capital of culture and ancient knowledge.

The Jews also were happy with the king. He allowed the three mosques in the Jewish quarter to become synagogues. However, they were concerned about the gifts Alphonso gave to the many foreigners who visited Castile. He was risking the financial well-being of the kingdom. The Castilian king consented to anything in order to gain European supporters in his imperial quest. Foreign delegations were coming to Castile, amazed at the luxury of the kingdom. The king even welcomed the Sultan of Egypt with great honors in Seville; in exchange, the Sultan gave him a lion and several exotic animals.

Lorenzo got used to the presence of the group in the tavern. As soon as they arrived. He prepared their favorite drinks. Often there was a poet among them and the evening became even more exceptional. When the troubadour appeared, Tirosh closed the tavern and the atmosphere became unique. The minstrel, after a few moments of silence, recited the sublime poems of Ibn Gabirol and other mystical authors. He delighted the members of the group with verses that touched them deeply. The poet entered in trance to speak verses like the following:

> *You are One,*
>
> *prior to all computation*
>
> *and ground to all figuration.*
>
> *You are One,*
>
> *and your oneness's mystery amazes the wise,*
>
> *who've never known what it was.*
>
> *You are One,*
>
> *and in your oneness*
>
> *know neither loss nor addition,*

neither lack nor magnification.

You are One,

but not as one that's counted or formed,

for neither enhancement nor change pertains to you,

neither description nor name.

You are One,

and my speech can't establish your boundary or line,

therefore I said I would guard my ways,

so as not to sin with my tongue.

And you are One,

sublime and exalted above all that might fall

that One might fall is impossible ...

After his performance, some of the listeners were so moved, they could not utter a single word. Others started to recite poems of Andalusian philosophers that brought them to a state of mystical contemplation. It was similar to what Lorenzo had felt in Gea with the Arab dervish. When the poetry session ended, the members of the group left the tavern, leaving behind an atmosphere that felt peaceful and blessed.

"Tirosh, are those people Jews?" Lorenzo asked him.

"Most of them are, but there are also a few Arabs and Christians.

"I sensed something special. They are different from the rest of the customers."

"I do not know much about them. I think they are part of a private group. Some of them are translators, poets, astrologers. One is a merchant, another is a financier... Some live in other parts of Castile."

"And do you know anything else about them?" Lorenzo kept asking.

"I do not ask what my clients do for living! They have been coming to the tavern for ages and I only serve them. I hardly know them," Tirosh answered, exasperated.

Lorenzo realized the importance of the Jewish community in Toledo, compared to the community of Teruel, Albarracin, or Cuenca. He also noticed there was great cooperation within the community; the people who were the most fortunate members helped the rest of the community in times of need.

However, the coexistence of the Jewish with the rest of the Toledans was challenging. The Christian farmers, peasants, and ranchers, who suffered the tax increases, attacked shops in the Jewish quarter; they blamed the Jews for the rising taxes and prices in Castile. They thought that the monarch's financiers and advisers were benefiting from the increases. They also accused them of witchcraft and sorcery. As a consequence, there were riots in the Jewish quarter and the Jews had to lock the gates, doubling the guard. The great rabbi Todros ben Yosef Halevi encouraged the rich to contribute, and they hired guards with trained dogs to patrol the streets and protect the houses during the hours of darkness.

Tirosh had to close the tavern during the evenings and the distinguished group stopped coming to the tavern. Lorenzo was disappointed. He searched for them in Toledo, but did not find any trace of the honorable group. It seemed that they had disappeared from the face of the Earth!

Wandering around Toledo, wondering where to find the members of the group, he heard a great hustle and bustle nearby. In a square, young men ran in front of bulls, while the noblemen, hidden safely, watched. All of a sudden, a humble friar, dressed in a simple tunic, faced a raging bull. There was a startling silence, and the monk, with great calmness and serenity, put himself in front of the bull.

With just his gaze, he hypnotized the bull. Then, he took the bull by the horns, and after calming the animal, he knelt in front of the beast. He praised the Lord, leaving the audience speechless. The noblemen showered him with alms, and his congregation built a convent in Toledo.

Lorenzo was so moved by that sublime encounter between the man and beast, that he sensed the friar had the same gift as the members of the special group: the Grace of God had touched him. Lorenzo's soul longed to receive that same Grace, but before he could, he needed to learn about the negative aspects of passion. He also had to pay for the emotional damage he had caused his former lovers.

25. PRETENDING

*L*orenzo had lost all hope, and stopped trying to find the members of the group. He concentrated doing his job as well as possible, and finding a partner woman with whom he could share his life. "Lord, I accept whatever life brings to me. If my task is to be a tavern man, I will be so, but at least with the company of a wife." That is how deep his despair was.

Lorenzo had difficulties meeting the refined women of Toledo. The delicate women seldom came to the tavern, and when they did, they arrived with a gentleman. Lorenzo did not even dare to talk to them on the street; they never gave him a sign indicating he could start a conversation. One day he shared his sadness with Carmen, Tirosh´s wife:

"Why do women in Toledo not even look at me?"

"Because of the way you dress," she answered, laughing.

"It is obvious you are not from here, and that you are not well educated. Your manners are primitive," the tavern keeper pointed out, stinging the pride of his employee.

"Lorenzo likes the refined courtesans. You can see how he looks at them when they walk around the street. They expect their men to dress with style and elegance," Carmen added.

"The courtesans are beautiful, aren´t they?" Tirosh asked him slyly.

"Many of them come to the court looking for a wealthy nobleman. Some come from aristocratic families in the north of Castile. Others come from nearby villages looking for fortune, pretending a distinguished ancestry," the wife explained.

"Looking how you do, they will not even look at you. Poor Lorenzo. My wife will help you buy the clothes to become a proper Toledan."

"Done, he needs a good smock, a cape of excellent quality, and elegant boots worthy of a nobleman. Next week we will go buy the clothes."

"He will spend all his money on clothing. I will have to advance him a half-year salary. Everything for Lorenzo, so he can become a charming gentleman. Let us toast to his health," the tavern man shouted, serving wine to all the clients, who were smiling at the embarrassed Lorenzo.

That same week, the princess Christine of Norway came to Toledo to marry Philip, the brother of Alphonso X. The marriage would seal the alliance between Castile and Norway. The city was beautifully decked out to welcome the princess. Everybody was looking to buy the best clothes and the prices were exorbitant. Lorenzo did not like to spend a fortune in his new wardrobe, but if he was to conquer his princess…

When the Norwegian court arrived, escorted by the Royal Guard of Castile, everyone admired the stunning beauty of the Nordic princess. She was much more beautiful that what they had heard about her. During her walk around Toledo, both peasants and merchants were astonished, sensing the aura that surrounded the princess. It seemed the woman came from another realm! Some people thought she was the incarnation of the Virgin Mary. Even James I of Aragon, when the lady passed by Zaragoza on her way to Toledo, fell in love with her; she was the most beautiful woman that the king of Aragon had ever seen.

Lorenzo asked permission to go to the Gate of Alphonso VI, to see the official welcome of the princess. His fantasies increased when he saw the lady, and he remembered the wish he had told the magician. After the official welcome, Lorenzo returned to work, fantasizing about his imaginary princess.

On his way back, he looked at a window in a convent, and saw the perfect face of a lovely nun, lit by the sun. The nun immediately turned aside, when she sensed Lorenzo was looking at her. The beauty of the nun moved Lorenzo, who wondered who she was.

The princess's welcoming committee organized many festive events and theatrical performances to flatter the Norwegian lady. Lorenzo, tidied himself up, smelling as good as any nobleman, headed off to attend the different events; his long blond hair and his blue eyes gave him the appearance of a handsome foreign prince. He went to one party in a noble mansion, where he introduced himself as an aristocrat from Aragon. Immediately his eyes landed on a tall, dark-haired, blue-eyed beauty, to whom he felt immediate attraction. He approached the beautiful woman:

"Good evening, lovely lady…" he saluted.

"Good evening, gentleman. I have not seen you before at these noble parties," she said with a captivating smile. "Are you a stranger in Toledo?"

"I am from Aragon," Lorenzo answered, unwilling to reveal his true circumstance.

"Looking at the way you dress, you must come from a noble family."

"It could be," he answered in a mysterious way. "What is your name?"

"Christine."

"Like the princess?"

"Exactly! Just like the princess…" she smiled seductively.

"And what do you do, lovely damsel?"

"I am a court poetess. Come to see me tomorrow, and we can converse," and then she bid him goodnight.

That night, in his room, the face of the poetess filled his thoughts, and he could not think of anything else. "Would she be my princess?" Lorenzo asked himself thrilled by the possibility. "The magician's prediction might become true," he thought.

At work, the next day, he was nervous and excited thinking about the date with the poetess. Tirosh and his wife smiled to each other, when they saw Lorenzo going out again, dressed so elegantly. The poetess made him wait for a long time before meeting with him. "By the way he dresses, he must be a noble man. I will give him a chance," the damsel thought when he saw him.

Lorenzo spent a small fortune wooing the courtesan. He also broke his promise of not drinking alcohol, and got drunk with the poetess, savoring the expensive bottles of wine. Lorenzo fantasized over his intimate encounter with the lady. The poetess dedicated several love verses to Lorenzo, who felt like a king. Even, being with such a beautiful lady made some of the other beautiful courtesans take notice of Lorenzo, something that had never happened to him before. With euphoria, he tried to kiss his muse, but she stopped him,

"Not so fast, gentleman. Maybe at another more propitious moment…"

Lorenzo was drunk and left. He hardly could recognize the way back to his room. The pain in his head and the hangover he suffered the next day prevented him from doing his work properly.

"Lorenzo, what is wrong? You look terrible," Tirosh asked

him.

"The most beautiful courtesan has fallen in love with me… poor lady," he answered with pride.

"But, does she know that you work at a tavern?" Carmen asked him.

"Everything in its own time…" he answered while the couple looked each other suspiciously.

During the weeks that followed, Lorenzo continued to behave and dress like a nobleman, and met the poetess in several occasions. He felt like a star, knowing that other men envied him for being with such an attractive woman. One evening, after dressing up with new clothes, he showed up where the poetess rehearsed.

"Kind sir, how wonderful that you have showed up! Come with me to buy a new dress for my performance. I need to dress according to the luxury of the Royal Court," the lady suggested, taking him to the expensive shops that sold imported silk clothes.

"This kind gentleman will pay for my dress," the actress told the saleswoman.

"Good choice," the saleswoman told Lorenzo, who promised to come back later to honor the payment.

Absorbed by her beauty and her influence, he could not refuse to buy the dress and the most expensive perfumes. He had to keep his image of a noble rich man from Aragon. He wanted to be with her at any price, although he did not know how to control the luxurious expenses she incurred. When he was on his own in his room he threw his hands up in despair, but his passion made it impossible to think clearly. He was spending all his savings…but she was so beautiful, and he felt so flattered by others when they were together. Lorenzo thought of a "master plan": she had to fall in love with him before he revealed his true job.

"I have put on the dress you bought me," the lady told him while showing him her slim neck, which Lorenzo attempted to kiss. "I would also need a matching necklace with the dress," she suggested turning away to avoid physical contact.

Lorenzo could not avoid buying her the necklace, although his face turned pale when he found out the price.

"Why are you so serious?" she asked him with affection.

"No reason," he answered, trying not to show the irritation he felt, for not being able to set limits to her expenses.

"If you are going to be in this mood, you had better not come with me today. Come back next week," the poetess told him after putting on her necklace.

Lorenzo left angry, but after a few nights, he showed up again at the Comedy Theater where she performed. Hidden, he watched with pain as the seductive courtesan mingled with young noblemen, and with an old widowed aristocrat. He returned to the tavern full of sadness, while his body was sending him warning signs that something was wrong. His chest hurt, but he could not stop thinking about the beautiful poet.

He paid her another visit.

"Don Lorenzo, how is it that you are here again?" the lady smiled when he saw the gentleman of Aragon.

"I just dropped by tonight. Would you like to have a drink with me?"

"Yes, let us have a bottle of wine," the lady answered.

They drank the most expensive wine, after which the poetess said,

"Now I need to go. It has been great spending this time with you. Come and see me another time," she said finishing off the last of the wine and blowing Lorenzo a kiss.

That night Lorenzo got drunk again. He was a puppet in the hands of an uncontrolled passion. A stylish woman with a seductive smile had captivated him. He remained in that state for several months, getting drunk, and feeling frustrated at not being able be with her. He did not know what to do. He wanted her to succumb to his whims at all costs, but it seemed that nothing was enough for her. Even when he had fulfilled all her wishes, she remained cold towards him. The more presents he gave her, the more she demanded; when Lorenzo managed to say no, she came closer to him, flirting and flaunting her affection for him. The game consumed Lorenzo and made him mad with love.

Although he loved the lady, one morning he decided not to see her again. Lorenzo prayed to God to grant him the strength to free himself from the obsession he had for her. Some days he asked God to make her fall in love with him, and other days, he asked Him to release him from her spell. Providence, being aware of his emotional shifts, answered the best way for his soul.

One evening, the beautiful poet went to the tavern with the widowed aristocrat. When she saw Lorenzo was the waiter, she was shocked; nevertheless, she kept calm and acted as if he were a stranger.

"Waiter, bring us the best wine. They say in this tavern we can find the best wine in Toledo," the demanding woman said, looking angrily at him.

Lorenzo wanted to bury his head in the earth. He was ashamed and had a strong stomach pain. Her words pierced his heart: the woman he loved hated him. He despised himself for trying to be someone he was not. With great professionalism, Lorenzo served the wine holding back his tears. Meanwhile she punished him by holding the hand of her older partner, while Lorenzo writhed in pain. Full of malice and spite, she allowed the dinner to go on for hours, only to increase his suffering. When they finished their extravagant dinner, she commanded Lorenzo:

"Waiter, clean up the table."

He did as requested, and while he was picking up the dishes, with tears in his eyes, he heard the following disdainful comment:

"Let us leave here. There are no people of our class in this tavern, and the barkeeper is vulgar and stupid."

Once the couple had left, Lorenzo was inconsolable, weeping bitter tears. His heart broken over the loss of his beloved. For the next while, he contemplated on what had happened, and contrary to what his heart told him, his soul felt an enormous relief: he did not need to pretend to be someone else anymore. He kept silent for several weeks, and then he went to the tavern owner.

"As Christians say, the habit does not make the monk," Carmen said.

"I am stupid. Sooner or later she would have discovered the lie, and I would have wasted money on dresses, wine, and expensive gifts."

"You are fortunate it did not last longer. You could have been in that situation for a much more time. If she had not come to the tavern with the widower, the situation could go on for ages. You were lucky," Tirosh concluded.

"She would never have fallen in love with you. Women have a sixth sense, and we know that wearing the shiniest clothes is not sufficient. You do not have the right look," Carmen added.

"Courtesans have a cold heart. They do not fall in love easily. They enjoy seducing and wielding their power over men. That is their game," the husband added.

The encounter with the courtesan was devastating. He knew Carmen was right. His way of looking was empty. He wanted to win a woman´s love with a false image.

Years later, Lorenzo met her by chance. He hardly recognized her. She had changed so much. Her external beauty had faded, and her body was a mere shadow of her former self. Her face was lifeless. Lorenzo then understood how blessed he had been. The hand of Providence, although painful, had placed him back on his true path.

Figure 5

26. OPPORTUNITY

*A*fter the painful love experience with the poet, Lorenzo left it to God to find him a wife. His last love affair had been a disaster. He could not make the right choice by himself, so he decided to dedicate his time to grow spiritually; that intention allowed Providence to open another door along his path. "By chance" he met the marvelous poet who had performed at the tavern.

"Poet!" Lorenzo exclaimed.

"Bar keeper!" the poet answered, surprised to meet him in the main plaza of Toledo.

"Why don´t you come to the tavern anymore? It was a great pleasure to serve you."

"We need to protect ourselves against attacks. Sometimes they blame the Jewish people for the kingdom's disasters, thus, we do not meet in public places."

"But what happens in the kingdom is not your fault. Everybody knows about the Crown's wastefulness. The king is reckless," Lorenzo added.

"The king wants to make everybody happy, and he is achieving the opposite result. The noblemen are upset, the peasants and merchants are unhappy, and even his father-in-law, the great James I of Aragon, is angry with him," the poet explained.

"Thanks to the king, the philosophers, astrologers, and

translators can do their work, but he is forgetting the basic needs of his people," he warned.

They both kept quiet. Lorenzo pondered what the poet had said. Then he spoke,

"I would give anything to meet with your group again. Each time you entered the tavern, the atmosphere changed." Lorenzo said.

The poet remained quiet. He knew he should not reveal the whereabouts of the members of the group.

"I would love to learn from them." Lorenzo said. "They seemed to be refined and exquisitely mannered people."

"My name is Benjamin of Seville."

"Lorenzo Diaz, at your service."

"My pleasure, I need to leave now. I wish you a wonderful day sir," and the poet said good-bye without making a commitment.

Disappointed, because he did not receive an answer from the poet, Lorenzo thought he might have done something wrong. He could not understand the reason for that excessive secrecy. He lost hope once more and was again discouraged. Meanwhile, the poet discussed with his companions if they should give Lorenzo an opportunity to meet with the group.

"Everybody deserves an opportunity to enter into a school of the soul," the leading teacher confirmed. "Since he asked to meet us with such a fervent desire, his soul is longing. Also your meeting in Zocodover was providential."

A few days later, a lad appeared in the tavern, asking for Lorenzo.

"Don Lorenzo Diaz?" the young man shouted from the door.

"Here I am." Lorenzo answered surprised.

"I've got a message for you!"

"Who has sent it?"

"I cannot give you that information. Here is your letter," the lad answered, leaving the tavern as quickly as he could.

Lorenzo was stunned when he saw the fine sealed envelope. He checked if the letter was for him. To his amazement, he saw his name in elegant handwriting. Excited, he opened the letter. It was the first time he had received an elegant message.

"The first Sunday following the next new moon, go to the Castle of Almonacid. Be there at noon."

There was no signature on the message, which confounded him. A hundred thoughts came to his mind, after rereading the letter, and paying very close attention. He was unable to move.

"Tirosh, where is Almonacid?" he asked without remembering that in his pilgrimage from Teruel he had already been there.

"It is half a day's journey south of here."

"The village is famous for the castle conquered by the Cid Campeador from the Arabs two hundred years ago. Don Isaac, the financier, has now the right to use the castle," one of the clients in the tavern said.

"The nobleman paid 45,000 gold coins to rent the palace for several decades. That gold helped the king in the military campaign of Jaen," another client added.

Lorenzo went to his room, overwhelmed by the mysterious letter. The moon was waning, which meant he had to wait for ten days to attend the enigmatic appointment. Several inner voices whispered to him during the following days and he struggled with his contradictory monologue. Still he was unaware of the importance of the appointment for his spiritual development.

"Maybe it is a joke. Maybe someone wants to steal me on the way to Almonacid; but, have I got a fortune?" he wondered. "What if a client from the tavern wants to take revenge out on me for something? Maybe they want to kidnap me and sell me to the Arabs as a slave in Africa. Do I really need to go to that appointment?" The roads of Castile are dangerous, but have not I made a pilgrimage from Teruel? Why is there no signature on the message? What if..." he tormented himself.

A few nights before the appointment, Lorenzo had a lucid dream. He saw himself in the center of a circle made by the members of that exceptional group, all dressed in white.

"There are not many chances to make contact with a spiritual school that follow a living Tradition," they told to Lorenzo in dreams.

"Is everyone given that opportunity?" he asked in the dream.

"Yes, at least once in the life, but most of the people are asleep and do not recognize the opportunity. Some prefer to remain in a safely ensconced in their little worlds, without making a decision that would question their imaginary stability," the spiritual group's teacher answered to him during the dream.

Lorenzo woke up in a state of clairvoyance. He related the dream to the letter he had received. Maybe he would have the opportunity to evolve and encounter what he had longed for since his youth.

The same day at the food market, he saw some delicious looking cheese.

"Do you make that cheese here?" he asked.

"No, a relative in Almonacid makes it," the shopkeeper answered.

Lorenzo took those words as another sign to keep the appointment. It seemed his life around was encouraging him to make a conscious decision.

During the days that followed he had several moments of panic, as well as a cascade of strange feelings: he had no appetite, could not focus on his job, did the accounts wrong, and felt cold, angry, excited... It was the fear of going through a door that would change his life.

Sundays were days of frenetic activity in the tavern. It was difficult to get the day off without a reasonable explanation.

A few days before the appointment, Lorenzo gathered his courage:

"Tirosh, I need Sunday off," he said.

"That is the busiest day in the tavern. You cannot go," Tirosh answered without hesitation.

"I have got a personal matter to resolve," he replayed firmly.

"Oh, is it because of a woman? Now I understand your lack of concentration. In that case, you can have the day off. I hope you make a better choice this time."

Lorenzo kept quiet so as not to lie.

"It seems that Lorenzo is in love and he is going to meet a lady on Sunday," Tirosh said with joy to his wife.

With the consent of Tirosh, Lorenzo cheered up. By Saturday, his fear had transformed into anxiety. He walked around like a headless chicken; his mind was everywhere, and he was hardly able to sleep. With the first light of dawn, he went to the Jewish Gate. He saluted to the sentinel and took the road toward Almonacid.

As he walked, he felt rejuvenated, and full of joy, but in the middle of the path, he felt an urge to stop. He thought about it for a few seconds, breathed deeply, and decided to remove the doubts out of his mind.

At noon, exhausted, he saw the castle of the mysterious encounter. He stopped and watched the monument illuminated by the sun. Impressed by the majesty of the building, he approached it, and noticed several others were there as well: the appointment was not for him alone. Everyone was dressed with refined clothes and he felt ashamed of his simple attire. The others all seemed to know each other and greeted joyfully. Lorenzo recognized some of the people who had been at the tavern and saw the poet Benjamin. His fears dissolved. He also saw the great rabbi Todros. There were also other people not from Toledo. He felt blessed and thanked God for being able to meet the ones that he had longed to see.

"Benjamin, poet, how are you?" he greeted him with delight.

"So, you received the invitation," Benjamin answered, smiling at him.

"Was it from you?

"You might say that."

"Who is the person that everyone greets with deference and admiration?" he asked, after noticing an elegant older man at the castle's entrance.

"Sorry Lorenzo, I need to go now..." and he left him alone.

Lorenzo did not know how to act. On one hand, they welcomed him; but on the other, no one paid attention to him. He went to speak with three people he recognized from the tavern, but they declined to talk to him. One of them placed his finger over his mouth, in a sign of silence, before quietly entering the castle. Lorenzo felt awkward. He wanted to talk to someone, but it seemed there was something more important for them. "If this is a secret meeting, why did they invite me?" he thought, again tormented by his doubts.

Since nobody said anything, he entered the castle and waited in the hall. The castle was magnificent, decorated with beautiful Persian carpets. There was a silver candelabra and a large gold Menorah with seven burning candles. Lorenzo sat in a chair and waited some direction, but none came. Confused, he tried to enter the room the others went, but the poet from Seville stopped him.

"Lorenzo, please, wait outside the room. Remain here in the hall," he told him.

They closed the door of the room. Hundreds of negative thoughts filled his mind. His pride misfired and he became angry. "Why is everybody inside and I am outside? What am I waiting for?" he asked himself, losing control. "They made me come here for nothing! I walked for a long time and now I am on my own, outside! This is not fair!" he complained in silence.

After a long anger filled wait, he decided to return to Toledo. He felt those people were looking down on him, the poet particularly so. Incensed, he stood up. As he was about to leave, the door opened. Around fifty radiant people came out. Their faces were shining and filled with peace. One of them, whom Lorenzo recognized from the tavern, came to talk to him:

"Good morning," the man said in a very refined manner.

"Good morning," Lorenzo answered, giving voice to his irritated state.

"Benjamin, the poet, has told us that you would like to see us again," the man, who seemed to own the magnificent castle, said to him.

"Yes. You do not come to the tavern anymore, and I loved your conversations... well, the little I could understand of them," Lorenzo muttered, stuttering.

"We do not go to the tavern anymore," the man replied.

"Is it because of the recent attacks to the Jews?" Lorenzo asked politely, when he realized that the man was considerate with him.

"It is not good to tempt fate."

"Well, I have received the letter and here I am," Lorenzo said proudly.

"Thank you very much for coming. This is enough for today. Come back here on the Sunday after the next new moon, at the same time," and then he said good-bye.

Lorenzo felt frustrated again, thinking he had lost one entire day.

Disappointed he headed back to Toledo, when he heard a familiar voice:

"Lorenzo, Lorenzo!" the poet shouted at him. "Here, take this is a present from the group: a candle and a candlestick."

"Oh!"

"Keep a candle lit on for a month, not letting the candle go out during thirty days. Focus on the flame. Although we no longer go to the tavern, this candlestick represents the group and the light symbolizes yourself and the divine spark within you," the poet explained.

"All right," Lorenzo answered astonished by the symbolic relation between the candlestick, the group, the light of the candle and the divine spark.

"Do you have a Menorah?" Benjamin asked him.

"I have a small one I found long time ago. I always carry it with me."

"Place the candle, the candlestick and the Menorah near one another. Meditate on the three objects. See you next month. Take care of yourself."

Now, Lorenzo would return to Toledo but not empty handed, as he had thought he would. He had a gift from the group and the trust and courage to accept this life enhancing opportunity. Now he would have to face a test of integrity and its temptations. If he conquered them, he would become a member of the school of the soul destined for him.

27. TEMPTATIONS

*T*he trip back to Toledo was a nightmare. Lorenzo got lost, hurt his feet, and stumbled on several occasions. He met a few merchants along the way, but no one wanted to take on a lone traveler on those dangerous roads. It became dark. He lost his way several times, and became angry with himself for having accepted the invitation.

He arrived in Toledo well into the night, but the sentinels who guarded the gate did not admit him. He yelled while waiting outside the wall for dawn to arrive. Luckily, some courtesans, who wished to attend a royal party, arrived. The guards still refused to open the gate, but the courtesans flirted with them, showing their legs. Entranced by the ladies' beauty, the guards finally opened the gate.

Lorenzo ran to the tavern where he arrived exhausted. Once there, he still had energy to place the candle near his Menorah. He lit it as the poet had suggested, after which he fell into a deep sleep. Because he was so exhausted he slept soundly, experiencing a profound dream. In the dream, he saw what happened in the room while he waited outside! Much to his surprise, he learned the group spoke about universal principles, the higher realms, and the path to full human realization. The wise man that led the meeting was explaining that self-realization means the discovery of our full human potential and becoming one with God.

Tirosh, the tavern owner, woke Lorenzo up at that precise moment. He was late for work. Lorenzo, despite Tirosh´s irritation, woke up happy, after receiving such a revealing dream. At last, he understood the purpose of his pilgrimage to Toledo. He would finally find answers to the questions that still resonated in his soul. With his aching body, wounded feet, but with a happy soul, he began his daily chores.

How was your date yesterday?" Tirosh asked once he calmed down.

"Good," Lorenzo answered, hoping to change the subject.

"You seem very tired. I heard you coming in very late."

Lorenzo did not like the questions. He tried not to answer and preferred to focus on his work. He took a long siesta and awoke with only one idea: to meet with the group again. He took great care changing the candle, so the light never went out. The exercised helped him sensing the presence of the group and the divine light within him.

The following weeks were tense. Tirosh, the Toledan, who had a developed high intuition, sensed that Lorenzo was changing inside, and that he soon would leave the tavern. Then, a negative force over took Tirosh, who did not want Lorenzo to leave; he considered him as his possession since he had employed him when the man was still a stranger. He started watching his movements, becoming his controlling shadow. Using the poor excuse the tavern was not making enough money, he demanded a scrupulous observance over his working hours, and reduced his time off.

Lorenzo knew then it was time to leave. Although he was thankful to Tirosh, he could not be a slave.

But before starting a new and vital chapter in his life, Providence tested him with two more situations. The first one involved a wine merchant who was a regular tavern customer. Seated at a table, he watched the increasing control, which reached unhealthy levels, that Tirosh exerted over Lorenzo. He also noticed the stoicism and calmness with which Lorenzo bore the situation. One day when Tirosh was not there, the merchant offered Lorenzo an improper deal.

"I have seen the pressure Tirosh exerts over you and I am sure he pays you very little for your work. Would you care to make some extra money?" the man suggested to Lorenzo, who listened with attention.

"I've got a great deal of wine. Could you take several liters from your barrel and pour them out into mine? Then, we will fill your barrel up with my wine. We can make this trade every week, when Tirosh is absent. The clients would hardly notice the difference, and you would make twenty maravedises. I imagine that is what you make in one month."

Lorenzo pondered the proposal for a few moments and he discretely declined the offer. Although he did not like how Tirosh was treating him, Lorenzo could not justify stealing from him. He would always be thankful for having offering him a job when he had newly arrived in Toledo.

"Sir, I think it is better that you should sell your wine in the market place. Tirosh is very careful with the quality of his wine."

"This is a common practice in many taverns!" If you do me this little favor, you could save a fortune and leave the man that is torturing you," the merchant insisted.

Lorenzo escorted the man to the door of the tavern, wishing him luck selling his wine.

Lorenzo's subtle way of dealing with the unpleasant episode pleased the heavenly watchers. He had passed his first test.

The second unpleasant situation occurred with a delegation from the city of Pisa who had come to Toledo to proclaim Alphonso X as the King of Romans. This title was a requisite to become emperor, but it did not guarantee the designation of the highest title on Earth. Alphonso X, flattered by the delegation's visit, showered the visitors with presents. The Castilian noblemen, who did not understand the advantage of Alphonso becoming emperor, allowed the lavish spending but with reservations, as they did not like throwing away thousands of maravedises satisfying the foreign delegation's cravings.

A Pisan couple arrived at the tavern. Tirosh had received the royal order to host them in the best room and give them the best food, chargeable to the Crown of Castile. Tirosh did not like the order, because he knew it would be difficult to recoup the money from the council. Nevertheless, he assigned the couple the most elegant room in the lodge, giving express orders to Lorenzo to treat them with exceptional consideration.

When the guests arrived at the tavern, Lorenzo recognized them immediately. The husband, bald and limping was getting on in years. By the way he dressed, he was a wealthy man. The woman, dark-haired with bright eyes, was attractive and much younger than her husband. They entered the tavern arguing, and Lorenzo realized the power the lady exerted over the old man. Each time he tried to speak, she interrupted with disdain. She did not like the fact the husband went to the organized events, games, and hunting programs for the Pisan men, while she was only invited to the evening banquets.

"I have married a man that cannot show his wife to have a good time," she reproached her husband.

"I am doing everything I can, but the day programs are only for men. This is a direct order from the king," he responded, over-whelmed.

The delegate left early the next morning, and his wife stayed in the room until noon. When she came down she had an entertaining conversation with Lorenzo. The smile of the woman delighted him. Lorenzo was attracted to her.

"Toledo is very beautiful," the woman said flirtatiously.

"Yes indeed."

"It is a pity nobody can show me the city. My husband is busy with the Pisan delegation, and I only will see him in the evening. On the other hand, staying in the lodge is not such a bad idea. In Pisa, we do not have such handsome waiters," she said coyly looking away, with feigned innocence.

Lorenzo wondered if the woman was trying to seduce him, and received an immediate clear response from his inner voice. It was a warning. "Trouble, trouble, trouble," he heard.

"Would you like to drink anything?" Lorenzo asked, pretending not to have heard her words.

"I would like to try your best meat and your best wine," she asked gently, touching Lorenzo's arm.

"I will prepare them for you straight away," Lorenzo said, also hearing in his head a voice warning him about the danger.

"When the food is ready, could you take it up to my room?" the lady asked.

"Yes, I will," Lorenzo answered, while his heart started beating at a frantic pace.

"I am still tired from the long journey, and my husband will be occupied at the games all day," she said, making suggestive moves towards him.

After delivering that subtle message, she climbed the stairs, exuding sensuality. While he was preparing her food, Lorenzo considered the consequences of unleashing his passion. He knew his body desired female companionship and yearned for release. He thought about the possibility of hiding the affair from her husband, but even in that case, would he be doing the right thing?" he worried, with the sensual image of the woman in his thoughts.

When the food was ready, he took it to her room. He was shaking as he ascended the stairs. His legs trembled, as he had never faced a desirable married woman before.

"May I?" Lorenzo knocked bashfully on the door.

"Come in," she answered with a sensual voice.

Lorenzo waited for a moment. Terrified, he entered the room and placed the food on the table. Then he left as quickly as he could. Nonetheless, he could not help noticing the half-naked woman on the bed.

"Thank you very much, handsome man," she said from her bed, laughing at poor Lorenzo, who almost flew back down the stairs.

"How much stress this job is causing me!" he thought. "A merchant wants to bribe me, Tirosh controls me without pity, and the wife of a strange nobleman wants to seduce me. How hard it is to behave properly! And I need to make sure the women does not take offense," he said to himself.

Lorenzo did a long meditation in his room and he managed to avoid another embarrassing encounter with the lady. He then changed the candle in its holder, so the light did not fail. He entered a state of profound stillness, controlling his body's carnal desires; still, it was difficult to ignore the image of the half-naked woman. After the calming meditation, he slept in peace.

The tests he had to undergo had not yet finished. The next day, the woman tried once more to seduce him, and asked Lorenzo to bring food to her room again. This time the lady waited for Lorenzo, standing in her room, naked, showing off her extraordinary curvaceous body. When he left the food on the table, the woman moved closer to him and touched him again. Lorenzo avoided her advances and tactfully backed away from her. This angered the woman, who was accustomed to getting her way with men.

Lorenzo went back to his room to calm himself. He prayed for several hours, asking the woman not cause him more problems; however, when he returned to the tavern downstairs, Tirosh was enraged.

"Our guest has complained about you," he shouted.

"She has no reason to complain. She asked for our best food, and I took it to her room, as she requested."

"You have to treat this couple with utmost care and attention. If the City Council hears they are not satisfied, they will not pay me, and will fine me."

"I can assure you I have treated them with all the utmost respect and consideration," he said, ending the discussion.

However, the testing continued. The next day, the woman, furious from his failure to respond, ordered food once more.

"Waiter, prepare me the finest food you have. We are the guests of the Castilian king," she said defying him with her look.

"Of course."

"Waiter, you are not preparing the food in the right way. In Pisa they know how to do it," the woman said loudly, to assure the other clients heard her. "Stop. Do not continue!" You are preparing the food incorrectly on purpose. You must apologize for this. I await your apology in my room," she said, trying to seduce him through force and fear.

The woman had to prove to herself she could control every man, but Lorenzo remained calm, and refused to succumb to her crude attempt at blackmail.

The consequences of his decision were easy to predict: the woman complained to her husband about the poor quality of the food and the lack of attention; they departed the lodge, and complained to the City Council. It was the perfect excuse for not paying their expenses, and fining Tirosh.

"Lorenzo, you are fired!" Tirosh shouted furious. "You must will leave the tavern."

Lorenzo felt hurt at the unfair decision, but it was just what he required to free himself from the job was enslaving him. Perhaps he would have never left the tavern of his own volition. For these reasons, he accepted Tirosh´s decision. For many people it would have been a disaster, but for Lorenzo it was the opportunity to follow his soul's destiny.

28. DOOR

$\mathscr{L}$orenzo's life was about to take an extraordinary turn. Attending the meeting at the castle had accelerated his development. In two weeks, he would lose his job and would move into a small room in the city center.

Tirosh felt terrible for having fired Lorenzo without a justifiable reason; he knew he had been an excellent employee for seven years.

During the following weeks, Tirosh did not look Lorenzo in the eye, nevertheless, he did not want to lose his power and control over him; as a consequence, he created a tense environment.

"On Sunday, you will come with me to pick up a large quantity of wine," Tirosh said.

"I am afraid I will not go with you, sir. I need the day off," Lorenzo answered standing firm, knowing there would a gathering at the castle.

"I am sorry, but you must work that day," Tirosh said.

It seemed that Lorenzo was meant to relive a past story. Tirosh was not aware that neither the bishop nor Diego could hold back the profound longing for freedom that lived within Lorenzo. His soul was ready to take the next step on his journey to freedom, and nothing could stop him.

On Saturday, Tirosh reminded Lorenzo that he should go

with him to buy wine, but Lorenzo refused to obey. He returned to his room and changed the candle for the last time. He was proud of himself for keeping the light burning for the full lunar cycle. He meditated by his Menorah and read the chapter of Exodus, which was opened before him. In fact he was traveling his own Exodus to freedom.

He put on the best clothes for the new meeting at the castle, and left the tavern without making any noise. At the Jewish Gate, he met a friendly merchant who offered to take him to Almonacid. Lorenzo arrived long before the meeting was due to begin. He sat down on a tree and entered a calm meditative state.

Minutes before the beginning of the meeting, he noticed the presence of the tutor of the group, who welcomed everyone at the castle entrance. Lorenzo approached him, noticing that his eyes shone with a brilliant intensity.

"Welcome. You must be Lorenzo," the group leader greeted him.

"Yes, that is right," he answered, surprised that he knew his name.

"I am Abraham. It is my pleasure to meet you," and shook his hand with great affection.

Abraham observed him intensely, perceiving the good quality of his soul. Then he greeted an unseen figure behind Lorenzo; the invisible guide also greeted Abraham.

"You are welcome to join us," he said.

When Lorenzo entered the main room of the castle, everyone was sitting with a profound inner stillness. He took one of the seats in the back of the room and tried to enter into the same calm state. Then, he had a feeling he had participated in similar gatherings, perhaps in past lives.

Abraham closed the room door, and spoke, asking the Holy Spirit to descend on those present. Lorenzo felt something extraordinary was happening, but he could not express it in words. The room became a chariot that carried them to another dimension, transporting people to an unseen, yet real realm. The room seemed to expand beyond its physical walls.

Abraham showed them an enigmatic and interesting diagram. Lorenzo wondered, fascinated, about the meaning of that composition. According to his limited understanding, it was a metaphysical representation of reality; it was a map of the manifestation, which explained the laws of existence. He realized the diagram also could be the reference to explain many daily situations. With the help of that map, called the Tree of Life, people could discern the forces and influences beyond each situation.

Abraham answered the student´s questions, and at the end of the session, the group again entered into a deep and profound silence. He gave thanks to the Holy One for what they had received, before closing the meeting.

When the meeting ended, Abraham called Lorenzo, and invited him to sit down near under a nearby tree.

"Lorenzo, this is a school of the soul."

"Oh," Lorenzo said, unaware of the existence of such schools.

"The work that we do here is to serve God, to help elevate consciousness around us, and to help people be free."

"And, how do you do it?" Lorenzo asked confused.

"By sharing the spiritual Teachings. The members of the group express them in several ways in the world. Some of them write books on the influence of the planets and stars; others write mystical poetry; others translate books of Greek, Jewish, and Arab philosophers. There are many roles; however, our main goal is to help people discover the path to the mystic union with God and beyond, towards total freedom.

"Is that the path of self-realization?" Lorenzo, asked.

"Yes, the path to self-realization is designed to help you develop all of your human potential, becoming a bridge between heaven and earth. But tell me a little bit about yourself," he asked.

Lorenzo told him his life's story. First, how, after his dream, he left Teruel disobeying his father wishes. Then he told him of his time as a businessman in Albarracin, and as a monk in Cuenca. He also talked about his time as a musician, and finally about his life at the tavern.

Abraham, delighted in hearing his personal story, realized Lorenzo's courage, and perseverance. He then said to him,

"Your journey now will no longer be horizontal through the roads of Castile and Aragon. Your journey will be vertical, upward, through the different subtle and spiritual realms."

"Are there really such paths?"

"Yes. Many people have explored those paths through the ages. Much has been written and many have created works of art illustrating the metaphysical truths. But you should know that spiritual work is not easy. You will need to work on yourself every day, wake up, learn to distinguish fantasy from reality, be responsible." Abraham said.

Abraham seemed to wait for a question from Lorenzo, but it did not come. The tutor received a sign from the heavens allowing him to keep talking.

"Your life has been a preparation for this meeting at this place. Your life experiences have been your training until now. Joining a soul school is the first step on the long ascending path."

"And what do I need to do to join the school?"

"You are already in," Abraham smiled.

"Really?"

"Yes, you have passed your tests."

Lorenzo wondered about the tests, and he remembered the episodes with the corrupt wine seller and the Pisan woman. He also told those stories to Abraham.

"If you had lied down with that woman or if you had accepted the wine seller dishonest offer, you would not be here. Now you need to continue to work hard. The goal is to become a refined instrument of divine expression," Abraham answered, finishing his talk.

Abraham stood up and left Lorenzo on his own, while he pondered on the words he heard. He approached a group of three people, who were concerned about the state of the kingdom. They were sharing their thoughts as they ate the food prepared for them. Lorenzo listened with great attention,

"King Alphonso is going to attack Granada," rabbi Todros, who knew the king intimately, said.

"I do not think so. The Granadian King pays a large vassalage, which is essential to Castile. Knowing the king's ambitions, it is possible he might wish to conquer Aragon betraying his father-in-law," the financier Don Isaac answered.

"If he does that, it would be disastrous for both the king and his kingdom. The queen would desert him and a civil war would ensue," the astrologer Yehuda ben Moshed stated.

"King James I of Aragon no longer trusts his son-in-law. Even his wife is angry with him because of his arrogance," the rabbi said.

"Things are not going well in Aragon either. The noblemen are unfairly oppressing the peasants. Many cities have united against the laws of the noblemen. A war against Castile would be a disaster for them as well. I am sure that James will make Alfonso see reason," Don Isaac said.

"Let us hope so. A war between Aragon and Castile would be a calamity for the Jews of both kingdoms," the venerable Yehuda ben Moshe affirmed.

Benjamin told Lorenzo the identity of the three people, which though modest, were among the most influential people of Castile: the chief rabbi of Toledo, the Europe's best astrologer, and the most important financier on the Iberian Peninsula. Lorenzo could not believe he was in their company. He also realized it was Don Isaac who had given him the candlestick the previous month at his first meeting. He felt foolish for having been angry at that time.

"One of the most important financiers had graciously given me a candle holder, and I behaved like a spoiled child," he admonished himself.

Benjamin told Lorenzo it was better he returned home alone, so he could ponder on the meeting. He did not mind walking back this time. He arrived home filled with joy, not having suffered on the road this time.

"You have treated me with no respect today," Tirosh yelled as soon as Lorenzo entered the tavern.

"I told you I was going to take the day off," and without giving him an opportunity to reply, he went to his room.

Lorenzo immediately forgot about the Tirosh's tirade. He basked in the joy from contact with a living spiritual school, and felt radiant. He could not stop thinking about the journey to the upper worlds. He was not yet aware that the journey upwards was in fact an inward journey, through the inner realms.

Tirosh hardly spoke to him during his final days at the tavern, showing his annoyance with him. On his last day, cold and aloof, he deducted a large amount of money from his pay, for his absence the previous Sunday.

Lorenzo packed his few clothes, the candle-holder, and the Menorah and politely bid him a goodbye. This phase of his life has ended.

Lorenzo rented a small room in the city center. He went in search of a job, and overheard a conversation among the friars regarding which was the best cathedral in Castile.

"If you want to see an authentic cathedral you must go to Burgos," one monk said, while the other boasted the cathedral in Toledo was the best of the world.

Lorenzo smiled and thought to be in touch with God, one does not need a cathedral. The Holy One is always present, like during the Sunday meeting in the castle.

Lorenzo offered himself as an apprentice to the artisans who made women's shoes near the cathedral, but the shoemakers rejected him because of his age; they thought he was joking. He got the same answer from other artisans.

He entered a tavern in the small Jewish quarter of Toledo, near the cathedral, and contemplated his future. He wondered about his possibilities. It was not going to be easy finding a job, and he faced reality: he was in his forties, unemployed, still single, and his only hope was a group of people he hardly knew.

His inner intuitive voice told him to find a job involving books. This was confusing to him, as he believed this was a job only suited for highly educated men. He abandoned that idea, and thought about becoming a soldier, although he was no longer young and the military campaigns were strenuous.

While he pondered his uncertain future, he overheard a conversation among some Jews in the tavern.

"King Alphonso, sublime if there ever was one, has granted us special permission to rebuild the main synagogue, the biggest and most beautiful in Castile," one Jew said, praising the monarch.

"Our synagogue, which has stood for hundreds of years, is going to be even more magnificent. We will call it "The Grand Synagogue of Toledo," and it will be even bigger than the synagogue of Almaliqim," another Jew said.

"Alphonso has disobeyed the pope, who does not allow building temples for non-Christians. He also has granted a pardon to two Jews sentenced to death," the first client exclaimed.

"Do not forget Don Isaac's and the rabbi's influence over Alphonso."

"Let me read you the text of Yehuda ben Shlomo al-Jarizi's," one of the Jewish clients said.

"I came to enchanting Toledo that shows off its beauty to all. There are many incomparable synagogues. Every soul praises the Lord in Toledo."

The comments about the synagogue, the rabbi, and Don Isaac, made Lorenzo wonder about the group of people of the castle. He sensed he had a deep connection with them. He thanked God for his good fortune for meeting them. At the end of the day, who was he: a simple barman, without a job.

He worried when he realized he would have a difficult time meeting these men again. His only reference was the Jewish tavern and he no longer worked there. He asked the Lord to meet these people again and he knew his profound faith would help him encounter the group destined for him.

29. SCHOOL

*L*orenzo spent the next three weeks looking for a job. He only could just live for six months on his savings. He worried, but the meeting with Abraham gave him hope. He knew he would receive the help needed. And so it was. A month later, by chance, he met the poet on the street.

"Benjamin! How nice to meet you! I did not know how to stay in touch with you. I lost my job at the tavern and feared that you would not find me," Lorenzo said excited.

"Lorenzo! Abraham has asked about you. He told me to invite you to our meetings," he answered.

"Thank you very much."

"We hold our weekly meetings in a house near the main synagogue. Sometimes we meet in other places, but we will let you know. There are also several events for outside Toledo, similar to the one you attended last time."

"Do I need to prepare myself in any special way?"

"The preparation is subtle. Enter a meditative state to receive the Grace before the meeting. In the gatherings, we receive what we need. You must be on time.

"I have noticed most of the members of the group are Jewish, but I was born Christian," he said, worried.

249

"The only real requirement is to be a mature and responsible person. It does not matter if you are Jewish, Christian or Arab, since we all are brothers. Look what happened in Toledo: Arabs, Christians, and Jews worked together bringing knowledge from the East, with their translations.

"Do you mean the works translated at the Court?"

"Yes. Adherents of the three religions work together to exchanging wisdom and knowledge. Everyone works for the Greater Good, regardless of their religion. Abraham also welcomes Arabs and Christians to his group, as long as they are respectful of others."

"Thank you very much, Benjamin."

"Another thing, you need to be discrete. It is forbidden to talk about what happens during the meetings. We endeavor to find mystical union with God, without intermediaries, something that every human being has the right to do, but very few are aware of it. If religious hierarchies learn about the group, they might feel threatened, and try to destroy it."

Lorenzo waited for the meeting day. He yearned to ascend the spiritual path. He arrived punctually at the synagogue, and met thirty people, many of whom he already knew. Benjamin of Seville introduced him to the rest of the group members, and Lorenzo apologized to Don Isaac for being grumpy on the day they had met. He also spoke with Yehuda ben Moshe, who not only was the kingdom's leading astrologer, but also the royal doctor. He also talked with several Arab astrologers from Cordova, and some famous Christian book illustrators. There were women in the group, which surprised Lorenzo.

"Men and women, if they are real spiritual seekers, are welcome," the poet stated.

"It is strange, since many religions degrade women."

"Women have an important role, because they balance the masculine energy, which sometimes lacks brilliance. A men's only group would be dry. Many women have been able to keep the flame of Tradition lit through history."

When Abraham came to the garden at the synagogue, the members of the group left in silence to a private room in a house nearby. They kept quiet, so people did not know they were meeting. Once in the room, Abraham invited the Holy Spirit to descend upon them. The atmosphere was solemn and respectful. He pointed out the importance of being still in the place where the Grace descended, and to balance the active and passive principles. Then he explained how the principles worked, using the example of what was happening on the kingdom.

"The king is very expansive, and if he does not develop limits, Castile will descend into chaos. He needs to apply discrimination to eliminate confusion. The king believes the kingdom has unlimited resources, and he is squandering them. The subjects and the noblemen are paying for his wastefulness, and sooner or later they will have enough."

Lorenzo tried to make a comment, because he wanted acknowledgment, but Abraham encouraged him to watch and listen before speaking.

"This is Lorenzo, and today he has joined our group," he said before continuing. "All excessive tendencies will balance. The danger is that the king will over-react towards the other direction, and will become rigid and controlling. In that case the kingdom will be an unbearable place, with heavy burdens for everyone," Abraham explained.

"The king believes everyone loves him. He is not aware the noblemen conspire against him, and the peasants doubt him. His own brothers want to overthrow him," Don Isaac added.

"When you advise him, you must be careful how to tell him

this information. He might react violently if he hears something he does not wish to hear," Abraham said to the king's advisers.

"The king is often difficult. His pride blinds him," Yehuda ben Moshe said.

"He might not realize it, but he is a divine instrument for bringing eastern knowledge to Toledo. We must help him, in a discrete way, to fulfill his task. Thanks to him, esoteric knowledge is transmitted here," Abraham said.

"Too much optimism can make the king spend much more than he has. He could undertake a new military campaign without evaluating his resources. Becoming King of Romans has inflated both his ego and his ambitions. He longs to be emperor no matter what the cost is!" Yehuda added.

Then Abraham commented on the importance of history and astrology. He changed the subject to explain the hand of Providence in human evolution.

"Our task is to be attentive to the signs of Providence. If we follow them, we will realize what is best and needed. That is why we must keep our channel with the spiritual realms free and clear of obstacles."

When the meeting ended, something had shifted inside Lorenzo. He knew, from deep within himself, that if he did things correctly, Providence would protect him. He noticed the meeting had also transformed the rest of the group members: their faces shone.

"Is everybody allowed travel the way to the higher worlds?" Lorenzo asked Abraham once their meeting ended.

"It works better in a group, since the path is not easy and there are dangers. Your companions can save your life, or stop you from going insane."

Lorenzo had just entered in another dimension. He had

begun his ascent through the subtle worlds, although he was not yet completely aware. He said good-bye to his soul companions, and went to his little room in a peaceful and happy state.

He remembered his young love, Ariadna. As he became closer to God, he was closer to his beloved, even though he had not seen her for decades. Both paths seemed to converge.

Lorenzo went to every meeting, never missing one. He sensed a special aroma in the room where the meetings were held. The more he listened to Abraham, the more impressed he was with him. He remained quiet during the sessions, as he did not want to make an ignorant statement among such evolved people.

"As a person approaches his spiritual awakening he has little to say," Abraham confirmed.

As he attended the group meetings, Lorenzo discovered the spiritual path had several phases, as Abraham explained,

"The doors open as the person is ready to accept new responsibilities. Each door is a test, each new one subtler than the last. A member of a group must accept the responsibility of being an example for others, since he becomes a channel between realms. Personal complacency does not have place here."

Lorenzo also knew Abraham's group of was not unique; on the contrary, there were several other groups meeting elsewhere in Castile and Aragon. There was a constant interchange of knowledge among the groups, and each of them helped Providence in their way. For that reason, Abraham invited several men of knowledge from Gerona, Barcelona, Zaragoza, Soria, Segovia, Avila, and Guadalajara. Thanks to those invitations, Lorenzo met many evolved mystics.

One day, after their spiritual session, Abraham spoke to Lorenzo:

"How are you?" he asked.

"Well, I love coming to the group. However, I lost my job, and can't seem to find another," he complained.

"Go to see a man called Metolitolah, at the Royal Chancellery."

Lorenzo dressed in his best clothes and went to the lavish book filled building. He met an old man, who carried the burden of organizing the books.

"Good morning, I am looking for a gentleman called Metolitolah. Abraham has sent me," Lorenzo saluted.

"I am Metolitolah. Abraham is a great man. Anyone sent by him is welcome. Yes, I need help."

"I am not sure if I am qualified to work here."

"What languages do you speak?"

"I know Arabic, Latin, Castilian and a bit of Hebrew. I learned them when I was younger, and I still practice whenever I can. However, I am not sure I can be of any help."

"The king hires us to translate books, particularly on astrology. There are times when the work is overwhelming, and I need someone to help me order and classify both the originals and the translations. The king has commissioned me to coordinate this vast project."

While Metoltolah was talking, King Alphonso entered the room, causing both men to become nervous in his presence. His blond hair, blue eyes, and his opulent outfit showed his royal demeanor, much as James I did in the woods of Albarracin. He was confident, and self-assured knowing how the world admired him. Lorenzo sensed the king had been born to fulfill a unique destiny.

"Metolitolah, I need you, follow me. I need you to take charge of the translation of the Quatripartito of Ptolomeo, and to organize Al-Ghazali's volumes," the king commanded.

"Excuse me, please. Come back next week, and we will talk more," Metolitolah said to Lorenzo, before leaving the room.

"Have I just seen the king? Can I help with such a vast undertaking?" he said to himself while his mind raced on. A window of hope had opened in before him, and he felt honored. "Am I capable of sorting the books and files? Would it be suitable for me?" he asked himself, doubting his abilities.

"It would be perfect for you," he heard the voice of his intuition, which spoke to his consciousness.

A few days later, Abraham spoke to Lorenzo,

"So, will you be working for Metolitolah? That is the right job for you, not the one in the tavern," he said proudly.

"I am not sure. I think they need help, but Metolitolah did not offer me work. I am not sure if I am qualified."

"Of course you are. Who could do that job better than you?" he answered reassuring him. "What other purpose brings you to Toledo, to find your princess in a tavern? At the Chancellery you will meet scholars, and wise ones seeking knowledge."

"I am not sure if I will be up to the task, even if the king is there, supervising the work."

"The king supervises the entire process of translations. He is very demanding and does not tolerate mistakes. You must stay awake and be alert."

In just a few weeks, Lorenzo´s life took an extraordinary turn. Thanks to God, and with Abraham's help, he would now enter a different world, full of ancient knowledge, which will build the foundation for the centuries to come. Lorenzo knew he must become a new man, responding to his new responsibilities. But not only was his professional life about to take a drastic turn for the better, but his love life was also about to change forever.

30. ENCOUNTER

$\mathcal{L}$orenzo went to visit Metolitolah. The wise man explained the translation process. Most of the translators worked in private houses in Toledo, and only few of them could access royal buildings. Metolitolah showed him several rooms in which scholars worked on literary works in silently with great concentration.

"Who are they?" Lorenzo asked.

"They are wise men, fluent in many languages. The king wants to employ the best scholars in Toledo, regardless of their religion. He had charmed the best translators in Castile to come and work here. There are wise men from Cordova, Murcia, Seville, Salamanca, plus a few foreigners.

"And do they all work in the same project?"

"No, these people here are working on books written in Aramaic, Greek, and Arabic. They edit philosophical, medical, botanical, and astrological works. In other rooms, people translate historical volumes. There is also a group of Christian lawmakers, while others produce book of chess, and arts."

"How many translators are here?"

"It is difficult to say. The king commissions works as they are needed and according to the books he brings into Toledo. The principal group consists of approximately twenty-five people, who are in charge of translating, compiling, and editing under the king's supervision. At times there may be more than a hundred scholars, depending on what is needed."

"And are all these works commissioned by the king?" Lorenzo asked, amazed.

"Yes, the king enjoys the translation process. Each new territory that he conquers, he brings the archives and libraries of those cities to Toledo. If Castile were not constantly at war, Alphonso would dedicate his full time to books, poetry and literary pursuits."

Metolitolah, became quiet and asked Lorenzo if he would care to be his assistant.

"It would be a dream come true," Lorenzo answered with great enthusiasm at the astonishing offer.

"The king pays the translators with land conquered from the Arab territories. I will try to have you paid in cash."

"If you accept my humble services, I will serve the king," Lorenzo answered, thinking he should be paying for the privilege of working there, instead of being paid.

"You can start next week. By the way, you will also need to help the astrologers draw their astrological tables, noting down the data."

He remembered the words of Abraham and he realized he was right. His departure from Teruel, his pilgrimage to Toledo, his several jobs, everything was a preparation for his new life that was starting.

Metolitolah instructed Lorenzo to classify books by language and subject. Day after day, he organized the works logically. He also helped the astrologers, who very much appreciated his work, especially Yehuda ben Moshe, who invited Lorenzo to San Servando´s Castle to observe the heavens with him.

"From here we observe the heavens, day after day, year after year. We note the movements of the planets and stars," the wise astrologer said.

"And how are the tables used?"

"We keep the data, and compare it with previous tables. Then we prepare books of astronomic tables, which help us to interpret horoscopes according to traditional ancient methods."

"And do you advise the king as well?

"Yes. First, we observe the heavens, and then we advise him on his decision making process. But do not tell anybody about this."

Yehuda asked him to observe the sky from the observatory.

"I will show you the different planets," and he pointed out the visible planets and their influence in relation to their relative positions to the Earth.

Lorenzo wanted to know more about the planets, and could not resist asking him about his natal horoscope.

"Your sun is in Sagittarius in the twelfth house, which means that you are a mystic traveler. You want to know the answers to the deepest questions Mystical and supernatural ideas attract you, and you need space for reflection. This explains your dream of coming to Toledo, and the longing to join a school of the soul."

Lorenzo was surprised about the precision with which the horoscope illuminated his life.

"Can you see if I will find a wife?"

"According to your horoscope, you are looking for someone deep, mystical, and special," Yehuda answered laughing, as Lorenzo visualized Ariadna once more. Although a long time had passed since their first encounter in Teruel, he had not forgotten his young love.

A short while later, Abraham led a guided meditation for his students and took them to the presence of God. Lorenzo used that intimate and direct contact with the Holy One to state the wish he was longing for; he asked God for a wife, although he knew it was not right to ask something by whim. Lorenzo was aware of the negative consequences of granting people's egoistic wishes, but he knew he had not been born to be alone, despite his long periods of solitude; therefore, his desire for companion was a true soul longing, and it was, therefore, right to ask. Lorenzo also thought that his companion should understand his spiritual work, since someone only concerned with material security was not a suitable partner.

Abraham explained that a celestial guide called Sandalfon was in charge of observing when a true petition came from the heart of a person; the archangel only passed the wish to God only if it was sincere.

"There is hope for you, be patient and the right woman will come." Lorenzo heard his inner voice say, and knew God heard his prayer.

A few weeks later, walking along a street, Lorenzo looked up at the top of a convent. He paralyzed when he saw a nun looking down at the street. It was the same face that he saw before the fateful encounter with the poet. He looked at her and their souls immediately recognized each other.

"Ariadna!" Lorenzo yelled.

The love of his life was in that convent, a few steps from where he lived. How many times he had walked by the front of that building, not knowing his beloved waited within. Nothing had changed about her face; it had the same youthful look Lorenzo remembered and had thought about so many times. The elegance, refinement, and purity of that woman was better than any Toledan courtesan.

Ariadna´s heart skipped a beat. She frightened, and retreated into the convent. She recognized the love of her life, whom she had not forgotten. That night she tried to sleep but her unease did not allow it. Deeply buried emotions arose from her soul. She knew she could not remain in the convent any longer.

Lorenzo came back to his little room stunned. "Is the nun actually Ariadna? Or is my mind playing tricks with me?" he thought.

He could not sleep that night. The woman's face remained frozen in his mind. He remembered, one by one, their meetings in Teruel. He looked at the stars and recognized hers. That night her star was shining brightly. The star always had been there, as a silent watcher of his steps. "Ariadna in Toledo...and in a convent...how could that be?" He wondered, amazed.

Lorenzo asked the Holy One, if it were His Will to meet Ariadna. Since that day, he spent as much time as he could near the convent. Each time he was near her window, his heart palpitated and he could not move. But she did not show herself again.

"Did I imagine her? Am I going crazy?" he often wondered. "Is this a heavenly trick?"

It could be worse. The nun was Ariadna, and she had forgotten him. "Destiny could not be so cruel," Lorenzo thought. "Would he meet her again, only to lose her for a second time? No, that could not happen. Would she leave the convent? What if she did not recognize him?" these thoughts spun in his head.

Lorenzo did not realize that Ariadna's was feeling even worse. In the convent, nuns were not allowed to look outside. The prioress was tough, and did not want the sisters to be distracted by worldly events. The vows obligated Ariadna to a life of silence, devotion, and faith. Years before, when her father tried to marry her to a gentleman from Huesca, she escaped to a convent, and promised no man would own her. She would not accept dying of exhaustion from taking care of an old man's family whom she did not love. She preferred to devote her life and love to God alone. After living in different convents, she was sent to Toledo to found a new congregation, but her world was shattered the evening she saw Lorenzo through the window. From that moment, she secretly went to the window whenever she could.

"Sister, the world outside is not for us. Only danger and temptation awaits there," the mother superior reminded her, when she saw her standing near the window.

"Yes, I know," Ariadna answered submissively.

Outside the walls, Lorenzo was trying to return to his life and forget the angel in the window. He did not want to be enslaved by a new fantasy, despite knowing his deep connection to Ariadna. One evening he felt compelled to walk on the street in front of convent. It was the same feeling he had as a youth, when he had followed the impulse to go to the stairs where he first met her. He approached the window and found Ariadna! They stood still staring at each other. Time stopped at that moment which lasted an eternity. Both, transported spiritually, once more, entered the higher worlds.

"Ariadna," Lorenzo sighed silently.

She gave him the sweetest smile. She was like an angel who had emerged from a fairy tale. Lorenzo gazed at her and thanked God for the opportunity of seeing her again. The heavens, also enjoyed the scene; it was a meeting of two spiritual souls who were going to carry out a mission. Their hearts recognized the eternal bliss they were receiving; two souls meeting again after their many travails. Ariadna, overjoyed to see Lorenzo again, hesitated a few moments, and she waved good-bye from the window. Her duties were calling her.

In the days that followed, Ariadna could not stop thinking about Lorenzo. She had closed her heart to the possibility of falling in love again a long time ago. Now, if she wanted to be true to herself, she would have to face the consequences of her decisions, and accept the changes that would follow. Her love, long suppressed, was still living deep within her soul. That explained her inability to reach the levels of ecstasy the other nuns experienced in their prayers; she had not been able to forget Lorenzo.

Lorenzo remained calm, since he did not want to rush. He needed a plan to be with Ariadna, but the convents were impossible to access. He prayed to the Holy One for guidance. Many people wait vainly their whole lives a meeting with the soul mate and they had already had two; for that he was grateful. Now, Providence would help them be together again, and carry out the spiritual task that awaited for them, but Lorenzo should put his heart and soul to accomplish the difficult mission to take Ariadna out of the convent.

Figure 6

• *Part Four* •

31. INDISCRETION

Lorenzo went to the convent. It was cloistered. He found the entrance in a secluded corner of the street. The door was locked. He knocked and shouted, but only received silence in return.

"I want to speak to Ariadna!" Lorenzo begged, unaware that his shouts were harming the woman he loved.

The mother superior, hearing Lorenzo´s shouts, assigned Ariadna the most difficult chores within the convent, hoping to make her forget the outer world. The superior also reduced her food to a minimum. The prioress hoped that through discipline and hard work, she forgot Lorenzo.

The opposite occurred; instead of focusing on her religious duties, Ariadna spent the day dreaming of him The prioress decided to move her to a convent in another city, so she could return to following a life dictated by the precepts of the order.

Lorenzo tried to reach her, but every time he approached the convent, he heard nothing, or the nuns chanting. This distressed him greatly. His highly stressed state resulted in making a serious error at work in the library. An elderly woman, named Luzmila, came to the Chancellery. The old lady, who acted as if she owned the place, picked up several books, flipped through them, and even tried to order the translators around…

"I want a book about mystical science of the Jews, the one the king praises."

"I cannot have access that book," Lorenzo answered, who knew she was talking about a book, written by the members of the group commissioned by King Alphonso.

"I am greatly interested in that knowledge, as my husband was. Do you know how I might meet the authors of that book?" she asked.

Lorenzo wanted to impress her so he spoke up saying,

"I often meet with them."

"I will join you next time you meet."

Lorenzo sensed an inner voice warning him to stop talking, but he did not listen, and continued:

"Tomorrow I will meet them in the main synagogue," he boasted.

"I will be there, as well."

When the old woman left, Lorenzo knew he had made a mistake. He asked Metolitolah about her:

"So, you have met Luzmila…" he said laughing.

"Yes, she seemed very interested in the books of Jewish knowledge."

"She is Diego Martinez de Aladren's widow, who was a royal judge. She obtained a permission to be here. She has nothing else to do, so she comes and misplaces everything. She must be the center of attention."

"And what does she do with her life?"

"She spends her husband's fortune. She drinks too much wine, and organizes parties for the noblemen and priests, who take advantage of her. Poor woman!" Metolitolah said.

The next day, Luzmila showed up drunk at the main synagogue, where she met Abraham´s group. Without asking for permission, she followed them, noisily making herself known. Once the session started, Luzmila compulsively asked many questions, without allowing Abraham to answer any of them. With great tact, the tutor tried to mirror her lack of balance, but she, intoxicated, dismissed his responses. Benjamin, the poet, invited her to leave the room, pointing out that she probably had more knowledge than the rest of the group. The woman left the meeting, offended. When the session finished, the oldest members of the group reprimanded Lorenzo.

"This is not a game. You have put the group at risk. Here, there are Christians, Arabs, and Jews who try to live as true human beings, but taken out of this context, this can be misunderstood," the poet warned Lorenzo.

"If that woman reports us, the Church will consider us heretics, and could punish us with death penalty. The Church wants crush all groups that do not conform to its rules," Yehuda ben Moshe said.

"The king still supports us, because he wants to learn the Traditional knowledge, but this is not always going to be the case. For many centuries, groups like ours had to meet in secret. Some people in former times risked their lives to pass on this Tradition," rabbi Todros said.

"This is unacceptable. You even told her where we meet. This is not the right way to introduce new people to the group," they further reproached him. "The admission to our circle is through constant inner work and because a deep longing in the soul."

Lorenzo went home worried, as he had a terrible premonition. As expected, Luzmila, came to see him the next day.

"Lorenzo, that group is heretical!" the woman shouted.

"Those people are seeking the truth," Lorenzo answered, regretting the consequences of his indiscretion.

"The Holy Mother Church teaches the Truth!" she shouted, out of her mind, making herself heard by everyone in the room.

"I lived in a convent in Cuenca and I know the Church very well."

"You also have humiliated me in front of people they dared to reject me."

"I invited you to that group because I thought you had interest in the Jewish mystical science, and you wanted to obtain a truer understanding of life, but…"

"But what?" Luzmila asked.

Lorenzo tried to hold his tongue, but he was unable to contain himself. In fact, he made things worse by saying something that should have never come out of his mouth.

"But…for a crazy woman like you this is impossible! You went to the meeting drunk, and constantly interrupted!" Lorenzo yelled. "A rich woman, who has inherited a great fortune and spends her time annoying others, this is what you are!"

After uttering those sentences, Lorenzo turned pale, realizing he had fallen into her trap. Luzmila had a perfect excuse to take revenge, and occupy her time in something other than organizing silly parties. The noblewoman, angry, spoke with the senior church officials, and reported Lorenzo, accusing him of participating in heretical practices in a non-Christian group. The Church, after exterminating the Cathars, wanted to find proof of other heretic groups in Europe.

Lorenzo repented a thousand times for his irresponsible action, especially when the consequences of his error came back to him. A church emissary issued him a subpoena: the bishop of Toledo wanted to interrogate him! Lorenzo trembled. He felt his life was at risk, as well as the continuation of Abraham´s group. Repentant and downcast, he informed Abraham about the bishop's summons.

"Many spiritual groups are born pure, but they end up as political structures. They do not want to liberate the person; on the contrary, they want to control people," Abraham explained to a sorrowful Lorenzo.

"Any person who seeks freedom becomes a threat. Sometimes, they can execute anyone under their legal framework," Yehuda ben Moshe said.

"They also demand large amounts of money to guarantee salvation, a gift which they consider themselves only bestowers. In this way they keep the majority of people morally and economically oppressed," Abraham regretted, who understood his student's test.

Lorenzo asked forgiveness with all his soul for his stupidity. On the way to the bishop's palace, he suffered a panic attack, experiencing uncontrollable heart spasms. When he arrived, he waited in the hall, while he looked at the luxurious objects from all around the world. After a few hours, the bishop's assistant came for him. Lorenzo recognized his old friend Julian, his companion in Cuenca, who now was the bishop's assistant in Toledo.

"Lorenzo! I thought I would never see you again," Julian said joyfully.

"Julian!" he said hugging him, happy to see a friendly face.

"What are you doing here?"

"The bishop wants to see me. He says…," and in that moment the bishop appeared.

"Do you know this man?" the bishop asked Julian.

"Yes, he was a member of our congregation in Cuenca. He

spent several years in the monastery."

"According to my information, this man belongs to a group that practices unchristian acts. He, as a good Christian, cannot belong to such group. He has the obligation, under the threat of severe punishment, to inform us of any heretic practices," the bishop warned, trying to frighten Lorenzo and get valuable information.

"Do not worry your Excellency, Lorenzo was always different, he used to ask strange questions," Julian interceded for his friend. "In the monastery he was in his own world, but his behavior was above reproach. His faith is real, I can attest to that."

"The punishment for heresy is death. We have advised the king to include the death penalty for all heretics in the newest set of laws, Siete Partidas. We will exterminate all heretic groups, once the king proclaims the law" the bishop said.

Lorenzo did not want to speak. He knew any word would lead to more questions.

"Have you anything to say?

"Your Excellency, I am not aware of any group that practices heresy..."

At that moment, a messenger from the king entered into the room, ending the interrogation. The hand of Providence intervened once again to save Lorenzo.

"Your Excellency, the king requires your presence. He wants to prepare a strategy to acquire the title of emperor when he meets with the pope."

"Alphonsito, Alphonsito, always bothering the Church," he mumbled in to himself, but perceptible to Lorenzo´s ear.

"Let this man go...for the moment," the bishop said. "We will watch this heretic," he concluded.

Lorenzo felt a great relief. He had never been under so much pressure. He cried, releasing the emotional tension that had accumulated within him. He thanked God for Julian's mediation.

"Julian, what are you doing in Toledo?"

"They have called me here. There is something extraordinary going on in the Toledo´s Church. We make decisions even before Rome. What about you?"

"I am helping with the translation of books of knowledge, coming from the East. It is something marvelous that is happening in Toledo."

"I am very happy for you. You have always tried to evolve. The bishop of Cuenca was angry at your sudden departure. He wanted you to convert in the name of Christianity and ordered men to find you."

"That task was not for me, Julian. I was not happy leaving as a fugitive, but I was afraid they considered me an enemy of the Church if I did not become ordained in the Militia Christy."

"I would like to see you. You have grown-up. You are a more mature man."

"I am in the Chancellery most of the time. Come and see me. It is a magnificent place."

Julian had saved his life two times. Lorenzo spent all his savings to buy him an extraordinary present, to honor him. He loved his friend, but he was sorry he was inside the church hierarchy.

Relieved, he told the other group members what had happened in the meeting, and asked for their forgiveness. Abraham spoke with Lorenzo alone,

"You must review your life and take responsibility for your irresponsible actions. You might not like what you discover," Abraham warned him.

Lorenzo did not like his tutor's words, although he thanked him for his desire to help him. Honestly facing his past actions, and acknowledging them required courage and integrity. Not everyone was capable of doing that.

"Accepting and forgiving our past mistakes is essential to our spiritual growth. Many people are not aware that what we do to others, we are, in fact, doing to ourselves. If you do not undertake this inner examination of your life, you will have to undertake it during your death process, probably with terrible pain."

Lorenzo went home intending to reconcile with himself. He made a list of all the people that he had hurt in his life. During a meditation, Lorenzo asked for forgiveness for them all, and he liberated himself of the burden.

Later, he asked Abraham to assign him a role that would allow him to be of greater service to the group, as a payment for all he had received. His tutor nodded, pleased, and commissioned him to prepare and clean the meeting room. This was a great privilege, since tidying the space where the Holy Spirit manifested would bring him great blessings.

Another door opened for Lorenzo. The astrologers told him some important news: one of the astrologers and advisers to the king, left Toledo, and his position was vacant. They showed him the king's horoscope, and asked him his opinion. They listened with great attention to his interpretation

"I believe that the essence of the king´s life is his spiritual quest, and the transmission of that knowledge, formerly reserved to elite circles, to the majority of the people," he answered humbly pointing the Sun in the king's horoscope.

"That is right, keep going," Yehuda ben Moshe said.

"But his desire for power and to be emperor is also strong, and that does not allow him listen to good advice," he continued pointing at the moon in his natal chart.

"Yes indeed, you are right," Yehuda said. "The king's ambition might risk the kingdom's future. You can see this by Jupiter's in conjunction with the Sun in Sagittarius. Those planets show he desires unlimited expansion to keep expanding his kingdom…"

"In addition he has authoritarian and vengeful tendencies, for the influence of Mars in Capricorn on his Ascendant. Saturn, also in the sign of Capricorn, gives him a strategic capacity, which can result in cold and calculated decisions," Lorenzo added.

Thanks to those accurate observations, Lorenzo passed the test. Then he answered with common sense other several questions about other horoscopes. After verifying his skill, they proposed him for the vacant position.

"Thanks Heaven. I hardly deserve this luck," Lorenzo said.

"It is easy to advise the king. His horoscope forecasts many problems in the second half of his life. Be prepared," Yehuda warned him.

Although he was thrilled by his new job, his thoughts were focused on his beloved Ariadna, whom he wished to rescue from her cloister. Lorenzo also needed all of God's strength to reunite with the love of his life.

32. LOVE

Lorenzo yearned to be with Ariadna. He wished they could walk together, to share their concerns, to be with each other... Every day he went to the convent, but it seemed only ghosts lived there.

He shouted but still got no response, although his sighs reached the most hidden depths of his beloved´s heart. The nuns worried about her, who struggled between her holy vows and the love was destined for. Ariadna sent one of her assistants, to give a note to Lorenzo, and risking much, she did so.

"Sir, sir! I have a message for you," he told him passing the note through the window.

Lorenzo read it eagerly.

"Are you my beloved Lorenzo? I always look at our stars on the horizon and they both continue to shine. I remember, as if it were yesterday, when we held hands that night in Teruel. Now, they plan to take me to a convent in Avila, and I do not know if I will say no to the mother superior. I cannot come to the window for fear of punishment. In three weeks, I will be heading to Avila. Yours, Ariadna."

Lorenzo became excited as he read the communication and decided to prevent her carriage reaching Avila. He would not lose his beloved again.

On the day of her departure, he took a sword, and as soon as they opened Alphonso VI´s Gate, he waited on the road to Torrijos.

Several wagons passed by until he determined which carriage carried his beloved. Lorenzo stopped the driver.

"Sir, this carriage does not carry jewelry, nor money!" Only religious women," the frightened driver told him.

"Take it easy, good man. I am not here to rob you. I just want to see one of your passengers. Ariadna!" he shouted.

Ariadna's heart was pounding. Without thinking twice, she left the carriage. Their souls rejoiced to be with one another again. Nothing had changed.

"This is the temptation that wants to take you out of your religious path," the mother superior shouted.

"Mother, this is beyond your understanding," she replied.

"Return to the carriage, Ariadna! How are you going to survive outside the convent?"

"I have suppressed this feeling for too many years. I know that my destiny is not in a cloistered convent. My path lies with this man."

"You will regret this decision! If you leave now, we will close the doors of the convent forever," the mother superior warned her.

"I will take that risk."

Her courage impressed Lorenzo. The mother superior, spiteful, ordered the driver to continue on to Avila, and the lovers stood before each other, overjoyed. Their faces were shining. They communed heart to heart, without the need to speak. Lorenzo and Ariadna returned to Toledo, walking calmly. They did not walk close to each other, since it was not acceptable that a nun walked with a gentleman. He took her to his favorite place in the valley. They hid, and Lorenzo kissed her, making sure they were not seen. He felt awkward being with a woman dressed in a nun's habit.

"We must buy you new clothes," he whispered.

"That is right, I will not wear this habit anymore. I will need time to get accustomed to my new life. You must be patient with me," Ariadna said, smiling.

They remained absorbed in one another until midnight, when they looked up at the sky.

"That star is you, and that one is me," Lorenzo said, pointing out the two bright stars. "The two stars will join and will become a brighter star," Lorenzo understood that they had been destined before they were born.

"We must be married soon."

"Are you proposing?" he said smiling. "My room is small, but I will sleep on the floor, and you on my bed."

Lorenzo could not believe his dream lover was with him. Her harmony and calm demeanor were extraordinary. The spiritual discipline he had developed over the years, allowed him to see her special light. He was blessed to be with her.

In that happy state, they passed the next months. It was the meeting of mature souls after a long separation.

"I have a special person who could marry us. He is my spiritual tutor," Lorenzo said.

"Are you friends with a priest?" Ariadna asked, still unaware Lorenzo belonged to a spiritual group.

He did not answer her question, as he was worried that she might not agree with his participation in the spiritual group. He knew if Ariadna did not approve of his path, they could not be together; Lorenzo had a spiritual destiny to fulfill and was determined to do so, even if he had to spend the rest of his life alone. Life could not be so unfair as to put him in this kind of predicament: to choose between the woman he loved and his spiritual path.

"Ariadna, there is something you should know before we marry," he said when he found the courage to speak.

"Would Lorenzo end this relationship? Was he married? Did he have another woman somewhere else?" she wondered, frightened.

After a long silence, Lorenzo explained himself.

"I am a member of a group of seekers after spiritual knowledge."

Ariadna could not imagine anything like that, and breathed a sigh of relief. She knew Lorenzo was different and wiser than others. She also had noticed he had not attended mass since they met in Toledo.

"Tell me more," she asked.

Lorenzo spoke, weighing his words carefully.

"The group I attend is spiritual, and it helps us to become aware of the presence of God, Who in fact is within us. Our goal is to be in union with the Holy One, as monks and nuns do, but living in the city."

Ariadna did not know what to say. She thought a life dedicated to God could only take place in monastery cloister. Was Lorenzo a heretic?"

Lorenzo tried to calm her.

"The group has helped me mature, and thanks to them I have found a job helping to translate books at the court."

Ariadna did not know what to say, so Lorenzo decided to introduce her to Abraham. In their meeting, Abraham was considerate with her and treated with great reverence.

"Good afternoon," Abraham said, sensing someone invisible behind Ariadna.

"Good afternoon," she answered, serene in front of the wise man.

Abraham gave Lorenzo a slight nod of approval. This allowed him to breathe easier and the evening was delightful. While they shared food, the soul of Ariadna realized that Abraham was a man of deep wisdom. Abraham's demeanor captivated her. She had never met such a human being, and her doubts vanished.

After that meeting, which they would remember the rest of their lives, the lovers, holding hands, took a walk around the Jewish quarter of Toledo. They were in their own world. Lorenzo heard his inner voice, "What are you waiting to marry her?" and he proposed to her. She answered with the most beautiful smile. Lorenzo went back to speak to Abraham.

"I am in love with her, I have been since the first moment I saw her," Lorenzo told him.

"You two belong together. No question about it"

"Would you marry us?"

"Of course, this woman will support and help you."

Following the New Moon in May, Abraham married them. And they asked the guests to be fully aware during the ceremony, so the Holy Spirit could descend upon them. Ariadna radiated a brilliant light, and the witnesses, both from the visible and invisible worlds, applauded and blessed the marriage.

Ariadna also asked Lorenzo to have a religious ceremony. The lovers went to see his friend Julian and asked him to conduct the wedding, but before doing so, he warned Lorenzo.

"Lorenzo, the bishop is asking about you all the time. He is obsessed with you. Watch out!

"Thank you for the warning, my dear friend. I am not doing anything wrong,"

"The Church is putting pressure on the king. They want him to approve the new code of laws following the ecclesiastic dictates, so they can persecute whoever does not conform to their form of Christianity," Julian added.

"I do not want to worry about that. This is Ariadna, my love, my beloved," Lorenzo said.

"I can see by the way you look at each other. You wish to be married, yes?

A few days later, Julian married them in the Church, and they spent ten days in the castle of Almonacid, gifted by Don Isaac as a wedding present. The lovers enjoyed each other where Lorenzo had met Abraham for the first time. Lorenzo was in a palace with his princess! His dreams had come true. He was the happiest man alive.

Once they returned to Toledo, Yehuda ben Moshe spoke to Lorenzo to invite him to meet the king.

"Dress in your best suit, and come with us to the meeting. Pay very close attention. Alphonso is unpredictable."

The king received the astrologers with great reverence, and when he noticed a new face among them, he spoke with him.

"You work with Metolitolah, correct?" he asked him.

"That is right, your Majesty. I help him organize the books," Lorenzo answered shyly.

"Lorenzo is also a great astrologer," Yehuda ben Moshe said.

"Welcome. Let us talk about a matter that worries me. I am

already King of Romans, proclaimed by the Pisa Embassy. However, the pope has not named me emperor yet. What are the stars saying about that?"

"Our advice, your Majesty, is that you focus on Castile, and be an example to the rest of Europe. Providence will grant you that title, if God wants," Yehuda said.

"It is my destiny to be emperor, and I will be! It is my right to be!" the king proclaimed, unaware he was a serious threat for the Roman Church.

"Your Majesty, we have seen in your horoscope that someone may betray you."

"Nonsense. Betray me? Impossible! Everyone loves me, the noblemen, the foreigners, my brothers…" the king answered, ignoring the true intentions of his close relatives.

During the meeting, Lorenzo noted the monarch's obsession to become emperor, and sensed disaster coming to Castile. The king no longer listened to advice, and spent large sums of money hosting ambassadors, and important people such Brunetto Latini, from Florence, the tutor of Dante Alighieri. Lorenzo remembered his premonitory dream before arriving in Toledo, and worried.

Lorenzo also had to take on new responsibilities in his spiritual life. Abraham knew his life was ending. Lorenzo´s tutor had plant a spiritual seed that had fructified. After watering for his whole life, the seed had become a spiritual school. In Castile, however, it was necessary to plant new seeds.

"Lorenzo, you have become matured. Your marriage, your work as a translator and as an adviser to the king is a proof of that. It is time you start teaching what you have learned. Start your own spiritual group."

"Me? But I do not know how to teach," he answered overwhelmed and flattered by his teacher's trust. "What can I teach?"

"There are people in need of spiritual instruction. Teaching is the way to learn. Your wife will provide you with the necessary support," Abraham said,

"And how can I start a group?"

"Start with a few people, where you live. I will announce that a new group is starting."

"But my place is very small," he replied.

"Do not worry. The people who want to explore the spiritual dimensions will find you. If too many people join, Heaven will provide a bigger space."

Abraham also warned Lorenzo that some people would come with the wrong motives, attracted by the spiritual light. He explained that many people, who fail to find success in the work life, try to occupy an important position in a spiritual organization.

"Ariadna, Abraham has asked me to start my own spiritual group," he said.

"And where are you going to do it?" she asked him.

"Here, in our little room."

"In our place. It is very small".

"Our mission is to serve. It will be a blessing for us the Holy Spirit to descend here."

During the months that followed, thanks to Providence, his hard work, seriousness, and Abraham's support, a dozen people came. It was a good omen. Lorenzo guided them humbly, and modestly. Abraham knew his new task would cause envy in some, and warned about the tests that every spiritual teacher must face.

Meanwhile, Lorenzo's fame as the king's adviser grew. It reached the ears of the bishop, who sent a cleric to follow him. The spy informed the bishop about the group Lorenzo ran in his home.

"You are mine. I knew you were a heretic and I am going to expose you," the bishop told himself. He was determined to finish him. The bishop became, in fact, the main opposition to the spiritual task Lorenzo was called to do.

33. EMPTINESS

*L*orenzo achieved much more than he had ever dreamed of doing. He was a member of an advanced spiritual group, he worked at the Royal Court as a translator, he was an adviser to the king, and was married to the woman he loved. Many people praised him, but his success also awakened the attention of the destructive forces, who lie in wait for people in their best moments. A painful emptiness over took him. It was the oppositional force, which wanted to destroy him.

Lorenzo continued to take part in daily life as though everything was fine, although it took a great effort to hide his negative emotions during the meetings with the king.

"I am considering launching an attack on Aragon," the king said coyly.

"Your Majesty, a war against Aragon would be disastrous. After conquering Seville, it would be better to advance towards the Puerto de las Salinas, Cadiz, and the Kingdom of Granada," a Christian astrologer from Seville advised him.

"King Muhammed I is my friend and pays much needed tribute. I will not attack Granada while he is the king."

"With the support of Rome and Aragon, you could strike the final blow and finish off the Arab lands on the Iberian Peninsula," the Sevillano added.

"I will ask the king of Granada a higher tribute. He will also have to cede Tarifa and Gibraltar. He cannot refuse. My plan is to cross the Strait of Gibraltar and launch a crusade in Africa!" proclaimed the king.

Lorenzo hardly took part in the meeting. He felt as though life was not worth living. He did not know why he was dying in what should be the most fulfilling time of his life. It was the bishop's sinister energy, focused on him, that generated these emotions. Even while translating, he made several serious errors, for which he was reprimanded. He also began to neglect his wife. Abraham noticed something was wrong with Lorenzo, and had a talk with him.

"Lorenzo, I have met with Metolitolah. He has told me there is something not right with you, it seems you are not present."

"I don't know what the matter is. I am unable to concentrate and I feel like an impostor," he replied.

"I see," said Abraham after sitting quietly for a few moments. "This is an important time in your life, in which a part of you is dying and trying to destroy the rest of you."

"What can I do?"

"Be aware the negative energy and how it is affecting you. When we start to guide others, these things happen. The oppositional forces pay special attention to spiritual tutors."

Lorenzo was not aware when someone becomes a spiritual teacher, he is more intensely tested. Providence needs reliable tutors who are able to face, with dignity, life's difficulties. Even Ariadna, in her convent, saw several nuns who lost their way in similar situations. Lorenzo prayed to God, but the dryness of his heart did not allow the connexion. It was as if God had disappeared from his life.

"Where are you?" Abraham asked him in a group meeting.

Lorenzo, off in his own world, only mumbled a response

"He is thinking humanity's lofty destiny," Abraham joked, provoking laughter in the rest of the group.

For the first time Lorenzo became angry with Abraham. He thought his teacher did not understand him, unaware Abraham had also undergone the same test. Benjamin, the poet, spoke with Lorenzo once the session had ended,

"Becoming angry is useless, but becoming angry with your spiritual tutor is the most foolish thing you can do. We all do stupid things in our lives, because we are human. The question is for how long do we keep repeating them."

Meanwhile, at the royal court, the monarch spent most of the resources on his African crusade and he reduced the amount allocated to the translators. In exchange, the king promised them land in the future African Kingdom. Lorenzo's income was already minimal, and acquiring land in Africa, was not an attractive proposition.

"Why am I following this spiritual way?" he asked himself, devastated.

His wife, due her experience in the convent, knew the best thing was to let her husband go through his existential crisis. She knew her task was to accompany him in his process. Lorenzo often cried during that period, without knowing the reason.

"What is happening to me? Does this make sense? Why don't I just die and go back to where I come from?" he tormented himself.

Deep within himself, Lorenzo knew he had to face the forces that wanted to block his progress, but confronting them frightened him. This unspoken fear caused him to avoid rather than accepting the responsibility of his new life.

One day, walking near the Pozo Amargo in Toledo, he saw his face reflected in the water of a well. He cried for no reason, in the place where a Christian had died of a broken heart from not being able to marry the Jewish girl he loved. The Jewess, trying to see the reflection of her beloved in the water, fell herself into the well. Since then, the water is as bitter as the Jewess's tears; and such was Lorenzo´s state of mind at that moment.

"Lorenzo, you are making great progress. Our mission is to return to the source, but not with apathy or negligence. Our task is to become fully conscious self-realized beings," his tutor told him.

"Yes, but nothing makes sense."

"That is the influence of the negative forces that try take us over. They provoke that pain."

"Then, what can I do?" he asked.

"Keep still, and pray for the strength to face that force. You are transitioning towards your new life."

"I have even thought about destroying everything, dear Abraham," Lorenzo confessed.

"Ascend to the spiritual realms to perceive the situation with greater clarity. Once you are no longer melancholic, you will be able to help other people. If you work on yourself, your presence will create harmony around you. This is your wife's situation, who is more mature than you."

"But how I can help others, if I cannot help myself?"

"How you are already doing it. Through your translations, and passing on the Teaching; in other words, helping those who come to you, as you are doing with your home group. This is how you contribute towards keeping the Tradition's flame lit."

"Is my job so important?"

"Yes. There are two parts to the Teaching: written and oral. With translating the books you help the written transmission. With your group, you help the oral transmission."

"Yes, but many people can do that job."

"There are always others who can perform a specific spiritual duty. Without being conscious, you have received a specific training for your role. In addition, the Jewish community is going to go through difficult times during the next few decades. The Christians will blame us for bankrupting the kingdom. It will be difficult for the Jewish community to continue passing on the Tradition. They will attack us. It will be easier for you, as a Christian. Although you must be very discrete," his tutor said.

"Then, was I born a Christian for a specific reason?"

"Of course. It is not a coincidence. But Christian, Jewish, or Arab, if you live in accordance with the Principles, you will live according to the Teaching."

"And if I refuse to continue," Lorenzo asked Abraham, testing his teacher.

"That is your decision, although you would be closing a door that has been opened for you so you could take a further step further in your evolution as a human being," Abraham answered.

The conversation with his tutor calmed him, and allowed him to see life with more optimism. His teacher's words became a source of strength for him. He knew he was right contributing to humanity's evolution. That idea renewed his hope. He asked for his wife's forgiveness for his inattentiveness, and from Abraham for being angry with him.

For the sake of the people near him, Lorenzo moved beyond the hopeless phase, wiser than before. He decided to dedicate body and soul to his spiritual path, and to use his talents in the correct way.

His astrologer companions noticed the improvement and they commissioned him to organize an event tied to the "Book of the Crosses." The book explained the influence of the stars and planets on earthly matters. The treatise described the three astrological methods used by the Arabs, which emphasized the importance of Saturn's position in the sky.

King Alphonso and his wife Violante chaired the event. Most of the Castilian noblemen, the military, ecclesiastics, and scientists attended. To begin the event the minstrels presented their comedies, the jugglers played popular tunes, and the poets recited poems to the Virgin. The king also performed religious songs that he had composed. Then, Yehuda ben Moshe took the floor and read from his prologue,

"Our Lord, and very noble King Don Alphonso, to whom God gave intelligence, knowledge, and understanding above the princes of his time. The Grace of God, from whom all things come, has given Alphonse the task of recovering lost studies, and for that reason God has shown his divine purpose in having him reign over the Earth."

After the speech, everyone praised the king of Castile. They knew the monarch was fulfilling the mission in translating the books of knowledge and sharing them with his subjects. He was making accessible to all the knowledge from scholastic elites, who had held on to them for centuries.

The party continued with beautiful courtesans, performing their courtly dances.

Nevertheless, the king could not enjoy the evening. Richard of Cornwall had proclaimed himself emperor, without the authorization of the pope. Alphonso, ballistic, called the astrologers to meet in private.

"Richard of Cornwall, who is not even a king, has dared to

proclaim himself emperor! The new pope had this promised to me!

The astrologers were speechless. They knew the king should not seek the title, but they were also aware of Alphonso's fixation.

"I am going to break the alliance with England!"

"Your Majesty, your life task is translating books. Do not worry about titles. Your spiritual mission is to complete the cultural work you are already performing," Yehuda ben Moshe said, trying to calm the king.

"The earthly title granted by the pope has no value in heaven. You already have worldly recognition," Lorenzo, shocked by the king's petulance, said.

Lorenzo called the minstrels to sing one of Alphonso favorites songs. It was a religious song composed by the king, dedicated to the miracles of the Virgin Mary. In the song, his beloved sister, the nun Berenguela, was mentioned. Lorenzo´s idea did not soothe him.

"I will immediately start a crusade against the Arabs! I will demonstrate to the world that I can defeat the Arab enemy on my own! They need to know who deserves to be emperor!

"Your Majesty, Castile is already in war against the Arab kingdoms of the Peninsula. If you announce a crusade, the king of Granada will be forced to ask for help to the emir of Morocco," Yehuda warned, after pondering for a few moments.

"The King of Granada will never betray me! First, I will conquer Cadiz and Niebla, and then I will defeat the North African Arab kingdoms! The Arabs will surrender when they realize I am going to conquer African lands!" Alphonso proclaimed in his crazed state of mind.

Lorenzo was concerned about the king's agitated state. While Lorenzo was pondering the consequences of the king´s intention, the bishop of Toledo came to talk to him.

"I understand that people come to your house with heretical purposes," the prelate told him.

"No, sir," Lorenzo said surprised of the accusation.

"We have finished with the Cathars in France. Now we are going to exterminate groups who think they can live outside the Church."

"We all have the right to be in the presence of God," he dared to say.

"I am watching you, Lorenzo Diaz. You cannot fool me. I know you are a heretic and a coward for escaping from the monastery of Cuenca."

Lorenzo realized someone was spying on him. When he arrived home, he panicked. Ariadna calmed him down.

"You are doing nothing wrong. People who come to your group want to be in the presence of God. Your mission is more Christian than what many people in the church experience."

"I am worried. Not only do we have to survive with little money, but now the bishop is spying on us and seeks to destroy us. I am not sure if it is all worth it."

"Have faith. God will help us," Ariadna said, supporting him.

He knew Ariadna was right. To teach the Unity of God and the possibility of a direct encounter with the Lord, beyond the political and religious structures was a praiseworthy task.

Lorenzo was in the sights of those who held religious power. He could not face them alone. The heavens decided to help him and open a new door along his way.

34. GUIDANCE

$\mathcal{S}$lowly, the shock of the meeting with the bishop faded away. Lorenzo focused on ordering books on history of Hispania. One of the works fell to the floor, and opened at the page, which explained the life of a former bishop of Avila. The priest, who lived in the Fourth Century, was a son of a noble family of Galicia and his name was Priscilian. He was a priest, who opposed ecclesiastic corruption, and believed that the Word of God should be available to everyone.

Priscilian, who thought the Church could not be the only interpreter of the Scriptures, organized private meetings which he allowed women and slaves to attend. He taught astrology, the Bible, and spoke about the relationship between God and human beings. His followers recognized something special in him, and his fame grew, creating envy in his Hispanic bishops, who put him on trial for heresy and sorcery. Priscilian went to Bordeaux to defend himself, but a fanatical mob stoned one of his followers and after a mock trial in Treveris, they decapitated him.

Pricilian consecrated his life to God, and experienced much opposition. Maintaining the purity of the spiritual Teaching, while preaching against the opulence and autocratic methods of the clergy cost him his life.

His followers kept secretly preaching Pricilian's teachings in Leon and Castile, and the bishop's influence continued for several more centuries. Upon reading the story, Lorenzo noticed many similarities between the teachings of Abraham and Priscilian, although there were eight centuries separating them.

"How little things have changed since then," Lorenzo thought.

One day Abraham suggested an exercise to his students. They had to take a walk trying to be conscious of each movement and they were to sit at a high place and contemplate the panorama of the city, watching the scenes unfolding before them.

Lorenzo sensed a presence walking along with him during his walk.

"Abraham, I have sensed a friendly presence near me when I walked."

"He is your invisible guide," Abraham assured him.

"My guide? Do I have a guide? Can I see him?"

"Yes, but only when you are ready. The light of the guides is intense and it can produce an overwhelming impact on your mind," he answered, knowing the difficulty of escaping the social conditioning that determines how we view reality. It is always difficult to accept the existence of invisible guides.

"And what do I need to do to see him?"

"Go into a profound silence and raise your consciousness," Abraham explained.

"And, are the guides always there?"

"We all have a personal guide who sends us signs. No one is left alone, but freewill is always respected. The problem is, some people, despite seeing the signs, do not follow them, and decide to live life in the shadows. Also, depending on your job, a specific guide can help you with a specific task."

"During my walking pilgrimage from Teruel to Toledo I felt that other presences were walking with me. Who were they?"

"They were disembodied beings following you. They were lost and wanted to make the transit to the upper worlds in Toledo. You did a good job helping them, even thought you were not aware of how you helped them."

After talking with Abraham, Lorenzo visited his favorite place in Toledo´s valley. He contemplated the river and the city. He entered into a profoundly calm state. Suddenly he felt the strong familiar presence.

"Is anyone here?" he asked.

"I am your guide," his invisible mentor answered, although Lorenzo was not able to hear clearly.

Lorenzo told Abraham what had happened. His tutor did not want him to force things; these types of experiences could cause a nervous breakdown. He told him to wait for the right moment.

"When you enter a meditative state, pay attention. If you cannot communicate with him, do not become frustrated. Forcing the meeting can make you mad," Abraham warned him.

That night, while meditating, Lorenzo asked his spirit guide to come to him. Lorenzo was excited and could not concentrate. The guide, sensing his excitement did not reveal himself.

The next day, in a calmer state, Lorenzo went walking, with the book of the bishop in his hands. Near the Tajo River country houses, he felt the presence again. With his eyes half-opened, he saw a wispy figure.

"Is anyone here? Who are you?" he asked, feeling a strong ringing in his ears, making visible contact with the figure from another dimension.

"Priscilian," the guide said, although Lorenzo could not hear him well.

Lorenzo opened the book by a random page. For his astonishment, he read the name of the bishop of Avila. He knew he was with him.

"Where are you from?" he asked to confirm what his instinct told him.

"I am from Galicia and I was the bishop of Avila," the figure answered him, as it slowly became visible.

"Are you my guide?

"Yes, I am here to help you in this life," he answered.

"Have we known each other before?" Lorenzo asked, thinking he was going mad.

"I have been with you for several lives; in some of them, you strayed from the path, and in others we worked well together. I am with you again during this life."

Lorenzo, overwhelmed by the solemnity of the moment, felt dizzy. His guide terminated the encounter. Lorenzo needed to calm himself down.

"That is enough for now. You can communicate with me anytime you wish," he told him, leaving quietly, so Lorenzo could assimilate the experience.

Lorenzo came back to reality on the mountains. He wondered if he was mad, and if what he saw was real. His inner voice confirmed him that it was, although he could not find a rational explanation for the event. Meeting his guide broadened his spiritual horizons. Now he had a substantial proof that he was not alone: someone from the spiritual world was interested in his spiritual growth.

He told his wife about his experience who, although she had not made a visible contact with her particular guide, knew Lorenzo was speaking truth. The most devoted sisters of her convent had had similar experiences. When Lorenzo told Abraham what happened, he gave him some advice:

"Now you may contact your maggid, which is how we call the guide. When you were little you had a connection with him, but during your childhood, you blocked the connection, although he was always close to you. Now can renew the bond."

"Yes, when I was young I knew I was connected to other beings. I remember a voice saved my life me when my parent's house caught fire."

Abraham did not want to give too much importance to Lorenzo's contact with the spiritual guide, and gave him some advice:

"You are not any more special for having a visual connection with your guide. This does not remove any of your responsibility; on the other hand, it increases it. It is even possible that you will face greater difficulties."

Lorenzo became accustomed to the conversations with his maggid. As he meditated, the communication channel with his guide was more open, and he received clearer answers.

Meanwhile, in the kingdom, the economic, social, and political situation became more complicated. Alphonso X started his personal African crusade, wasting the kingdom's resources, sending both soldiers and clerics into battle, and transferring the court to Seville for a short while.

"The king no longer trusts us. He has told me to focus on my translations and nothing else. He has other advisers now," Yehuda ben Moshe told the group of astrologers.

"The king trusts you. You are one of his most respected men. Do not worry. He wants to prove the Europeans that he can conquer the Islam on his own," Lorenzo told Yehuda trying to get some perspective on the situation.

"I know, but I am his private doctor, and he has changed. The lust for power has overtaken him. He was never this arrogant before."

"The king has borrowed heavily from Don Isaac to finance his crusade, and the financier could not say no. Things are reaching a climax," the Jewish astrologer said.

In Abraham's group, there were also upsetting influences. After a meeting, Lorenzo saw several people from the group talking in the main street of the Jewish quarter. One of them was an ex-Jewish lawyer, named John of Sicily, who converted to Christianity to obtain a notable position in the court. The lawyer helped to draft new unfavorable laws against non-Christians.

Lorenzo found out he was leading a secret group, and he charged his students large amounts. Abraham had accepted him in the group, believing he had a real interest in a true spiritual path, but recently, he was posing many questions to test his tutor. Lorenzo wondered why Abraham allowed him to continue attending the meetings since it was obvious that the lawyer's goal was to take Abraham's place and take advantage of his efforts.

John of Sicily was secretly undermining the wise man's reputation.

"Abraham is wrong. He repeats things and he is boring. There are more knowledgeable groups in Toledo," he said behind Abraham´s back to new members of the group.

"Really?"

"Yes, in my school, we teach real knowledge. Why don´t you

come by?" he shamelessly invited them.

The lawyer wanted to steal good students from Abraham´s group and have them joined his group. John wanted to feel a sensation of power, by taking advantage of the student's naiveté. He did not want to help them to be free, on the contrary, his intention was to enslave them.

"Abraham is old and unaware of the newer teachings," Lorenzo overheard him say.

Worried about the corrosive tactics of the Sicilian, Lorenzo spoke discreetly with Yehuda ben Moshe.

"Yehuda, it seems that there is another group within Abraham´s group."

Yehuda, who was not aware of that matter, paid great attention to Lorenzo's words. It could be a serious thing.

"But probably Abraham is already aware of what John of Sicily is doing," Lorenzo continued.

"I am sure about it," Yehuda answered, getting the subtle message.

In the next session, Abraham explained the consequences of our choices on our incarnations.

"Reincarnation is the process by which human beings may raise consciousness, life after life."

"Nonsense. We are all predetermined!" John of Sicily exploded.

"And who has predetermined you? dear friend John" Abraham asked.

The Sicilian started babbling, not knowing what to say, exposing himself.

"Let us stop this nonsense! I have been listening to your foolishness for years!

"Nobody forces you to stay here. You are free to leave," Abraham continued calmly.

"Some people here think as I do! In my school, we deal with important matters and not with crazy stuff!

John of Sicily left, urging the rest to follow him. About one third of the people, to Abraham´s dismay, stood up and left with him. Abraham watched how they closed the doors to the spiritual worlds. Lorenzo was even more surprised: Abraham had changed his life and did not understand how someone could act in such a way. He asked God that John of Sicily did not harm anyone.

When the session finished, Abraham talked to Lorenzo.

"Thanks for warning Yehuda. These kind of things often happen in spiritual groups. It is the forces opposed to the Tradition that want to lead the students astray. It is a test for everyone."

Lorenzo never expected that type of betrayal in a spiritual group. Priscilian also affirmed what had happened during his life.

"The way I died, martyred, was an example. The truth had to prevail. That is why I accepted my destiny," Lorenzo heard from his guide.

"And the Teaching was the same before?"

"The principles are similar, since they come from the same source, but the way they are expressed is different. I lived in a Celtic culture, with Greco-Roman influences; therefore, we expressed the Teaching accordingly. In my age, we linked the Teaching to rituals related to earth and nature."

"And now in Castile?"

"Now life is more refined, based on Judeo-Christian culture, with Arab and Greek influences. It is great what is happening in Toledo. The degree of refinement is exceptional. Abraham's group expresses the principles exquisitely."

Abraham pondered the group's situation after John of Sicily's rebellion. He knew his cycle was coming to an end, and was worried about the situation in Castile. In a meditation, his guides revealed very significant information.

"The kingdom of Castile is at a critical point, and it will stagnate during the next three generations. Afterward, the Castilians and Aragons will have another opportunity to lead the world, if they heed their lessons," Abraham heard.

Indeed, the situation was worrisome. The kingdom was bankrupt due to the constant waste. The nobleman intrigued against the king, and the monarch was obsessed with his unnecessary crusade. It took nine months, much more time of what Alphonso had expected, to conquer the small kingdom of Niebla. His attack on Sale, a small town in the north of Africa, was also a disaster. The pope and the Christian European kings criticized him severely. The attack on Sale was on Ramadan, and it turned out a brutal pillaging of a defenseless city.

Reviewing the dangerous situation, Abraham received new advice from his guides.

"We must plant seeds in other places, so the Tradition can continue. Evolved men should depart to other kingdoms."

"What is going to happen in Toledo?" Abraham asked.

"In the future, it will not be the spiritual center of humanity. Even so, there are many years of plenty ahead. The translations themselves are of great importance."

Confirming what his guides told him, Abraham received a

letter from Nahmanides, the rabbi of Gerona. He explained the reason why he had been exiled; his arguments on a theological dispute in Barcelona were considered heretical. Nahmanides was forced to leave the kingdom, although King James compensated him well for his debating skills. Abraham was aware the exile of that extraordinary human being was part of the divine plan. That also confirmed his cycle as a teacher was about to end. Abraham would end it harmoniously, after preparing his students to follow the Tradition.

35. PEACE

*L*orenzo often spoke with his maggid. The conversations helped him to discover their reasons behind several events of his life. One time, he received the following message:

"You need to explore your past lives," he heard to his surprise, from his invisible guide.

"My past lives?"

"The soul has memories of past lives, especially if the events were dramatic or intense. We cannot understand many of our current situations if we only consider our present life. Previous lives contain valuable lessons."

Priscilian took him on a trip using his imagination, to a room full of books. Each book represented a past life. Lorenzo took down one of the books at random, and read the life of a ship captain in China. He knew it was himself in a past life. Another book was about a monk in Rila, Bulgaria.

"Each life has a specific lesson for us to learn," he heard from Priscilian.

Lorenzo was curious about the last book on the shelf. It told the story of a man in the Danish Court. He was the spiritual adviser of King Valdemar the Great. During that life, instead of fulfilling his mission, he wasted his time in seducing lovely courtesans. They shortened his life to prevent him from doing more damage. While he read the story of that life, Lorenzo felt a strong pain in his chest.

"Why do I feel this pain?" he asked his maggid.

"The pain is related to that life's lesson. Once you have learned the lesson, and acknowledged the mistake, the pain will go away."

That night a large bruise appeared near his sternum. He dreamed he was with a beautiful Danish lady. Lorenzo had left the woman pregnant, and had failed to accept responsibility for the baby. The child died from a serious illness. During the days that followed, the pain became unbearable; he experienced the torment he had caused the lady and her son. He asked for forgiveness, and after a week had passed, so had the bruising and the pain, healing the actions of that past life.

Lorenzo also reviewed other previous lives. Some of them brought him very pleasing memories. For example, in Tuscany, he saved a mother and a daughter from a murderer, putting his own life at risk; he was justly rewarded for that. One after another, he healed his lives until he had cleansed his emotional realm.

"It is enough. Healing past lives is all right, but it is more important what you do in this one. After each life, we go through a process of recapitulation that helps the cleaning process."

Lorenzo felt lighter. He was shining without intending to.

Abraham, on his part, initiated the process to put an end to his cycle. His guides rewarded him for fulfilling his mission. His physical body was not working as well as before, and his time was about to end. He organized a farewell gathering.

"We must prepare a special meeting in the castle of Huete. Talk with Don Isaac, and ask him to speak to the Lara family about using the palace," Abraham asked Lorenzo.

The members of the group set off for Huete to attend the event. When he arrived at the Duke's Palace, Lorenzo remembered his time there as a minstrel; the kind of happiness he felt now was more profound and lasting, compared with the temporary satisfaction of his sporadic romances. The housekeeper gave Lorenzo white clothes and a letter with instructions; he should keep quiet, trying to be in a contemplative state to receive the Grace of God during the encounter.

After greeting each other, they went to castle of Huete to participate in the sessions, which lasted for several days. During the day, they pondered on how the actions of Providence, had brought them to this meeting. At the end of the day, Lorenzo felt an immense compassion and love for his soul companions.

They also shared mystical poetry. Benjamin recited, accompanied by the music, several mystical poems such as "Keter-Malkuth" composed by Ibn Gabirol. The attendants were very awake during the recitations. Lorenzo felt the Divine Presence alive within.

"To reach that state is not difficult. Everybody can reach it. The difficulty is to keep yourself in that state of higher awareness," Abraham told them, while his eyes shone brighter than ever.

Lorenzo held onto the consciousness of the Presence the whole evening. During the night he dreamed that he walked along a path. At the end of the road, he stood before an arch. God spoke to him like a friend.

"Lorenzo, I am with you, although you might live through difficult times, you will receive the assistance you need."

God blessed him and he woke up feeling extremely peaceful.

"Some dreams offer an extraordinary source of revelation," Abraham explained after listening to Lorenzo´s dream.

On another day, they held an exercise of personal observation. The students who were too expansive had to plan, and apply discernment in their lives; on the contrary, the more severe people, who tended to judge others, needed to cultivate more compassion and mercy. At the end of the day, they shared food like brothers.

To close the event, they had a farewell ceremony, which also was an initiation ritual for each of them. Abraham blessed everyone. The ceremony ended his cycle. Lorenzo embraced him, thanking him for all the years he had dedicated to the Tradition. He was at peace in the presence of such a developed human being, who had changed his life. Abraham invited everyone to remember the event as a special landmark on their paths to self-realization.

Lorenzo returned to Toledo in a state of inner silence. During his return trip, he had a vision that Abraham would die soon. He had never thought about that possibility. He trembled thinking about being on his own, without his main spiritual reference point, but he knew it was not right to force Abraham to stay more time than he had set.

During the days preceding Yom Kippur, his guides told Abraham he was going to leave in a few months. He prepared himself with great care for his transit, with profound peace filled meditations. During his last weeks, his light was brilliant. He had reached a fully enlightened state! He embodied the divine qualities. Before he passed away, he told his students they should be a reference for people on the same path. He also met with Lorenzo.

"Lorenzo, there are difficult times ahead for the Castilian Jews. There will be obstacles to the Teaching," he said with a worried tone in his voice.

"But there are already many groups of knowledge who are already passing it on, in Guadalajara, Burgos, Avila, and Segovia," Lorenzo answered.

"Yes, but there is great chaos in Castile. The structure of the kingdom is collapsing, and they will blame the Jewish. In addition, some of my richest compatriots are taking advantage of the chaos, corrupted by luxury and richness."

"Is the situation so serious?"

"Yes, the Jewish communities are getting weak by the constant excommunications among the rabbis. They are disputing over faith and reason. Also, several rabbis are breaking the principles," Abraham added, worried

"Then, what can I do?"

"Work honestly to keep the flame of Tradition lit. Wait until better times come. You will get help from within."

"Thank you very much for your trust in me. I am not sure if I am worthy of it," Lorenzo said, deeply touched.

The last moments of that meeting were beyond words. While silence prevailed in that eternal moment, both recognized each other as human and divine beings.

Lorenzo knew the way someone died was a sign of how they lived their life.

A few weeks later Abraham passed away. Due to his exceptional spiritual work, his transition was noble. Without any pain, in complete awareness, he left from his body with dignity. He was also an example during his process of death. Abraham had dedicated his life to helping the evolution of humanity. He was one of the Just of his time!

During the following days, Abraham met several people in his ethereal body, to say good-bye to them. He visited Lorenzo in his dreams. He told him of the extraordinary happiness and freedom of the other realms, without being limited by the physical body. In those unforgettable vivid dreams, Lorenzo said good-bye to that extraordinary human being; he realized how fortunate he had been to share part of his time.

The death of Abraham meant a great transformation in his students. They had to take on new responsibilities. Even so, unknown forces in Abraham´s group came to light. Some members tried to takeover Abraham´s position. Astonished, Lorenzo watched in silence as several members positioned themselves to take on Abraham´s leadership role. He felt sorry for them that they had forgotten that the objective of the group was to serve others. After an inner power struggle, Yosef Barchillon, who had been with Abraham for more than ten years, convinced the rest of the group members he should be the new leader. Yosef preferred not to start his spiritual group from ground zero, since that was an arduous task. It was easier to occupy Abraham's vacant position.

Soon after he died, Abraham paid a visit to his group. He shook his head when he saw how Yosef put himself in front, without being worthy of the position. The most sensitive members sensed Abraham´s presence and his annoyance. Nevertheless, Abraham was instructed to leave the room and focus on his own after-life process; it was the group member's responsibility to stop Yosef who, sooner or later, would pay the consequences for his narcissism.

The new tutor attempted to impose new rules. He also told Lorenzo he wanted to oversee his group. Lorenzo, with great diplomacy, denied the request, since not even Abraham had dared to ask such a thing. Since Lorenzo's denial, Yosef considered Lorenzo his enemy and undermined Lorenzo´s reputation. Due to the Yosef's corrosive force, other members of the group began to treat him coldly as well. Lorenzo felt lonely, but tried to look at things with philosophy; he knew the destructive principle had possessed Yosef. He decided to ask direction from Priscilian, and his maggid told him he should watch in silence and learn what not to do.

Yosef attacked Lorenzo, not only with words and gestures, but also with direct psychic attacks. One night, in his dreams, Yosef visited him using forbidden magic. Lorenzo felt a freezing terror when a sinister figure tried to possess his physical body; luckily, a tremendous white light emerged from his heart, and the specter disappeared.

After pondering the situation, Lorenzo realized that he had to grow stronger. He did not reply to the attacks, avoiding a hand-to-hand fight in which everyone would lose. He decided to live with dignity in his isolation, letting silence put things in its proper place. Now Lorenzo, for no reason, had two powerful enemies: Yosef, and the bishop, who kept finding evidence against him.

Meanwhile, Alphonso was losing everything that his father Ferdinand III had achieved during his reign. As his astrologers had predicted, the king of Granada betrayed him. First by refusing to surrender the cities of Tarifa and Gibraltar, he then asked for help from the Muslim kings of North Africa. He also incited the Arab cities of the Peninsula to rise up against Alphonso. The king of Castile, whose wife fled to Aragon, led the attack against the rebels in person and was almost killed in battle. He did not ask the pope for help, since he did not want to jeopardize his chances of becoming emperor.

Alphonso´s army´s emerged victorious; this improved the King´s mood. As soon as he had recovered, he summoned his astrologers,

"Your Majesty, we are old and only want to focus on the astronomic tables that will carry your name. We kindly request to be exempted our roles as astrological advisers," Yehuda ben Moshe and two other Jewish astrologers begged.

"You are exempted. I understand you wish to finish those magnificent works, but, what advice do the other astrologers offer?"

"Your Majesty, maybe it would be wise to put the kingdom's

finances in order," Lorenzo said, surprising everyone else with his nerve.

"I already had it in mind. What else do you see in the horoscope of Castile?"

"Maybe it would be wise to conquer Granada, since the king has betrayed you. Pope Clement IV will support Castile," the Christian astrologer of Seville added, receiving a disapproving look from the king.

"I will not attack him, but I will increase the vassalage for his gross betrayal; instead of one hundred and fifty thousand coins per year, he will pay me two hundred and fifty thousand. I need his money to extinguish the revolt in Alicante."

"Also it would be advantageous to cooperate more with Aragon," the king's clergyman suggested.

"That´s it, Aragon has helped Castile with the revolt in Murcia, and James I, despite inner pressures, honored our treaty. Murcia now belongs to Castile. It is good I did not make an enemy of Aragon," he said looking to Yehuda, thanking him for his advice.

After the meeting, Alphonso called Zag de la Maleha, a wealthy Jew from Cordova, and appointed him as the kingdom's new treasurer.

Yehuda ben Moshe, Don Isaac, and the rabbi Todros warned him, "Zag, be careful in the new role you are undertaking. The kingdom is close to bankruptcy. Watch for the signs. The commercial fair of Medina del Campo was a disaster. The prices of the basic goods keep raising, and there is a great deal of corruption among the privileged classes," Don Isaac warned him.

"I know how to deal with the situation," Zag answered arrogantly.

"You are not aware of the risk you are accepting. You will be responsible for what happens in the kingdom. And, because you are Jewish, they will blame it on us," the rabbi warned him.

"The king has made this request and I will accept the role."

"To be the treasurer of a kingdom in bankruptcy is risky. You expose yourself unnecessarily. You already have a fortune and do not need to take on a public duty. The king is unpredictable," Yehuda warned him.

Zag, ignoring his friends, accepted the offer. Initially, things got better. The new treasurer stopped the robberies of the caravans of vassalage from the Arab kings, and the waste in trivial things in the court. But those were only provisional measures. He needed many more to stop the impending disaster.

The improvement of the economic situation in the kingdom was a propitious moment for Lorenzo to give a present to Ariadna, and celebrate the happy years of their marriage. He suggested to the monarch that he should go to Seville and Cordova to bring him back some books. The king accepted and paid the trip's expenses. Escorted by two royal guards, they headed to Cordova. Lorenzo and Ariadna enjoyed the scenery and the hospitality of the people of Ciudad Real, Las Navas de Tolosa, Linares, and Lucena.

When they arrived in Cordova the beauty of the city amazed them. Centuries before, great rabbinical academies, and schools of knowledge were established there; there were around four hundred thousand books in more than seventy libraries. Abdurrahman III made Cordova, two hundred years before, the most brilliant European city. It outshone Bagdad and Constantinople.

The couple visited the public baths, mosques, and libraries. Lorenzo took with him works of Jewish and Arab philosophers, and books of history written by the Arab chroniclers. Ariadna and Lorenzo visited the Jewish quarter and sensed its greatness, before they had to leave it and travel northward.

The couple journeyed on to Seville, where they had great respect for Alphonso. Lorenzo wished to contemplate the sea at least once in his life, and went to visit Santa Maria del Puerto. He was amazed when he saw the ocean. It was a gift of God. Ariadna and he, holding hands, spent a long time contemplating the waves, feeling an immense peace. Lorenzo tried to hold that image in his memory, and felt a true deep peace, for which he had so long yearned. Now they would need to maintain that elevated state in the busy capital, this only being possible for advanced and balanced souls.

36. PRESSURE

$\mathcal{L}$orenzo watched how the group was developing with great disappointment. Yosef Barchilon made decisions based on the external form of the Teaching, and created rigid rules. He forced everyone to dress in a certain way and to recite sentences in Hebrew without the understanding the true meaning. He also demanded the non-Jewish members to convert to Judaism.

Some of the oldest members discretely left the group, as they did not agree with Yosef's decisions. Lorenzo was not sure if he was right to dissent, although he felt constrained by Yosef's strict rules. In just a short time, Abraham's exceptional group became a military-like regiment, taken over by an impostor. While in a state of deep meditation, Lorenzo received guidance from Priscilian that he should leave the group. With great sorrow, he presented his respects to the Tradition and to the true seekers. He informed Yosef of his decision.

"Leave the group if you wish, but you cannot teach anymore. You do not have authorization to continue with your group," Yosef blurted out.

"You have no authority over me."

"Then, I will use other measures to enforce you."

"I only bow before the Tradition. If I am wrong, Providence will take me off the path," Lorenzo said. He knew that only heavens, after hard personal work, could grant spiritual authority.

Yosef continued his night time psychic attacks against Lorenzo. When he saw how strong Lorenzo's psychological protection was, he focused on Ariadna. He conjured psychic attacks against her during the night. She was upset by the interference on her psyche, which made her question their spiritual path, and the difficulties they were going through.

"This is very different from what I experienced in the convent."

"You were protected there. It was a safe place for you; however, here with so many forces in the city, the learning is extraordinary. The spiritual path is not always a peaceful and loving one. Having to face real forces makes us stronger and provides us with greater knowledge. We can face anything together."

"I hope so, because I am very nervous during the day. My stomach hurts to the point of vomiting," she said.

"Do not worry, my love, God protects us. We only need to get stronger."

"Lorenzo, I am also overwhelmed in this small place. I cannot live like this anymore!"

He calmed his wife down during the night. They shared an amazing meditation and their souls danced together once more in the divine realms. They asked for protection against all evil and God heard them. They felt that God was with them and their anxiety disappeared.

During the next days, they strengthened their physical bodies with long walks. This helped them not only physically but also psychologically. After a few months had passed, Yosef's attacks could no longer annoy them.

Lorenzo met the king and gave him the manuscripts from Seville and Cordova, so the monarch could finish his historical chronicles of Spain and the world; but Alphonso gave him bad news.

"I am cursed by the evil eye. I have hired three new advisers. They will put an end to my curse," he told him with his look fixed on the infinite.

The king introduced him to his three new astrological advisers: a Christian convert from Murcia; a Christian priest who was an expert in exorcisms; and a magician from Naples. Lorenzo could sense a black shadow behind them, who was relishing in the disintegration of the kingdom.

"The priest is going to rid me of the evil eye, and he will exorcise the Castilian evil forces. The bishop highly recommended him," Alphonso exclaimed.

Lorenzo could not believe what he was hearing. He knew that the disastrous influences of the new advisers would destroy the kingdom and bankrupt Castile.

"And what about the other advisers, who have been with you until now?" Lorenzo asked worried about his Jewish friends.

"They will no longer be my advisers."

After meeting with the king, Lorenzo knew his days as an adviser would soon end. The exorcist, friend of the bishop, told him,

"I have heard many things about you. Your references are not good, and heresy is a capital crime."

Lorenzo kept quiet and did not allow himself to be provoked; he knew, in time, the destructive forces that over took the king would manifest.

"Ariadna, we need to live more humbly."

"More? I lived better in the convent."

"Soon I will no longer be one of the king's adviser, the

bishop is hunting me, and one of his friends is the new adviser. In addition, Yosef is attacking us. I am sorry you have to share in my problems, but this is part of my spiritual process."

"Of our process" she asserted, trying to be as consoling as possible. She showed, that in spite of the hardships, she faithfully supported her husband.

Lorenzo knew he was doing the right thing, and he should not be afraid. He knew Providence needed strong people, who were able to face down evil forces. The study group in his house continued to go well. He had the privilege to see the Holy Spirit descend on his home, which gave him energy to continue his work.

Meanwhile, the king received disastrous news: his best friend, Nuño Gonzalez de Lara, whom he had defended on several occasions, convinced the Christian nobility and his bitter enemy Lope Diaz de Haro, to depose the king. The kingdom was in shock. Lorenzo heard a heated discussion in the Lodge of the Blood.

"The noblemen are aligning with the Arab king of Granada and the Arabs are going to fight Alphonso with the help of the Castilian army, although the monarch forgave him and granted him his life after his betrayal!"

"The noblemen do not want to obey the king's rules! They have betrayed the King Alphonso!" a peasant yelled.

Alphonso, devastated, watched helplessly as his kingdom collapsed. After hearing the news, he regretted he did not finish off the Granadan king when he had the opportunity, as the Jewish astrologers suggested. He could not understand the noble's revolt. The new set of laws benefited business, shepherds, and foreigners. They unified the laws of Castile, and everyone would know how to behave in all parts of the kingdom.

"I never expected my best friend's betrayal! Seventeen noblemen and my own brother are against me!" the king complained to his father in law, James I.

"The noblemen waited for the moment of greatest weakness to overthrow the king. That is their nature. They did it with me when I was a child, but I faced them," the monarch of Aragon reminded him.

"Why is this happening to me? I have been good to everyone..."

"You believed you were someone that you were not; and you did not foresee the consequences of your actions. Your new set of laws took power away from the nobles, and they have rebelled against you. Nothing new."

James I disapproved of Alphonso's behavior, and criticized him for promising things without fulfilling them, as well his lack of planning, and not appreciating the consequences of his actions. King Alphonso came back to Toledo discouraged, although he knew changing the course of his reign was impossible. He succumbed to the noblemen; he gave up and abstained from publishing his new set of laws. By doing so, he pleased the noblemen, whom immediately abandoned the king of Granada and returned to Castile.

"Alphonso is absolutely destroyed. He has agreed to everything the noblemen demanded, even hundreds of ridiculous petitions," Lorenzo overheard in a conversation in the main plaza.

"The king is a puppet in their hands. Now they have betrayed the king of Granada, who sheltered them and rewarded them with many gifts."

"The Arab King feels humiliated by the Castilian nobles. Angered, he has called upon the emir of Morocco, and they are going to start an Arab crusade in Castile. The Moroccan will attack with great fury," Lorenzo heard, and became worried.

"Castile is defenseless, everyone is fleeing to Navarra and France, and presenting themselves to those kings; also the Jews are leaving by hundreds to Navarra. They know they will be blamed for the current situation," added another businessman.

So, it was, that Castile was at the mercy of circumstances; the king of Granada and the emir of Morocco from the south, and the king of France with the support of the Castilian noblemen, from the north, could conquer it. Alphonso, facing the unfathomable situation, called upon Lorenzo and the new astrologers.

"My son Ferdinand, has just sealed an alliance with France; now I need money to convince the noblemen to come back from Navarra and face the Arab crusade," he said but the anxiety showed through in his voice.

"Impose a service tax as an emergency measure. The people of Castile will pay a fixed amount to finance the army," the three new advisers proposed.

"But the people are already suffering terribly, a new tax will only make them rebel against Your Majesty," Lorenzo warned.

"Don Alphonso, people must pay."

"Your Majesty, the kingdom is suffering from a declining population. A new tax will only result in more people leaving," Lorenzo replied, knowing the Jews were already leaving.

"The king knows his duty. This disaster is the result Jewish influences. Those sorcerers, who, by the way, also killed Christ..." the priest answered, stabbing Lorenzo with his look.

After the meeting, the three astrologers raged at Lorenzo.

"Do not disagree us again in front of the king, we are now his principal advisers."

"I am offering my opinion to resolve a difficult situation."

"What can a heretic offer?" the priest, responded. "By the way, if I were you I would be more concerned with your personal situation."

Lorenzo left the meeting worried about what was about to happen; he wondered if he was doing enough to help prevent impending disaster befalling Castile.

"Am I doing my job well enough? I am not sure I am doing the right thing," he asked Priscilian in a meditation.

"You are doing well. What happens in Castile is normal. It is the natural cycle of events. Kingdoms are born; they grow, flourish, and decay," the voice said clearly. "Once the kingdom has performed a specific task, then it decays. It is a fact of life."

"Is there something I could do to help improve the situation?"

"It is difficult, the king and the noblemen's decisions are wrong. You have already done enough through the maps and the astronomical tables. They will be of great use in the future to help navigate towards new lands."

"But, the known world finishes in Finisterre."

"You have said it, the known world..." he heard, surprised from his maggid.

The collapse of the kingdom caused many people draw nearer to Lorenzo. They needed spiritual guidance beyond that offered by the ecclesiastic hierarchy. Even some of the members of Yosef's group wanted to join his group, which increased Yosef's hostility towards Lorenzo. The energy Lorenzo put into his group was exhausting work. He had to deal with several forces as well as the fear and anxiety of the members. How difficult it was and how easy Abraham made it seem. With the help of his wife, he could remove the obstacles with dignity. Ariadna's presence provided a peaceful harmony among the students who came to their home.

Some students started to become difficult; for example, one of Lorenzo's first pupils wanted to take over the group. Lorenzo could sense the man's desire, and accepted it as part of the student process. The man sent him critical thoughts trying to force Lorenzo to leave his role as the tutor; Lorenzo remained quiet. The student was not aware he could not force himself into that role; and if he were to succeed, he most likely would be abandoned on the path, without a real spiritual reference.

As had happened to Abraham, he also suffered an inner revolt, initiated by three people he respected. The leader of the revolt was a scholar, who had recently started pointless debates to show off his intelligence. The three left the group, trying to convince other members to follow them.

"Ariadna, are their assertions correct? Have I done anything wrong?" he asked his wife, when he heard what his students were saying.

"It is possible that sometimes you might be rigid, yet on other occasions you do not set proper limits. It is probably their jealously and their fantasy that push them to carry on with the revolt," she answered calmly.

"I am worried about confusing true searchers."

"You do not confuse them, Lorenzo. Tradition is clear and you are fulfilling its Principles well."

Soon, the three men who left the group fought amongst themselves about the way to impart the Teaching. One year later, they only sewed confusion, and failed to do anything productive. One of them approached Lorenzo, and asked for forgiveness and he allowed him back in the group.

Under so much pressure, Lorenzo contemplated the difficulties of his life; the kingdom was collapsing, Yosef was using magic to attack him, the bishop was stalking him, his students were rebelling, and his wife complained about their living circumstances. Still, his faith and optimism were resilient. In that moment, he knew his endurance and his ability to face adversity were being tested. Without a doubt, this was the right moment to give the best of himself.

37. LONELINESS

$\mathcal{T}$he death of Richard of Cornwall fed Alphonso's fantasies. He decided, despite the kingdom's precarious situation, to visit the pope, and claimed, once again, the title of emperor. The Pope, Gregory X, did not grant it to him. The pope left the title empty, thinking Rudolf of Habsburg would be the best choice. He believed Alphonso was a threat. The Church knew of his ambition, and they preferred to have him at their service rather than granting him the imperial title.

While Alphonso was away, his son Ferdinand died, preparing to fight the Arab crusade. The death of the prince devastated the king, and from then, Alphonso lived in an unbalanced state. His second son, the infant Sancho, proclaimed himself the heir to the throne. That proclamation provoked a civil war in Castile between the supporters of Sancho and the supporters of the deceased prince Ferdinand's children. Alphonso developed gout and isolated himself in Toledo, avoiding to face the kingdom's problems. He only dedicated his time to complete his poetic and historic works.

The crisis in Castile also affected the Jews. As Abraham warned, the Jews experienced tremendous hardships; the Christians blamed them for the kingdom's sad situation. The attacks on the Jewish quarter were frequent, and the Church forced the king to impose heavier taxes on the Jews, while separating them from the rest of the city. Some of the Jewish translators, including Metolitolah, left their jobs. Lorenzo, as a tribute to his friends, decided to compile the older books of Philosophy and Jewish poetry. When the king saw what Lorenzo was doing, he went ballistic:

"Lorenzo, my new advisers have told me about your bad behavior. The bishop is also suspicious of you! You can no longer be one of my advisers!" the king blurted. "The Jews have had malevolent influence on you!"

"Your Majesty, I only try to allow God to be present in my life, but as Your Majesty wishes, I will cease advising you."

"That will be the best."

After meeting with the king, Lorenzo cried: the destructive influence of the new astrologers had succeeded. The astrologers, after reading the king's horoscope, told the monarch he would be assassinated by a man of his own blood and he would be disinherited from the throne. When he heard the prediction, he ordered, out of control, to kill his brother Fredrick, and the nobleman Simon Ruiz. He blamed them for the noblemen's recent betrayal. He tortured his brother in prison, and sentenced Simon Ruiz to be burnt alive. In addition, he commissioned his son Sancho to execute the sentence, to teach his son a lesson.

Panic over took the kingdom's inhabitants, who thought they were being ruled by a mad man; only a crazy man would kill his brother based on an astrological prediction. The situation was not sustainable...

When he pondered the difficulties, Lorenzo wondered if the path that he had chosen was the right one. If he had stayed in Teruel to live the life chosen by his father, he would have lived a much calmer life, but he would have lost the opportunity to develop and meet Abraham. He also had a conversation with his guide about the possibility of having joined the Militia Christi in Cuenca:

"Alphonso X and James I were in Castile and Aragon, to

carry out a specific mission. Had you been a soldier, you would have helped them to conquer more land. But your mission is spiritual," his guide told him. "You must pass on the Teaching to the next generation and help those whom, by the Grace of Providence, you meet along the way."

"I will try my best, but my room is too small for the many people who are coming to the meetings. Houses in Toledo are very expensive..."Lorenzo said.

"Maybe it would be a propitious moment to find your own home," he heard from Priscilian.

The chaos continued in Castile. The kingdom was bankrupt and ruled by a mad man. The king's mood became even more bitter and violent, and his wife Violante left him. Following the advice of the new astrologers, who practiced exorcisms to finish with the Jewish curse, the king promulgated incoherent laws. He tried to fix in a few months the disaster he had created in decades. Everyone abandoned the monarch, who took ever more unpredictable decisions. His son Sancho, seeing his father's disastrous condition, convinced the Church, his mother, and the noblemen of Castile to appoint him as the new king. Alphonso was enraged and initiated a disastrous military campaign against his son.

Things only became worse. The emir of Morocco, Ibn Yusuf, took advantage of the chaotic situation in Castile and invaded the Iberian Peninsula. He devastated all territories as far as Seville. Alphonso tried to reconquer the land, supported by a strong naval force. Despite his excellent strategic position on the Guadalquivir River, the supplies did not arrive on time. The Arabs burned the remarkable fleet, and the king was almost killed.

The treasurer of Castile, Zag de la Maleha, had disobeyed the king's orders; instead of using the money to equip the fleet in Seville, he delivered the money to the queen in Aragon, following her orders. Alphonso, enraged by the treasurer's disobedience, had him executed. He also, as a punishment for the treasurer's misconduct, imposed a daily tax of twelve thousand maravedises on the Jews, and confiscated most of their properties.

Lorenzo went to see his Jewish friends, the poet Benjamin, Don Isaac, and Yehuda ben Moshe. The four sat down in the garden of the main synagogue. It was a special encounter.

"The situation in Castile is insane. Everyone is against Alphonso and supports his son Sancho, who was proclaimed the new king, by the Court of Valladolid. Only Seville, Murcia, and Badajoz are loyal to the old monarch," Yehuda ben Moshe said.

"Sancho is not going to be a great monarch, but after the murderer of Zag, and the confiscation of our properties, we cannot support Alphonso anymore. He is hurting us. Soon we will leave for Navarra," Benjamin added.

It was the last time Lorenzo would see his Jewish friends, who deeply regretted having to leave Toledo. They would depart knowing they would be welcomed in Navarra.

"I am sorry the treasurer's error has forced you leave this wonderful city," Lorenzo expressed sorrowfully.

"That is the history of our people. They will blame the Jews for the kingdom's disasters," Don Isaac said sadly.

"Will the rabbi leave as well?"

"No. Todros will stay, but his son will settle in Talavera. He will continue with the Tradition."

Lorenzo was touched, and embraced his friends. They remembered Abraham in silence; and felt his presence. With great respect for his former teacher, they honored his dedication. Because of his teachings, they had matured together. Benjamin broke the silence,

"Before I leave, I would like to offer you a gift. Please come with me," the poet said.

Benjamin took him to a house, near the main synagogue. The house had two floors, an inner patio, a stable entrance and a large main room. Downstairs was a large fireplace for cooking as well as heating. From the upper part of the house, they could contemplate the stars. It was a dream house.

"Welcome to your home. Before it becomes a property of the Church or the Christians, I give it to you" Benjamin said, knowing Lorenzo's important spiritual mission.

"But…this house is wonderful…I," he answered, contemplating the Tajo River from the upper stories of the house.

"Here. Take the keys. You may move in whenever you wish. I hope that your wife likes it."

"I will use this place to keep the flame of the Tradition alive, and to fulfill the Divine Will," he promised solemn.

Lorenzo said goodbye to his friends, in a moment he would remember forever. His soul companions had to leave Toledo, due to the king's poor governance, and the treasurer's folly. The three men were proud of themselves, for their role in humanity's evolution, and for continuing with his work and dedication. Lorenzo prayed for them.

After the meeting, he went to see his wife and told her the news. Ariadna was saddened by the departure of their three friends, whom she respected. Now they owned an excellent home, suitable for the spiritual gatherings. Lorenzo also had a small library. In that moment, he recalled Daniel, the astrologer's room of Teruel, and replicated it as his study.

He announced to the students that the meetings would move to a new location. It was a blessing. Happy, he organized the initiation ritual to welcome them in their new home. The Teaching would expand from there. Abraham, in his psychological body, came to the inauguration, and the most sensitive group members felt his presence, who blessed them all.

A few days later, Yosef Barchilon, who had heard about the new home of Lorenzo, paid him an awkward visit.

"I had warned you. You do not have the authority to teach. I am the leader of this line of Tradition!" he exclaimed in a threatening tone.

"The Teaching is one, and thus, we also have the right to live this Tradition, if it is in our hearts. Spiritual Teaching is not anyone's personal property."

"You are not even Jewish," Yosef said dismissively.

"I am not. Christians, Arabs, or Jewish, we all have the same right to receive the Grace. We all come from the same father. We are all brothers," Lorenzo answered, saying good-bye to Yosef, firmly but respectfully.

Yosef left, angry, while his group was collapsing, caused by his strictness. Instead of asking himself why it was happening, he kept up his night time attacks on Lorenzo, to try to push him off balance. He could not tolerate the Turolense's success, and could not acknowledge that Lorenzo's hard work had paid off. But Lorenzo's spiritual protection caused that the disasters Yosef had planned for Lorenzo, to manifest on his own body: Yosef did not realize that what we wish for others, finally happens to us. He continued to be obsessed with Lorenzo, and tried to prevent Lorenzo from teaching. Finally, he sent a letter to the bishop, accusing Lorenzo of heresy, alleging that he had correspondence with enemies of the Church. Meanwhile the group of Yosef, slowly dried up, and after a few years, disappeared.

Lorenzo received other sad news. His old great friend Julian called him one evening. He was sick and dying. When he arrived, he found the priest in bed, waiting for him to say good-bye. When he entered the room, his face brightened,

"Lorenzo, you are an example for me..." Julian said in an agonizing whisper.

"You have been also for me," he answered, deeply moved and proud of the man in front of him.

"I admire your courage and your search of the truth, beyond the norms."

"I could not have carried out my spiritual task without your help. You saved my life twice, and taught me many things."

"I have spent too much time dealing with political and administrative issues..." he regretted, making a great effort to speak. " Instead of dedicating my life to live in the presence of God and be an instrument of the Divine, I have spent my time with tedious bureaucracies and political machinations."

Lorenzo thought this was the big lesson from Julian´s life. He would need to deal with it in his next incarnation, but he chose to remain silent as the Christian Church denied the concept of reincarnation.

"My friend," Julian sobbed, holding the arm of Lorenzo.

"Thank you, my friend," he answered with a lump in his throat.

Julian took a final breath and passed on. Lorenzo closed his eyes, and prayed deeply within his heart. After looking at his friend's aura, he knew he would have a good passage through the higher worlds.

Lorenzo took the passing of Julian as a sign. He knew his time on Earth was not infinite, so he decided to dedicate his body and soul, to go through the last stages on the path of self-realization, and to show the path to those near him. Night after night, he connected with his Priscilian, and Abraham. In his meditations, he learned to watch mundane events objectively, and to understand the historical cycles. He became an impartial watcher of the forces on Earth; he was truly a silent witness.

Meanwhile, the bishop, who was still obsessed with Lorenzo, followed his every movement.

"What have you learned about Lorenzo?" the bishop asked his spy.

"He is living in the Jewish quarter. How a true Christian can live there?" the assistant asked, stoking the bishop's envy.

"Exactly! He is not following the Church's doctrine, and he is teaching heresy. He also corresponds with heretical Jews, such as Abulafia, who tried to convert the pope," the bishop added, after reading Lorenzo's intercepted letters.

"Abulafia had been sentenced to be burned at the stake, in Rome; while awaiting his execution, the pope had a heart attack, after which Abulafia was released. Who knows what kind of sorcery that man used?" the assistant insinuated.

"Stop talking about the Jews, and prepare a warrant for Lorenzo's arrest. Meanwhile I will continue collecting evidence against him. The fact that a Christian has joined the traitors is a disgrace to this city."

While the bishop focused on Lorenzo´s case, the tension in Castile spilled over. Alphonso cursed his son Sancho, and asked for a loan to the Emir of Morocco, Ibn Yusuf, to pay for the war against his son. Lorenzo went to see the rabbi to better understand the situation, since the Jews were the first to know what was happening in the kingdom. The rabbi tried to convince Alphonso to lift the daily levies on the Jews, which already provided over one million gold coins.

"Everybody has gone crazy! The emir of Morocco is financing Alphonso against his son Sancho," Todros told Lorenzo.

"Even the new pope is participating in the collective madness. He is supporting the Arab Emir and Alphonso against Sancho, who waits in the north supported by the Castilian Church."

Lorenzo could not imagine the king and the Arab army carrying Vatican flags, destroying Castile, with the help of Alphonso X. The king had lost his mind! "The situation could not endure for long," Lorenzo thought.

The chaos was uncontrollable. The hysterical monarch became ill, and spent his last nights alone with his nightmares. He struggled to remember how he had acquired so many enemies: his brothers, his sons, his wife, the noblemen, the Jews, the Church, everyone was against him! His only friends were his natural enemies: the Emir of Morocco and the Vatican.

Days before his death, the king was wracked in pain throughout his body, so he could feel the suffering he had caused the people of Castile through his decisions. His stubbornness only increased his pain. Alphonso's death was painful and agonizing, increased by his own demons. The image he created of himself, as the most powerful man on Earth, would not let him go in peace. His pain was only alleviated when he thought about the impressive cultural work he had carried out, and the creation of the Honest Council of the Mesta, which helped the Castilian ranchers and shepherds.

Finally his agonies ended. Racked with pain, the king surrendered and could assess his successes and mistakes. He finally accepted his responsibility and initiated a process of forgiveness, which helped him free his soul. The monarch, before dying, requested his heart to be buried in Jerusalem.

Alphonso X, known in his reign as "El Estrellero" or the Astrologer, died at the age of sixty-three in Seville, completely alone, without any friends or relatives with him. In the beginning, he was a fair man, but his ambition to become the most powerful man on earth lead to the collapse of both the kingdom and himself.

38. PREPARATION

The death of Alphonso X brought relief to the people of Castile and they proclaimed Sancho the new king. Although he lacked the charm and the charisma of his father and grandfather, he tried to bring order to the kingdom. Still, Castile remained divided between those who supported him and those who supported the offspring of his deceased older brother. Nevertheless, the situation was better than during the preceding years.

Sancho realized that without the support of the Jewish financiers, the bankrupt of the kingdom was impossible to resolve. Therefore, he turned to Rabbi Todros for help. With the support of the Jewish community, the commercial enterprises between the Castilian cities returned to normal. The economic improvement brought tranquility to the Jewish quarter, which helped Lorenzo to carry out his spiritual task.

The new king Sancho told the older translators he would not commission any new works, therefore Lorenzo bid farewell to the task he carried out for several decades. He thanked God for the opportunity to have participated in the greatest translation undertaking in European history. Lorenzo had more time to teach, and other study groups of other cities invited him to guide them. He had meetings in Zaragoza, Burgos, Segovia, Avila, Medinaceli, Guadalajara, and Ciudad Real. Fulfilling his spiritual obligations, he planted many seeds in both Castile and Aragon.

Now, his home was always filled with people, but as his

group grew, so did the problems. Lorenzo had to learn to deal with the forces that some of his pupils, unconsciously, carried with them to the study sessions. One of his students believed that he was the Messiah, and spoke with Lorenzo,

"I am here to carry out a great mission. I know that for sure," he told Lorenzo.

"The greatest missions are within; once you transform your inner self, the external self will reflect your enlightened state. Trying accomplish a great mission without being ready, can lead to madness," Lorenzo warned him.

"But I was born to do something great!

"Maybe you should look at yourself honestly," Lorenzo suggested.

The man did not want to listen and left the group. He tried to create a group of followers, and while he saw himself as the greatest man on Earth, the rest of the world only saw him as a mad man.

Lorenzo also carried the projections of several students, as had happened to Abraham. Against the custom of the age, Lorenzo allowed women to attend his meetings. Some tried to seduce him, and while some believed that Lorenzo was their soul mate, he did not separate from Ariadna, his true soul companion.

Another student tried to make Lorenzo stop teaching in public and dedicate all his time to him, in exchange for a large amount of money. The rich man believed he had the right to receive the Teaching exclusively, since he did not want to mix with other people. Lorenzo explained that spiritual knowledge is not exclusively for any one person.

"You are welcome to attend the meetings, but you will be treated like everyone else, in spite of your social standing and possessions. The Teaching is for the true seeker," Lorenzo told him, and the man left in a huff, without realizing that he was not as special as he believed.

With time, practice, and his spiritual work Lorenzo not only was able to visualize Priscilian, but also his pupil's guides. When he spoke to his students, he could tell them their guide´s messages. In one meeting, he could see Ibn Gabirol, the famous mystic and philosopher, who was guiding one student. In another session, he verified the prophet Elijah, who came to oversee the session. This prophet sometimes appeared in a spirit form to help groups searching for realization, as had happened to the groups in Gerona during the preceding centuries.

The bishop, for his part, monitored Lorenzo's activities closely. He sent several people incognito to get information about his meetings and find incriminating evidence. The bishop had already convinced the new king that the heretical groups were responsible for the Alphonso's madness and he should exterminate them. The prelate criticized Alphonso heartily, not only for not closing those groups, but also for supporting, financing, and letting them publish books which disputed the Christian doctrine. When the bishop had enough evidence against Lorenzo, he called him to his presence:

"Don Lorenzo Diaz, you must report to the bishop as soon as possible," a messenger from the prelate ordered him.

Lorenzo went to the palace of the bishop, but this time he was not afraid. Thanks to his meditations, he already knew he was much more than his physical body and he no longer feared death. He was ready to face his destiny, whatever it might be.

The bishop, after a cold greeting, pressured him,

"We know you live in the Jewish headquarter. As a good Christian you should live where other Christians live, otherwise people will mistake you for a heretic…" the bishop warned him, trying to threaten Lorenzo.

"Living in the Jewish quarter is not illegal. It is more illegal to confiscate the goods and properties of honest people," Lorenzo answered, referring to the appropriation of properties by Alphonso X during the final part of his reign.

"I have received detailed information about what you do. You invoke the Holy Spirit, make astrological predictions, practice forbidden heretic sciences, and even you have lured a nun away from her path."

"Only God can judge me," Lorenzo responded, challenging the bishop.

"The norms of the Church are crystal clear in relation to those teachings. King Sancho is already aware he must be strict with the heretics. We are helping him in matters of the spirit, so he will apply capital punishment to save the souls of people like you."

"I do not understand why you tell me such things. I am not aware of the existence of any heretics."

"Your group must cease; it is dangerous for those practices to continue, beyond the norms of the Holy Mother Church."

"Is it dangerous, for whom?" Lorenzo asked calmly.

"The first person in danger is you. I can put you on trial and you will be found guilty of heresy; however, I am not interested in you, since you are already old. I want to end all those practices, so Castile will be a pure place to live in the future."

"And what are you going to do to prevent the light of God from illuminating all men and women equally?"

"The Church is the only institution with the authority to preach the Word. As you can see, I am favorably disposed towards you. Your arrogance may have already cost you a grave punishment, but I want to make a deal."

"What is it about?"

"I want a list of all the people who participate in your group. If you give us that list, you and your wife will be free, and you will live peacefully the rest of your life."

"I see…"

"Think about it. Give us the list and you will live in peace."

"And if I do not deliver the list?"

"I will subject you to a public trial, and the probability of being found innocent is highly unlikely. The evidence against you is overwhelming. My influence with the king and the city councilors will preordain your sentence," the bishop said to Lorenzo.

Lorenzo remained quiet and bade him farewell in a dignified manner. He was concerned as this was a serious matter. He regretted that he was not more diplomatic during the meeting. The bishop wanted to finish off the true spiritual searchers, but he would never denounce his students, even though it would mean the end of his own life.

When he arrived home, he told Ariadna about the meeting. She became frightened because of their situation.

"Dear Ariadna, Spiritual Teaching is both theory and practice. We need to pass these tests to see if we are true. Keeping alive the light of the Tradition is not easy."

"But I am afraid of what might happen to you," she cried.

"The physical body sooner or later will die. The question is if we live and die with dignity," he said calmly.

"This is unfair. What is happening is not right! You have not done anything wrong. You help men come closer to God," his wife cried.

"I understand it is difficult, but look at the situation with perspective. We are not born to drift during our life; our task has its rewards. Look at how we have developed."

"I only want to live peacefully and rest. We are always having problems. Life was much easier in the convent."

"We can rest when we die. While we are here, our mission is to carry on the spiritual work, and learn as much as we can. What is your true fear?"

"That they will take away everything, that we have to move, and even that they will execute you," Ariadna said with tears in her eyes.

"Fear is opposite of love; do not worry, I love you and God will help us."

Lorenzo knew Ariadna was going through a test of her faith, although they were together for providential reasons. He tried, now that he could see the situation with greater clarity, to return her support.

Some of his students tried to convince him to leave Toledo, but he was not going to run. He had escaped many times before arriving in Toledo, but now he would not avoid his fate, whatever that might be, including the possibility of a dramatic ending. Lorenzo received instructions from Priscilian, so the Tradition would continue.

"They will hunt your students, therefore you must pass on the Teaching along two lines: one within your group, training new teachers to keep the light alive; and the other in meetings in cities in Castile and Aragon."

"I know that when I die my students will have a difficult time, the same as your students did. I am already training teachers in Toledo and other places."

"Some of your students will need to remain in Toledo, and others will need to travel across Europe and the north of Africa. Focus on teaching the Principles of the Tradition so they are not lost. Subjectivity can distort the Teaching," he concluded.

After the conversation with his maggid, Lorenzo sent letters to several students who resided outside of Toledo. In his letters, he addressed reincarnation, astrology, and matters of faith. The bishop intercepted some of those letters, addressed to people considered heretics by the Church. That was the final evidence the bishop needed. His association with dangerous people and his unorthodox views allowed him to proceed. He initiated the process leading to a civil trial and the execution of Lorenzo. After receiving the authorization from the council, he sent soldiers to arrest him.

Lorenzo waited calmly in his house, preparing for his life's final test. He knew that his death should be an example for his students. It was essential to keep alive the light of the Tradition.

39. TRIAL

*T*wo gentlemen from the Lodge of the Brotherhood knocked on Lorenzo´s door, and asked him to accompany them. He did not resist. He said good-bye to Ariadna, and calmly left his house. Escorted by the guards, they proceeded along the streets of the Jewish quarter, to the archbishop's palace. Sensing the inevitability of his execution, Lorenzo, in silence, said good-bye to the city.

While they walked, the members of the Brotherhood wondered what Lorenzo had done. They normally dealt with violent and dangerous criminals, but Lorenzo cooperated and offered no resistance. When they reached the palace, they felt a great compassion for him and he kindly said good-bye.

The bishop had everything prepared for Lorenzo's trial and execution.

"Do you have the list of the people of your meetings?"

"Yes I do," Lorenzo answered, taking the bishop by surprise.

The bishop smiled maliciously thinking Lorenzo had betrayed his students. He thought Lorenzo could not cope with the pressure and had lost his dignity. That was normally the case with other people, but when he read the list, his faced turned white.

"Priscilian, Saint Francis, Elijah, Ibn Gabirol," the bishop read loudly, becoming more infuriated with each name he read out. "What is this farce? All those people are dead. How can they attend your meetings? Are you mocking the Church?"

"No," Lorenzo answered.

"I see what you are trying to do. You want to make fun of the Holy Mother Church!"

"It is not a joke. The list is true."

"Do you swear in front of God and the Church that those people on your list attended your meetings?" the bishop inquired.

"I swear," Lorenzo answered.

"All right, I will give you a public trial, and I will charge you with perjury, heresy, and sorcery."

The bishop communicated his decision to the city council and launched the process. The main judge, noticing Lorenzo's good manners and educated demeanor, asked the prelate if he was sure about his decision.

"What is this man accused of?" the judge asked.

"Heresy and perjury in front of God and the Church," the bishop answered, explaining the list of names Lorenzo mentioned under oath.

The judge was stunned, and thought Lorenzo was mad, but a public execution was an unreasonable punishment. Even so, the bishop kept putting pressure on the judge, knowing his influence could cost him his post. The judge, intimidated, yielded to the pressure.

"All right. He will undergo the red-hot branding iron test. If he fails it, we will execute him for the crime of perjury," he stated.

The test consisted of applying a burning iron to the body of the accused. If the iron left a mark, it meant he had lied, and therefore, he was guilty and executed. On the other hand, if the incandescent iron did not leave any mark on the defendant's skin, it meant he was telling the truth, and that the hand of Providence had saved him. The bishop agreed because he loved the idea of Lorenzo suffering.

While Lorenzo waited in a cell of the bishop's palace, he entered into a deeply meditative state, reaching a point of total clarity and awakening. He accepted his destiny, whatever it might be. He had never felt so alive before, and he shone with an extraordinary inner spiritual light. As had happened to Abraham, the divine qualities shone from within him. During those hours, he thanked God for this monumental experience, and for the way he had been able to serve Him. He was in His Presence.

The Council invited the whole city. The public trial was about to take place in the cathedral plaza that evening. It had been a long time since the last public execution. The council and the king knew the majority of the population enjoyed the trials. When the people had their minds focused on them, they could unleashed their darkest emotions and their worst passions, forgetting about attacking the ruling elites.

Before sunset, the main plaza was packed. They assembled a stage and three members of the Council and the bishop seated there. The blacksmith prepared his tools. Lorenzo walked calmly to the stage. He was not afraid, and was able to watch the performance without an emotional reaction. He looked at himself as an actor in a play; he ceased to identify with the role that destiny had compelled him to play. He observed several of his students, and his beloved wife, who were sending him love and support. He also saw others, violent people, paid by the bishop, who heckled him. Despite all the noise around him, his calmness and tranquility were apparent: he was in a deep state of inner peace.

"Lorenzo Diaz, you are accused of heresy and perjury before of God! You are subject to the test of burning iron and, if the result is not satisfactory, you will be executed!" the bishop shouted.

"Before proceeding, you will undergo an interrogation, so the entire population of Toledo will witness your answers," the main judge shouted out.

"Being a Christian, have you helped people of the Jewish race?" the bishop starting inquiring.

"Instead of my helping them, they have helped me," he answered with sincerity and gratitude, thinking particularly in Abraham, his former teacher.

"Do you live in the Jewish quarter? You must be aware that a Christian should live with other Christians."

"Yes I do."

"Heresy! Heresy! Heresy!" the people yelled, after they heard a Christian had close bonds with the Jews.

"Have you participated in meetings of non-Christian cults? We have the testimony of the Yosef Barchilon, a respectable Jew who affirms you have participated in such meetings.

"There were not meetings of Jewish cult. The meetings helped people to fully develop as human beings," Lorenzo answered, watching Yosef Barchilon enjoying his moment of revenge.

"Have you organized private meetings invoking the Holy Spirit?"

"I am a human being and therefore I am entitled to this; God and the Holy Spirit are inside of each of us. To invoke Them means to connect with that inner part that is within each of us."

"Your testimony is convicting you by itself. You are giving yourself away. This trial is going to be very short. Are you aware that the Church is the only authority allowed to do that?" the bishop continued.

"No one has the exclusive authority to bestow spiritual teaching. It is Providence who supervises the people that carries out that task," he answered fearlessly, astonishing the council members with the heretical words he was pronouncing.

The bishop exploded.

"This man is a heretic! He is confessing his sins before hundreds of people. He deserves capital punishment! We need to save the soul of this devil! Let us burn him for God´s sake!"

"Heresy! Heresy! Heresy!" the crowd of people shouted throwing stones at him.

The members of the Lodge of Brotherhood tried to maintain order among the mob. One of the stones hit the face of Lorenzo, who bled severely, but he remained quiet; with dignity he wiped away the blood, and the trial continued.

"Have you participated in heretical meetings?"

"No, being in the presence of God cannot be a heresy. There is no need of an intermediary between human beings and God," he said as the people went mad.

"Have you carried out any kind of magical rituals?"

"No, sir. Magic is forbidden for a true spiritual searcher."

"And why do you organize those heretical meetings?"

"Those are not heretical meetings. We ask God to be present in the lives of attendees."

"Which God are you talking about? The God of the Jews, or the Father, Son, and the Holy Spirit?"

"There is only one God, the Absolute. The manifestation of God can take several forms according to different cultures and traditions."

"Do you agree then with the God of the Arabs?"

"That God is an expression of the Absolute. They express God according to the Arab form."

The words of Lorenzo stirred the people's passions even more. They were sure he was a Christian traitor. The crowd stomped on the ground in unison, shouting.

"Have you ever practiced sorcery or witchcraft?"

"No sir, witchcraft would be to burn someone in the name of God," Lorenzo said calmly, attacking the ecclesiastic practices, and firing up the bishop even more.

"This man is a liar, practices magic, and commits heresy! Only someone of his kind would dare to speak such words in front of a Christian crowd. I ask the death sentence for heresy, according to the doctrine of Rome. We accuse him of invoking the Holy Spirit in private places, talking about sacred matters without ecclesiastic preparation and supervision, promoting heresy among young people and women, and perjuring in front of the Christian God, the only true God!

Then, the main judge of the Council, as he promised, asked to proceed with the test of the burning iron. The blacksmith had made it white hot.

"Lorenzo Diaz, do you claim that Priscilian, Ibn Gabirol or Elijah were in your meetings?" the main judge asked him.

"Yes I do," he answered firmly, leaving the members of the council and the crowd astonished.

"Are you aware some of those people are already dead for more than a thousand years?" the judge asked Lorenzo, although he could not help but think he was not in his right mind, despite his refinement and dignity.

"I know, and I assure you they have been there," Lorenzo answered with conviction.

"Do you claim in your group you do not do any magic? Do you claim you have never done any act of sorcery? Do you claim you do not practice anything considered heresy?

"Yes I do."

"Do you claim that Allah and the God of the Jews, are the same one as the God of the Christians?"

"The three are an image of the Absolute God."

The crowd yelled hysterically. They could not believe what they were hearing.

"All right, we will proceed with the test of the burning iron. If you are telling the truth, the iron will not leave any mark on your chest. Open your doublet and the shirt," the main judge ordered, still stunned by the words of the accused.

Obedient, Lorenzo uncovered his chest, and the executioner moved the iron closer. The crowd could already feel the heat of the metal. They waited to hear the shout of pain from the accused. A silence fell over the plaza as the crowd held its breath. As the blacksmith moved the iron near his chest, some people yelled, crazed by the drama of the situation. The bishop posed a question again,

"Lorenzo Diaz, do you swear in front of God, the Holy Church and the people of Toledo that Priscilian, Ibn Gabirol, or Elijah were in your meetings?"

"Yes I do. I swear."

Lorenzo closed his eyes and focused on the love of God. He felt a divine cape protecting him, sensing an astonishing white light. He experienced the Presence of God. Meanwhile, the blacksmith put pressure on his chest with the burning iron. Lorenzo was not concerned. He was in a trance enveloped by the Divine Presence, and felt love for all men, even for those who wanted to execute him. He knew he could not suffer any harm. The executioner moved the iron away. The crowd was stunned. There was no mark! A member of the council knelled before Lorenzo.

"This is not possible! It is a trick of his heretical magician! Sorcery!" the bishop exclaimed outraged.

The bishop abruptly took the iron from the smith, and after checking that it was hot enough, pushed it into Lorenzo's chest.

"Let's see if God saves you now," he said venting his rage, pushing the iron with all his power.

"Why are you doing this to yourself?" Lorenzo asked the bishop, who was even more astonished at those words.

Two thirds of the people in the crowded plaza knelt. They knew they were witnessing a miracle. The bells of the Cathedral started ringing unexpectedly, and the eyes of Lorenzo were shining, showing unconditional love for the world. His face was the face of a compassionate child taking all the pain away from humanity, and transforming it into understanding.

The bishop tried again with all his strength. Lorenzo, fell in the floor and fainted. The face of the bishop turned white, knowing he had murdered him, and he would pay for it. He observed Lorenzo's chest again, and to his dismay, it did not have any mark. Everyone, but the bishop, knelt. Never had anyone had passed that test. They had witnessed a miracle. The judge somberly proclaimed,

"This man is telling the truth. He has passed the test of the burning iron. Lorenzo is a free man!" after which the crowd shouted with joy.

The bishop, outraged, started kicking him and swearing at Lorenzo, who lay unconscious on the floor. The members of the

Lodge of Brotherhood took the mad and unhinged bishop to his palace. The bishop could not forget the compassionate look Lorenzo had on his face while he had pressed the iron against his chest. He went crazy and had terrible nightmares for days. Everyone left the bishop alone, since they knew he had murdered a Toledan Saint. After suffering a week of terrible physical, psychological, and spiritual pain, the bishop ended his own life.

40. ASCEND

*A*riadna and Lorenzo´s students came to view his body, laying immobile on the plaza. They tried to revive him. Lorenzo was unconscious. They carried his body home. It was already night, and hundreds followed carrying torches, in a silent procession to the Jewish quarter. Some of them touched Lorenzo´s chest to confirm the miracle: there was no sign of a burn from the iron.

One man, after realizing he was witnessing a miracle, sang a beautiful melody, which touched the hearts of all his followers. Everyone joined in, and a celestial chant filled the streets of Toledo. The members of the Lodge of Brotherhood, confused by what was happening, followed the crowd to keep public order. The ecclesiastic hierarchy tried unsuccessfully to stop the spontaneous procession.

Upon reaching Lorenzo´s house, they placed his body on his bed. He seemed dead, although his vital signs were normal. Ariadna knew a miracle had happened and asked everyone to leave the house, and not disturb her husband.

"His life is in God's hands," she said.

Many of his supporters waited outside his house praying for him. Rumors of what happened spread all over Toledo, and hundreds of curious people came to see the saint. Lorenzo's students spent the whole night praying and reciting religious chants and the Jewish quarter was transformed during for the evening.

Yosef Barchilon, skeptical, also came to the house. He could say nothing because he did not know how to express his emotions: the situation overwhelmed him. His desire to kill Lorenzo had been for naught. He knew, that even if the person he envied most died that night, Lorenzo would remain alive to all his followers. He knew he had initiated the trial against Lorenzo by sending the letter to the bishop. He realized what he had done, and had a moment of repentance.

Lorenzo reached out to the upper worlds, and his guide Priscilian appeared to him.

"Now we are going to teach you one of the great secrets. Do not worry about your physical body," his maggid said.

Lorenzo entered another dimension while his body remained below. He went to a place from which he contemplated the path that all the spiritual pilgrims journeyed until they reached the Veil of Heaven. He took Lorenzo in front of the Great Assembly of Just Men, who welcomed him. Those spiritual saints and sages, who watched over the development of humanity from the heavens, thanked him for the mission he had been carrying out. They congratulated him for becoming a divine instrument and a bridge between heaven and Earth.

Then, he met Enoch, the first human being who had reached full realization, who acknowledged him. Lorenzo then saw the cosmic forces which create and maintain the forms of the manifestation, and he felt an enormous respect for them; then he saw the forces in charge of destroying the forms, and he trembled. Enoch told him not to worry, since both forces are necessary for the process of the manifestation of Existence. Beyond time and space, Lorenzo contemplated the moment when everything returned to its source, in an indescribable setting. He felt the profound love God has for his creation, and realized that love was much more intense than he had ever felt, thought or imagined.

In his psychological vehicle, Lorenzo spent more than one month in the celestial realms, where they crowned him. The profound peace he felt, pushed him to fly freely. He wished to die in that precise instant, but Priscilian called him.

"Your time has not arrived yet. You must go back to complete your work. The Tradition must continue…"

After forty days in that profound contemplative state, Lorenzo returned from the heavens. His physical body was weak, although the celestial guides had kept it alive and healthy. Meanwhile, in the Jewish quarter, many of his followers lost hope of seeing him alive again, and only a few supporters kept a vigil near the house. The rest of the students, little by little went back to their daily routines, forgetting about the miracle they had witnessed.

One morning, Lorenzo opened his eyes and found his beloved Ariadna praying for him beside their bed. Lorenzo had gone through a complete transformation. He was fully conscious and lucid. The movements of the world no longer attracted him, and, at the same time, he loved everything. The change in his perspective was astonishing.

"Dear Ariadna," Lorenzo said.

"Dear beloved," his wife answered.

"My time has not arrived yet. I need to finish several things."

"I knew that you could not leave without saying goodbye," Ariadna said, deeply touched.

Lorenzo's state also provoked a profound transformation in his wife. She vibrated on the same harmonic note as her husband, and in that moment her fears evaporated. Lorenzo knew a human life on Earth represented only a small instant in the universe.

"We must be discrete. Only call my closest students. I need to talk to them, but I must not leave the house. I want to avoid excitement and remain in retreat," Lorenzo asked.

He received some of his students, of whom he asked complete discretion. They noticed a remarkable change in their teacher, and some were even afraid to be near him, because of the intense light that shone from him. Lorenzo could see his student's entire lives in just one moment: the pupils were transparent, and could hide nothing. He told each of the students the exact words they needed to hear. He had become an instrument of perception and divine transmission. Those who met with him experimented a profound transformation.

Lorenzo knew Toledo would experience difficult moments. The force of opposition incarnated by the bishop, would manifest again through others in the future. There would always be a force to test spiritual seekers. Those who followed his same journey would not have an easy life. He wondered who would continue to keep the flame of Tradition alive when he passed away. He thought about three potential candidates and he assigned each of them several tasks: one would be in charge of the Toledo group and gave him specific instructions; the second student would travel to Castile and Aragon to compile all the spiritual knowledge in one book for future reference; and the third candidate's mission would be beyond the Iberian Peninsula; he would move to Jerusalem, to take the Tradition back to its source.

He also said good-bye to his native city Teruel. He lovingly remembered his infancy. While meditating, he visited Teruel and said goodbye to the places of his youth. He saw several gates, and saw in his mind's eye, the wall where he walked with the astrologer Daniel. Teruel had prospered. Happy, he went in his dream state to his familial house, which now belonged to his sister. He recognized his sister Leonor and she was lovely. She chose not to follow the religious life his father planned for her; and turned the house into a happy home. Before returning to Toledo, he blessed his beloved sister.

Once he finished his duties, he knew his time had come to an end.

"Ariadna, my time has come. Please pay close attention to the process, it is going to be a unique moment," Lorenzo said calmly to his wife, who could hardly speak.

While he was preparing for his passage, Ariadna tried very hard to contain her tears. She could see a light around him, and communicated with him through her eyes. She knew they would always be together walking hand with hand in the spiritual realms. Despite the pain of the moment, the sadness of Ariadna disappeared when she realized the unbreakable bond she shared with Lorenzo.

"Thank you very much for everything you have done for me. I love you." Lorenzo said, pronouncing his last words.

The room filled with a dim light, and Ariadna knew his passage to his next life was imminent. Priscilian tried to calm his student, and told him,

"Do not worry, there is nothing to fear."

Lorenzo was breathing at a constant rhythm. With a last intense look, he said good-bye to his wife and closed the eyes forever. Ariadna could halt the flow of her tears.

"Follow my instructions. Sometimes fear can freeze the process," Priscilian said. "Breath in harmony. You do not have any unfinished business, and thus, you should not suffer."

Lorenzo entered into another state of consciousness and his perception changed. He was between two realms. He had access to the invisible worlds, and could see his wife in the room, even though his eyes were closed. He saw Ariadna's energy field, and understood the kindness of the person nearest him. Her dedication and compassion were overwhelming.

"During the process you might meet different images and forms. But, do not worry, this is normal," Priscilian continued.

Calmly, Lorenzo watched several weird beings approach, attracted by the spiritual light that permeated the room. They attempted to prevent his transition. Immediately, Priscilian expelled them from the room. Meanwhile, Lorenzo's breathing became more labored. Brightness from a lighthouse called him, and he heard the celestial chorus. Ariadna could hear the choir and knelt before the immensity of the moment.

Four invisible beings eased Lorenzo from his physical body. He had only a few breaths remaining. Each of them lasted what seemed to be an eternity. Within an instant, he lost control of his body: to resist was pointless. There was no reason to stay in his mortal body and something made him fly. Then he saw each of the moments of his life as if projected on a screen. His incarnation was condensed into millions of images, which he contemplated as an impartial spectator. The beings of light helped him, and supported him on his transit. He noticed that he was receiving new information without the use of a language, and entered a state of great lucidity. He could communicate at great speed. He started to fly, and he saw Ariadna kneeling, contemplating that moment. He sent a message of love that his wife felt.

Lorenzo allowed the guides take over his vehicles of expression, and they took him from his body. He saw himself as being outside his physical body, joined by a small silver cord that was breaking. He experienced an unconditional love and felt the eternal mercy of God. He knew he had nothing to fear and he projected light to his wife, friends, and enemies. He was now a being of light and love. The perception of having enemies was gone, and he understood that all the people who had entered his life had been there to help in his development, consciously or unconsciously.

A great eye, which was growing larger, beckoned him: it was both an abyss and a gate to another dimension. At the end of tunnel, he found himself in front of an enormous light. There was no possibility of returning after entering into the immensity of the ocean of light. He approached the light and met several guides who acknowledged him for his courage and for having kept alive the flame of the spiritual Tradition. The celestial chorus welcomed him. It was an eternal instant before entering into a mystical ecstasy with God, which he perceived as a whole eternity. When he took his last breath, he exclaimed AUM, an expression that revealed the manifestation of the four worlds. He finally broke his connection with the physical body and he felt an enormous happiness and freedom. His final breaths were a transcendent experience, much more than he had imagined when he was on Earth.

He now could move freely to any place, without being subject to the physical laws of gravity; although he still had control over his ethereal body, and decided to visit his house in Toledo. He realized the enormous amount of energy the physical body required. It seemed like an eternity but only a few seconds passed since his physical death. He felt an overwhelming happiness to see his wife. He wanted to share his freedom with his beloved, who was crying beside his body.

"Ariadna, that body is not me," he said to his wife.

She was still in shock, but felt her husband's presence, and understood his words.

"Ariadna, my physical body has started the process of disintegration. It no longer has the vital spark. It is now only flesh and bones."

Priscilian called him to meet with his loved ones in heaven, who were ready to welcome him. He saw himself in a garden near a fountain. Suddenly his mother was there, with whom he shared an emotional embrace; he saw his brothers, the astrologer Daniel, and the shepherd Arturo, whom he thanked for the early teachings. Then he met his beloved friend Julian and thanked him again for twice saving his life. Later his teacher Abraham appeared, whom he thanked for the mission he had carried out on Earth. Several friends and deceased students came to greet him, thanking him for his help. In one spontaneous movement, they began to praise him. The emotion was overwhelming. It was the recognition of all his work during his life.

"Where is my father?" he asked.

"He is not here, he is somewhere else," Priscilian answered.

"Why is he not here?"

"He has to go through his own healing and repentance process. As long as he remains in denial, he will not able to leave the place he is."

"May I see him?"

Priscilian took him to a dark place, where his father was whispering, lonely, trapped in his own thoughts, believing he was a victim of life's circumstances.

"He is going to need more time before he realizes the opportunities that he squandered, and the ones he took from others. He is a victim of his own actions."

"I understand," Lorenzo answered, feeling great compassion for his father.

Priscilian then told him,

"Now you must summarize of your life."

Three guides of high hierarchy called Lorenzo. They showed him several events that had happened in his life, and his failures and successes. Some of his mistakes were difficult to acknowledge. He also saw times in which he had lost his center, losing his dignity. He repented for those times. He knew the only way to evolve was to acknowledge the mistakes, which he did, although it was far more difficult than he thought it would be.

He also went through a list of people with whom he had unfinished business. One after the other he asked for their forgiveness, and forgave the others mistakes, even the bishop's.

"What happens with people who deny what they have done during their lives?" Lorenzo asked.

Priscilian showed him the dismal places where those who put themselves in denial go. He did not want to stay there long; it was freezing cold.

"Now you should put your life in perspective with regards to your past lives."

Lorenzo knew his life was the end of a cycle.

"All lives have a purpose. This one was important for you. You have made the most of it. You have fulfilled your purpose well. You are ready for the next phase of evolution. Congratulations! You have followed the signs, which was not easy, and developed your potential," the main guide told him.

They took him to a very beautiful place where he enjoyed a well-deserved rest. He lived for some time with great sages and philosophers in a celestial city, full of wonderful vistas and a golden light. There he met his tutor Abraham, with whom he shared extraordinary conversations; there was so much knowledge he learned in a short time in heaven!

After a long period, they called him to a celestial academy, where highly developed human beings planned the spiritual evolution of humanity.

"It is time for you to prepare for your next mission," they told him.

Humanity on Earth is still very young and most human beings are like little children. They need lots of care and love."

In the celestial school Lorenzo learned about hundreds of generations of human beings who lived on Earth for centuries. He watched how the law of cause and effect worked and the consequences of each act of every individual on the rest of humanity.

They also showed him how the evolution of the school of the soul was developing in Toledo. They analyzed the history of Castile and told him they would need great spiritual help in the year 1492.

"We need volunteers to go down on such important date for humanity."

He volunteered himself, although he knew incarnation was not easy and he should not take that decision lightly.

"You will not be alone, we will send Abraham and your beloved spouse Ariadna. We need a group of evolved souls to help in such a critical moment. Abraham will put an end to the cycle of the school in Toledo in 1492, and will prepare the followers of the Tradition, who will have to leave Castile and Aragon."

Lorenzo was happy with the thought of the possibility of sharing the adventure with some of his beloved friends; however, he still had a great surprise before starting his next mission.

"Come, you need to welcome someone," Priscilian told him.

Seven years had passed in Toledo, although for Lorenzo it seemed only a few months. Time in heaven goes more slowly than on Earth. A person with an angelical face appeared. It was his beloved wife Ariadna. Lorenzo was delighted to welcome his soul mate.

"My love, are you here?" Ariadna, who was overjoyed to meet him again.

"Yes, are you not aware we are soul mates? We run the same path of evolution."

Lorenzo looked at Ariadna and felt they were one with God.

God was with them and they realized how close He is to human beings, despite the many moments they forget Him.

The two lovers contemplated the prodigy of Existence and melt in another eternal moment presided by the love of God. The miracle of life would start again. The guides applauded Lorenzo and Ariadna's courage for their willingness to return to Earth. Now they were going to be prepared to take on a new act of love and help humanity on an important date on Earth.

"It will not be an easy task, but we will guide you from here," Priscilian told them.

While they felt the extraordinary love of God, Lorenzo and Ariadna prepared, from the subtle words, to realize again the will of the Holy One, and to help humanity to continue the path of return to the divine source. They would take another step to return to the origin of everything that has been, is, and will be. God, through them, contemplated his Creation on the Mirror of Existence. Love.

Thank you for reading this book

You can contact the author of the novel in the following e-mail:
info@thecallingnovel.com

Ilustrations

· Figure 1: «Hispania nach aller seiner gelengenheit in bergen wassern stettne volckern künigreichen und inseln» (Sebastian Munster - 1544). Información geográfica © Instituto Geográfico Nacional.

· Figure 2: «Teruel – Atalante español» (Bernardo Espinalt y García – 1778). Biblioteca Nacional de España (B.N.E).

· Figure 3: «Albarracín – Atalante español» (Bernardo Espinalt y García – 1778). Biblioteca Nacional de España (B.N.E).

· Figure 4: «Sign of King Fernando III» Historical Municipal Archive of Toledo, Spain - 1219

· Figure 5: «Sign of the King Alfonso X» Historical Municipal Archive of Toledo, Spain - 1254

· Figure 6: «Illustration of Toledo made by José Arroyo Palomeque around 1720. Published in the book by Julio Porres Martín-Cleto, Rafael Juan del Cerro Malagón, and José Luis Isabel Sánchez». Historical Municipal Archive of Toledo, Spain.